the *secret*

french recipes

of *sophie valroux*

WITHDRAWN

Samantha Vérant

BERKLEY
New York

BERKLEY
An imprint of Penguin Random House LLC
penguinrandomhouse.com

Copyright © 2020 by Samantha Vérant
Readers Guide copyright © 2020 by Samantha Vérant
Penguin Random House supports copyright. Copyright fuels creativity, encourages diverse voices,
promotes free speech, and creates a vibrant culture. Thank you for buying an authorized edition of
this book and for complying with copyright laws by not reproducing, scanning, or distributing any
part of it in any form without permission. You are supporting writers and
allowing Penguin Random House to continue to publish books for every reader.

BERKLEY and the BERKLEY & B colophon are registered trademarks of
Penguin Random House LLC.

Library of Congress Cataloging-in-Publication Data

Names: Vérant, Samantha, author.
Title: The secret French recipes of Sophie Valroux / Samantha Vérant.
Description: First edition. | New York: Berkley, 2020.
Identifiers: LCCN 2020002370 (print) | LCCN 2020002371 (ebook) |
ISBN 9781984806994 (trade paperback) | ISBN 9780593097731 (ebook)
Subjects: LCSH: France—Fiction.
Classification: LCC PS3622.E7325 S43 2020 (print) |
LCC PS3622.E7325 (ebook) | DDC 813/.6—dc23
LC record available at https://lccn.loc.gov/2020002370
LC ebook record available at https://lccn.loc.gov/2020002371

First Edition: September 2020

Printed in the United States of America
1 3 5 7 9 10 8 6 4 2

Cover design by Eileen Carey
Cover photographs: woman by Rolando Caponi/EyeEm/Getty Images;
french buildings © Chris Reeve/Trevillion Images
Book design by Alison Cnockaert
Interior art: wreath by gst / Shutterstock

This book is dedicated to my grandmother Dorothy "Dotty" Thomas, my beloved Nanny, and to all the other grandmothers in this world who inspire us with unadulterated love and nourishment.

———— ⚜ ————

Author's note: Champvert is a fictional village that is inspired by my life in southwestern France.

L'Amuse-Bouche

———❧———

Every woman should have a blowtorch.

—CHEF MARY BERGIN TO JULIA CHILD

I

fall

The thing about all my food is that
everything is a remembered flavor. Maybe
it's something I had as a child or maybe it's
something I had in Milan, but I want it to
taste better than you ever thought.

—INA GARTEN

I

counting stars

A ZUCCHINI FLEW OVER my head, missing it by a few centimeters.

Miguel, my commis, caught the torpedo of a vegetable with flair, swaggered over to the Bose sound system, and changed the music from Vivaldi's *The Four Seasons* to Madonna's "Lucky Star." Nobody whipped Miguel's ass with a kitchen towel or slugged him on the arm as he danced his way back to our station. Instead, after exaggerated moans and groans from a few of the macho men, the brigade sang along, Miguel using the zucchini like a microphone.

Insanity, momentary madness, spread like wildfire. Vegetables were launched in all directions, a few tomatoes thudding on the floor with a healthy *splat*. Freedom. Chaos. The rules went out the window. I smiled so wide my cheeks hurt.

Miguel set the zucchini down on a chopping block and then he nudged my ribs. "Look at you, Sophie, you're always so serious. But right now you look like that weird Cheshire cat in the Disney movie— all teeth and crazy eyes."

"This is my wonderland," I said, sweeping out my arms.

"Wonderland? You sick?" He placed the back of his hand against my forehead. "You're looking a bit pale and skinny."

"I've always been pale and skinny," I said with a laugh.

When I'd first stepped foot into this kitchen five years prior, the entire brigade made fun of my whiter-than-white complexion and teased me, saying they'd expected me to break like a porcelain doll. But I proved to them that I was far from fragile—conquering late nights and early mornings, not to mention all the burns, cuts, and bruises. It wasn't long before they dubbed me Scary Spice, the guys having learned never to drop their pants in front of a woman wielding an oyster knife.

"*Dios mío*, Sophie, I never, ever thought I'd be a part of something like this," said Miguel. "Do you think we'll get it?"

I couldn't respond because I was praying with my heart and soul we would.

Rumor had it that any minute now we'd find out if we'd received our third star before Michelin released next year's New York red guide. Renowned chefs throughout the city were already receiving courtesy calls—a few of them gaining stars, and a few becoming starless. Judging by the six-month wait to dine at Cendrillon NY, this third star was shooting right toward us in all its shining glory. I clasped my hands together and lowered my head, my spine tingling. I wanted this more than anything. I wanted to be blinded by the light of this magnificent event, the splendor.

"*Chica*, you've zoned out," said Miguel, hip-bumping me. "Do you think we stand a chance?"

"Well, we deliver the ultimate dining experience," I said, floating back from my galactic-inspired fantasies and coming back down to earth. "The third star is in the bag. For sure."

Miguel made the sign of the cross with his right hand, exuberantly—up, down, left, and right.

"Pray to the food and wine gods," I said, and we both snorted.

Miguel grabbed me by the waist and we sambaed. Or we did our best with my two left feet. Yes, this kitchen was my crazed wonderland.

Normally, we were a well-oiled machine, operating with precision—the way any Manhattan-based Michelin two-star restaurant should run. If Auguste Escoffier—the French chef who'd codified the brigade system for the hierarchy of kitchen staffs in the early 1900s—were still alive today, he'd have flambéed our crew of eighteen one by one. But today was an exception, and perhaps even Auguste would have cut us some slack. I'm sure he strived for his dreams, too. If Michelin decorated Cendrillon with its third star, every kitchen door in the world would swing wide open for me, and the thought of running my own restaurant sent chills down my spine. The kitchen was the only place that made sense in my world, where I had control and could make people happy with my cooking. The kitchen was my life.

A cough came from the doorway. Miguel raced to the Bose and turned the music off. The brigade froze as Chef O'Shea sauntered into the kitchen. He stood in silence for one of those moments that felt like an eternity.

Barrel-chested and broad-shouldered, O'Shea's appearance was more similar to a redheaded street boxer from Southie than that of a two-star chef. We'd joke he was part pit bull, part man, but not when he was around. His hands were enormous—it was amazing he could handle his knives with such grace. The man could fillet a yellowfin tuna in under a minute. And while he may have left his South Boston life behind him when he came to New York as a venerable chef, he still had the temper of a kid from the streets. But this guy, this man, was a culinary visionary. Regardless of the fear factor he imposed, we were working with—and for—the best.

"Is this the kind of kitchen I run?" O'Shea asked with a hiss. "No more messing around. We have a busy night ahead of us."

"Yes, Chef," came our nervous answer.

Instead of going off on one of his tirades, when his face would turn beet red and his large nostrils would flare, O'Shea broke out into a wide grin. "I can't wait to show those French pussies in Paris what an American thug from the docks can do. A third star will seal the deal for opening a Cendrillon in the City of Light."

Pots and pans banged.

O'Shea turned on his heel and headed to his office in the back of the kitchen. "I'll join you in twenty for the family meal. Get back to work."

I set the commercial immersion blender on high, puréeing my velouté to creamy perfection. As I squeezed a lemon to add a dash of acidity to the base, a hot breath on my neck sent shivers of dread down my spine. Catching his musky scent, a mix of cologne, sweat, and cigarettes, I didn't have to turn around to know Eric stood behind me—too close for comfort. "So, have you thought about my offer?" he asked.

I turned to face him, putting a few inches of needed space in between us. "Have you told O'Shea you're leaving yet?"

"Nope," said Eric. "But it's not like he can hold it against me. He was—what? Seventeen when Jean-Jacques Gaston discovered him at the fish market? And he left *Le Homard* shortly after it received its second star—"

"We all know his rags to riches story. And it seems he's passing the torch on to you," I said with sarcasm. "Moving on up from chef de cuisine to an executive chef with your own restaurant. May the stars be with you."

Eric placed a hand on my shoulder. "Our stars, they align. Leave Cendrillon to work for me. And then we'll take things from there."

"You have to be joking," I scoffed, pushing his hand off me.

"I'm not," said Eric. "Every time I look into those gorgeous green eyes of yours, I get lost. Do me a favor, think about all the good times we had."

Good times? Was he nuts? He'd had them with other women.

"Oh my God, what the hell have you been smoking?" I choked back my laughter and yanked out my necklace from underneath my coat. Attached to the chain was an engagement ring, complete with a sparkling five-carat canary diamond the color of glistening butter. "You do realize Walter and I are engaged."

"Rings are worn on fingers."

"Not one as big as this. Don't want to lose it in the soup," I said, tucking my necklace back into my jacket. I let out an annoyed huff. "You seem to have a new flavor of the month every week."

"They mean nothing to me," he said. "Brain-dead food groupies. Starved for attention."

Eric crossed his arms over his chest, the black ink of his tribal tattoos peeking out from under his sleeves. "What kind of relationship do you have with a stale, boring attorney, anyway? You never see him. You're always here in the kitchen with me." He tugged my braid. "We were so good together, Sophie. And now we can be even better. A real team. Don't forget I was the one who took the risk and convinced O'Shea to hire you after your *stage*."

"I proved my worth during my internship. And he hired me, not you," I said.

"Sure, Sophie," he said. "Whatever you want to think."

For a moment, he almost had me, the way he locked onto my eyes. Still, we were over. I was never going to go through that pain again—no matter the temptation of his perfect smile.

Lanky with a goatee and tribal tattoo arm sleeves, Eric broke the mold when it came to sexy chefs. His eyes were dark, the color of dried cloves—dark brown and hard—his eyelashes were long, and his body was buff. In the beginning, when I was young, dumb, and full of hope, his charm and charisma had drawn me to him, right into his bed. I'd loved watching him rule the kitchen, clipboard in hand, acting with finesse even when under pressure.

But, unfortunately, up-and-coming chefs in New York City were like rock stars, and our personal relationship had flamed out. After Cendrillon received its first star, Eric was written up in the *Times* and *Post* almost as often as O'Shea was, and he attracted food groupies looking for fresh meat. When O'Shea traveled—opening new restaurants or appearing on cooking shows—Eric's status of chef de cuisine became equally important and he ran everything. After the second star came a year later, his ego exploded like an overcooked soufflé. Women went nuts for Eric. One evening, I overheard one say to her friend, "I'd have sex with that sexy chef in front of my husband." *Cendrillon* meant "Cinderella" in French, and Eric's foot fit right into the proverbial glass slipper. Such a shame serial cheating also came in his size.

Although Eric's many, and I mean many, betrayals hurt me to the core, my culinary aspirations were more important to me than the state of my heart. Only one percent of restaurants had women navigating the helm of a Michelin-starred establishment and it was my lifelong dream to become one of them. With Eric leaving Cendrillon to strike out on his own, I stood a chance to take over his position of chef de cuisine, build up my name in the culinary world, and eventually create my own empire just like the female chefs I'd idolized over the years.

"I've worked here for five years. And I believe I've held my own," I said with a beleaguered sigh. "Look, Eric, we work well together in the kitchen. But we never, ever worked well as a couple. Speaking of work—I'm trying to get things done."

After Eric placed his hand over his heart and pouted with mock hurt, he dipped a spoon into the soup I was preparing: roasted potimarron—a chestnut-flavored squash—velouté, one of the restaurant's signature fall dishes served with orange-and-ginger-infused lobster. He spit out his mouthful, wiped his lips with a kitchen towel, and said, "The base is absolute shit. Did you even season it?"

"Of course," I said, taken aback. "I followed Chef's recipe to the letter, like I always do."

He shoved the spoon toward my mouth. "Taste it," he said and I did, mostly because I didn't have a choice.

"It's fine," I said. "Just the way it's supposed to be."

"Fine? Are you questioning *me*? I'm still the chef de cuisine here, not you," he said, pointing his finger in front of my face. "We don't do *fine* here. We serve the best, and your velouté is completely bland. Did your taste buds take off on a vacation?"

Although I didn't trust Eric as a man, I did trust his palate. I smacked my lips together and grabbed a clean spoon. "I guess you're right," I said, adding more cinnamon, cumin, and paprika into the base. After a quick stir, I held out a healthy-sized mouthful of the velouté. "Better?"

He tasted the velouté. The way he licked his lips made me cringe.

"Thatta girl, Sophie. It's perfection," said Eric. "Finish up the velouté and get on tonight's entrée for the tasting."

"Yes, Chef."

Eric nodded perfunctorily and stormed toward Alex, the sous chef. They whispered in the corner by the walk-in, up to their usual colluding. Probably talking smack about me but I didn't care. Soon, Eric would be out of my life, out of this kitchen, and my lifelong dream would be within reach.

Miguel's eyebrows shot up. "Your history with him has been dead for years. Why doesn't he pick up the hint? What's his problem?"

"He's an egomaniac. And there are far too many problems to list." I forced a smile. "Let's focus on tonight. Can you grab a few more lobsters from the tank while I head into dry storage?"

2

never trust a skinny chef

C ENDRILLON SPECIALIZED IN seafood, so we had four fish stations: one for poaching, one for roasting, one for sautéing, and one for sauce. I was the chef de partie for the latter two, which also included making our restaurant's signature soups.

O'Shea planned his menu seasonally—depending on what was available at market. It was fall, my favorite time of the year, bursting with all the savory ingredients I craved like a culinary hedonist, the ingredients that turned my light on. All those varieties of beautiful squashes and root vegetables—the explosion of colors, the ochre yellows, lush greens, vivid reds, and a kaleidoscope of oranges—were just a few of the ingredients that fueled my cooking fantasies. In the summer, on those hot cooking days and nights in New York with rivulets of thick sweat coating my forehead, I'd fantasize about what we'd create in the fall, closing my eyes and cooking in my head.

Soon, the waitstaff would arrive to taste tonight's specials, which would be followed by our family meal. I eyed the board on the wall and licked my lips. The amuse-bouche consisted of a pan-seared foie gras served with caramelized pears; the entrée, a boar carpaccio with eggplant caviar, apples, and ginger; the two *plats principaux*, a cognac-flambéed seared sea scallop and shrimp plate served with deep-fried goat cheese and garnished with licorice-perfumed fennel leaves, which fell under my responsibility, and the chef's version of a beef Wellington served with a celeriac mash, baby carrots, and thin French green beans.

As I lit a match to flambé the scallops, Alex and Eric raced around the kitchen, checking everybody's stations. Alex always looked as if he was sweating profusely, out of breath. Not to mention the way he'd leer at the waitresses working the front of the house. When Eric left the restaurant, O'Shea couldn't want this lecherous creep to be the face of Cendrillon, could he?

My match fizzled out. I lit another one.

Damn it. I'd paid my dues. I started off as a garde manger, making salads, hors d'oeuvres, canapés, and terrines. Then it was on to entremetier, a commis under the chef de partie in charge of all the vegetables. I worked hard and soon I was a commis to one of the three *poissonnières*—fish cooks. Not many people can handle seventeen-hour-long shifts, wake up, and do it all over again the next day. And, more to the point, not many women could or even wanted to endure the abuse, especially under a brute like O'Shea. But I'd learned my way around a testosterone-infused kitchen and I held my own. I worked twice as hard as the men, my hands rough and calloused. Rule number one: no crying in the kitchen. I never shed one tear. I did what I had to do and I got it done—no matter the occupational hazards, which also included avoiding Eric and his advances after we broke up.

Sure, as chef de partie I was lower down on the totem pole than Alex. But speed, precision, and consistency were the most important traits in a kitchen like this and Alex was lagging, mostly due to his severe cocaine addiction.

I grabbed a handful of tarragon and closed my eyes, inhaling its sweet fragrance. I could almost feel my grandmother next to me, smell the aromas embedded into her poppy-print apron, taste her creamy veloutés. Thanks to her, my skills in the kitchen started developing from the age of seven. I'd learned how to chop, slice, and dice without cutting my fingers, to sauté, fry, and grill, pairing flavors and taming them into submission.

Just as I'd experienced with my grandmother's meals, when people ate my creations, I wanted them to think "now this is love"—while engaging all of the five senses. For me, cooking was the way I expressed myself, each dish a balance of flavors and ingredients representing my emotions—sweet, sour, salty, smoky, spicy-hot, and even bitter. My inspiration as a chef was to give people sensorial experiences, to bring them back to times of happiness, to let them relive their youth, or to awaken their minds. Although I was only telling O'Shea's tale, I hoped one day I'd get the chance to author my own culinary narrative.

When this third star came in, my *grand-mère* would be jump-over-the-moon-and-swing-from-the-Michelin-stars proud of me. Pinches of guilt tweaked my heart. I hadn't spoken with Grand-mère Odette in ages and I'd never properly thanked her for her tutelage. She had inspired my culinary career, and now everything I'd worked so hard for was within my grasp.

O'Shea's voice knocked me out of my olfactory-induced trance. He held six bottles of champagne, three in each of his enormous hands. "I think we should celebrate early."

The brigade shouted out a whoop, followed by the beating of pots and pans. Somebody popped open a bottle of champagne. In an instant, corks flew across the kitchen. I made a mental note to call my grand-mère.

As the bottles were passed around, the phone on the wall blinked green. Our hostess Bernadette's sultry voice interrupted our celebration. "Excuse me, Chef, but you have a call," she said.

"Take a message," said O'Shea. "I'm in a staff meeting."

"I think you'll want to take this," said Bernadette. "It's Gabrielle from Michelin."

I willed my heart to stop racing and prayed again to the kitchen gods. *Please, make me the youngest female chef de cuisine at a Michelin three-star restaurant in New York. Let me become a part of culinary history.*

"Put the call through." O'Shea's eyes widened and he held up a finger. "Guys, simmer down. Not a word. I'm putting the call on speaker." He clicked the line open. "Dan O'Shea here."

"Good afternoon, Dan. First, as you know, this is a courtesy call before next year's New York red guide is released, which is tomorrow—"

O'Shea's eyes crinkled into a smile. "Yes, yes, an exciting time."

"I'm happy to inform you that two of your restaurants, Cendrillon Las Vegas and Cendrillon London, have received rising stars, and Cendrillon Los Angeles has received its second *étoile*."

O'Shea nodded his big head and shot us the thumbs-up. "And Cendrillon NY?"

"Dan, I'm afraid I have some not-so-wonderful news to deliver." Eyes darted back and forth. O'Shea grunted. "Yes?"

"Consistency is very important to us here at Michelin, and I'm afraid Cendrillon NY did not receive its third star," said Gabrielle. "With that said, I'm devastated to tell you that Cendrillon is not only *not* gaining a star, I'm afraid it's losing one."

Time stopped for a moment. We couldn't contain our surprised and disappointed groans. There was nothing worse for a chef than losing a star. It burned the ego, damaged reputations, and destroyed identities.

"I'm sorry, Dan. I wish I was the bearer of better news," said Gabrielle.

"Thank you for your candor," said O'Shea. He cleared his throat. "I guess I have some things to sort out."

"At the very least, congratulations on your other achievements."

"Thank you, Gabrielle."

O'Shea did not hang up the phone. He ripped it right out of the wall and smashed it to the ground. He sank to the floor and cradled his head in his hands, sobbing.

I gulped.

When you see someone strong and powerful shatter, it's haunting; you see the ghost of a man with his dreams dying. You want him to get up, to put disaster behind him, but he's crumbling right before your eyes. A deep sadness slowed down my heart. I found myself wanting to say something. But what words would be appropriate? It's like when you hear somebody has died and all you can come up with is "My thoughts and prayers are with you" or some other contrived shit like that. It's not that you don't care; you just don't know what to say. Most of the brigade rubbed their eyes with disbelief . . . or looked down at their clogs.

Eric and Alex exchanged a glance, and then nodded. Alex walked up to O'Shea. "Chef," he said. "We're a team here." He paused, wiping the sweat off his brow. "And I've been wondering if everyone here has been playing on it."

"What are you talking about, Alex?" asked O'Shea, his voice weak.

"I don't have proof, but I think Sophie has had it out for you, for all of us. She's got a chip on her shoulder."

My jaw unhinged. My heart raced. My words came out as a barely audible wheeze. "He's crazy, Chef. I don't have it out for anybody—"

"I've been thinking the same thing," said Eric. "I think she spices her dishes after I taste, adding in additional ingredients. Last week a guest, one of our regulars, requested to see me and told me they loved how much cinnamon was added into the potimarron velouté." He paused. "And we—Alex and me—believe it's happened more than once. It would explain the inconsistency."

"Eric, *you* told me to spice," I said, every muscle in my body tense. It took great effort to raise my hand to point a shaky finger with accusation. "You—"

"She's always talking about her grand-mère Odette's soups, how much better they are than yours. Bland. That's what she said. Your recipes are bland," said Eric, and then the skinny bastard shrugged. His twisted grin, the one he was trying to hold back, gave him away. His betrayal hit me. He'd set me up. My legs were about to go from under me.

"Chef," I said, bracing myself. "Please, give me a chance to explain. Eric—"

O'Shea smashed his fist on the prep table and I nearly jumped out of my skin. "—would never stoop so low. He didn't have people pulling strings for him after he graduated from a fancy cooking school. He *knows* what hard work is because he didn't pay to play," said O'Shea. He shook his head as if to clear it and then, with his face turning bright red, he barreled over to my stove. He picked up a spoon, tasted the base for the soup, and spit it out onto the floor. "The proof is right here. Your station. Your velouté. Not my recipe. You think you're better than me?"

What O'Shea said didn't make any sense. Eric was always holding the fact that he'd convinced Chef to hire me over my head. There were no strings. "But—" I began.

"Don't say another damn word."

I took in a sharp breath, feeling as if razors lacerated my throat.

O'Shea picked up the pot and threw it into the sink. Orange poti-marron dripped off the walls and onto the floor, splattering every-where. I was rendered immobile, staring into the face of a man who looked like he wanted to skin me alive. O'Shea's nostrils flared like a bull about to charge at a red flag. And I was the flag. For every step O'Shea took toward me, I took one back. And then he cornered me.

O'Shea's baseball-glove-sized hands were just about to wrap around my neck when two of our roustabouts pulled Chef away and dragged him to the back of the kitchen. O'Shea stood in the door-way, panting. "Get your sabotaging ass out of here before I hang you up by your ankles and gut you open like the dirty, disgusting, and disloyal pig you are." He turned around on one heel and entered his office, his last words: "Your career in the culinary world is dead. I'll make sure of it."

Breathless. I was breathless.

All eyes were on me, glaring, heads shaking. I whipped around to face Eric. Alex stood by his side. They both wore smirks on their faces. My hands curled into tight balls. "The two of you planned this? Why? Why would you do this to me?"

Alex cut me off. "Miguel, you've worked under Sophie. Tonight, you'll take over her station. And who knows what else the future will bring?" he said. Alex's posture challenged mine, the way he crossed his arms over his chest, the way he planted his feet.

"Miguel?" I questioned, turning to face him. "You heard Eric tell me to spice. You were standing next to me. Help me out here."

Miguel's posture caved, his shoulders slumping. "Sorry, *chica*, I need this job."

Alex clapped his hands together. "Guys, we have a busy night ahead of us, and now, with this stars debacle, we've got our work cut out for us. Everything has to be perfect. Consistent! Miguel, clean up the mess and get on that velouté de potimarron."

"Yes, Chef," he said, head down. He shuffled over to my station and began picking up pots and pans, organizing them on the aluminum shelves. Miguel couldn't bring himself to meet my panicked gaze.

I braced my hands on my knees. My eyes darted to each member of our eighteen-person brigade. "Nobody is going to back me up? Nobody?"

"I'd grab your knives and get the hell out of Dodge before O'Shea comes back," said Eric.

"Come on, guys," I pleaded, wheezing in between each word.

Not one person spoke up. Instead, they went back to chopping or sautéing or doing whatever the hell they were doing. The clatter of knives slamming against cutting boards. The sizzle of the fryer. The silence of nobody speaking up; it was deafening.

"I'm going to talk to him," I said, making my way to O'Shea's office.

"You'd risk your life to do that now?" said Eric. "I thought you were a smart girl."

"I'll take my chances."

Alex gripped my arm, stopping me in my tracks. "Get your stuff and get out of this kitchen. You are not seeing O'Shea." He twisted his grip, burning my forearm. "I mean it."

When the rest of the brigade crossed their arms over their chests, their eyes shooting daggers, I knew I was doomed. "The truth will come out. I'll make sure of it," I said.

"Whatever you want," said Eric with a laugh. "Hey, that's the slogan for that hamburger and pizza joint. Maybe they'll hire you there."

A harsh reality shook me to the bone, to my core. The brigade blamed the loss of the star on me, and along with this thrashing came a lofty pay decrease. Part of me wanted to fight—but not against eighteen guys. I didn't stand a chance. With no other options aside from certain death, I bolted to my station and grabbed my knives too quickly, cutting my hand in the process. I raced to the changing room, stuffed my street clothes in my bag, and skulked out the back door among the rats. I walked in the pouring rain, each drop burning and pricking into me like needles. Still dressed in my checks and toque, blood streaming down my hand, I muttered and swore under my breath.

A text alert buzzed. I grabbed my phone out of my sack, hoping things had been set right. Eric and Alex couldn't get away with this. Somebody must have fessed up. We weren't ostriches cooking with our heads in the sand. Everybody knew everybody's business in that kitchen. I clicked open the message, praying with every fiber in my heart, in my soul, only to find myself sucker punched by *his* words.

> I was kidding about the burger joint. Still, nobody in their
> right mind will hire you once word gets out. And it will.
> O'Shea's on damage control. My offer still stands.

A taxi whipped by, launching a tidal wave of putrid water over my head, drenching me. I was too angry, too flipped out, to care. My body filled with a palpable rage. I stood on the corner of Sullivan and Prince, raised my arms to the sky, and screamed so hard I thought my lungs would burst. Tears pricked at my eyes, but I refused to let them fall. Lightning crackled in the sky, illuminating the buildings and bringing me back to my senses. An icy clarity washed over me. Eric wanted me back in every sense, and would make sure I had no other options but him. Soaking wet, I forced my legs to move and walked the four miles home to the Upper East Side, oblivious to the downpour, to the cold, trying to figure out a way to set the record straight. Until he cooled off, talking to O'Shea was out of the question, if he'd even give me a chance to explain what I thought went down, what I knew in my bones went down.

I'd found my heart in the kitchen. The only real relationship I had in my life was with food, and without my dreams I had nothing. Eric knew that. Now my heart was shattered into a billion pieces.

3

the jig is up

IGNACIO, MY FRIENDLY doorman from the Bronx with a gap-toothed smile, frowned when he buzzed me into the lobby. By now, the cut on my hand had stopped bleeding, but my chef's coat was bloodstained, my toque had flattened on my head like a deflated balloon, and my black Crocs dirtied the polished marble floors, leaving a water trail with each step I took.

"Good lord, Sophie, you look like you've been through a war," said Ignacio, clucking his tongue, worry speckling his usually cheerful tone. "Is that kitchen life of yours that dangerous?"

"In more ways than you can imagine," I said with a long sigh.

"You hurt?"

"Only a flesh wound," I said, feeling as if somebody had torn my heart out of my chest and seared it to a crisp. "Just a little cut."

I didn't want to be rude to Ignacio—he was always so nice—but I wasn't in the mood for small talk. I just wanted to get up to my apartment, change out of my bloody, wet clothes, and plot my revenge against Eric. I pressed the button to call the elevator. "I guess I should get upstairs and clean myself up," I said, rocking self-consciously on my heels, water squishing in between my toes. "I'm making a mess in the foyer."

"Don't worry about it. Water dries," said Ignacio with a sympathetic smile. "Have a nice evening. Tomorrow will be another day."

"Thanks," I said and stepped into the elevator, thinking about the old adage "The early bird gets the worm." In my case, this conjured up a bottle of mescal, tequila's smoky big brother. If the manufacturers of this potent libation hadn't drowned the worm found at the bottom of some bottles, the worm would have metamorphosed into a butterfly. The knot in my stomach tightened, so painful I couldn't breathe. I shook my head, the scene from Cendrillon flashing into my mind like some kind of hallucinatory nightmare, so dizzying I almost fell down. My prayers to the kitchen gods had gone unanswered, unless it was their intention to turn me into a sacrificial lamb, left gutted and slaughtered. Everything I'd worked so hard for had evaporated in less than five minutes. I slithered out of the elevator and onto the floor, trying to will my heart to stop from breaking.

Frank Sinatra crooned and the sound of laughter came from inside the apartment. Walter was home and I really needed to talk to him. Unfortunately, he was probably entertaining one of his highbrow clients, preferring home meetings or restaurants where he could get them liquored up outside the confines of his stuffy office. Thankfully, there was only one apartment on each floor, the elevator opening up with a key into a private foyer, so I wasn't risking exposing myself to anybody unless Walter or his client opened the front door. The laughter inside got louder. I figured I was safe.

Shivering with cold, I kicked off my clogs, tore off my drenched socks, and changed into my street clothes—jeans, sneakers, and a pale blue cashmere sweater. Then, I pulled out a brush and re-braided my hair so tight my temples throbbed. It wasn't my best attempt at cleaning up, but I no longer looked like I'd gotten into a knife fight in the back of a dark alley. I balled up my wet and bloody clothes, stuffed them into my bag, and unlocked the door. Two glasses of champagne stood on the coffee table. There was no sign of Walter or his guest.

"Walter?"

He popped up from the couch like a surprised prairie dog, his head darting around in every direction. He wore a pair of silk boxer shorts with whales on them, nothing more. "Sophie? What are you doing here?"

"I live here, remember?" I said, dropping my bag to the marble floor in the entry.

"Yes, but you're never home this early," he said.

"And you're never this naked at seven p.m.," I said, eyeing the clock in the kitchen, realizing I'd just walked more than an hour and forty-five minutes in pouring rain.

A man with nutmeg-colored freckles peered over the couch and waved. "My fault," he said, his nose scrunching.

It was Robert, Walter's longtime friend from Stanford Law. He was also Walter's boyfriend. And he was also half-naked in his Calvin Kleins. After a long hiatus, they'd gotten back together a few months ago. They scrambled around the living room, throwing on their pants and buttoning the buttons on their matching—yes, matching—Façonnable blue-and-white-checked dress shirts with stiff white collars.

As they dressed, I walked over to the kitchen and ran the water to clean the cut with soap. Thankfully, the knick wasn't too deep. I wrapped a piece of gauze—a staple in our cabinets—around my hand.

"Did you hurt yourself?" asked Walter.

"Just another one of my klutzy moments."

"With a knife?" he asked, and I shrugged. "Let me have a look."

"I'm fine," I said. "You're not a doctor, you're a lawyer."

"You're going to be more than fine in a minute," said Walter, grinning like a fool. "Robert and I have some exciting news to share."

"Oh, I think it might take more than a minute for me to be fine."

Robert clapped his hands together and grinned with childish glee. "The charade is up! You don't have to be Walter's beard anymore. He finally came out to Nicole tonight!"

"Your mother? Wow. How did she take it?" I asked, gobsmacked.

"As well as can be expected," said Walter. "She's pretty disappointed I'm not marrying a beautiful French-born chef, and won't be able to entertain her ladies who lunch. You know how Nicole is, she's all about appearances." He threw up his hands. "Let's face it. Deep down, she always knew I was queer, but she didn't want to come to terms with it. Thankfully, having a gay son is de rigueur now. She'll snap back. I'm pretty sure she's already planning our wedding. It'll be a huge event."

"That's great," I said, my throat constricting. His beautiful French-born chef was in total ruin. Walter didn't need me anymore. My culinary career was in the crapper. I didn't have a job. I didn't have a fake fiancé. I really had nothing. They were probably buttering me up before they kicked me out. "Just swell."

Walter smiled, which drew attention to the adorable dimples in his cheeks. His thick black hair brought out the brightness in his clear blue eyes.

"Here's to my Sunday gal," said Walter.

He and Robert raised their champagne glasses and clinked the bottle that I had picked up. Suddenly, the cut throbbed with a shooting pain. Instead of reaching for a glass, I chugged the Dom

Pérignon straight from the bottle. Robert eyed me with a bit of disgust, but didn't say anything.

"Here's to Sunday," I said.

"Do you remember the first day we met? Robert and I were talking about it earlier."

"I do," I said.

"Grab one of the gorgeous Baccarat crystal glasses you bought me for Christmas last year, Sophie," said Walter. "Didn't your grandmother tell you it's the only way champagne should be served?"

Robert smirked and pointed to the buffet. "We certainly don't drink Dom straight from the bottle."

"Yeah, yeah, yeah," I said. "How crass of me."

I meandered over to grab a glass—a *coupe de champagne*, the oldest design, preceding flute and tulip glasses. Legend had it that the bowl of the glass was modeled after the breast of Marie Antoinette. I settled back on the couch and Walter poured.

"Cheers to our Sophie," he said. "I don't know what I would have done without you."

Lone moviegoers, Walter and I had struck up a friendly conversation at a French film—*Manon des sources*—at one of the local theaters two years prior. That night, we ended up back at his $3 million loft, where we drank wine and listened to Edith Piaf and Nina Simone. He was kind, sensitive, and liked the same things I did. As a chef working long hours, I didn't have time to meet anybody, let alone date. And, other than a few chefs from the CIA—not operatives for the government, but students at the Culinary Institute of America—who were scattered across the country, I didn't have any friends. I gave up going out with the brigade for nightcaps at Blue Ribbon Brasserie, a late-night hangout for chefs in the city and open until four a.m. Eric always lurked around, trying to convince me he was a "changed" man. His pleas to get me back in his bed got old real quick and bordered on extreme sexual harassment. Sometimes he'd corner me, placing his hands all over my body. I thought I'd just deal with it by keeping silent. That was probably a big mistake. I figured I had thick skin and if I worked hard, I'd be fine. Regardless, I thought I held my own, demanded respect. But that wasn't the case. Eric never respected me.

With Walter things were calm, different. A new friendship developed. For one month we spent our Sundays together, talking and laughing. I knew he was gay from the get-go and we weren't going to have a steamy romance, but I needed a friend I could actually talk openly to. Walter needed the same from me.

It wasn't long before Walter offered me a very tempting proposition. A rich trust-fund kid from Greenwich, Connecticut, he was terrified of coming out to his old-money family, especially to his mother, Nicole, who wanted nothing more than for him to have grandkids she could tote around. He'd felt pressure—too much pressure—to live up to her expectations. While he gathered up his courage, he decided to live a small lie. I'd receive an amazing apartment to live in and pretend to be his fiancée. It was as if the universe had thrown Walter right into my lap. Eric and I had recently broken up and I'd been staying in a modestly priced hotel while looking for an apartment of my own. I really liked and trusted Walter, so I agreed to his plan. Plus, since I was his fake fiancée, he provided an excuse I could use to fend off Eric's advances.

But now the jig was up. I sank onto the couch, wondering what I was going to do. Where would I go? Why would Walter want me to stick around? What did I have to offer him anymore?

"Walter," I said. "Honestly, I don't know what I would do without you."

I was hoping he'd say, "I still need you" or "you still have me."

Instead, Walter continued, "So I bit the bullet today and I did it." He grabbed Robert's hand. "We actually did it. I picked up Robert and we went to see my mother. You should have seen her face when I told her Robert was my lover."

"With all the Botox, I thought she was a tad expressionless," said Robert. "But her mouth did drop a little bit."

"You don't know how amazing I feel," said Walter with a laugh. "It's like I'm free. Free to be me."

As Robert tied his ascot around his neck, I let out a wicked laugh and jumped up from the couch. "I guess we should call off our engagement," I said, fingering the five-carat diamond ring hanging from my necklace. Walter hadn't given it to me. We'd found it in my mother's affairs and thought it would be a great prop for our charade. The diamond was probably fake, but it served its purpose. Now it was useless—like me. I chugged more Dom Pérignon too quickly, choking on the bubbles.

"Sophie, what's wrong?" asked Walter. "You should be happy, thrilled even. You're my best friend. You don't need to play along with this charade anymore. Isn't it great? We can live the lives we want to live. No more hiding—"

"In the closet," said Robert.

I held up a finger. "I get it, and I'm happy for you two. I am. But I'm having a really bad day—a momentous, life-crushing day."

"What's going on?" asked Walter, deep concern flashing in his eyes. "Sit down, Sophie. Stop pacing. Tell me what happened."

"Oh, it's really bad. Worse than bad. Epic," I said. Gripping the bottle of champagne, I slumped on the couch and stared at the ceiling, the devastation of what had happened rolling in like ten-foot waves and pulling me under. My voice shook as I recounted what went down at Cendrillon.

Walter sat quietly in thought. He tapped his fingers on his thigh.

"Maybe you should take a vacation. When was the last time you took one?""

"That would be never," I said.

"Go somewhere. You're always working so hard. Everybody needs a break," said Walter. "What about Monica? Your chef friend in Los Angeles. Give her a call. Maybe a change of scenery is what you need. Until things cool down."

He'd said exactly what I feared; he didn't want me to stick around. "Now that I'm fired as your fake fiancée, are you booting me out, too?" I asked.

"No, never, not in a million years. You can stay with us for as long as you want. Forever even. We owe the world to you—"

"We do," said Robert. "Tonight, we're having cocktails at the Boom Boom Room and a celebratory dinner at Le Coucou." He paused, giving me the once-over. "Go get yourself cleaned up and come along."

"Thanks," I said, feeling more cuckoo than "hey you" or "peek-aboo," the French translation of *coucou*, and pronounced the same way. "But I'm not in the shape, form, or mood to go anywhere. I'm going to make myself something to eat, watch a movie, and go to bed. Go have fun. I'll be fine."

But I wasn't fine. I just wanted to forget everything.

4

*flat champagne bubbles
and broken dreams*

A FTER THE DOOR shut behind Walter and Robert, I polished off the bottle of champagne and shuffled over to the freezer to retrieve a half pack of old cigarettes. I'd given up the social habit two years ago, considering I was never social, but I figured my life was already in the crapper. One or two, maybe three, cigarettes wouldn't hurt me.

The cigarettes were the long English brand—Sobranie Cocktails—with colorful pastel encasings and a gold band around the filter, the same kind my mother, Céleste, had smoked. I lit one up, thinking of her. Sometimes she'd used a long black holder, a vision conjuring up glamorous movie stars from the golden age of film. Her lips would purse and she'd inhale, finally blowing out the smoke from her raspberry-red lips in a *whoosh*, her posture always straight. When she smoked, she was graceful, even elegant, whereas I was not. With each inhale, I coughed and hacked. I snuffed out the butt in an ashtray.

I kept the only photo I had of her tucked away in my top drawer underneath my socks. I fumbled my way to my room, pulled it out, and made my way back to the couch. A few people had said I look like her. Similar in appearance to me, she had large green almond-shaped eyes, high cheekbones, a defined jawline, full lips, and long black hair, but people had also said that I was rougher around the edges. Perhaps it's because I rarely wore makeup, my hair was usually in a messy braid, and, for the most part, I was always dressed in chef's threads. Not exactly the epitome of glamour. I stared at the picture, gripping the corner between my thumb and forefinger.

We were holding hands and skipping down a path in Central Park. In the background, there were a couple of ducks in a pond. She was twenty-four at the time, wearing a black flowered sundress that tied at the neck; I was around five, wearing a pinafore dress, a white shirt, and black Mary Janes with lacy white socks. She looked down at me with a grin; I looked up at her with awe. Even in this picture, Céleste carried herself with the kind of grace only French-women know how to pull off.

We'd moved from France to New York when I was six months old. I didn't recall much of those early years, too young to remember, obviously. But I do remember the days when I was older, like in this picture. My mother had just gotten a bit part in a movie, playing the role of the clichéd sexy French maid. A method actress, she was scrubbing down the kitchen when she sat me down and asked, "Do you know what dreams are, *ma petite*?"

"A big ice cream sundae," was my answer.

She shook her long black hair and giggled. "My darling girl, dreams are much bigger than that. I'm going to be a star."

I was entranced, wondering if I could swing from the stars or carry moonbeams home in a jar, the tune my mother hummed. My eyes widened like saucers. "A star? Like one in the sky?"

"No, not like a star in the sky, something bigger and brighter. I'm going to be famous one day. Mark my words." She winked. "*Ma petite*, we come from noble blood. Your great-great-*grand-père* was a *comte* and now your grand-mère has the world at her feet. It's my turn to shine."

"Ma grand-mère?" I'd asked. "Where is she?"

"Oh, don't you worry your little mind over her. You wouldn't like her. She abandoned us. Just as if we were stray cats prowling on the streets." She held up her manicured fingernails and made a clawing motion. "She's like that witch, the mean one, in the movie you love so much, the Wicked Witch of the West."

"The Wizard of Oz?"

"Yes, that's the one." She looked out the window, humming.

At five years old, I didn't think much about this grandmother I'd never met. Thanks to my mother comparing her to the Wicked Witch of the West, I'd envisioned her as old and decrepit with a green face and skeleton-like hands. I didn't want to come face-to-face with her. My dreams were comprised of sweet treats and swinging on the swings. I was seven years old when I finally met her. To my delight, she didn't have a green face or long decrepit fingers with curled nails.

I tried to remember my mother's smile, the days when she was happy, the memories hard to come by. I slammed the photo onto the coffee table facedown.

This photo was a lie. Her dreams never came to fruition and my life was filled with broken promises. When my mother was up, she lit up the room. But when she was down, spiraling into depression, the days and nights were hard. I always thought it was my fault, something I did. But I knew now that wasn't the case. My mother was never happy. She was good at being a faker, at pretending, especially when she smiled her closed-lip smile. I could see her eyes were dead.

I wanted to shake off the memories of her that were invading my mind. I got up, made my way to my room, stuffed the photo into its drawer, and jumped into the shower, needing to be proactive, not reactive. I ran the water cold to offset the fire searing my chest.

Clean, but not exactly refreshed, I threw on a pair of flannel pajamas, turned the gas fireplace in the living room to a blaze, and picked up the phone to call Monica, my closest friend from the CIA. A dynamo in the kitchen, she was elevating Mexican cuisine to new gastronomic levels. She had opened her restaurant, El Colibrí, two short years ago. At first people thought she was nuts—then they tasted her dishes. Billing her cuisine as "not your mother's tacos," she'd introduced gourmet Mexican food to Los Angeles, and you didn't eat her creations—like the lobster tail served with the pomegranate mango salsa, served on a blue corn tortillas—with your hands, especially with her secret version of a chimichurri sauce. A hint: truffle oil along with olive oil. The girl genius was an alchemist in the kitchen, creating elixirs and blending ingredients like a mad culinary scientist.

"Hola, babe," she said. "It's a bit nuts here. I only have a few minutes."

"Are you looking for a sous chef?" I asked.

She went silent for a moment. "Jesus Christ. I'm so sorry, Sophie. I just heard the news."

My throat constricted. "Already?"

"What can I say? News travels fast in the culinary circles. Everybody knows everybody's business."

"Eric was behind it." Once again, I repeated my sad, pathetic story.

"I always hated that skinny, diabolical bastard. Never knew what you saw in him."

"You and me both," I said. "So, back to my question. I'm thinking a change of scenery and a new job would do wonders for my psyche—"

"Babe, you know I love you. I do. But I simply can't take the risk right now. What were you thinking?"

"I wasn't thinking. It was Eric," I cried. "I've screwed myself, haven't I?"

"It's not the best of scenarios." Monica sighed. "I hate to drop this on you on a day like today, but you're going to find out anyway. El Colibrí is on the rising star list."

"Oh," I said, gripping the phone. My voice shook. "Congratulations. You must be thrilled. You're part of the one percent."

"I'm sorry. I know it's been your dream, too. A dream that would have come to fruition if Eric the skinny rat weasel hadn't—"

"Don't apologize. I'm happy for you." I gulped, even though jealousy tweaked my heart. She'd done it; I hadn't. I was ruined. "I'm thrilled. Really. You deserve this."

"Well, I was jumping over the moon until I heard what happened. Really kind of flattens the champagne bubbles, if you know what I mean." Monica paused. "If you're serious about a change of scenery, you're more than welcome to come stay with Esteban and me for as long as you want. I can put you in contact with some chefs I know—chefs doing exciting things."

"Nobody is going to touch me with a ten-foot pole. Eric has turned me into a liability, an outcast. I'm so screwed."

"Things will simmer down soon. As they say, time heals all wounds. Believe me, the truth always has a way of rising to the surface. I'm just so sorry I can't offer you a position here."

A long silence lingered. The chatter of a man's voice in the background interrupted our conversation. Monica grumbled something and then got back to me. "Babe, I'm so sorry, but I've got to bolt. As you can imagine, we've got a huge night ahead of us—"

"I understand," I said.

"I'll call you tomorrow morning when things are calmer, okay?

And think about visiting Esteban and me for a few weeks. A few months. Whatever you need. *Mi casa, tu casa.*"

"Thanks," I said.

"Ciao, babe. We'll talk tomorrow."

The line went dead. I sat on the couch, a deeper depression sinking in.

My culinary life was dead.

My dreams were dead.

And I wanted Eric dead.

Before I ended up in jail for killing the bastard, I needed to figure out next steps. I could email one of my food critic contacts at the *Times* with a fake email account, tipping her off as to what really happened at Cendrillon; I could pretend to accept his offer of working for him, and then poison him with arsenic; and, of course, I could cut off his balls and feed them to stray dogs in the alley. (The last option brought a twisted smile to my face.) I was tempted to send him a few texts, laying into him, and I even typed a few out; it made me feel better.

> You are the biggest prick on the planet.

> I'm putting a curse on you.

> Your restaurant will fail.

I deleted all but one.

> You destroyed my life.

Still reeling from the buzz of champagne, after I sent the message, I thought, What life? Although running a restaurant as part of the one percent of women had driven me all these years, I didn't have a life. I'd been a beard for a gay man. Aside from Walter, Robert, and Monica, I didn't have any friends. I definitely needed a big change. Maybe I even needed to change? When was the last time I was happy? Truly, madly, and wonderfully happy? When was the last time I laughed? Felt free? The answer hit me like a thunderbolt: those summers in southwestern France cooking with Grand-mère Odette.

My life in the kitchen began with my grandmother in the village of Champvert in the Tarn-et-Garonne department of southwestern France, the town so small you'd need a magnifying glass to find it on the map. I'd sit on a tall wooden stool, wide-eyed, watching Grand-mère Odette in her navy-blue dress and black ballerina flats, her apron adorned with *les coquelicots* (wild red poppies), mesmerized by the grace with which she danced around her kitchen, hypnotized by all the wonderful smells—the way the aromas were released from the herbs picked right from her garden as she chopped, becoming stronger as she set them in an olive oiled and buttered pan. She'd dip a spoon in a pot or slice up an onion in two seconds, making it look oh so easy, and for her it was. But my favorite part was when she'd let me taste whatever delight she was cooking up, sweet or savory. I'd close my eyes, lick my lips, and sigh with happiness.

Sometimes Grand-mère Odette would blindfold me, and it wasn't long before I could pick out every ingredient by smell. All the other senses came to me, too—sight (the glorious plating), taste (the delight of the unknown), touch (the way a cherry felt in my hand), and hearing (the way garlic sizzled in the pan).

"You are a chef," she'd say.

"One day, I want to be just like you," I'd say.

Her pale green eyes, which reminded me of the freshness of spring, would crinkle as she smiled and she'd tousle my hair. "*Sophie, quand tu es en France, il faut que tu parles français.*" (When you are in France, you must speak French.) Then, she'd mumble something about how that traveling star-chaser of a mother of mine had ruined my education and how, thankfully, I spent the summers with her so she could put the pieces back together, to get me in touch with my roots. After all, I was born in France, so I was French in Grand-mère Odette's eyes and not an American, and not, heaven forbid, a New Yorker. Much to Grand-mère Odette's chagrin, the facts were the facts and I was all three.

Those formative years, all the summers spent with Grand-mère Odette in her kitchen in southwestern France, fueled my dreams of becoming a chef, the love of cooking running like the sweetest of cherry juices through my veins. Thanks to the skills I picked up while soaking in Grand-mère Odette's every word like the greediest of sponge cakes, I graduated at the top of my class from the Culinary Institute of America.

The more I thought about Champvert, the lighter my anger became. Unfortunately, it was three a.m. in France, too late to call Grand-mère Odette, and I wasn't quite sure if she'd be happy to hear from me. We hadn't spoken all that much in well over six months because I'd been too busy with work, pushing for a promotion I'd never get. She'd call, but I'd brush her off with "I'll call you tomorrow. Got lots on my plate." Unfortunately, her hours didn't match mine, not with the six-hour time difference. In a failed attempt to drown out my misery, I opened up a bottle of wine, poured, and then stared off into space, trying to think of happier times.

Something overtook me. At first, I thought the ceiling was leaking, my face splattered with a few wet droplets. And then it was like somebody had turned on a faucet. My body rocked, shaking my entire core. I cried for the death of my career. I cried for not being a better granddaughter to Grand-mère Odette, the only person in my world who fueled and supported my dreams. The last time I'd seen Grand-mère in person was when she flew out for my graduation from the CIA five years ago. Although she didn't like to fly, she'd taken the long journey across the Atlantic. She was so proud of my achievements—the fact that I'd graduated at the top of my class. Yet I'd just set my grandmother to the side, thinking she would always be my pillar of strength. Too obsessed with my culinary career, I kept delaying a trip to Champvert, thinking she'd always be around. But the days were passing by and she *wouldn't* always be around.

By the time I polished off the bottle of wine, guilt and plans for diabolical ways to get back at Eric replaced the memories of France, my mind filled with vengeance. Exhausted and angry, I finally made my way to my room and, after tossing and turning, I passed out stone-cold.

5

---

when bad things happen to good people

I T WAS A little after seven in the morning when I came to. The wine had left a sour taste in my mouth; there were no feelings of euphoria, no buzz, just the pulsing pressure of a severe headache, nausea, and a mouth full of cotton. I desperately needed coffee. I shuffled my way to the kitchen, passing the living room.

An ashtray full of half-smoked cigarettes sat on the coffee table, and next to it, the empty bottle of wine. That, in addition to the champagne—I'd definitely gone overboard. The past ten hours flashed in my mind, a hazy blur of distress hitting me in waves. Yesterday wasn't a nightmare; it was real. I eyed my cell phone and groaned when I picked it up, my eyes focusing on the screen. Why on earth had I texted Eric? Of course he'd responded.

> I didn't destroy your life. I offered you an opportunity. It's up to you to take it.

I threw my phone across the room and punched the cushions on the Roche Bobois couch while trying to muffle my screams. Walter padded into the living room wearing his pajamas—plaid pants and a long-sleeved thermal top. He rubbed away the sleep from his eyes and let out a cough.

"Sophie, what did the couch do to you?"

It was his attempt at humor; I didn't laugh. I grunted and sank onto the couch. "Sorry, did I wake you?"

"You know me, I'm always up at the crack of dawn."

"Did you have fun last night?"

"We did, but something was missing at our celebration," he said with a sweet smile. "You."

"Sorry," I said with a feeble shrug. "I wasn't in the best shape."

"Never apologize. I understand." Walter shuffled over and sat down next to me. He put his arm around my shoulders and pulled me in to his chest. He always smelled like fresh lemons and oranges, which was comforting. I wanted to stay curled against him forever and never have to face my stinking life. As he stroked my hair, he said, "I know things appear really terrible right now, but today will be another day."

"A worse day." I bolted upright. "The entire culinary world knows about Cendrillon and me, the supposed sabotaging chef. They just don't realize the blame is being placed on the wrong person." I gulped. "You're an attorney. Can I sue him? Can I sue Eric?"

"I practice family law, Sophie."

"I know. But maybe somebody at your firm practices—what is it? Defamation of character?"

Walter let out a worried huff. "Let's look at the facts. Do you have proof that Eric told you to put the spices in the dishes?"

"No, not exactly."

"Is there anybody who would corroborate your story?"

"Miguel might," I said, and then thought of his earlier actions. He couldn't even look at me. No, loyalty was a one-way street in a kitchen like Cendrillon NY; it went to the chef. And, after Eric left, that chef would most likely be Alex. "Then again, probably not."

"And would you really want to walk down that road? All the money you'd have to fork out? All the bad publicity? A trial that could last years? It would be Eric and Alex's word against yours. Even though I know you didn't do anything, the press would drag your name through the mud. Do you really want to go through all that?"

I thought about it.

"Why not? I'm already ruined. I have some money left over from when I sold my mother's apartment. Plus, thanks to you and to my lack of shopping, and mostly eating at the restaurant, I've got two years of pay saved up. I have to do something." The words gurgled out of my throat. "Anything."

Walter raised an eyebrow. "Soph, I'd think about this a little more when things settle down. Little girls plot revenge. Smart women sit back and let karma do its job."

"I hope karma is a bloodthirsty bitch," I mumbled, my jaw clenched.

"Me, too," said Walter with a laugh. His joy was short-lived. When he saw me huddled over, breathing hard, he became serious. "Just don't do anything rash in the heat of the moment. You'll only be adding fuel to Eric's fire. Let the dust settle."

"I guess you're right," I said, my head pounding. "I mean, it's not like I can do anything now. It's a he-said, she-said dilemma and O'Shea is listening to that He-Man bastard right now."

"Think about the silver lining," he said.

"Is there one?"

"We don't have to get married."

"I would have done that for you," I said, wiping my nose with the sleeve of my pajamas.

"I know you would have, and that's why I love you so much," he said. "Let's get the day started with some goodness. Coffee?"

I nodded, really needing to clear my head. "I'll make it."

"No, take it easy. You look spent. Hey, I may be the world's worst cook, but I can handle a cup of joe."

Robert padded into the living room, his pajamas matching Walter's. He let out a roar of a yawn. "Oh, thank the lord, coffee! We didn't get home until three in the morning. Make it extra strong, Walter," he said, and then kissed me on the cheek.

We sat down at the counter, watching Walter fumble with the grounds and the French press. It was a good half hour before our daily doses of caffeine were set before us. "Oh, you're spoiling me, my love," said Robert. "*Times* here yet?"

Walter shrugged.

Robert shuffled over to the front door. He grabbed the paper and made his way back over to us, rummaging through it. His eyes darted to Walter's and he whipped a segment behind his back. My heart plummeted into my stomach. I jumped off my stool. "What's going on?" I asked. "Is today Wednesday?"

Walter let out a groan. I could feel the color draining from my cheeks. It *was* Wednesday—the day the *Times* printed the Food section for the English-speaking world to see. "Hand it over."

Robert held the paper above my head. I jumped and snatched it from him, ripping the pages. "You really don't want to read this," he said. "Not today." He grabbed the segment back.

"Robert?" I said, crossing my arms over my chest. "If you don't hand it over, I'll never speak to you again."

He was in the process of trying to shred an article when I snagged it from his grip. I sank to the floor, putting the pieces back together like a jigsaw puzzle. On page one, my worst nightmare hit me so hard I felt like I'd been sucker punched in the stomach with a sledgehammer.

The headline: SABOTAGING CHEF DE PARTIE SOPHIE VALROUX COSTS CENDRILLON NY A STAR.

A picture of me smiling with one arm latched onto Eric's, and the other onto O'Shea's, accompanied the text. The photographer had taken the picture right after Cendrillon had received its second star.

> Today Michelin released its New York red guide and a few of the most notable restaurants in New York City are in a tizzy. Some restaurants, like M.D.M., have gained a star and a few restaurants, such as Blink 214, have become starless. But one restaurant in particular has the culinary world on edge: Cendrillon NY.
>
> Cendrillon NY was expecting its third Michelin star, but instead of gaining one, it lost one. In his press release, Chef Dan O'Shea has pinpointed the reason why, outing the culprit for ill-fated plates, a saboteur by the name of Sophie Valroux, a chef de partie (pictured center).
>
> According to Chef O'Shea, "She [Valroux] seasoned my recipes to her liking. She broke the rules. She was always trying to prove herself, always trying to one-up the men. Sometimes egotistical chefs with a chip on their shoulder get out of hand. I can assure the public and the culinary world that this will never happen again. I've given Valroux her walking papers and I'm taking a more active role with all of my restaurants, especially Cendrillon NY. We will get our second star back. And we'll eventually get that third star, too."
>
> At the time of printing, we could not reach Ms. Valroux for comment.

What? I scrambled on the floor like a squirrel looking for a hidden nut, finally finding my phone. Eight calls had come in when I was passed out. I'd flipped out over Eric's text, and too busy finding out a way to block his number, I didn't check my voice mails. Plus, nobody ever called me.

"Hello, this is Trevor Smith from the Times. *We'd like to get your thoughts on what happened at Cendrillon—"*

Delete.

"Ms. Valroux, this is Trevor Smith calling from the Times. *We're about to run the piece. Could you please call me back at your earliest convenience?"*

Delete.

Nausea gripped me, rocking my core. My face went hot. Drops of perspiration coated my neck and back. I stared straight ahead. Walter rubbed my shoulders. "You okay? You look like you're going to be sick."

I could only gurgle out a yes before running to the bathroom and emptying out the contents of my stomach. This was so much worse than anything I'd ever imagined. Eric and O'Shea had eviscerated my entire life. The whole world was going to think that I was a sabotaging chef. A pariah. Walter tapped on the door. "Are you okay, Soph?"

I threw the door open. Walter jumped back. "I'm fine," I said.

"You don't look fine," he said, his smoky blue eyes wide and fearful.

I could only imagine how I looked—angry and crazed.

"I will be fine in a minute." The people in my neighborhood, the people I said hello to every day weren't going to find out about this. At least the people who didn't have the *Times* delivered to their front doors. I raced to the entryway, throwing on a pair of boots and my coat, grabbing my purse.

"Where are you going?" asked Walter. "You're wearing pajamas. You can't leave the apartment like this."

"I know," I said. "But I am. There's something important I need to do."

Everything in my vision blurred. I raced past Frank, our day doorman. I bolted out the door and looked around frantically. Darting through traffic like a crazed frog, I scrambled up to our local newsstand and purchased every copy of the *Times*. Out of the corner of my eye, I saw a man swaggering down the sidewalk. I'd recognize that walk anywhere. Eric. What was he doing on the Upper East Side? This was not his neighborhood. The devil of a douchebag lived in Hell's Kitchen. His eyes widened when he saw me. I froze. Before I could get away, he ran toward me and grabbed my arm. I whipped it away.

"Don't touch me. Don't talk to me. Don't even look at me."

"We need to talk," said Eric with surprise—as if he'd actually believed I'd race back into his arms after what he'd done.

"What are you doing here? How did you get my address?"

"We do have records at the restaurant," he said smugly, his breath reeking of whiskey. It was clear he'd been out all night. He eyed the stack of papers. "Since you didn't respond to my text, I was going to drop off a note, extending my offer for you to work for me. Your choices are limited, Sophie. Extremely limited."

We stood in front of one another, me wanting to claw his eyes out.

"Don't look at me like that," he said. "I did what I did for us."

"After you killed my career? I'm never talking to you again," I spat. He grabbed me by the arm once more, gripping it tightly, pulling me closer. He smelled of cheap perfume and cigarettes. I yelped. "Let go of me, Eric."

"Sophie, I need to tell you—"

"Save your lame-ass words for somebody who wants to listen to them," I said, whipping my arm from his grip. "You are certifiably insane."

"I'm not the crazy one here, Sophie. You are. I'm thinking it must run in your family."

His words delivered a punch, rendering me numb.

He ran his hands through his hair. "You'd be nothing without me. A complete zero. I'm the one who taught you everything you know. Let's face it, you're just a talentless lackey. I'd be surprised if you made it into cooking school on your own."

"Of course I did," I said, mostly trying to convince myself. I'd gone above and beyond to get into the CIA. Nobody had pulled any strings for me because there wasn't anybody to pull them. I'd done everything on my own. "I worked my ass off, graduated at the top of my class. You were the one who sought me out."

"You sure about that?"

My blood boiled with an all-consuming rage I'd never felt before. I slapped Eric as hard as I could with my free hand.

I turned to bolt into my building, a cab nearly running me over as I dashed across the street. Once inside the protection of the lobby, I glanced over my shoulder. Eric stood on the sidewalk, a smug grimace twisting his face. When I returned to the loft, Robert and Walter eyed the stack of papers shaking in my arms. "Should we have a bonfire before we head off to work?" asked Walter.

"Yes," I said with a whimper, "and I'm never leaving the apartment again."

6

flambéed with a capital F

FOR WEEKS I stayed holed up in my room, which was filled with half-empty containers of meals I couldn't bring myself to finish. Thankful for the fact that I lived in the city, I could order in anything—Chinese food, tampons, and Chunky Monkey ice cream. I lived in my pajamas, because when I wasn't scouring the Internet reading about what an abomination I was, I slept. I tried calling O'Shea numerous times, but the second he heard my panicked voice saying, "Chef, Chef, please let me explain," he hung up. And I gave up. My breakfast, which usually came at one in the afternoon, consisted of some kind of sustenance like a poached egg with a side of vodka and orange juice, which I also ordered in. I wanted to sleep forever, oblivious to everything.

Walter and Robert would come into my room, trying to cheer me up. Whatever they did—bringing me flowers or chocolates or telling lame jokes—never worked. Walter would sigh. Robert would say, "Let her grieve."

"For how long?" Walter would ask.

I'd answer, "For as long as it takes."

"Give her time," Robert would say. "She'll snap out of it."

No, I thought, not when I've snapped. They'd shuffle out of my room, eyeing me with pity. They didn't get it. They didn't understand. Everything I'd worked so hard for—my wonderland, my dreams—had evaporated right before my eyes. I couldn't pick up the pieces of my life when I couldn't even pick myself up. Self-doubt ran through my veins, making me question everything. Eric had made sure of that. Perhaps I was a talentless lackey. A charity case he'd felt sorry for. Still, if I was such a cretin, a waste of kitchen space, why did he want me to come work for him so bad? The answer hit me hard. Eric wanted to break me because he wanted to win, wanted to make sure I didn't have a voice. Well, he'd succeeded. He'd won. And I was broken. As I spiraled down a well of broken dreams, thinking nobody would believe my story, I played possum. And I did it well.

I was alone in the apartment when my first panic attack gripped me in a vise of fear. My heart raced so fiercely I thought it would jump out of my throat. The tips of my fingers tingled. I couldn't catch my breath, and for a good ten minutes I thought I was having a heart attack. I collapsed on my bed and squeezed my eyes shut, certain I was going to die. As I focused on my breathing, willing my heart to calm down, I remembered that my mother had suffered through episodes like this. She used to breathe into a paper bag, which stopped her from hyperventilating and passing out. Thanks to many deliveries, there were plenty of paper bags strewn all over my floor. Once the attack subsided, I realized I was being pulled into a dark place I desperately needed to get out of.

This wasn't me. I had to do something. I wasn't my mother. I reminded myself I did graduate the CIA at the top of my class.

I meandered into the kitchen, ready to dig in, ready to convince myself my life and everything I'd worked so hard for was worth something. For a moment, I stood numb, looking at the glittering copper pots and pans Walter had purchased for me, the beautiful stainless steel stove, questioning my skills, which was easy to do with Eric's and O'Shea's words pricking at my head like a swarm of angry bees.

"Talentless."

"He didn't have people pulling strings for him."

"I'd be surprised if you made it into cooking school on your own."

"You'd be nothing without me."

I needed to prove them wrong. Prove to myself that I wasn't a zero. Prove to myself that I was something, that I was anything. I grabbed my knives, a cutting board, and opened up the refrigerator to see what was on hand. Apparently, Walter and Robert had been ordering in from a food delivery service supplying all the fresh ingredients to make predetermined recipes. I frowned when I noted the boxes were marked for two, feeling left out. Then again, I hadn't exactly left my room. What I should have been doing was shopping at the market and cooking for them instead of turning into an angry hermit.

The box I commandeered was packed with chicken, zucchini, ras el hanout sauce, garlic, saffron, capers, raisins, couscous, and Greek yogurt. I didn't bother looking at the recipe; I was going to make this dish my own. I wanted to turn these ingredients into something truly delectable.

Wasn't I the woman who could do every single cut with her eyes closed? Dice, mince, julienne, and chiffonade? I unpacked the box, placing everything on the counter. I surveyed the ingredients—a nemesis of sorts. I used to love cooking and creating. Now it was almost as if I hated it.

Prove you can do it, Sophie.

I picked up the zucchini and began to chop. While slicing, I nicked the tip of my thumb. I dropped the knife and sank to the floor, curling up into a pathetic ball. The cut wasn't deep, but it was the kind that flowed and oozed for forever and a day unless you did something about it. The only thing I'd proven to myself was that I was a failure. I couldn't even bring myself to get up. My tears fell like a thunderstorm. It angered me that I was now a crier; I hadn't used to be one. I used to be strong.

My best friends came home to find me bleeding and crying. Walter lifted me off the floor and ran my finger under cold water while I sniffled and wiped my nose with my free hand. He wrapped my finger in gauze and tried his best to console me, but it was kind of hard to console the inconsolable. "Take a shower. Get out. Stop feeling sorry for yourself. This will all blow over," Walter said, his eyebrows furrowed. But even he knew the truth. This situation wasn't going to settle down anytime soon.

"It's never going to blow over! Look at me. I can't do anything right."

Walter slammed his hand on the table. Then he gripped my arms and shook me. "Sophie, I love you, but things have to change. I can't keep living like this. Robert can't keep on living like this. And neither can you."

I'd never seen him angry, not like *this*. He was always so level-headed. I bit down on my bottom lip to try to keep from crying. Still, hot tears rolled down my cheeks.

"Are you kicking me out? I wouldn't blame you," I said, my voice coming out in a pathetic whimper. "Just get it over and done with."

"I'd never kick the Sophie I love out, but this new you, this obstinate, self-pitying creature you've become, needs to change, and quick."

"I'm sorry, Walter," I said. "You know I am. I'm not myself. Eric killed me."

"Eric didn't kill you," said Walter. "You're standing right in front of me—alive and well and rather obnoxious. Pull yourself together. If you don't, you'll end up like her."

I knew he was talking about my mother. Aside from Eric, he was the only person I'd talked with about her death. "That's a low blow, Walter," I said, even though it was exactly what I'd been thinking.

Walter embraced me in a tight hug. "Come on, you're not acting like the Sophie we know and love."

"And we do love you," said Robert, placing his hands on my shoulders. "Do you want to clean yourself up and come to dinner with us? You really should get out of the apartment, breathe in some fresh air."

"Maybe tomorrow," I said.

"We don't like leaving you alone," said Walter.

"Don't worry," I said. "I'm not like her."

"I left the number of a therapist on the counter," said Walter. "Maybe call her, and talk through what you're feeling. You know, an unbiased ear who will listen to you and offer some advice." He kissed me on the cheek. "We'll be back in a few hours. If you need anything, just call."

I nodded.

After the door closed, I clung to my knees. I'd lashed out at my only friends in the worst of ways. To add fuel to my dumpster fire of a life, I couldn't bring myself to call the one person I needed most, and it wasn't a therapist: it was my grandmother. She'd just say "I told you so" and make me feel as if I were incapable of making decisions. Perhaps she would comfort me. But I wasn't ready to be comforted. I wanted to wallow, to be angry with myself and everyone else in the world, including her. It ticked me off she hadn't called; surely the news had reached every corner in the world, even the remote village of Champvert, France.

Still, I missed her. I needed her.

My summers with Grand-mère Odette in France came to an end when I was thirteen, an age when everything mattered—the pimple on your chin, the awkwardness, and, worse, the loneliness. During those years, when my mother was passed out in her bedroom or zoned out from popping pills, my escape was the kitchen. Embarrassed with my life at home, I became a loner, the quiet girl who kept her head down and didn't talk to anybody. Cooking meant everything to me.

I was eighteen when I found my mother's body in the bathtub, blue and bloated, a bottle of pills scattered on the floor. She didn't leave a note, aside from the word "Sorry" scrawled onto the bathroom mirror with her signature red lipstick—Chanel's Rouge Allure. There must have been something wrong with me. I hadn't shed one tear. I just wiped the mirror off with toilet paper, and after I called the paramedics, I called Grand-mère Odette.

Although we hadn't spoken since my last trip to Champvert when I was thirteen, my grandmother agreed to fly out and help me with the funeral arrangements. Our conversation was short, clipped. When I met her at the airport, the first words Grand-mère Odette had said to me were, "I'm surprised you called. I didn't think you wanted me in your life."

"Who told you that?"

"Céleste did. She said you didn't want a thing to do with me. I begged and pleaded for you to come to France."

"She told me you didn't want to see *me*," I said. "And that if I was a good daughter, I'd stay home and take care of her."

"I see," said Grand-mère. "Well, she was a sick, sick woman. *Évidemment.* Now that she's gone, I want you to come to France for good. To your home. You are the only family I have left. After your mother took off and your grand-père died, I've felt quite alone."

This was the first time she'd mentioned my grandfather. I didn't have any memories of him. Nothing. Nada. He was an invisible entity to me.

Her lips pursed. "If you are wondering," she said, "he died of a broken heart. When Céleste took off with you, it crushed him. Does family not mean anything to you?"

My head had dropped with guilt. I had plans. Big plans. Part of me wanted to go back to France, but a bigger part of me wanted to follow my dreams. And we were never the happy, picture-perfect family. Far from it. I was estranged from my mother and barely knew anything about her life in France before I was born. She made sure of that. Aside from visiting my grandmother over those summers, I didn't really know Grand-mère all that well. She hadn't made an effort to step in when I'd really needed her. I wondered if I was missing out on something, but I was eighteen and full of piss and vinegar, obstinate and stubborn. "My life is here, in New York," I said.

"And such a life it is."

"Grand-mère, I've just applied to one of the best cooking schools in the country, in the world—the Culinary Institute of America. I'm hoping to get in. With all my heart, all my soul. I haven't forgotten one thing you taught me."

She straighted her posture, her chin lifting high. "France has the best culinary schools. You should attend Le Cordon Bleu."

"But I want to go to the CIA," I said.

"I see," she said. "If that's what you wish for, I'm sure it will happen."

As we sorted out my mother's estate, she never again brought up the subject of me moving to France, although she did drop the occasional hint. "Champvert is so much cleaner than this dirty city of yours." Or, "Food is healthier in France. Look at those strawberries! They are the size of oranges. It's not natural. And they aren't even in season."

Neither of us cried over the death of my mother. The only time my mother's name was brought up was when I asked if we should have a funeral. Grand-mère Odette's face flushed bright red. She gripped her rosary beads. "What Céleste did was a sin. No funeral," she'd said. And that was that.

Two weeks later, Grand-mère Odette returned to France and I picked up my mother's ashes at the crematorium. As I held the black plastic box in my hands, the tears still wouldn't fall. I resented—no, hated—my mother. She'd never wanted to be a mom, this I knew. When I was a child, she'd told me to call her Céleste, not Mom, in public. She thought my calling her Mom would "age" her. I think she told people I was a stray cat she'd found on the streets. And she'd laugh her tinkly laugh. I scattered her ashes in Central Park and threw away the box. In a way, I felt relief. I'd taken care of her for so long I finally had the chance to take care of myself.

My own mother had sabotaged my life. And now Eric had, too.

Sabotage, of course, ran rampant in the food world. A rival chef once booked dozens of fake reservations and ruined the success of a certain chef's opening night. Angry chefs have turned up ovens to five hundred while cakes were baking. Adding salt or pepper into dishes has been a favorite.

While I might have been mad at Eric and had more than a few unresolved feelings for my mother, I was even angrier with myself. Perhaps I'd deserved this fate. A good chef always paid attention to every detail. Cooking is a science, and it's up to the chef to be continuously aware of every ingredient and every dish, tasting often, and I never tasted the velouté after Eric told me to spice it. I trusted his instincts when I never should have trusted him at all.

The facts were the facts. Eric *did* sabotage me; I'd trusted him, his palate, and the fact that he was chef de cuisine. But I should have trusted my gut and I didn't. I hadn't paid attention to anything. It was in this moment I realized that, along with Eric, I, Sophie Valroux, had sabotaged myself.

7

once burned, twice shy

WALTER AND ROBERT were right. I couldn't continue like this. I didn't want to end up like my mother. I thought of my grandmother. I thought of her strength. I thought of how disappointed she would be if she saw me like this. I'd tried calling or texting Monica; the phone just went to voice mail and she never responded. Go figure—at the CIA she was always in constant competition with me. Now I wasn't a threat. I got it. She didn't need to keep tabs on me anymore. My weakness disgusted me to the point of vomiting out the contents of my stomach daily. But then, one day, when I was hunched over the porcelain god, I had an awakening. That aha moment. This wasn't me. Just because my career was in the crapper didn't mean I needed to ruin everything else, such as my closest friendships—my only friendships.

It took me a good two hours to clean my room, throwing away the empty bags and containers of rotting Chinese food and sludge-like ice cream. I showered. I put on fresh pajamas. Although I'd cleaned myself up a bit, I was still hesitant to leave the apartment—

not with the puffy bags under my eyes, not with the terror of being recognized sparking my mind.

After ordering in supplies for a killer breakfast, I set my alarm for six a.m., my plan to make amends with Walter and Robert. I may not have been the most loquacious or poetic when it came to apologies, but food was my way of communicating, my way of showing my love. On the menu—*œufs cocotte* with ham and chives, bacon, and roasted rosemary potatoes with truffle oil, my gourmet version of hash browns. By seven, the coffee was percolating and filling the kitchen with its earthy aroma. As I prepared my makeup meal, Walter pulled up a chair at the counter, eyeing me curiously.

"You're up?" he questioned.

I shot him a closed-mouth, apologetic smile and poured him a cup of joe.

"You showered? And you're making breakfast? For me?" he asked, and I shrugged. "There is a God. Is that bacon I smell?"

"Yep," I said. "With *œufs cocotte*. It's my apology—"

"Never apologize. Is my Sophie back?" he interrupted. "Because I really want her back."

"I'm getting there—one step and one shower at a time. But I'm missing my heart—"

"You're not missing your heart."

"Without a kitchen I am."

"Where are you standing right now?"

"In a kitchen," I said with a huff. "And it's not the same thing. Look, now that you and Robert are free and clear to live your lives, you have no need of me."

"Yes, we do," he said.

"I'm sure everybody wants a walking nightmare in their lives," I said, my tone a bit snappish. Perhaps I was trying to test Walter's friendship. If he didn't love me, he'd send me away. And I wouldn't blame him.

"You've been a bit terrifying lately, but you're still my best friend."

A tear slid down my cheek. "Some friend."

Smoke filled the kitchen and the fire alarm went off. I'd burned the potatoes and my eggs were overdone. I grabbed a kitchen towel and waved it over my head. "For Pete's sake, I can't even cook anymore. I've lost my cooking mojo."

Walter grabbed a plate, placing an overdone ramekin of eggs and burned potatoes on it. "I'm sure it's still edible." He picked up a forkful of potatoes and chewed, grimacing. "A bit overdone, but delicious."

Robert stumbled into the kitchen. "What's that horrible smell?" he asked.

"My life," I said, throwing up my hands with resignation. "Up in smoke."

"You still have a lot to be thankful for."

"Like what?"

"Me and Walter," said Robert.

If I were them, I would have pushed me out the front door, slammed it shut, and never opened it again. But they didn't. They just exchanged kind, loving smiles and then directed them at me. Walter winked at Robert. Something was up.

I placed one hand on my hip and paced, my other hand gripping my hair. "Let me get this straight. You don't want to kick me out? Even after this breakfast from hell?"

"Not in a million years, Sophie. You're like the deranged sister I never had," said Robert. "We're with you for the long haul."

I pinched my lips together, not able to meet their expectant eyes, so I turned my back on them and picked up the pan of burned potatoes, throwing them into the trash. I didn't deserve their support. As the disaster slid into the garbage, I hung my head, ashamed.

"Thanksgiving is in a few days," said Walter. "We're going to have a party here. It'll be a major feast."

I whipped around to face Walter. "Wait. Hold the phone," I said. "The two of you barely know how to boil water. I'm assuming you want me to cook?"

This was nuts. I couldn't even get a simple breakfast right. And Walter and Robert's friends were super judgmental, especially when it came to food. I couldn't face another setback. Not now. Not ever again. I clenched my jaw so tightly, my teeth hurt.

"I don't think our delivery service does Turkey Day, and if they did, I'm thinking it would be abominable," said Robert, fanning his face dramatically. "We want the real deal—with all the fixings."

"You're the chef here, Sophie," said Walter. He placed a hand on my shoulder. "And you're the best chef I know."

My eyes darted to the stove, nasty smoke still filling the air from the pan of burned potatoes—the odor of defeat. Although I didn't want to let them down, my confidence was shot.

"I don't know what I am anymore," I said. "I'm not sure if I'll ever be able to cook again."

"You're a chef and you're also my best friend." Walter smiled, his eyelashes fluttering. "Plus, you are family."

Family, I thought. My mother was dead. I didn't know who my father was. All I really had was Grand-mère Odette and I was terrified to call her. At least Walter and Robert were on Team Sophie.

"So, Thanksgiving?" said Walter, puffing out his bottom lip. "Please?"

Robert followed suit, letting out a whimper like a puppy.

They had me. I groaned. "Fine. But if it's inedible, don't blame the chef. She's kind of a hot mess right now. Plan B: we'll order in Chinese."

"Plan A will be fine," said Walter.

After Robert and Walter left for work, thinking of family, I googled my grandmother's château. What I found had to be a different home. Even on the small screen, it was so much bigger than I remembered it to be. This château had two restaurants, Les Libellules and Le Papillon Sauvage, and was listed as being a part of La Société des Châteaux et Belles Demeures. I blinked back my confusion. Clearly, I was hallucinating. It had been too long since I'd visited my grandmother. Things couldn't have changed that much. Still, I needed to hear her voice to ground me for a moment, though I knew it would be tinged with disappointment when I told her what had happened.

It was now two thirty p.m. in France. As I remembered from my childhood years, she would have already finished her morning duties in the garden, had lunch, and was probably having a *café crème* in the kitchen.

After staring at her name for a few minutes, I finally gathered the courage to call. My fingers shook as I punched in the number, listening to the phone ring and ring, that strange European drone. I was about to hang up when somebody answered.

"*Allô?*" came the response on the other end of the line. The intonation didn't carry the throaty huskiness of my grandmother's voice.

"*Oui, bonjour,*" I said, my words slurring a bit. I straightened my posture and continued after clearing my throat. "*C'est* Sophie, *la petite-fille d'Odette.* Clothilde? *C'est vous?*"

Clothilde had been by my grand-mère's side for as long as I could remember. Even though I hadn't spoken to her in years, I thought I recognized her voice.

"*Oui, oui, oui, c'est moi,*" she said. "You must be some kind of clairvoyant. I was going to call you in a few hours," she said, her voice catching in her throat. "It's your *grand-mère.*"

Clothilde's breath came heavy and it took me a few seconds to make sense of her words. Aside from food terminology and the rare occasions when I talked with my grand-mère, I hadn't spoken or heard real French in over thirteen years. One by one, I translated her words in my head. Panic rose in my chest. I sank off the couch onto my knees. "What? Is everything okay? Is she okay?"

"No, I'm afraid everything is far from okay," she said, her voice shaky. "Your grand-mère had a stroke a few days ago." Clothilde sniffled. "This morning, they moved her to a larger hospital in Toulouse from Gaillac so she can get the care she needs."

Was it possible for your heart to be sucked out of your chest? I couldn't feel mine anymore. I was certain my grand-mère had heard I was a sabotaging chef and this distressing information had caused her stroke.

"No, no, no," I said. "This can't be happening. Not now."

"I'm afraid so, dear," she said. Clothilde inhaled deeply, clearly trying to find her breath. In between gasps and sobs, she said, "Dr. Simone is doing everything she can. Thankfully, due to the aneurysm's small size and location, she is going to treat it within the blood vessels using a mildly invasive procedure. And she's hoping to stop the bleeding."

"Why didn't anybody call me?" I spluttered.

"*Ma puce,* we didn't want to worry you until we had all the facts."

"I'll book a ticket the instant we hang up."

"No, don't worry. Your grand-mère wouldn't want you to feel like it's an obligation."

"Obligation" was an easy word to translate, the same word in English just with a different pronunciation. The phone was about to slip from my hand and I almost dropped it. "She doesn't want to see me?"

"You have your own life to lead. I'm sure she'll be fine. I'm praying she'll be fine."

"Clothilde, don't be ridiculous. I'm booking a ticket."

"If you insist," she said with a sigh. "Call me once you have your flight information and I'll send Rémi to pick you up."

"Rémi? Rémi Dupont?" I asked. I hadn't thought about him in years.

Clothilde's voice caught for a moment. "The very one. I'd come and get you myself, but I need to be at the hospital—"

"I understand, Clothilde," I said, choking on my words. "I'll get back to you as soon as possible."

Numb, I hung up the phone and called Air France. If something happened to Grand-mère Odette, if she didn't make it, I'd never forgive myself. I booked the ticket, worried and skittish as if I'd had too much coffee.

IN TERMS OF my wardrobe, I really didn't have much of anything notable—just a few dresses to throw off Nicole, and her ladies who lunched; three pairs of jeans; and sweaters. As for shoes, I had a pair of ballerina flats, two sets of heels—one kitten, one high—my woolly winter boots, and Keds—all of them black and dark like my mood. I shoved everything into a bag, not quite sure what my plan was. I didn't know how long I'd be staying in France. A week? A month? Longer? Whatever. Did it matter? Save for Walter and Robert, there was nothing left for me in New York anymore.

I thrust my knives into their roll bag carrying case. Once treasured tools of the trade I took everywhere, the knives now carried bad karma. I could barely look at them. But a chef never goes any-where without her knives. I wondered: Was I still a chef? Would I be one again? I didn't know. Regardless, Grand-mère Odette had given me these knives after I'd graduated from the CIA, and even if I never cooked in a restaurant kitchen again, if I never julienned one more vegetable, they meant something to me.

My mother's affairs, at least the things I'd kept of hers, were stuffed in the back of my closet in a big blue suitcase. I decided to bring it with me, thinking maybe my grandmother and I could go through her things together. Going back to Champvert conjured up memories of her and so many questions. I knew why I had problems with my mother. I'd lived with her, taken care of her. But I'd never understood why she and Grand-mère Odette were estranged.

As I zipped up my bag, a soft knock came and Walter opened my door hesitantly. "Oh, good, Sophie, you're here. I was worried about you." He eyed my suitcases curiously. "Going somewhere?"

Waves of sadness and guilt washed over me. I let out a few ragged sobs and fell to my knees. My words came out in a garbled, nonsensical mess. Even I didn't understand what I was saying as I tried to explain my grandmother's serious situation.

Walter sucked in his breath. "Oh dear." He pulled me in for a hug. Instead of talking, he just held me close and caressed my head. When Walter finally released me from his embrace, he had tears in his eyes, too. He wiped them away with the back of his hand.

We flopped down on my bed, lying side by side. I wondered if I'd ever see this beautiful room again. The wrought iron four-poster bed with billowy white curtains. The whitewashed wooden blinds. The antique dresser with the white marble top and the bronze Degas bal-lerina, a replica of *La petite danseuse de quatorze ans*, resting on it. A lithograph print of Josephine Baker in her famed banana skirt. Knowing of the passion I had for my French roots, Walter had designed this room wanting me to feel comfortable before I'd moved in for the big charade.

Walter finally broke the silence. "When does your flight take off?"

"Eleven o' clock," I said with a sniffle. "It's the red-eye."

"When are you coming back?"

"I don't know. I booked a one-way ticket."

Walter gulped. "You know this is your home. When you come back, we'll welcome you with open arms."

"I know. Thanks, Walter. For everything."

"Can I at least reimburse you for your flight? It's the least I can do. And I want to do so much more."

"It's okay," I said. "Your friendship has meant the world to me. Without you, I wouldn't have anybody."

The truth of this statement hit me in the gut.

"I don't know how long you're going to be gone, but I'm going to miss you, even if it's just for a day. I'm pretty used to having you around—even when you're a pain in the ass." He swallowed hard, his Adam's apple bobbing up and down. "Robert has to work late. He's going to be so upset he wasn't able to see you off."

"Give him a big smooch from me."

"I will," said Walter, wiggling his brows. "Maybe even in public."

Despite my own troubles, I managed to grin, happy he'd finally found his courage to live his life the way he wanted to—out in the open. "I forgot to tell you that I'm proud of you."

"I know you are," he said. "If you need anything, anything at all, call me, text me, or send a carrier pigeon. I'm here for you."

"I will," I said. "And I'm sorry I won't be here for Thanksgiving. I probably would have made a disaster of the meal anyway."

"No, you wouldn't have."

"I'm not so sure about that." I squeezed my eyes shut, trying to keep my tears from falling. "I've ordered everything you'll need from Zabar's for twelve people—a pre-roasted turkey and all the fixings, a couple of desserts, plus a few nibbles for an *apéro* like smoked salmon, foie gras, and grilled shrimp. They'll deliver everything on Thanksgiving morning."

"What am I going to do without you, Sophie?"

"Between you and Robert, you've got this. All you need to do is heat what needs to be heated up."

"I meant I'll miss you." Walter's eyes went all watery and he swallowed hard. "And, Sophie, *you've* got this. You're an amazing chef. Sure, you've been thrown off your game, but with everything that happened, it's no wonder. You'll start over and become a bigger, more badass chef than ever before. You'll rise from the ashes like a culinary phoenix!"

My lips quivered when I forced a smile. Although Walter's statement was one of support, it reminded me, yet again, that I'd suffered a career destruction of mythical proportions.

8

au revoir, new york

I FLEW ON my first international flight when I was seven, my mother by my side. She didn't pay attention to me, just read fashion magazines and didn't take her sunglasses off. I wiggled in my seat with my coloring books, a stuffed rabbit, and my favorite blanket. Although I didn't have any memories of her, I was excited to spend time with my grandmother, a phantom I'd been aware of but had only met when I was an infant. I didn't sleep, just sat in my seat wide-eyed, giddy with excitement.

My mother walked me off the plane and into the terminal, where Grand-mère Odette waited. She was easy to spot—an older, plumper version of my mother, her gray hair pulled back into a tight chignon. Relief washed over me. Definitely not the Wicked Witch of the West. My grandmother and my mom didn't greet each other like normal people. An icy friction volleyed between their cold stares that even I, as a child, could feel. There were no hugs, no kisses. Just tension.

"It's nice to see you're well, Céleste," said my grandmother.

"I wish I could say the same thing to you." My mother pushed me forward. "This is Sophie."

My grandmother crouched down to eye level. "What a beautiful child. I hope your mother hasn't ruined your education—"

"Mother, don't start up or I'll take her with me." My mother's eyes narrowed into a dagger-shooting glare, the same one she gave me if I didn't clean up my toys. "Everything is all sorted?" my mother asked.

Grand-mère Odette handed her a file. "Yes. And I'm glad you finally agreed to allow Sophie to visit with me."

"I wanted to spend some time in Paris anyway. As you know, she'll fly as an unaccompanied minor on the way home. Which is in New York, not in France. Don't get any ideas. Make sure she's on the plane." Her red lips pursed. "The key to the apartment?"

"It's in the folder."

"And the money? I'm twenty-five now. It can no longer be blocked."

"The *notaire* has transferred it to your account."

"*Parfait*," said my mother. Before she walked away, she said, "Sophie, I'll see you in a few months."

She didn't bother to kiss me. She just left. Grand-mère Odette took me by the hand and we watched her disappear into the crowded terminal, her heels click-clacking on the floor, men giving her appreciative looks. Grand-mère Odette smiled. "It's about time you find your roots, *ma chérie*," she said.

Together, we hopped on another flight to Toulouse, where I inundated her with questions.

"Is it true we are noble?"

"Yes, but only in name. Your great-great-grand-père was a *comte*, which is the same rank as an earl in England, and your great-great-grand-mère was considered a *comtesse*. We are the Valroux de la Tour de Champvert, but titles in this day and age are silly, pretentious, and don't mean a thing."

Visions of my favorite Disney characters filled my little head. "Am I a princess?" I asked.

She kissed me on the cheek. "You are *ma princesse*."

The summers that followed until I was thirteen were absolute magic. I'd swim in the river or the lake with Rémi, the boy close to my age who lived on the farm down the road. Sometimes we'd chase fat geese and chubbier rabbits on his farm. Sometimes we'd catch and release slimy frogs. But my favorite thing to do was picking plump black cherries in the orchard for grand-mère's clafoutis and homemade compotes.

Part of me was excited now to get back to Champvert, but not under these conditions. My stomach twisted in knots. There was no way I'd get any sleep until I was in France and until I knew Grand-mère Odette was okay. Plus, how was I going to explain what had gone down in New York? I wasn't ready for an onslaught of I-told-you-sos. I knew all of the decisions I'd made so far had blown up in my face.

I crammed myself into the tight window seat and took in my surroundings. A few businessmen in suits. A family with two unruly children. Well-heeled women. Perhaps it was my imagination, but the plane appeared to freeze with all movement. It could have been supreme paranoia, but it seemed like everybody around me—even the kids—had stopped what they were doing and were staring at me. A sudden fear gripped my heart. I put my sunglasses on to avoid making eye contact with anybody, hoping I wouldn't be recognized.

After the flight took off, I stared vacantly at the television monitor, flipping through films with the remote and never settling on one. I couldn't sleep, my mind racing between my grand-mère's health and my ruined career.

SEVEN HOURS LATER, the immigration officer in Paris regarded me with a quizzical expression when I handed over my American passport. "You have a French last name, *non?* Are you French?" he asked.

"I am," I said, explaining that I was born in France but lived in New York. He asked to see my French passport, which made me a bit nervous, as it had expired a decade ago. I handed it over. He studied both documents for a minute, a scowl on his face.

"*Alors*, your name is Sophie Valroux on your American passport and Sophie Valroux de la Tour de Champvert on your French passport?"

"My mother changed our name in the US," I said. "For her career. Uh, she thought our last name was too long—"

"But she didn't change your name in France?"

"No, not in France," I said, worried I'd have a problem with this one. "She hasn't been back here in nineteen years."

"*Ah bon?*" he said, his eyebrows lifting as if saying he found it extremely bizarre a Frenchwoman would eschew her roots, especially noble ones. "Welcome home," he said with a sympathetic smile and handed the documents back to me. "While you are here it might be a good idea to renew your French passport."

"I will," I said. "*Merci.*"

One two-hour layover later, I finally stepped off the plane in Toulouse.

UNBELIEVABLY, MY TWO suitcases were the first ones out at baggage claim. I grabbed a token from a machine and commandeered a cart, wondering how on earth was I going to recognize Rémi. Rémi—the clean-cut farm boy with thick black eyelashes most women would be envious of. Rémi Dupont. A spark of remembrance lit my chest as I thought about my first kiss. I was thirteen. Rémi was fifteen. We'd just gone swimming in the lake and he'd pinned me down on the bank behind the willows. I remembered the look in his caramel eyes—dreamy and mischievous. I'd liked the kiss, but it had shocked me. I scrambled off the ground and ran into the vineyard, Rémi chasing after me. He caught up to me and we laughed. "Was my kiss that bad?" he'd asked and I'd blushed twenty shades of crimson.

"No, I've never done that before," I'd said, meaning with a boy. My stuffed animals, on the other hand, had received their share of passionate smooches.

"I'm going to miss you, Sophie," he'd said with a bashful grin. "I can't wait until next summer."

Unfortunately, I'd left Champvert the following day and never went back. I was looking forward to catching up with Rémi, to see how my first crush had changed. I snorted at the thought. We had a lot to share, I was sure of that. Would he laugh at how young we'd been? And how awkward our first kiss was? As I recalled, he wore braces and they'd cut my lips.

I pushed the cart through the automatic doors and glanced around hoping to see a familiar face. A few old men and women chatted at the exit. A couple of families waved their relations over. No Rémi. There was nobody there to greet me. Not a soul. Clothilde and I hadn't exactly planned out my arrival well. I stood in the hallway for a good hour, searching for him, when a heavily bearded man wearing army fatigues walked directly toward me with purpose. Blood stained his clothes. Underneath the scruff, I noted he was good-looking, maybe even exceptionally so. But so was Ted Bundy. The man stopped directly in front of me and went in for *les bises*, where he air-kissed each of my cheeks.

"I'm late," he said in French.

"Rémi?" I asked. He was taller and more built than I remembered. And hairier.

His brows furrowed. "What? Did you not recognize me?"

"Um, *désolée*, but no I didn't." I stared openmouthed at his clothes.

"I went hunting early this morning. The *sangliers*"—(wild boars)—"are destroying the fields in the region and the deer are running rampant," he said, his French quick. "You're not afraid of dogs, are you? They're in the car. I've come directly from the chase."

His words swam around in my brain, one expression and conjugation at a time. To my knowledge, Rémi didn't speak one word of English and, even if he did, his scowl made it clear he wasn't going to make an effort for me.

"Only hunting wild animals, I hope," I said with an awkward donkey-like laugh, trying to muster up my best French.

"*Alors*, I haven't shot a person yet," said Rémi, looking like he wanted to kill me. He scorned my cart, pushed it out of the way, and grabbed my luggage. Unnerved, I followed him through the terminal and out into the parking lot, his pace brisk. We made our way to a white Ford Ranger, where two black Labrador retrievers with sloppy drool trickling down their mouths bounced in the back seat. On the sides of the truck, the emblem of my grandmother's château caught my eye.

"You have an American car?" I asked.

"The motor is French," he replied. He threw my bags into the back and then jumped into the driver's seat. He rolled the passenger window down further. "What are you waiting for? *Le Père Noël*? Get in," he said.

No, I wasn't waiting for Santa Claus. I wanted to get to Grand-mère, so I did as I was told. "It's so great to see you after all these years," I said as I settled into my seat and buckled up.

Save for a grunt, he ignored me and peeled out of the parking spot. We exited the lot and sat for a good five minutes as we made our way onto the autoroute. Rémi focused on the road ahead, his mouth curled into a sneer. I stared at him, my mouth agape.

"Why are you looking at me like that? It's rude," he said, his voice clipped.

Who was this guy? This wasn't the Rémi I remembered.

The Rémi from my childhood had been a skinny, cute boy with sparkling eyes and an infectious laugh—a practical joker. I recalled the time he tricked me into eating a live snail, explaining that snails were a delicacy in France, and if I were to develop a true palate, I had to eat one. It wasn't until later that I learned they were, indeed, delicious, but one didn't just pick up a snail from the garden and put a dash of salt on it. Snails were eaten after a long curing process and served after they were baked in loads of butter, garlic, and parsley— *les escargots de Bourgogne*. Rémi had laughed so hard he fell to the ground and called me *la mangeuse de bave* (the slime eater) the rest of the summer. He'd laughed even harder when he told me that he made that expression up when I'd used it. "It's not even a French expression," he'd said.

I shot him the occasional glance. Gone was his silly grin, his mouth carved into what appeared to be a permanent frown. He had no laugh lines bracketing his eyes, just an angry, deep furrow digging into the space between his eyebrows. His hands were rough and calloused. His shoulders were broad. He was big, mean, and surly. Surely, he couldn't have changed that much.

"What have you been up to all these years?" I asked as one of the dogs drooled on my neck. I wiped the slobber off, cringing.

"D'Artagnan, Aramis, sit," said Rémi, and the dogs did.

"Do you want to go back the château or head straight to the hospital in Toulouse?" he asked pointedly.

"The hospital. I need to see my grandmother."

"But your jeans are ugly. There are holes in them," he said, each syllable he uttered dripping with disgust. *"Tu l'as acheté, comme ça?"* (You bought them like that?) he asked with disbelief.

In fact, I hadn't purchased these jeans. They'd been a gift from Eric when we'd dated. He'd told me to get with the program, to possess an ounce of cool. For a second, I debated changing. My grandmother would hate what I was wearing and now I hated what I was wearing. I sat dumbfounded at his rudeness, picking at my cuticles. "Regardless of what I'm wearing, I'd like to go directly to the hospital, if that's okay with you."

"D'accord," he said, blowing out the air between his lips. "Clothilde will drive you home. I'm heading back to the château and I'll bring your suitcases up to your room."

"Merci," I said.

Rémi turned on the radio, setting the volume to high, and hummed along to the '80s French band Indochine's *"L'Aventurier,"* which was played at every party I'd ever attended in France when I was a kid. Before I was able to reminisce over any good times I'd had in France, Rémi pulled up in front of the hospital and pointed. "You enter through those doors right there."

"Thanks for the ride," I said before jumping out. "I appreciate it."

Aside from an impatient grunt, he didn't say a word. Maybe he'd had things to do and was irritated he had to pick me up? Maybe he was having a bad day? He waved me away with an impatient flick of his wrist. "You should go," he said.

"I will."

The second I closed the door, the car peeled out of the parking lot. I stood there for a moment in the dust the tires of his truck had kicked up. The more I tried to excuse his behavior, the more I realized he'd changed into a person I didn't particularly like.

This was not the welcome I'd expected.

9

lost in translation

I HURRIED INTO *l'accueil*, my lungs pumping so hard I thought I'd have a heart attack. Not only was I stunned by Rémi's behavior toward me, hospitals flipped me out. I hated everything about them—the smell of ammonia, the sterility, and the fact that, sometimes, people didn't leave them alive. I hoped that wasn't the case for Grand-mère.

"*Bonjour,*" I said, panting. "I'm looking for my grandmother. Odette Valroux de la Tour de Champvert? She's expecting me."

"*Pardon?*" the woman at the information desk asked.

I didn't realize that in my rush I'd spoken in English, which she clearly didn't understand. I repeated what I'd said in breathless French, cognizant of my New York accent. She nodded and typed a few keys into her computer.

"Ah, *oui*, your grandmother, Madame Valroux de la Tour de Champvert. Her room is on the third floor," said the woman. "Take the elevator, turn right, and head to the nurses' station."

"*Merci,*" I said before racing down the hall.

A female doctor wearing a white lab coat and black slacks rounded the corner as I exited the elevator. She was probably in her midforties (not that I was the best judge of somebody's age) and wore funky green glasses, with her chestnut hair wrapped in a French twist. "Madame Valroux?" she asked, and I smiled, noting her use of "madame."

As I recalled, former Prime Minister François Fillon had dropped the term "mademoiselle" from official contexts a few years prior, stating it referenced a woman's matrimonial situation, whereas "monsieur" simply signified "sir." Of course, this order came after a strong campaign by two French feminist organizations, *Osez le féminisme!* (Dare to be feminist!) and *Les Chiennes de garde* (The Watchdogs).

"Yes," I said. "But please, just call me Sophie."

"*Alors*, Sophie, Emma from *l'accueil* alerted me to your arrival. Permit me to introduce myself—I'm Dr. Simone. I'm the endovascular surgeon responsible for your grandmother's treatment, care, and recovery."

A nurse wearing pale green scrubs rushed down the corridor. A loud beep came from one of the rooms. More nurses followed her into the room. Jaw clenched, I met the doctor's kind gray eyes, hoping my grand-mère was okay. What if I'd arrived too late?

"Can you tell me what happened?" I said once I found my voice.

"Yes, your grand-mère gave us permission to share her medical condition with you, Madame Girard, and Rémi Dupont. *Alors*, we ran a computed tomographic angiogram and found that your grandmother had an aneurysm, which caused bleeding in the brain. Thankfully, we were able to get it under control with a mildly invasive surgery."

"And the prognosis? Could it happen again?" I asked.

"I'm not going to lie to you. There is a fifteen to twenty percent chance another aneurysm can occur. Because of her age, I'd like to monitor her condition for a bit and, perhaps, perform a follow-up angiogram in two months just to make sure she's stable."

I went silent for a moment as I took in what the doctor had said. I'd half hoped the doctor would brush off her condition, say it was nothing serious, that Grand-mère Odette would be back to her usual self in no time. But that was a dream. Grand-mère Odette was eighty-two years old. To me she had always been ageless, timeless. I blinked back my tears. I'd put off this visit for far too long.

"What do I do? How can I help her?"

"For now, keep her comfortable, surround her with love, and don't let her overexert herself during the recovery time." Dr. Simone smiled. "She's a feisty woman, that one."

"That she is," I said. "When can I see her?"

"She's in her room. I'll take you there," she said, and we turned to walk down the corridor.

Clothilde clicked down the hall, holding a small paper espresso cup. I immediately recognized her—chubby and wearing silly flats covered with ladybugs and a blue-smocked housedress. In her early seventies, and almost ten years younger than my grandmother, she'd aged, but her hair was still the same shade of bright red and coiffed in tight curls. My grandmother's sidekick, the Betty to her Veronica, the Scarecrow to her Dorothy, ran up to me, her coffee spilling on the tiled floor. "Sophie, you're here!" exclaimed Clothilde.

"Oh, Clothilde, it's incredible to see you. I can't believe it's been so long. How is Grand-mère Odette?"

"Wonderful, wonderful! She's doing much better!" Clothilde pulled me in for *les bises*, kissing my left cheek, then the right, all while making a lip-smack sound—*mwah*. "I see you've met Dr. Simone."

"Yes, she was just explaining Grand-mère's condition," I said.

Dr. Simone handed me her business card. "I'll leave Madame Girard to escort you to your grand-mère's room. Please feel free to call me if you have any questions."

"*Merci*," I said. "And thank you for taking such great care of her."

She shrugged. "I'm a doctor. It's what I do."

As Dr. Simone turned on her heel, Clothilde embraced me in a tight hug. "Oh lord, are you skinny, Sophie! About the same size as when I last saw you. I thought Americans ate big meals."

"I guess I follow the French rules of portion control," I said.

"Come with me. I'll take you right to your grand-mère, *ma petite puce*." I smiled. Clothilde had always called me her "little flea," a term of endearment. She raced down the hall, her ladybug flats clacking on the tiled floor, speaking with breathless exuberance. "She's so excited to see you, Sophie. You should have seen the smile light up her face when I told her you were coming."

I couldn't stop my words before they escaped my mouth. "That's good. Because Rémi wasn't so happy."

Clothilde nudged me in the ribs. "Don't mind him. He can be a surly one, that boy. He's always working and a bit of a loner." She lowered her voice to a whisper. "Not that I'm one for gossip, but I've heard all of the single girls in town and the next towns over are after him."

"Why?" I asked, grimacing. "He's a bit rude—"

"But very good-looking, *très beau*, indeed." Clothilde giggled like a schoolgirl. "Let's get you to your grand-mère. A little warning first—her speech is a bit slurred and she forgets a few things, but she snaps back."

I stopped in my tracks. "Wait. What if her condition doesn't improve?"

"*Ma puce*, don't think about the what-ifs. They'll frazzle your beautiful mind. Your grand-mère is a strong woman and she'll be back to herself in no time." She pinched my cheeks, like she'd done when I was a child sitting on my stool in the kitchen watching Grand-mère Odette cook.

My head dropped; I missed those days. I was petrified to see the state my grand-mère was in. My body shook and trembled. What if?

Clothilde placed a loving hand on my back. "Ready?"

"As I'll ever be," I said.

When I opened the door to her room, my grandmother's eyes brightened the instant she saw me. I exhaled a worried breath before regaining my composure. The pale green color of her eyes was the only recognizable thing about her. Where had the beautiful regal queen I'd held like a snapshot in my mind gone? Her gray hair was thinning, so fine I could see her scalp. She must have weighed less than a hundred pounds. She wasn't a pillar of strength; she was weak. Pushing the guilt of not visiting sooner into the deepest corners of my mind, I forced a smile and sat on the side of her bed. I took her hand; it was cold and fragile, the skin almost like a thin sheet of paper, her grip weak. I needed to keep my surprise veiled. The last thing she'd want, and this I knew, was pity.

"Grand-mère, I just arrived this morning," I said, worried about the pallor of her complexion as we exchanged *les bises*. "How are you feeling?"

"Better, *ma chérie*. Much, much better now that you're here." She broke into a wide grin, reminding me of the woman I remembered. Her speech was indeed a bit slurred, but I could understand her words as clear as a bell. "You came back to me, my darling, my beautiful Céleste, the light of my life. You've forgiven me."

I shot Clothilde a panicked look. She shrugged and spread out her arms as if she didn't know what to do. Clothilde whispered, "Memory loss and confusion are two of the symptoms we're hoping will go away."

I wondered why my mother would need to forgive my grand-mother as I lightly squeezed her hands, trying my best to smile through the worried and gut-wrenching knot tying up my stomach. "Grand-mère, *non*. It's not Céleste. It's me, Sophie, your grand-daughter. Céleste's daughter."

Her hands ran across my face and down my neck. She placed her palms on my chin lovingly. "Oh, yes, yes, *ma chérie*, how could I make such a mistake?" Her pale green eyes darkened with fear. "I'm sorry, my love, I'm not feeling like myself. Lately, I forget things—so many things. And then this happened. I really should have paid more attention to the warning signs."

"There were warning signs?" I asked.

"Debilitating headaches, a bit of numbness in my arms, a bit of dizziness," she said as if it was no big deal. "I really should have gotten myself to the doctor sooner, but we've been terribly busy at the château. I figured my problems came from stress, that the feel-ings would pass."

No wonder we had lost touch. We were both consumed with work.

"You have to take care of yourself," said Clothilde, and I agreed.

"*Ah bon*, I know," said Grand-mère Odette before returning her attention to me. "You are the spitting image of your mother, my darling. *Les chiens ne font pas des chats.*"

"Dogs don't make cats" was a French expression that was similar in meaning to "The apple doesn't fall far from the tree." It always made me smile. Through the window curtains, sunlight poured into the room, illuminating my grand-mère's weakened state, although she appeared brighter, almost glowing. I leaned forward, clasping my hand around hers.

"That's an interesting piece of jewelry," said Grand-mère, eye-ing the ring hanging off my necklace. "Quite beautiful."

"It was my mother's," I said, shifting uncomfortably. I cleared my throat. "I brought some of her things with me. Maybe when you're better, we can go through them together?"

"I see," said my grandmother pointedly. She then changed the subject, clearly not wanting to talk about my mom. "When did you arrive?"

"Today. For you."

"That fancy New York restaurant of yours gave you time off?" Her eyes widened a bit, but she didn't seem all that surprised.

"You could say that," I mumbled. "It's kind of a forever time off."

"What did you say? I didn't quite hear you."

"Oh, it's nothing." I forced another smile. "I'm happy the doctor says you're on the mend."

"How long are you here for?" she asked.

"For as long as I'm needed."

"Well, that would be for eternity. When you're not by my side, my heart crumbles." She smiled and struggled to sit up, but couldn't. "And, now that you're here, you can get me out of this damn hospital. *On y va.*" (Let's go.) "Right now."

I was pleased to see my grandmother's spirit was strong, but her leaving the hospital wasn't going to happen. I'd never seen my strong, bullheaded grandmother look so fragile. "The doctor said she has to monitor you a little longer," I said, and Clothilde nodded her head with enthusiastic agreement.

"Bah, *je suis pleine de vitalité. Regardez-moi,*" said Grand-mère Odette.

I was looking at her and she wasn't exactly full of vitality—in fact, far from it. Her hands shook like a blender on the verge of exploding. Her speech was slurred—not to mention the mistake she'd made when she mistook me for my mother. My dead mother.

"I'm sure you'll be home soon," I said. "But right now it's important for you to get better. Doctor's orders."

"*Mais*, we have a houseful of guests arriving tonight. There's much to do—"

"Don't worry, Odette," said Clothilde, rushing over to grab her hand. "Sophie, the rest of the staff, and I will take care of everything, won't we, dear? You'll help manage the kitchen."

My eyes went wide. I sucked in my breath, willing the impending panic attack to settle down. I wasn't sure if I'd ever be able to walk into a kitchen again. And now I was supposed to manage a kitchen I wasn't familiar with?

"Without me, I'm sure the château needs management," said my grand-mère. "I've been doing my best while being cooped up in this horrible room, but I can only do so much. Sophie, I'm counting on you. Can I?"

There were so many questions I wanted to ask, but, a bit shell-shocked, I didn't want to sound accusatory, and panic sparked Grand-mère Odette's eyes.

"How many people does the restaurant seat?" I asked.

"Forty," answered my grandmother. "Can you handle forty covers?"

"Er, yes, definitely," I said, feeling the need to give her reassurance.

"*Bon.*" Grand-mère Odette pulled out a notebook and flipped through it before locking me in her gaze. "For tonight's special, I was planning on making a *daube de biche* for the guests. Do you know how to make a *daube*? Or do you just make fancy seafood dishes with strange foams?" I didn't answer right away, so Grand-mère Odette patted my hand and continued with a heavy sigh. "You are my granddaughter and I have faith in you, my dear. It's almost eleven. The two of you better be going, as the guests are set to check in at four. Dinner is set for seven thirty p.m. sharp."

"But I just got here. I want to spend time with you," I said. I meant it, but I also wanted to procrastinate getting back to the château. How was I going to make a *daube de biche* when I couldn't even get *œufs cocotte* and roasted potatoes right? I wasn't ready for this.

"*Ma chérie*, I'm quite tired and won't be much of a conversationalist. You'll just be watching me sleep," she said. "Plus, it is paramount things are handled with the business—the entire village counts on us. And since I'm stuck in this awful hospital bed, it's you who must take over while I'm incapacitated."

"Okay, but this is all so surreal. I'm coming to visit you tomorrow."

"*Hors de question*" (Out of the question), she said, lifting her chin with defiance. "There's too much to do for our guests. I'll be back at the château before you know it." She crossed her arms over her chest. "Clothilde, show her where my kitchen notebooks are. She's going to need them."

"But you don't let anyone touch your notebooks—except for me," Clothilde said, her fingers fluttering to her neck. "Are you sure?"

"My recipes are a part of Sophie's heritage," Grand-mère said before her eyelids fluttered closed.

My heart stopped beating for a moment. In that instant, I thought she'd died. I placed my ear over her mouth and my hand on her heart. "Please, you can't leave me now," I whispered.

A soft hand stroked my back. "*Ma puce*, she just needs her rest," came Clothilde's soft voice. "*Ne t'inquiète pas.*" (Don't worry.) "*Elle ira bien.*" (She'll be fine.)

I wasn't so sure about that. Save for the guilt pecking at my heart, I wasn't sure about anything.

10

the grand chef

As we settled in Clothilde's dented old orange Deux Chevaux, I tried to keep my wits about me and swallow back the worry pounding in my throat for grand-mère's health. Clothilde straightened her posture and stuck her key in the ignition, and, after a loud roar, the car rumbled to life, jolting us backward. My eyes widened with fear, and not just because of the rickety state of this tin can of death.

Clothilde spluttered out a laugh and gripped the stick shift. "Don't worry, she'll get us back to the château in one piece." She switched the gear into first, then second. "These cars have traveled deserts, crossing over sands. They've gone through wars. Safest drive in the world, although not very comfortable. Still, they are collector's items—if they are in good shape. I love my Jasmine."

"You named your car?"

"Of course I did. She's a beauty."

A spring in the seat pinched my butt as we bounced along the road. It hurt. I'd definitely have a bruise with my pale skin. I grimaced.

"Are you okay, *ma puce*?"

"I'm fine. I just can't believe I haven't been back for so long," I said, placing my hands under my butt. "What's been going on at the château?"

"Oh, *ma puce*, it's been very busy. A lot has changed since your last visit thirteen years ago."

"Can you tell me about the restaurant?" I asked.

"You'll see. And there's not just one, but two."

I couldn't believe the place I'd found online was, in fact, my grandmother's château. "I wanted to come back, but—"

Clothilde patted my hand. "I know, *ma puce*. You had your own life to create and you were never far from your grand-mère's heart. She knows you were busy."

I bit down on my bottom lip, feeling guiltier than ever. My world was in shambles. I had nothing. I'd worked so hard, and for what? Death was knocking at my grand-mère's door and I'd been too busy for family, too driven to make a name for myself. Without her, I wouldn't even have a name. Without her, I wouldn't have followed my dreams. But what were my dreams now?

"And what's this about the entire village depending on the château?"

"All our livelihoods depend on it. We all work with or for Grand-mère Odette," she said. "After your grand-père Pierre passed away just after you were born, Bernard and I sold our farm to her and we've been living in the guesthouse right on the property. You may remember visiting us there?"

"Vaguely," I said, which was a lie. I didn't remember. I did recall the guilt trip my grand-mère tried pulling on me in New York after my mother had died. Perhaps I was selfish for following my dreams when my grandmother needed me in her life, but I figured she'd be fine without me. And look where I was now. My big plans, my big goals, had backfired.

Clothilde cleared her throat. "At any rate, Bernard still manages the vineyard. And I help out your grand-mère however I can."

Her husband's full name had me chuckling softly to myself for a brief moment—Bernard Girard. Perhaps even his parents found it funny when they named him. Way back in France in the time of Napoléon Bonaparte, it was necessary to have names approved so the outcome wouldn't have a negative impact on the child's life. Even in recent times, first names like Fraise, which meant "strawberry," were declined, the judges ruling that the girl could be picked on with the expression of *"ramène ta fraise"*—a slang phrase roughly translated to mean "get your ass over here." No, the government prohibited names like Nutella or Manhattan, too. But, even though it rhymed, Bernard Girard had made the grade.

Clothilde gripped the steering wheel. "Plus, with you and your mother, rest her soul, in New York, we didn't like Odette living on that big property all alone."

I stared out the window feeling like the monster the *Times* article had made me out to be. Not to mention the interview on Eater where Eric had slandered me, gutted my reputation with his digs. Part of me wanted to go back to New York to fight for my life—but not when Grand-mère was fighting for hers.

As if sensing my discomfort, Clothilde shifted gears and gripped my hand. "You had your own life to lead. Don't worry about us old folks—*les vieux.*"

"I don't understand how so much could change without me knowing about it. Why didn't Grand-mère Odette tell me about any of this?"

"It's all out there, right on the Internet."

"I'm not really into all that. I don't even have a Facebook account," I said.

"I'm thinking you should get out of that New York kitchen of yours. Even I have a Facebook account. So does the château."

"Oh?" I said with a loud yawn.

Clothilde shot me a glance, worry pinching her mouth into a concerned frown. "Why don't you get some rest, dear? You look absolutely exhausted, a bit green in the face. I think it's better if you see the château to get a fuller understanding. And we have quite a bit of work to do before the guests arrive."

"But I have so many questions," I said.

"You'll get your answers, *ma puce*. For now, just rest. We really need all hands on deck today, including yours."

"Okay. . ." I said, struggling to keep my eyes open, the motion of the car soon rocking me to sleep.

FORTY-FIVE MINUTES LATER, Clothilde's orange Deux Chevaux bumped off the highway and shook and rumbled onto a winding country road, waking me up. The brakes screeched. Short and squat, Clothilde could barely see over the steering wheel and we had a close call with a fluffy white sheep standing on the side of the road. His loud *bah* startled me, as if he was pissed off we had the nerve to interrupt his leisurely stroll. Watching him walk into the bushes, I noticed the backside of his flank was tattooed with an Occitan cross, a symbol of the region—the coat of arms for the Midi-Pyrénées— along with what I assumed were his owner's initials. A bell jingled around his neck.

"He's always getting away, that one," said Clothilde with a sigh. "I don't know how he escapes his pasture. I'll have to talk to Monsieur Martin. Again."

At that point, I'd have offered to drive, but as a New Yorker who took taxis and the subway, I didn't have a driver's license and I didn't know my way behind the wheel. Instead, I rolled down the window to take in the crisp November air—not warm, but not quite cold yet. We passed by vineyards with perfectly spaced vines, the trunks knotty and twisted, the branches hanging onto wires. The leaves on the trees glimmered in a kaleidoscope of colors—bright oranges, yellows, reds, and greens. I'd never visited Champvert in the fall, and the natural beauty—the bubbling Tarn River and foliage—astounded me. Winter would arrive soon. I closed my eyes, imagining all this beauty lightly dusted in snow. For an instant, I felt different, like somebody had miraculously lifted a thousand pounds off my shoulders. I was out of the pollution of the city, breathing in fresh gulps of air, and nature's bounty surrounded me, filling me with a sense of calm I didn't realize I needed. No honking taxis, no busy sidewalks with people pushing and growling for you to get out of the way, and, more important, no Eric. I shuddered at the thought of him.

Maybe I was selfish. It took a family emergency to bring me back here, to a place I loved. And would I be here if I hadn't been canned? Of course, I would have. Wouldn't I? Even on her hospital bed, even in her fragile condition, Grand-mère Odette let me see more of myself in her than I had ever seen in my mother. I'd always felt that way.

We passed through the town of Champvert. There was a small church with a steeple reaching into the cornflower-blue sky, the stone *hôtel de ville* (city hall), one bar that also served as newsstand and *tabac*, and a small grocer that sold vegetables from wooden stands exploding in fall colors. By the looks of it, squashes of all sizes were in season—pumpkins, butternut, and, sunlight bouncing on their orange waxy skin, potimarron.

I grumbled, apparently out loud.

"Is something wrong, *ma puce*?" asked Clothilde.

"No," I said. "I'm fine. Feeling better—just a bit woozy."

"Understandable, after your long travel day," she said. "I've never traveled more than six hundred kilometers from Champvert."

Hopefully she hadn't been driving then.

Clothilde swerved the car and the sudden movement had me holding on to to my seat. We bounced down a familiar lane with evenly spaced plane trees, the leaves and branches forming a canopy above us, the trunks tall like soldiers standing at attention awaiting our arrival. Clothilde slammed on the brakes hard, stopping. Once the dust settled, the tall, bronzed gates of the château towered over us, oxidized a bluish green over time, the scrolled dragonfly symbol of the château smack-dab in the center. Etched into one of the tall stone posts was the name of this magnificent home—CHÂTEAU DE CHAMPVERT—with the date XVIII SIÈCLE under it. Clothilde pulled out a remote, pressed a button, and the gates opened.

"As I said earlier, a lot has changed since you last visited," she said. "A lot."

"I can see that," I said. A brass sign plastered onto the other column caught my eye. I wanted to get a closer look. "Do you mind if I hop out and walk for a bit? I feel like I've been cooped up and some fresh air will do me good."

She smiled and nodded her head, her curls bouncing. "*D'accord, ma puce*. I'll meet you at the house. Just come on in. I'll be in the kitchen. We have about forty-five minutes before we need to get started with the preparations for tonight's dinner service."

In my confusion, I'd almost forgotten about the guests set to arrive. My mouth went dry.

"I'll be there in a few," I said.

I kissed her on the cheek and hopped out of the car. Clothilde's Deux Chevaux rumbled into the parking area, one with clearly marked places for at least twenty or thirty cars. For a moment, I stretched my arms and legs, taking in my surroundings and breathing in the crisp air. Then I walked over to the plaque, traced the brass fleur-de-lis and the words inscribed, *La Société des Châteaux et Belles Demeures*, with my fingertips. Over it rested a smaller plaque with my grandmother's full name in raised letters, ODETTE VALROUX DE LA TOUR DE CHAMPVERT, and under that, the words *Grand Chef.*

Grand Chef? What in the world? I didn't know if I should be proud of her or disappointed she hadn't shared the news of receiving this honor with me. My heart raced, giving me a burst of energy. I ran down the driveway, my sneakers crunching on the gravel. Breathless, I stood in front of the family seat, feeling ridiculous for calling a massive residence like this my grandmother's home.

Four stories high, the château itself must have been at least twenty-four thousand square feet, maybe more. An imposing double staircase, one side of which had been converted to a wheelchair ramp, led up to the first floor and main entrance, above the garden-level ground floor. Constructed out of pink-hued bricks and stone with a slate roof and turrets reaching into the blue sky, the château also boasted seven Juliet balconies, three on the left, three on the right, and one in the center.

As a kid, I hadn't realized just how impressive the château was. Perhaps the dust of time covered my childhood memories with hazy recollections. I remembered the château being enormous, but a bit run-down and under constant construction. Now, as an adult, I was floored. Every detail seemed larger-than-life—even the sky, the horizon stretching out for miles and miles.

I took another deep breath, gulping in the air, trying to absorb everything and feeling quite disoriented. With my heightened sensitivity to smell, there were too many aromas to take in at one time. Pine. Apple. Cedar. Smoke from the fireplaces. An onslaught of sensorial experiences. All the odors blended together into one and, although wonderful and fresh, it was dizzying and my nose twitched from overload. My eyes focused on the orchard, the trees still laden with apples. *Je vais tomber dans les pommes*, I thought, thinking of the French expression "I'm going to fall in the apples," which meant to faint. I needed to move, get my bearings.

Before heading inside, I climbed to the top of the hill to get a better vantage point. Surrounded by willows and hundred-year-old olive trees with thick, knotty trunks, the lake sparkled in the distance. To my left, there were sweeping views of the Tarn River. The land appeared to be limitless, rolling with hills and a forest filled with towering pine trees. After walking by the large pool set up with tables and wrought iron sun loungers resting under white canopies, I rounded the bend, noting all of the other buildings— the clock tower, the guesthouse where Clothilde and Bernard lived, the large brick barn, and the winemaking facilities. The greenhouse shimmered in the hazy sunlight like a beautiful mirage in a desert oasis. I didn't recall it being so substantial. The well-manicured gardens were laden with a maze of bushes carved into fleurs-de-lis— one of the best-known symbols of France. My footsteps crunched on the white gravel as I walked toward the vineyard in the distance. Seeing it devoid of grapes, I realized I'd missed the harvest, that I'd never witnessed it, and that I wanted to take part in it. I looked at my watch and made my way to the front of the house, deep in thought.

Why had I suppressed the memories of this enchanting world? Because I'd been happy here and didn't think I deserved happiness? Because my mother was never happy, and I blamed myself for her misery? She'd had me too young—I'd been her cross to bear? Aside from fighting for my now ruined career, my mother's death—

her suicide—was the real reason I'd avoided coming back to France, to the house she'd grown up in. Champvert reminded me of a life I no longer had, a world I'd never truly been a part of. A world where I'd never been loved by my mom. In the past, with nobody to talk to, I'd become my own psychoanalyst, and I'd just locked up my feelings and thrown away the key. The kitchen had been my escape, my salvation, the way I avoided uncomfortable situations.

But I was here now.

Rémi's white truck rumbled down the driveway. He pulled into a parking spot, jumped out of the driver's seat, and, after letting the two Labradors out, slammed the door shut. I wanted to give him the benefit of the doubt, thinking some people, like me, had very bad days, and shot him a hesitant wave. The dogs ran toward the lake and dove in. Rémi didn't even look in my direction, just walked away, carrying a large crate.

"My God," I muttered. "What is his freaking problem?"

I swung open the heavy wooden doors of the main entry and stepped onto freshly polished marble floors, immediately noticing the dining room on my right—an immense salon with an ornate silver tin ceiling carved with fleurs-de-lis, the cornices with an elegant ropelike pattern; sparkling chandeliers dripping with crystals; oak herringbone parquet floors; and a massive marble fireplace I could walk into.

Three men and two women, varying in age from their late twenties to late forties, bustled around, setting up for dinner service. I didn't recognize any of them, although they certainly knew who I was. Whispers of *"Elle est là"*—(She's here)—*"l'Américaine, la petite-fille, la New-Yorkaise"* echoed softly in my ears. They said quick *bonjour*s, not quite looking me in the eyes, and scrambled back to work. I noted their uniforms—soft charcoal gray slacks or skirts with crisp white shirts. Elegant. Like I'd remembered my grandmother.

I walked up to one of the tables. Silver dragonflies decorated all of the glasses—champagne, water, and wine, as well as the pewter-rimmed plates. Reminiscent of the Belle Époque, sterling silver-ware with flowers carved in relief amazed me. It was lovely, every last detail perfection, including the iridescent silver-gray napkins the waitstaff had folded into the shape of seashells. I had to confess, my grandmother had done an amazing job, overlooking no exquisite detail. I just wished she'd told me what she'd been up to all these years. Rubbing my eyes with disbelief, I floated into the kitchen as if pulled by an unseen entity.

II

—⁕—

a world of confusion

NOTHING HAD PREPARED me for *la cuisine*, which like the salon had doubled in size. The stainless steel workstations sparkled, as did the prep areas, the line, and the plating station. There were heat lamps, reach-in coolers, two walk-in coolers, and an HVAC system. A grilling station. A broiler. A fryer. Heated holding units. Two four-burner hot plates. Not to mention the two beautiful powder-blue Lacanche ranges with double ovens and warming cupboards—five burners each, a cast-iron simmer plate, plancha, and flame grill.

This setup, this gleaming kitchen, was worthy of a Michelin-starred restaurant and capable of serving at least two hundred covers. "What in the world?" I said under my breath.

Clothilde looked up from beating an enormous piece of meat. "Oh, sorry, *ma puce*, I didn't see you come in." She slammed her knife into a carcass and wiped her hands on her apron.

"I think the deer is already dead," I said, a lame attempt at humor.

"Thankfully, Rémi skins them and empties out the organs. I

don't know if I'd be able to stomach that." She held up the butcher's cleaver with a wild look in her eyes. "Don't worry, this one has been aged. Your grand-mère Odette usually prepares the meat." Clothilde paused. "Are you hungry, *ma puce*? Would you like something to eat? You look a little peaked."

My growling stomach answered for me. She winked and pulled out a stool, ushering me to sit down. I sank into my seat. This was the same stool I'd sat on as a child, the same wicker strands pinching into my legs. When I was a kid, I always had a pattern of dips and crevasses embedded into the back of my thighs.

"Besides being a little older, you haven't a changed a bit." She scurried around and then set a tray of cheeses and a baguette in front of me. "Everybody—and I mean everybody—works for your grandmother. Madame Truffaut makes the bread and croissants, but she bakes them at her home and brings them here. Madame Bouchon makes the yogurt, same scenario, although she makes the compotes here. And Madame Moreau prepares the foie gras, the sausages—"

As Clothilde explained the workings of *les dames*, my mind went dizzy as I recalled all the familiar names, trying to remember who was who. I couldn't place them. Their names and faces blurred together into one. I spread some fresh goat cheese onto a baguette and bit into it. The bread was flaky and buttery, clearly freshly baked this morning, and the cheese was tangy and tart. For an instant, the cheese, the taste, transported me to my childhood, to the kitchen I remembered—the one with the red-and-white-checked curtains—to many days of happiness, to the cheese I was eating right now. I didn't remember it tasting so good.

"Oh my God," I mumbled with this mouthful of excitement, so delicious it was sinful.

"*Ma puce*, is something wrong?"

"No, this is the best meal I've had in weeks," I said. "It's sublime."

"Bah," she said. "It's simple. But sometimes simple is the best, *non?*"

I couldn't have agreed with her more. I wanted—no, needed—simple. Lately everything in my world was so complicated; I prayed for simple.

"Madame Pélissier makes our goat cheese right on her farm—also other fresh cheeses like *le Cathare*, a goat cheese dusted with ash with the sign of the Occitania cross, as well as a *Crottin du Tarn*, which is the goat cheese we use for the pizza, and *Lingot de Cocagne*, which is a sheep's milk cheese. Do you want to do a little tasting of her cheeses?"

"Would I? You bet."

Clothilde ambled over to the refrigerator, returning with a platter of lumpy cheese heaven straight from the cooking gods' kitchen.

"*Et voilà*," she said, placing it down and bringing her fingers to her lips, blowing out a kiss.

There were veiny cheeses marked with blue and green channels and spots, soft cheeses with natural or washed rinds, and fresh and creamy cheeses, like the goat cheese. The scents hit me, some mild with hints of lavender, some heavily perfumed, some earthy, and some garlicky.

"*Merci beaucoup*, Clothilde," I said, my mouth full and crumbs sprinkling onto the table. "This is amazing."

"It's wonderful to have you back even under such circumstances. It feels like yesterday since you visited with us, but many yesterdays have passed." Clothilde pinched my cheek. "I remember when we couldn't keep you out of the kitchen. We'd urge you to go play and then find you hiding in the servant's staircase, watching us cook and prepare the Sunday lunches. Such a shame you missed the last one of the season," said Clothilde. "It was two weeks ago."

"I'm sorry I missed it. I loved them when I was a kid," I said, suddenly longing for them.

On Sundays, we'd have family lunches, inviting practically everybody from the tiny village of fifty or so people. The day started at ten in the morning, not ending until dusk, when the bats and barn swallows swooped in the sky and the moon and stars began to twinkle. Villagers arrived early in the morning with whatever they had—eggs, fresh fruits and vegetables from their gardens, ducks, chickens, rabbits, and homemade sausages. The men would play *pétanque*, France's version of bocce ball, on the field. Grand-mère Odette and the women would cook up a storm—whatever was fresh and in season, whatever was brought to the doors. They'd shoo me away with their aprons, urging me to have fun. Sometimes I hid in the stairwell, watching them laugh, chop, and cook, licking my lips as delicious smells enveloped me, hugging me in a spicy embrace. We ate at picnic tables covered with beautiful French linens. I remembered the laughter and joy from those days like it was yesterday, as Clothilde had said. Too bad I was having problems placing anything else. Save for mentioning the Sunday lunches, my grandmother hadn't told me anything—that she was a Grand Chef or that she was now part of the famed group La Société des Châteaux et Belles Demeures. Or that she ran two restaurants.

"Can you please tell me what's been going on at the château? Everything's changed so much. I feel like I'm on another planet."

Clothilde's laugh twittered like a small bird's. "I'm afraid it's your grandmother who will have to answer your questions. *Je m'occupe de mes oignons.*" I mind my own onions—or translated in English, "I mind my own business."

"I hope she's around to—" I started to say, but cut myself off when Clothilde's mouth formed into one of the saddest pouts I'd ever seen.

She fluffed up her curls, ignoring my statement. I wanted to hug her, to apologize, but didn't know how to do so; it was out of my arsenal of emotions. Apparently, all I knew now was how to take a defense position, and I didn't do it well.

"We've got a full house booked this weekend, plus a wine tasting and the cooking demonstrations, and we'll need all the help we can get," she said. "I'm sure you'll find the kitchen is very well equipped with everything you need."

I wasn't so sure about that. My last attempts with cooking for Walter and Robert were complete failures. "Who is in charge of the wine tasting?" I asked, worried it would fall under my responsibility, worried I'd pissed her off. I knew enough about wine, the basic tasting notes, but I knew nothing of the wines of Gaillac, and had absolutely zero knowledge of the varieties created at the château.

"That would be my Bernard," said Clothilde, and relief washed over me. Her eyes met mine and she pinched my cheeks again—not too hard, but enough to tell me she cared about me and, although I'd offended her, any conversation regarding the state of my grandmère's health was over.

"Do you remember I named my bear after him? *Bear*nard."

Clothilde twittered her birdlike laugh, her red curls bobbing like coiled springs. "Oh my! *Oui*! The English word for *l'ours* is 'bear.' Between you and me, my husband is a bit of an animal. You should hear him snore! He shakes the entire house."

I laughed. And, honestly, it felt good to laugh. I couldn't remember the last time I'd done so.

"And the cooking demonstration?" I asked.

"I'm in charge of those," she said. "We like the guests to experience everything the château has to offer—wine tastings year-round, picking grapes during the harvest, skeet shooting or hunting—even gardening," she said. "You'll get the hang of things around here once you settle in a bit more."

I swooned at all this information, feeling dizzy. My grand-mère had created an empire. And I felt like a bystander, an intruder.

Clothilde walked over to a corner and bounced lightly on one of the old oak planks, the one with the twisted knot. She dropped to her knees and lifted the board, chucking it to the side. *"Et voilà,"* she said, her breath heavy. "Here are your grandmother's kitchen notebooks. Her recipe for the *daube* should be in one of these. I'm just not sure which one."

After struggling with their weight, Clothilde handed me around twenty dark brown leather-bound notebooks tied with red leather cords. They were beautiful, like pieces of fine art, splattered with water spots and food stains.

"Why do you keep them hidden in the floor?"

"Because of the war—when the Germans occupied northern and western France. Your grand-mère's family was from Bordeaux, and although she was just a young girl of five years old, she remembers her mother hiding valuables to keep them safe." Clothilde wrung her hands. "It was a difficult time, one she doesn't like talking about."

"She doesn't like talking about a lot of things," I said. "Especially my mother."

"As I said, *je m'occupe de mes oignons,*" she said, forcing a nervous smile. She patted a notebook. *"Alors,* your grandmother painstakingly wrote all of her recipes down for well over twenty years. And we don't want anything to happen to them now, do we?"

"Why are you talking about her as if she's already gone?" I said, and Clothilde's face crumpled. My heart dropped into my stomach. I'd made a major faux pas and could only backpedal after being so rude to Clothilde. "I'm sorry. I didn't mean for it to come out that way."

"I understand. You're worried about her. I am, too, and I pray every day she'll pull through. Now that you're back, you've given her something to fight for. More than anything, she wants to spend time with you," she said, blinking back her tears. "Open the notebooks, *ma puce*. Like your grandmother said, these notebooks are part of your heritage."

With shaky hands, I opened up one of the notebooks and thumbed through the creamy pages filled with my grandmother's beautiful handwriting to find no recipes, but rather names, dates, and what people ate, what they liked and didn't like. I let out a gasp when I found my name. Pages upon pages were filled with mostly likes and a few dislikes. I hated *tête de veau* (boiled cow brain), and who wouldn't, but loved escargots in a creamy garlic, butter, and parsley sauce. The word "cerise" was underlined four times, along with the words "*Ma petite-fille Sophie, elle aime n'importe quoi avec les cerises*." Cherries. I still loved them.

My visits to Champvert always coincided with cherry season, and Grand-mère Odette always made sure a bowl of plump black cherries sat in front of me. When I wasn't tasting one of her wonderful creations, I'd stuff one cherry after another into my eager mouth and spit the pits into a bowl, reveling in the juicy and sweet explosions hitting my tongue. As she whisked the batter for her clafoutis, stating how important it was to keep the pits in the cherries or the dessert would lose its nutty flavor, she'd tell me about some of her other recipes, the ingredients rolling off her tongue like a new exotic language I wanted to learn every word of. Saffron, nutmeg, coriander, paprika, and kumquat—what were these things, I wondered?

As I thumbed through the pages, I realized how dedicated my grandmother was to me and the other people surrounding her. To take the time to gather such information proved it. She wanted to make sure everybody was happy when they were under her roof and, more specifically, at her table. I placed my head in my hands, rubbing my temples. I traced my name with my finger, trying to burn Grand-mère's loopy scrawl into my memory. Unlike her, my handwriting looked like chicken scratch. One thing we had in common, though, was the love of cooking.

The recipes I'd cooked as a child floated in my brain, like making succulent duck and cooking potatoes in duck fat—a standard in southwestern France. From chicken to sausage, pork loin to lamb, duck fat gave savory ingredients a silky feeling on the tongue. Again, the visions I was having transported me back in time, right to when I first tasted Grand-mère's special duck-fat-drowned French fries. I'd been a goner ever since. After my palate exploded with joy, Rémi and I had run down to the lake, jumping right in, the cold water burbling over our heads in tiny waves.

"Those were the best French fries ever," I'd said. "I can't believe it."

"Believe it," said Rémi, splashing me. Then I dunked him. Those days were long gone.

Clothilde peeked over my shoulder. "Oh, *ma petite puce*, you'll want the notebooks with recipes. These notebooks are old."

A rogue paper slid out of the notebook onto the floor. I scrambled off my stool and picked it up. All somebody had written on it was Sophie1993. My first name. The year I was born. I held out the slip and looked at Clothilde with my eyebrows raised in question.

"Most of the information you were just looking at pertaining to the guests has been entered into the computer. Your grandmother likes to keep track of everything—their likes and dislikes, anniversaries, birthdays—"

"Why?"

"To her, every guest becomes a member of the family when they stay under her roof," said Clothilde. "Speaking of guests, there's work to be done. Did you find her recipe for the *daube*?"

I hadn't. "Just give me a minute," I said. A minute to take in all of the childhood memories flashing before my eyes. A minute of happiness. A minute to catch my breath.

12

the pressure cooker

I'D JUST FOUND the recipe for the *daube* when a young, elegant blond woman with steely blue eyes walked into the kitchen carrying a basket filled with fresh herbs—the scents of rosemary, thyme, basil, and tarragon infiltrated my nostrils. I wondered how in the world this woman could garden in kitten heels while keeping her nails manicured and her hair perfectly coiffed in a lacquered French twist. She eyed me up and down, locking on to my ripped jeans. "I see the prodigal granddaughter has returned."

I was expecting French, not English, to come out of her mouth. I also wasn't expecting to be insulted. After Rémi, the odd whispers of the waitstaff, and now this woman's attitude, it seemed nobody aside from Clothilde and my grand-mère was all too thrilled I was back.

"I'm Sophie." I was about to say, "Nice to meet you," when she cut me off.

"I know exactly who you are. I'm Jane," she said, her smile faker than a Louis Vuitton bag purchased on Canal Street. "We can't wait to hear all about your life in New York. You were a Michelin chef, yes?"

By her smug expression, she knew exactly what had gone down in New York. I shifted on my stool uncomfortably and cleared my throat. "No, I worked at Michelin-starred restaurant," I said. "A chef de partie."

"How exciting," she said.

"She learned everything she knows from her grand-mère," said Clothilde, nodding her head of curls. "We're very proud of her."

A brunette with blue-violet eyes the color of pale hydrangeas trailed in a few minutes after Jane. She carried a large crate filled with mushrooms similar to porcinis. "I went foraging this morning and the cèpes are still in season! There must be hundreds, all of them exquisitely beautiful," she said with excitement. She placed her bounty of mushrooms on the prep table and looked up, taking notice of me. "*Bonjour*, Sophie! I'm Phillipa, Jane's twin."

My upper lip twitched with disbelief. Granted, I was happy to have a break from speaking French, but I wasn't expecting two English twins.

Complete polar opposites, Jane and Phillipa didn't share any similar traits. Whereas Jane was tall and elegant with a swan-like neck and had a figure most women would kill for, Phillipa had cropped, shaggy hair, and was as skinny as a French green bean, *un haricot vert*, perhaps even skinnier than me if that was possible— and went au naturel with her makeup. By means of explanation, Phillipa said, "We're fraternal twins."

"Oh," I said. "When you hear the word 'twin,' you expect—"

"Two of the same kind, cut from the same mold," said Phillipa, her cockney accent strong. "Nobody ever believes us when we tell them."

"Well, nice to meet you," I said with a pause. "If you don't mind me asking, where are you from?"

"Bibury, England. Ever hear of it?" said Phillipa.

"Sorry," I said. "I haven't."

"No worries. Not many people have. It's lovely, located on a river and, in a way, it reminds me a lot of here. Except we have much better weather in Champvert."

"How long have you been working at the château?" I asked, my curiosity piqued.

"Our parents retired and bought a small home in the next village over, Sauqueuse, about ten years ago. You get a lot more for your money in France than in England. There are quite a few of us *rôti de bœuf* in the area. Grand-mère Odette says we're invading the Tarn-et-Garonne. Anyway, a few years ago, I lost my job, so I escaped England for France and I've been working for Grand-mère Odette ever since. Jane, too."

"You do realize *rôti de bœuf* is quite an offensive term? It means 'roast beef,'" said Jane. Unlike Phillipa, Jane's accent was reminiscent of the Queen of England and peppered with exaggerated snobbery.

"I know," said Phillipa with a nonchalant shrug. She locked her gaze onto mine and winked. "And I, for one, find it absolutely hilarious. Sometimes I call your grandmother a frog. She gets a kick out of it. Probably because the word '*grenouille*' doesn't roll off my tongue." She repeated the French word for "frog" five times until she got it right. Phillipa smiled, her blue eyes clear and friendly. "I was so excited when I heard you were here. I've been looking forward to meeting you. You're all your grand-mère talks about when she's not talking about the château or food."

"How long are you staying on at the château?" asked Jane, leaning forward a bit menacingly.

"I'm not sure," I said. "At least until Grand-mère gets better."

"Your grand-mère is under the impression we need your help. She thinks we can't manage without her."

"I don't know anything about running a château," I said.

"I'm sure you don't," said Jane.

This woman wasn't making it easy for me to like her. "Are you a chef?" I asked.

"Me? No, but Phillipa is one, or rather, wants to be." She lifted her chin so high I could see into her flared nostrils. "I run this place—do a bit of everything."

"So, you're a Jane of all trades?" I asked with a nervous laugh, trying to see if I could lighten up her attitude.

Jane's mouth curved into another fake smile as she chortled out an even faker laugh. "Clever."

"It was," said Phillipa, with a clap of her hands. "And now that that's settled, I'll fill you in. Clothilde and I are Grand-mère Odette's sous chefs, and Jane, who *thinks* she runs the château, will check in the guests. In season, Jane and I live in the clock tower. The granny brigade and Gustave should be arriving around two, but we should get started prepping." She smiled. "I'm really excited to learn from you, and I, for one, am thrilled you are here."

I liked Phillipa and her effervescent personality and chatty optimism, but Jane sat with her arms crossed over her chest with her upper lip curled.

"*Moi aussi*," said Clothilde. "I've picked up some English from these two. I don't understand everything they say, but I get the general gist of it."

"Who else is coming in?" I asked. Clothilde had mentioned *les dames*, whom I could only assume were the granny brigade, but Gustave was a foreign name.

"The rest of the kitchen staff," said Jane pointedly—as if I should know who was who and what was what.

"I just arrived today," I said.

"And you don't know a lick about this place," said Jane. "In fact, you look a bit jet-lagged. Maybe you should get some rest."

"Jane, you don't even know how to boil water. We need Sophie's help," said Phillipa, turning her attention to me. "What do you want us to do?"

I didn't even know where to start, but by Phillipa's eager expression, the way her eyes widened, I knew she was counting on me to take charge. I couldn't move. This was too much pressure. I couldn't be head chef or anything else when I wasn't myself.

Clothilde cleared her throat. "The guests arrive in three hours and the *daube* must *mijoter* for at least four hours. Dinner is set for seven-thirty, so we have just enough time. Plus, we have the wine tasting, which comes with an *apéro*, and all of the other dishes to prepare."

"Is there a planned meal?" I asked.

"It's right over there." Clothilde pointed to a large chalkboard.

My eyes scanned the menu and my heart stopped when I saw one of the entrées written in white, the words flashing like a neon light—a roasted potimarron velouté. Any early pinch of optimism I'd felt vanished. I glared at the board, blinking.

"*Ma puce*, is something wrong?" asked Clothilde.

"I don't know if I can do this," I said, the back of my neck covered in a thin sheet of perspiration.

Jane let out a wicked huff.

"Of course you can," said Chlothilde, shooting Jane a look. "You've learned from the best, your grand-mère."

Rémi walked into the kitchen carrying a burlap sack, distracting us. He pulled down a kitchen scale from one of the shelves and, with his back to me, said, "Nearly two kilos," then, turning on his heel like a trained marine, he stormed out of the kitchen, sack in hand.

"He's not very friendly," I said under my breath, and Jane scowled at me.

"He's invaluable," she said.

"Are you a couple?" I asked, thinking they'd be perfect for one another—both of them rude, crude, and annoyingly good-looking. Jane's ice-cold eyes flashed onto mine, but she didn't answer. "I really hope I don't have to see him too much," I said.

"Impossible," said Phillipa. "He lives in the stone house just down the road, the one at the far end of the property, and when he's not there, he's always here working."

"Great," I said. Just great.

Phillipa, Clothilde, and I sauntered up to the scale. Every muscle in my body tightened. With Rémi's attitude toward me, I wouldn't have been surprised to find a dead rat. I picked one of the black dirt-encrusted beauties up and breathed in its earthy, sensual scent. This gift of gourmet delights, worth its weight in gold, was clearly delivered by the cooking gods.

"D'Artagnan and Aramis are not only hunting dogs, they're wildly talented truffle trackers," said Phillipa.

Thanks to the *Times*, I knew dogs had mostly replaced pigs years ago on the quest for truffles because they were easier to train and didn't chow down on the fungus after they found it. Plus, if you had a pig on a leash, it advertised what the hunter was doing. And truffle territory was highly protected by those who had claimed a territory. I did the math in my head. The two kilos Rémi delivered came with a rough street value of around $7,000.

Phillipa's eyes dilated with truffle-drugged excitement. "Maybe we can grate a little bit into the velouté tonight? I'm thinking it would definitely raise the bar."

The muscles in my hand holding the black beauty went rigid. Once burned, twice shy, the last thing I wanted was for my grandmother to boot me out of her kitchen because I'd disrespected her recipes. After what went down at Cendrillon, I didn't want to take any chances. "I don't think it's an ingredient in Grand-mère Odette's recipe," I said firmly.

"But Grand-mère Odette says recipes are only guidelines, that being creative in the kitchen is what makes for a great chef," said Phillipa, not backing down. "She's inspired me and taught me to bring flavors and aromas together in complex ways, to cook using my senses. And my sense of smell is screaming that we should use the truffle in the velouté."

I pursed my lips, remembering Grand-mère Odette telling me the exact same thing years ago. At the time, she said she'd learned the lesson that recipes can't be duplicated the same way exactly again, that the process, timing, and ingredients needed to be adjusted, from famed chef Jacques Pépin. Not long after this, Grand-mère Odette bought me one of his books, *La Technique: An Illustrated Guide to the Fundamental Techniques of Cooking*, and, when I was only ten years old, Jacques Pépin became one of my cooking idols. Throughout the years, there would be many more chefs who provided inspiration, namely female chefs making their mark, including my grand-mère and Julia Child.

"As I recall, Grand-mère Odette added truffles to the velouté last year," said Clothilde.

"Then it's settled," said Jane, tilting her head to the side. "After all, this isn't a Michelin restaurant being judged by *consistency*. Cooking isn't linear. If we're making something better, we are going to do so. The truffles are going in. End of discussion."

She just had to twist the knife in my back and mention consistency. The scene at Cendrillon flashed in my memories—the soup dripping off the walls, Eric's smug grin, O'Shea's anger. Clothilde tapped me on the shoulder, breaking me out of my angry trance. "Are you okay, *ma puce*?"

"I'm just a bit out of my element," I said with a gulp.

"Long flight. Worrying over your grand-mère's health. All this." Clothilde swept out her arms. "Taking over this kitchen from the word go. It's a lot of stress. We're so very thankful you're here to help us man the ship."

Jane smirked. Phillipa nudged her side.

My finger shook like it was made of gelatin when I pointed to the board, to the potimarrons on the counter. The nape of my neck went hot. My breathing turned rapid. I couldn't be head chef. "No, I can't do this. I'm sorry. But I can't."

"Some master chef," said Jane, rolling her eyes. "Go ahead, leave. You couldn't cut it at Cendrillon and you're not going to ruin things here."

"Jane," said Phillipa with a gasp. "Not appropriate."

My knees were about to go out from under me. They all *knew*. I'd thought maybe in Champvert I could escape the drama my life had become for a while. But the truth was you could never escape your past no matter how far you ran. Which was exactly what I was going to do.

I raced out of the kitchen and straight up the servant staircase, heading for my room. Unfortunately, I'd left the door open, and I overheard Jane as I scurried up the steps, her words echoing in the stairwell. "What? Don't look at me like that. We all read the stories, saw the videos. It's probably best she stays out of our way. We have a business to run here."

"Give her a chance," said Clothilde. "You don't even know her. And this is a family business. She's Grand-mère Odette's pride and joy."

"I know what I read," said Jane. "And as far as family goes, I've been more like a granddaughter to Odette. Sophie abandoned her, never even came back for a visit."

"I'm sure there's more to the story," said Phillipa. "We haven't heard her side of it yet."

"I agree," came Clothilde's voice.

"We all just saw what we saw. The way she shook and trembled," said Jane. "She's mad as a box of frogs—completely barmy."

I placed my hand on the wall, trying to find my balance. The panic attack setting in was worse than any of the others. My breath came hard and fast. I couldn't breathe, couldn't move my feet. The last thing I remembered were my knees hitting the concrete, French words and translations swimming in my head.

Je suis tombée dans les pommes.

I fell in the apples.

I fainted.

II

winter

❦

Cooking is the art of adjustment.

—JACQUES PÉPIN

13

———✦———

the puppet master

A WEEK HAD passed since I tumbled down the staircase. My ankle throbbed and my body was bruised from head to toe, the welts dark and purple and unforgiving like crushed blackberries rotting on the ground after being stepped on. Housekeeping came into my room, but I'd send them away. They couldn't change the sheets on my bed when I didn't want to get out of it. I thought of visiting with Grand-mère, but she'd only be disappointed in me because I'd let her down. Just like in New York, I stayed in my room, avoiding everybody but Clothilde, who brought me meals and updated me on my grandmother's health, and Phillipa, who tried her best to snap me out of my funk. One morning, she brought a red poinsettia into my room.

"It's almost Christmas. We're going to get into the spirit of the season," said Phillipa, setting the plant down. "What are you asking *le Père Noël* for?"

"A new life," I said with a grumble. "Nobody wants me here."

"I do."

"Why?" I asked.

She tapped the side of her head with her finger twice. "It's my sixth sense. I have my instincts."

"Is it telling you to run for the hills? To get away from impending danger?"

"You're funny when you're depressed." She snorted out a laugh and then turned serious. "I'm really sorry for what Jane said. I'm sure she didn't mean it."

"What is her issue with me?" I asked, thinking Jane had meant every word she'd uttered with her holier-than-thou accent.

"She has issues with everybody. Don't let her get to you," said Phillipa. "When we were children, I used to call her JJ."

"JJ?" I questioned.

"Judgmental Jane," she said with a cackle. "And she hated it. Did you faint because you overheard her?"

"It's not like she pushed me. I fell," I responded. "It was an accident. And what she said was true," I added, pulling the covers over my head.

"I don't think so," said Phillipa. "Your grand-mère told me she taught you everything she knows. And if you can cook like her, you're one of the best. So, once you're feeling better, I, for one, can't wait to see what you can do."

"I can ruin things," I mumbled.

Phillipa didn't catch my pathetic comment. She pulled the duvet off my face. "What?"

"Thank you for the plant," I said.

"It's the little things in life that make us happy," she said with a shrug.

Although Phillipa left my room with a smile, thinking she'd cheered me up, the nightmare I left behind in New York still haunted me. I could hear O'Shea in my sleep, threatening to gut me open like a pig. I could see Eric's twisted grin when he called me a talentless lackey. Sometimes I'd stare out the window and watch *les hirondelles* (barn swallows) swooping in the gray skies, executing quick and sudden turns, almost as if they were diving right to the ground. I'd wonder if they'd crash, hitting a low point, like I did. They didn't have doctors for broken dreams or broken hearts and I didn't know how I'd ever be fixed. My thoughts went back to New York and how I wanted to catch the first plane out of France once Grand-mère was on the mend. If I cleared my name, I could go back.

I reached into my purse and pulled out my phone to text Walter—something I'd forgotten to do. The second I switched my cell phone off airplane mode, more than twenty alerts came in, beeping incessantly.

> Walter: Did you get in okay? How is your grandmother?
>
> Walter: I haven't heard from you. Text me!
>
> Walter: Where are you? I'm getting worried.

I quickly texted Walter back: I'm so sorry I haven't gotten in touch with you. I'm here. Grand-mère is still in the hospital, but doing better. Me? I feel like I'm on another planet. Lots to fill you in on. I'll call you later. Xox

> Walter: Great news! Robert has moved in with us! We have
> to store a few things in your room until we figure out
> where to put them. Let us know when you're coming home
> and we'll sort things out before then.

Home. I couldn't move back to New York without a job and become a freeloading roommate to a couple starting their lives together. Home? I felt as if I didn't have one anymore, that I was just an unwelcome visitor.

At the very least, my bedroom—a large suite comprised of a salon with a fireplace, a children's nursery, a bedroom, and a bathroom—was familiar and, after everything I'd seen and experienced so far, I needed a dash of familiarity. I regarded the same faded damask wallpaper; the same queen-sized wooden bed with the same green jacquard comforter; the faded, milky Aubusson carpet with floral patterns.

A couple of weeks after my failure in the kitchen, Clothilde barged into my room without knocking. "*Ma puce*," she said, "you've gotten your rest. It's time for you to join the world again."

I rolled over and pushed my face into my pillow, muffling my voice. "You're all doing fine without me in the picture."

"We all know of the troubles you had in New York. It's time for you to get over it." Clothilde rolled me over to face her. "Now get up and get on with your life."

"I don't think I will ever get over it."

She placed a loving hand on my shoulder. "Maybe your difficulty is our gain. You are here now and your grandmother—all of us—are depending on you." She held me in her gaze, a look that said "no messing around."

"How is she?" I asked with a sniffle.

"I'm glad you asked. She's doing better than you are right now," she said. "But like her, you have the fire of the Valroux de la Tour de Champverts running through your veins."

I wasn't so sure about that. All I knew was that I'd gone down in flames—not once, but twice.

"Such a long, ridiculous last name," I said. "No wonder my mother shortened it when we moved to New York."

"Your grand-mère says the same thing, which is the reason she insists most people call her Grand-mère Odette." She crossed her arms over her chest. "But in France, the longer the name, the more it proves just how noble you are."

"I'm not noble," I said. "I'm a coward. I didn't stay to fight for my honor. I ran away."

"You didn't run away. You came back to Champvert to serve a greater purpose. You're here for your grandmother, for your family. That's a big difference. I'd get used to the idea, and quick. You're home now and you are surrounded by people who support and love you." She clucked her tongue. "Stop playing the victim like a petulant child and get out of bed. This is Champvert, not New York. Tomorrow, I expect for you to be up and dressed by nine a.m. I'm taking you to see your grand-mère. Or did you forget you came here for her?"

With that, she spun on her heel and left, leaving me in my thoughts and feeling guilty.

My teddy bear sat on a chair. Large, fuzzy, and brown like caramelized sugar, *Bear*nard was my "here" bear. Grand-mère Odette wouldn't let me take him back to New York, no matter how much I begged and pleaded. I picked up Bearnard and hugged him to my chest, smelling a very faint hint of lavender, the scent of my childhood.

I WAS NINE years old when I harvested the lavender with my grandmother. She'd explained that she'd purchased her plants in Provence, on a route where a sea of purple flowers bloom in mid-June. She'd told me of the beauty, how she wanted to bring it back to Champvert so she could add it to her special homemade mix of *herbes de Provence*, and promised to take me to the Routes de la Lavande so I could see and experience the magic myself. I'd asked if we could go the following day, and she'd smiled and said, *"Pourquoi pas."* We packed a picnic lunch of homemade baguettes with ham, butter, and Emmental cheese along with a large container of cherries in the early morning and drove the six hours in her Mercedes, passing fields of happy sunflowers along the way.

"This was the last trip I took with your grand-père before he left us for the angels," she said. "We'll stay in the same château." She patted my hand. "Roll down your window, breathe in the air, *ma chérie.* We're almost there."

The car rounded a corner and the landscape was just as she'd described it, the air strongly perfumed. Fields upon fields of lavender plants, sometimes offset with sunflowers or poppies, burst over the rolling terrain, the colors and scents so vibrant they took my breath away. Grand-mère stopped the car on the side of the road in front of a small shack selling goods like oils, bouquets, and Provençal textiles. I stood in awe, excited like the many bees buzzing through the flowers. It was here Grand-mère had purchased my teddy bear and her poppy apron.

Smiling wistfully at the memory, I inhaled Bearnard, letting the soothing effects of lavender calm my nerves down. With the bear tucked under my arm, regardless of everything, I thought of my grandmother and how I had to pull myself together for her, which Clothilde had reminded me of when she called me petulant.

But Clothilde was right. And I'd promised her I'd snap out of this funk; I was going to keep my word, no matter how uncomfortable I felt.

AS I DRESSED the following day, I looked out my window, surveying the land, the buildings, and the beautiful gardens, feeling out of place. Perhaps it was time for me to try to fit in. I threw on a navy-blue midi dress with long sleeves that tied at the waist, and never wrinkled—the one I'd worn for Walter's mother's lunches—and my one and only pair of black ballerina flats. With no guests wandering around the château, I wanted to explore before Clothilde took me to see my grandmother, and I found myself in the hallway standing in front of an elevator, blinking back my astonishment. I pressed the call button and the doors opened. The interior of the compartment was elegant and sleek and modern, the kind you'd find in an upscale hotel in New York or Paris, with burgundy leather walls adorned with Chesterfield buttons, a modern stainless steel chandelier, and LED lights. Music played. Bach.

I knew my grandmother came from money, but I didn't know she had this kind of money.

In France, the ground floor is the *rez-de-chaussée*. Instead of heading to the kitchen, I made my way to the third floor—which was actually the fourth, a fact that still didn't quite register in my American mind—one floor up from mine, and also where my grandmother's suite was located. I exited the lift and ambled down the hall. A member of the housekeeping staff—dressed in a pale gray dress with a crisp white shirt and carrying a bucket of cleaning supplies—rushed by and whispered a quick, *"Bonjour, madame."* She swung a heavy wooden door open and I couldn't help but peek into the room.

"Holy *merde*," was all I could utter.

There was an Italian-style bathroom, including a shower and large Jacuzzi tub made of beautiful white French marble with thin gray veins. Billowy white curtains surrounded a beautiful, ornate wrought iron bed, and on the mattress made up with white French linens were white flower petals. The floors in this room were inlaid marble, red and black. The windows opened to the Juliet balcony. There was so much open space I could have done a cartwheel if I wasn't such a klutz.

My grand-mère's suite was locked, but I opened up a few more doors to find that every room in the château was just as grand and beautiful. I explored each floor, finally making my way down to the *rez-de-chaussée*, where complete shock set in. The entire space had been renovated into a hammam spa and decorated with intricate blue, green, and ivory Moroccan tiles. I don't know what surprised me most—the two small pools or the bubbling Jacuzzi or the rooms overflowing with orchids and set up with massage tables. When I wasn't rubbing my eyes with disbelief, I was trying to catch my breath. My grand-mère had created an empire, but how vast was it?

With my curiosity piqued, before I headed to the kitchen to look through grand-mère's notebooks, I meandered into my grandmother's office. The room was as opulent and refined as the rest of the château. Dark paneled walls. Beautiful paintings. A large Louis XIV desk with a red leather top and gilded accents on the wood, complete with a matching chair. On the desk sat her computer—an iMac with a twenty-seven-inch screen.

On the wall above the desk hung a diploma from Le Cordon Bleu. I gasped and looked closer at the date: 1994. Wow. My grand-mère had attended France's premier culinary school a year after I was born? Why hadn't she told me about this? This piece of information made me realize I didn't know anything about her life—not really. I knew she loved to cook. I knew she loved me. But that was about it. I wanted to know more.

I fired up her computer. There were three log-in accounts—one for Jane, one for my grand-mère, and one for a guest. I opted for my grand-mère's account, trying Sophie1993, the code I'd found when it slipped from the kitchen notebooks, not sure what I was doing or exactly what I was looking for. In the corner of the screen, a dozen email alerts came in, my eyes darting to flashing blue squares. My legs were about to go out from under me when I saw *his* address pop up: kitchengod1990@gmail.com. Eric had emailed my grand-mère? What? And why? I'd forgotten she'd met him when I'd graduated from the CIA. Afterward, we'd eaten dinner at Cendrillon NY, as I'd wanted to show her the restaurant where I'd be working. I knew going through somebody's email was wrong, but so was corresponding with the devil.

Shaking with confusion, I sat down, opened up her mail, and read through the thread.

From: KitchenGod
To: Château de Champvert
Subject: Your Granddaughter
Date: 1 octobre 2019

Dear Madame Valroux de la Tour de Champvert—

I don't know if you remember me, but I met you in New York when Sophie graduated from the Culinary Institute of America. As you know, we lived together for two years and then we broke up, due to my arrogant ways. I'm opening a new restaurant called Blackbird in a few months and I'd like her to come work for me. She's one of the best chefs de partie in the city. But she won't listen to me. If you have any advice on how to convince her, I'd really appreciate it. Sophie and I make a great team.

Many thanks,
Eric

From: Château de Champvert
To: KitchenGod
Subject: Re: Your Granddaughter
Date: 7 octobre 2019

My granddaughter, like all the women in our family, is a very independent woman—fierce, strong, and stubborn. If you are serious about wanting to convince her heart to work with you, she'd need to depend on you.

Bonne chance.

From: KitchenGod
To: Château de Champvert
Subject: Re: Your Granddaughter
Date: 30 novembre 2019

Dear Madame Valroux de la Tour de Champvert—

I took your advice, but Sophie won't have anything to do with me. Is she in France? I need to speak with her.

Many thanks,
Eric

Reeling with mixed emotions, I searched through her account, finding a folder called "Letters for Sophie" with emails addressed to the Culinary Institute of America—letters of recommendation for my admittance from famous chefs, including Jean-Jacques Gaston, O'Shea's mentor. He'd also ensured I got the *stage* at Cendrillon.

Strings. There they were. My grand-mère was a puppet master and I felt like a little marionette. I also felt terrible. My grandmother had helped me achieve my dreams from afar, even though she wanted me back in France. And I was an ingrate. Putting the confusion I had about her correspondance with Eric to the side, I felt dizzy with guilt and placed my head in my hands.

A huff came from the doorway, and I flinched when I looked up.

"You're not supposed to be in here," said Jane. She placed her hands on her hips, her eyes locking onto mine. The veins in her neck pulsed and throbbed.

"I needed to use the computer," I said, quitting out of Grand-mère's email and logging out.

"You have the password?" she asked.

"I logged on as a guest."

Jane postured herself like a peacock defending its territory. "Next time, use one of the computers in the business center. I have work to do," she said, eyeing me warily. "Clothilde is waiting for you in the kitchen."

"Then I guess I should go," I said.

"I guess you should."

14

poker face

ALTHOUGH MY HEAD still pounded with the information I'd just learned, I set off for the kitchen for my date with Clothilde. Until I spoke with my grand-mère, I needed to keep my wits about me and put my best game face on. Clothilde had been nothing but nice to me. I couldn't begrudge her. She was rummaging through cabinets, mumbling to herself.

"*Bonjour*," I said, forcing the best smile I could muster. "What are you looking for?"

"Cumin," she said, her tone frazzled. She threw her hands in the air. "I wanted to make Bernard a tajine tonight and I don't have any at our home. And you can't make a tajine without cumin, ginger, and turmeric. It's the trifecta of ingredients—like a *mirepoix*."

"Moroccan?"

"No, Algerian. Bernard and I were, as they call us, *pieds-noirs*. We lived there during the French rule in the late fifties." She sighed. "We'd just married and we were so young then. He was in the military, *tu vois*?" She flipped her red curls with her hand. "We moved back to France after the war ended in 1962. Times were tough, but Bernard, *hélas*, still loves his tajines."

I did, too. A tajine was a spice-infused Maghreb dish named after the earthenware pot in which it is cooked. I hadn't had one since I was twelve. Grand-mère had introduced me to a few international recipes, wanting to expand my cultural horizons.

I shuffled around the kitchen, found the cumin, and handed it over.

"Oh, thank you, *ma puce*," she said, her smile bright. "Did you look outside? It's snowing!"

I glanced at the window. Giant powdered-sugar flakes of snow tumbled from the sky, sticking to the ground, the trees weighed down with frosty cream. In a few hours, the whole world had changed and everything was covered in white—like a clean slate. It was the most beautiful scene I'd ever witnessed, like a fairy tale or a snow globe, but unlike a snow globe, my life had been shaken up and nothing had settled. I wanted a clean slate.

"*Ma puce*," said Clothilde, "put on a coat or you'll catch a cold." She glanced at my feet. "And you might want to wear a pair of boots. There are some in the closet about your size. Can you manage with your ankle?"

I'd forgotten about my ankle. Oddly, it didn't hurt too much unless I twisted it to the right. I headed to the closet in the hall, kicked off my flats, and pulled on some rubber wellies. After grabbing my coat, I asked, "Are we off to see grand-mère so soon?"

"No, not quite yet. Bernard is meeting us at Le Papillon Sauvage for breakfast."

"Oh, Bernard, I'm dying to see him. How is he?"

Clothilde closed her eyes, a wistful smile carving on her lips. "Wonderful, as always. Even after fifty years of marriage it still feels like yesterday," she said. "*On y va?*"

I nodded. "Yes, let's go."

"Follow me," she said, turning toward the back door.

I followed her outside, nearly slipping on the rocky steps. "The other restaurant in the barn? Can you tell me about it?"

"There's not much to it. Le Papillon Sauvage serves simple country food at a fixed price," said Clothilde. "Last year, the restaurant received an award from Michelin." She cackled. "*Eh ben*, I've never understood what tires have to do with food."

My heart skipped a few beats. "Did you say 'Michelin'?"

Before she could answer, I jumped through the snow and raced to the barn. The sign was plastered right on the front door. Le Papillon Sauvage had received a Bib Gourmand. Not quite the same as gaining Michelin stars, this honor was reserved for restaurants serving exceptional meals at moderate prices. According to the framed menu hanging in the window, one could eat here for the price of twenty-nine euros, including wine from the château's vineyards.

With my heart galloping like a herd of wild and unruly horses, I opened the front door and walked into the space, taking everything in, one breathless gulp at a time. Rustic and charming, the restaurant screamed country French. Porcelain roosters and chickens adorned the long, wooden community-style tables with bench seating. Wrought iron lighting fixtures. Aged wine barrels and other antiquities like an old oak washing tub in the corner. Copper pots hanging from a rack. An open and well-equipped kitchen. A woodburning oven. Antique transfer plates in various shades of blue hanging on the brick walls along with lithograph prints of butterflies.

It was beautiful—but Grand-mère Odette never mentioned the Bib Gourmand. Granted, I'd been caught up in my New York life, but we did occasionally talk on the phone. Why so many secrets?

Clothilde scurried up behind me. Hunched over, I put my hands on my knees, bracing myself. "Clothilde, tell me what in the world is going on at the château." She shrugged, and as I caught my breath I pointed to the sign plastered by the door. "A *Bib Gourmand*?"

"*Oui*, that's what the award is called."

"And she didn't tell me? About this?"

"I don't see what the big to-do is," said Clothilde.

"It's a huge deal. Enormous," I said. "It's Michelin."

Before she could respond, Bernard burst into the restaurant. He still wore the bushy mustache that curled up on the edges like Salvador Dalí's and still had bright blue eyes that sparkled with decades of laughter. He kicked the snow off his boots and raced up to me, twirling me around.

"Be careful," said Clothilde with a tsk-tsk. "She had a fall."

"*Je sais, je sais, mon amour, mais elle est là!*" (I know, I know, my love, but she is here!) he said with a wink, setting me down with care. "And she is so skinny. We need to feed her." He patted his portly belly. "*Tu as faim*, Sophie?"

"*Oui, un peu*" (Yes, a little), I said. Mostly, I was starving for anwers.

"Come sit down next to your *tonton*," said Bernard, referring to himself as my uncle, like he'd done when I was a child. "My beautiful wife will get us sorted out."

"I should help her," I said.

"*Non*," said Clothilde. "I can manage. You're just getting your strength back. And we need you to be strong."

"For what?" I asked. Were they trying to fatten me up as an offering to the cooking gods? If so, take me now, because my prayers in New York had gone unanswered.

"Why, the wedding weekend, of course."

"Wait. Hold the phone. What wedding weekend?"

"Hold the phone?" she asked. "I feel quite lost half the time with you young girls. What an odd expression."

Probably like the one twisting my face. "Wedding? I thought the château was closed for the winter season—"

"It is—unless we book a private event," she said. "We'd like for you to plan the menu."

"You cannot be expecting me to cook," I said with too much force. "You saw me a few weeks ago. You know I can't do anything. I-I-I—"

"Need to stop playing the victim. And you will do this for *me*. No questions. No arguments. No pity party. You are a talented chef. I need your help. That is all."

Bernard shook his finger and winked. "A little advice. Don't argue with my wife."

Good lord, great God almighty, what had I roped myself into?

As Clothilde darted around gathering our breakfast, I sat rigid. Finally, she placed a platter of croissants, yogurts, and a French press of coffee on the table. There was another drink, the earthy scent hitting my senses immediately. "I made you a *chocolat chaud*," she said. "You loved them when you were younger."

"I still love them now," I said.

She placed the bowl in front of me and I took a sip, the chocolaty goodness sliding down my throat, each gulp a memory. I found myself getting lost in my childhood—when I was free and happy with no cares in the world. Seven years old—the first time I tasted a real hot chocolate, and when I whirled around with unrestrained glee, begging for more, the cocoa melting on my tongue. I remembered when my grand-mère served me my first one, and the way she laughed at my delight. I remembered her words.

"It's the simple things in life that make us happy," she'd said.

So I wondered, why was everything so damn complicated now?

"*Ma puce*, you remind me of your grandfather in so many ways. I see him in you," said Bernard, pulling me back from the past into the here and now. "You have his eyes, a strength."

"What was he like?" I asked.

"Strict and very serious, but passionate with a zest for life. He was a very giving man. A lot of people were struggling financially in Champvert, and he helped all of us, especially Clothilde and me. He paid for our son, Victor, to move to Paris for university and mentored him through business school. He bought our farm and invited us to live in the guesthouse. He gave us back our lives. In fact, he bought most of the properties in Champvert." Bernard paused. "I miss Pierre every day, especially during the harvest, which you unfortunately missed. I hope you'll be able to experience the magic someday."

"I hope so, too," I said, only now realizing how indebted the villagers of Champvert were to my family. The feelings that came with knowing my grandparents controlled everything like land overlords unsettled me. Granted, they were noble; I knew this. But it was like the entire community was enslaved to them. I wondered about my mother. She did everything she could to get out of Champvert. Was it their control she was trying to escape from? I wanted answers and only my grand-mère could give them to me.

"We'll have to give you a proper wine tasting one of these days," said Bernard. "Unfortunately, it's only nine in the morning."

"I could use some liquid courage now," I mumbled, which Bernard clearly didn't hear.

"It's time to fatten you up," said Bernard, pointing to the tray. "*Mange-le.*"

"Aren't Frenchwomen supposed to be skinny?" I asked.

"*Bah*, not in the southwest of France. The food is too good here. And women with a little meat on their bones, like *ma poule*, are full of life."

The way Clothilde smiled at Bernard lifted my spirits for a moment. It was inspiring. I'd never experienced love, not this way. Eric had shown me his "love" in bed in an animalistic way, never through kind actions or words. It wasn't love; it was just sex. Pushing the thoughts of him out of my mind, I grabbed a *chocolatine* and inhaled its fragrance, the buttery flakes crumbling in my fingers. Food had always been my way of showing love, but I'd lost the desire to cook. I wondered if I could get it back again.

Right when I was chewing, Rémi appeared in the doorway of the restaurant, arms crossed over his chest. He'd shaved off his beard and wore black slacks, a crisp white shirt, and, from what I could tell, a black leather belt with a silver Prada buckle. The boy could clean up. His eyes bore into mine. "I'm supposed to take you to visit with Grand-mère. Clothilde asked because she's uncomfortable driving in the snow."

Buttery crumbs fell from my mouth, chocolate sticking to my tongue. My gaze shot to Clothilde's. "I don't want to go anywhere with him."

"Fine by me," said Rémi. "I have many things to do."

Clothilde slammed her hand on the table. "The two of you are going to the hospital together. No arguments."

Bernard raised his hands in resignation. "Never argue with my wife."

Rémi turned to leave, but didn't. He stood in the doorway, his back to me, his breathing labored. "*On y va*, Sophie" (Let's go, Sophie), he said. "Now. I haven't got all day."

After scarfing down my *chocolatine*, I scrambled out of my chair and grabbed my coat. "So sorry to take up your precious time, Rémi," I said.

Rémi pushed open the door. "You shouldn't talk with your mouth full," he said. "And, believe me, I have better things to do than chauffeur you around. Not everything is about you, *princesse*," he said, and stormed down the driveway.

Just like at the airport, Rémi's pace was brisk and I had to scramble to keep up with him, nearly falling in the snow a dozen times. He didn't look back once. He bolted right to the truck and jumped in. From the inside, he opened the passenger door. As I crawled into my seat, his upper lip curved into a snarl.

"Look, I'm not happy about this either," I said, meeting his glare. "But I need to see Grand-mère and I can't drive with my ankle. Well, there's that and the fact that I don't have a driver's license."

"*Quoi?*" he asked, mouth agape. "How could you not know how to drive? You are twenty-six years old."

I let out a huff. "Well, I lived in the city—no need for a car. I took taxis or the subway and never learned."

His eyes flashed onto mine for a quick second. He brushed back a loose strand of thick black hair off his forehead. "*Et alors*, you are here now," he said. "Maybe you should learn."

"Oooh," I said. "Was that a full sentence?"

"I believe I've spoken three, maybe four," he said.

I went silent, staring straight ahead, until he started up the engine. I could handle a forty-five-minute ride, even though it was colder in this truck with his attitude than it was outside.

"Yes, I am here now," I muttered. "Might as well make the best of it."

"Here today, gone tomorrow," he said. "Like your mother."

If I had a craw, Rémi had definitely gotten into it. He pushed my anger to heightened limits. How dare he bring up my mother. Hot tears threatened to explode, but there was no way I was going to cry—not in front of him. "Whatever you want to think," I said. "Let's just get to Grand-mère."

"*D'accord, princesse.*"

"Stop calling me that."

"Do we need rules?" he asked, and I nodded. "Don't speak."

"Fine," I said, wanting to get the last word in.

Rémi peeled out of the driveway. We sat in silence for the forty-five-minute drive to Toulouse, me with my forehead pressed against the window, my breath fogging up the glass. Screw Rémi. Screw Jane. Screw Eric. And screw the world. I needed to find the courage to ask my grandmother some questions when I didn't have much of it.

15

chasing dreams

GRAND-MÈRE'S EYES LIT up when Rémi and I walked into her room. She looked as if she was doing much better. Her hair was coiffed and her cheeks had a rosy tint. "Oh, my heart may burst. My two precious darlings have come for a visit," she said. "Sophie, Clothilde told me you had a fall. Are you okay? I was very worried."

"You shouldn't worry over me. I'm just a little bruised and my ankle hurts, but I'm fine," I said, and kissed her cheek. "I'm worried about you."

"You shouldn't be," said Rémi with an annoyed huff. "She's on the road to a complete recovery. Just look at her."

I didn't know if he said this for his benefit or for hers. Or to drag me under the rug. Whatever the case, his modus operandi worked. Grand-mère's hand latched onto Rémi's and she smiled. "That I am, my darling boy. I'm doing much, much better, and I'll be out of here in no time."

I wondered what my grandmother saw in Rémi. Maybe he had two personalities—one for the rest of the world, a Dr. Jekyll, and one for me, the murderous and violent Mr. Hyde. I hoped Rémi only hunted wild animals, because he was gunning for me. Rémi and my grandmother swapped *les bises* and he excused himself. "I'll let you and Sophie speak alone," he said.

My grandmother nodded and we both watched him leave the room. "I think of Rémi like a son. He's a very handsome fellow, is he not?" said my grandmother with a chuckle. "Much nicer than the fellow I'd met in New York. What was his name again? The chef you were working with?"

"Eric," I said with a pause. She knew exactly who he was and she'd opened the doorway to the conversation I wanted to have. I was going in. "Grand-mère, I know what you did. And I'm not happy about it. How could you?"

Her gaze didn't waver from mine. "How could I do what?"

I cringed. "You told Eric to sabotage me. I found the emails you exchanged with him on your computer."

Grand-mère went silent for a moment, taking in my confession. Why didn't she say anything?

"I can't believe you told Eric to destroy my career."

"I said no such thing," she said. "Eric saw what he wanted to see in my words. I told him you were independent. Is that a lie? Is that not true?"

"Yes, but you wrote to him, saying if he wanted to win me back, he needed to make me dependent on him."

"And then I wrote *bonne chance*, did I not? Is the boy so thick he doesn't understand sarcasm? If I were you, I'd read my response to him again," she said. "You are a Valroux de la Tour de Champvert. You are *my* granddaughter. We are independent women. This isn't the 1950s."

I didn't need to read through the emails again; I'd memorized them. My guard was up higher than the gates at the château; I needed to lower it. I needed to trust somebody, anybody, starting with my grand-mère. I was sick of feeling as if the whole world was out to get me. I wanted to believe her, to understand her motives.

"No, it isn't," I said. "I'm taking it that you know what happened in New York?"

"*Oui*," she said. "I may be old and sick, but I monitor the news—especially when my granddaughter is involved."

I was getting tired of repeating my side of the story, but sat down and did it again, reliving every hellish and painful moment. "I didn't sabotage the restaurant," I said, ending my woeful tale.

"I know you would never do anything like that," she said, her eyes squeezing shut. "When I read that article in the *Times*, my heart broke. I had a feeling you'd been set up and that Eric had something to do with it."

"You've been monitoring me?" I said, shell-shocked.

"I have nothing but love for you," she said, and my heart plummeted into my stomach. "We don't talk often and I wanted to make sure you were well, especially after your mother's grand escape from life. I have your name on Google Alerts. I've read about your triumphs and, *alors*, this situation. If this makes me a bad person, I don't know what a good person is."

"You could have told me," I said. "I mean, you didn't even ask me if I needed letters of reccomendation for school. You just did it."

"Ah, so you found those, too," she said, and I flinched. "Maybe I meddled in your life. Do you blame me? Am I supposed to sit back and watch you suffer?"

"Keeping secrets is just as bad as lying," I said. "You've been keeping so much from me."

"Sophie, when was the last time you were here? When was I ever given the chance to speak openly and honestly with you?" She gripped my hand with such strength, for a moment I forgot how sick she was. "We're both guilty of pushing each other away."

My brain felt like a thousand-pound weight was pulling my head down. "Because of my mother," I said, hunching over and scrunching my body into a tiny ball, hugging my knees to my chest. "And what she did."

"Yes, *ma chérie*," she said. "But I don't want to talk about Céleste. It upsets me."

"But we have to talk about her. I need to talk about her."

"And one day we will. But that day is not today."

I snapped upright. The truth was she never wanted to talk about my mother. At the time, with my head spinning, I didn't either, so instead of pushing, I changed the subject. "I wish you had told me about all the changes you've made—the restaurants, the fact that you're a Grand Chef with the famed Société des Châteaux et Belles Demeures. The Bib Gourmand? Why didn't you tell me anything? I feel like an outsider—and not a very welcome one."

"You had your own dreams to follow. I wanted you to come back here of your own accord, to see for yourself everything I've done," she said. "I didn't want you to feel obligated to follow my plans and dreams."

"Well, that didn't exactly happen," I said, clearing my throat.

"Whatever the circumstances, you're here now and that's all that matters to me." She turned her head, glancing at me briefly. "With my health, death might come knocking on my door sooner than later."

"Grand-mère, please don't speak of such things."

"But I must. It's time for you to know the truth about your inheritance," said my grandmother. "French inheritance laws protect children, not the spouse. Céleste didn't care about her father. All she wanted was his money. I knew what she'd do with her funds—

waste them on useless things. Or do something rash like move to New York. Which is exactly what she did when she received her inheritance after my father passed away. Your grandfather and I went directly to the *notaire* to protect your interests. If we didn't do this, your mother would have inherited two-thirds of the estate, the cash in the bank totaling the equivalent of 15,000,000 euros at the time, only one quarter left to me. Of course, the inheritance left to me by my parents is not included in this sum, and I have lifetime rights to the château, so it can't be sold until my death."

"I don't understand. What does this have to do with me?"

Grand-mère fixed me in her gaze, unflinching. "After Céleste left with you, construction began—a new roof, the greenhouse, the renovations to most of the rooms, and the conversion of the barn. We poured money into the château. We bought new property in my name. And now with your mother deceased, after I die, you, *ma chérie*, will receive the total of the estate, save for fifteen percent, which will be allocated elsewhere, according to my wishes. But the château will be yours."

Mine? The château would be mine? The idea had never entered into my head, not even in my wildest dreams. My breath came out in ragged gasps. I couldn't even run a kitchen. How on earth was I supposed to manage a château? The pressure was just too much. "This is a lot to take in," I said.

"I understand," she said, clasping her hands around mine. "If my blood pressure stays stable, the doctor is letting me leave right around Christmas under the strict orders that I don't overexert myself. I'll enlighten you on the inner workings of the château as best I can. I know you have a lot to think about."

"Grand-mère, I'm not sure if I want the château," I said. "I'm not even sure I'm a chef anymore. I'm nothing. I didn't even get into cooking school on my own."

"Perhaps I meddled ensuring your enrollment," she said. "But everything you did after that, you did on your own. You did graduate at the top of your class, *non?*"

I did. I worked harder than anybody. I threw myself into my culinary education. I should have been happy my grandmother cared about me enough to go out on a limb for me.

"You are like me. Cooking for you is love, and it's all I've ever wanted for you. Love. Right now, you have to think about what I've done for you. It's all about love."

"Me? I'm like you?"

"Yes, and you are my everything. And if helping ensure your dream of going to that school was wrong, I'll die today. But when I die, I want to see my life, our family's life, grow and prosper. Your mother broke my heart when she left—" she started but couldn't continue.

I gripped her hand. "I think—no, I know—that I need to understand why she did what she did. I don't want to end up like her. I have so many questions. Can you promise me we'll talk about her when you're ready?"

"*Oui, ma chérie,* but let me get a bit of my strength back," she said with a wheeze. "Please send Rémi in now. I'm quite tired and I'd like to speak with him before I fall asleep. And you, my dear, have the wedding weekend to plan. I've told Clothilde you will be in charge of planning the menu and all other menus to come."

Drowning in my self-imposed drama, I'd completely forgotten about the wedding weekend.

"I don't know, Grand-mère. You're putting me under a lot of pressure."

"It's good for you," she said. "Be strong, like the woman I know you are."

"Why do you think I'm strong? I'm nothing lately. I'm weak—the weakest link."

"Are you not my granddaughter?"

"Yes."

"That's how I know."

"But my mother—"

"You are not your mother. And we will not be talking about her now. Please send Rémi in."

ON THE RIDE home, I sat in numb silence, staring straight ahead. Rémi, per his usual surliness, didn't say a word either, and I wondered what he and my grandmother had spoken about. Upon our arrival, the château's iron gates loomed above, foreboding in the gray winter sky. The truck rumbled down the driveway, and when it came to a stop, I scanned the façade of the château. I wasn't prepared for taking over all of this and didn't know if I'd ever be. Paralyzed with shock and knowledge, I couldn't move. Rémi opened the passenger door with a look of impatience.

"Get out," he said. "We're here."

"Why do you hate me so much?" I asked, narrowing my eyes into a glare.

"I don't hate you."

"Could have fooled me."

"I just don't like you," he said.

"Ditto," I said, seething with anger.

Rémi stormed off toward his home on the far side of the property, leaving me to hobble to the front door. The sky darkened, changing from light gray to black, and the rain came down hard. The wind whipped through the pine trees in howling whooshes.

The sudden change in the weather camouflaged the tears streaming down my cheeks.

I stared at the forbidding château, its turrets and slate roof, thinking how crazy this was. Most people of sound mind would be thrilled to inherit all of this. The thought of running away crossed my mind, but where would I go? To New York to an even bigger nightmare where I was a pariah? I didn't want to go to my room. I didn't want to head into the kitchen. I just wanted to be alone. The rain let up and I wandered the grounds to the river, the color a bluish gray, the water boiling and bubbling like my raging emotions. A fallen branch nicked my bad ankle. I grimaced and sank to the ground in pain—and not just physical. This water, the way it flowed and splashed against the rocks, reminded me of my mother and the fact that she was gone. Every time I thought of my mother lately, the thought of ending it all—just like she did—crossed my mind.

A Eurasian magpie—*une pie bavarde*—landed on a tree, followed by a few more, their black, blue, and white feathers glistening in the rain, their tails pointing accusingly down at me, their crow-like faces and pointed beaks menacing. They squawked from the trees loudly— a *chac-chac-chac*—as if I was encroaching on their territory. They were one of the most intelligent birds, and I knew from my childhood summers they could become quite aggressive, especially when protecting their nests. Perhaps grand-mère was like a *pie bavarde*. She did say she was only trying to protect me from afar. Yet the French word *bavarde* meant "talkative" and, although she was being more forthright, she always evaded the subject of my mother.

The wind howled and screeched. I could do it, end it all right here. I leaned forward and touched the ice-cold water. The birds, maybe sensing the danger looming in my mind, snapped me back into reality with a chorus of *chac-chac-chac*s. I shook my thoughts off and ran back to the château, the wet grass slurping under my feet.

I wasn't my mother. I was still alive.

Back in my room, I sought out the few things of my mother's that I'd kept, stuffed into the big blue suitcase. Tucked in between sparkling evening gowns, designer dresses, and her white mink coat that I probably should have stored, considering it reeked with a musty scent, I spotted her jewelry box. It was where I'd found the engagement ring I wore around my neck. It was filled to the brim with imitation diamond necklaces and bracelets. I recalled the words she used to say: "If you want to be a star, you have to look, act, and dress like a star—diamonds, rubies, sapphires, and emeralds included."

But she was a fake, just like her jewelry. No, I wasn't like her. If anything, it had been my goal in life to be nothing like her. After the thoughts I'd had at the river, I knew something in me needed to change, and quick. I'd found my heart in the kitchen; it was high time for it to start beating again before I lost everything.

16

fight or flight

I T WAS JUST after noon when I meandered into the kitchen, glassy-eyed and limping on my bad ankle. Jane and Phillipa were eating baguettes slathered with ham and butter. I joined them. Jane stiffened when I sat down next to her. She didn't say hello or even glance in my direction.

"Hungry?" asked Phillipa, and I nodded. "Dig in. We have some wine, too. Don't know which one, but it's good."

"It's the château's 1994 dry white," said Jane. "Really, Phillipa, you should start educating yourself if you want to be a chef."

"Oh, I am a chef, my darling sister," said Phillipa, pouring me a glass and handing it over. "Sophie, this is one of the perks of working here."

I held up the glass to the light, swirling its golden contents around. The tears—*les larmes*—stuck to the side of the glass like honey. I took a sip, and a chorus of hallelujahs infiltrated my taste buds. "Wow. Delicious. So smooth."

Jane let out a snooty huff. Her mouth formed a tight line and the words she wanted to say but didn't rolled in my head. *"Oh, you're such a connoisseur of wine."*

"I'm so excited for this weekend," said Phillipa, mumbling in between bites of her sandwich. "And I'm also glad to see you're feeling better. Clothilde tells us you're joining in on the madness?"

"My grand-mère didn't exactly give me a choice," I said. "I'm doing this for her."

"You always have a choice," said Jane. "Unless you are a programmed robot without a mind of your own."

The New Yorker in me wanted to tell her to go screw herself, or at least give her a hip slam so she fell off of her stool. But I refrained and made a sandwich. I couldn't let this snotty twit get to me. I'd dealt with worse types. Like Eric.

"Does this mean you're staying on in Champvert?" asked Jane.

"The jury is still out debating that question," I said with a shrug. "But I'm here for now. Might as well make myself useful."

"Brilliant," said Jane, rolling her eyes. "Just brilliant." She jumped off her stool, smoothed out her skirt, and sashayed away.

"What is her freaking problem?" I mumbled.

"It's just Jane being Jane," said Phillipa.

"Maybe she should try on a new persona, because I want to slap the snot right out of her," I said, immediately regretting the words that had tumbled from my mouth. "I'm sorry. I shouldn't have said that. She's your twin sister."

"My evil twin sister." She laughed. "And, really, no worries. There have been days when I've thought the same thing. She didn't used to be such a snob. I think your grand-mère might have given her too much power and, ever since then, she's been on a power trip." Phillipa let out a sad sigh. "I miss the old Jane. She was sweet and nice, warm and bubbly."

I couldn't imagine this fictional Jane. Not even for a second. "Does life at the château change people?"

"Only if you're Jane. I'm still me, the wacky girl from a small village in England," said Phillipa.

"Do you ever miss your life in Bibury?" I asked, wondering if I missed New York. At first, the silence of the countryside comforted me. Now, it just made me feel alone and disconnected. I missed the busy streets, the fast-paced life, the way people said exactly what was on their minds instead of throwing in digs, like Jane, or dancing around a subject, like my grand-mère, that made them uncomfortable.

"I did at first," she said. "When I first moved here, I felt completely out of my element. I think moving to a foreign country has stages. You have the honeymoon stage, where everything is perfect, followed by culture shock, isolation, acceptance, and, finally, integration."

I picked at my fingernails, massacring my cuticles. Phillipa grabbed my hands. "You shouldn't do that."

"I know, I know. It's a nasty habit," I said, tucking my hands under my thighs. "Do you think it's possible to skip the honeymoon stage? Because I'm only feeling culture shock and isolation right now."

"Sophie, you came back under very hard circumstances."

A huge part of me wanted to like it here. But I was being pulled in so many directions I felt as if I'd fall apart—like a dog's chew toy. "Does it get easier?"

"I think it took me about five or six months to get into the swing of things. My true happiness—that bingo moment—came when your grand-mère hired me. I started on the waitstaff, and then she tested me to see if I had any talent in the kitchen because the château was getting busier and busier."

"Of course she tested you," I said. And I was being tested as well, only if I failed it would kill her. I wasn't going to be responsible for that. I already had enough guilt. "What did she make you do?"

"She asked me to make something French. I made crêpes, although we Brits call them pancakes. *Et voilà.* That's my story. But I'm tired of talking about me. I'm boring." She leaned forward and whispered, "Look, now that we're alone I wanted to ask you about what happened. Because I have a feeling."

"A feeling about what?"

"You. It's my instincts." She tapped her forehead with her index finger twice. "There are two sides to every story and I haven't heard yours," Phillipa said, her eyebrows lifting. "Care to share what really happened in New York?"

I nodded, head down. Perhaps confiding in Phillipa would make me feel better. Plus, I liked her. I shared my sorry tale and Phillipa's eyes filled with tears. "I knew it," she said. "I knew something was up." She paused. "This Eric sounds like he has narcissistic personality disorder. What he did and said to you? How he brought you down to bring himself up? It's a real sickness. And, seriously, if you're such an appalling chef, why did he want you to work for him?"

"I've been wondering the same thing," I said with a shrug. "I don't know."

"Oh, I know why. He needed you because you're better than him—more talented."

"I'm not so sure about that. I've lost my way in the kitchen."

"Then it's time to find your way back," she said with force. "I don't know him from Adam, but I want to kill Eric for what he did to you."

"Me, too," I said, but then thought of what Walter had said. "But, instead of going postal, I'm going to sit back and let karma do her job."

"I hope karma is a raging lunatic and a ball-busting bitch."

"I said almost the exact same thing to a friend of mine."

Our eyes locked and we burst out laughing. For the first time in weeks, I laughed so hard I almost fell down. Phillipa clasped my arm before I did. In between gasps and wheezes, I managed to say, "Thank you, Phillipa. I needed this pep talk."

"Good," said Phillipa. "What have you got planned?"

"I don't even know where to begin." Every cooking failure I'd had flashed before my eyes. I wanted to tell Phillipa everything— all my deepest, darkest secrets. I also didn't want to scare her away. She held my one chance at friendship here. I'd said enough. I didn't want to lose her with my wavering insecurities.

"Well, thankfully we've got three days to figure it out. Two five-course meals—one on Friday night, which will be a fish. And the other on Saturday, which will be typical meals of the region— probably duck and beef, along with an *apéro* for both evenings."

"Who is in charge of what around here?" I asked. I had no clue. "I kind of skipped out before . . ."

"I don't blame you. I would have gone running for the hills, too."

"You would have?"

"Holy *merde*, yes," she said, and the tension wrapping my entire body unwound.

"Tell me what to do."

"Me?"

"Yes, you. You know your way around here. I don't know where to turn." I raised my hands with resignation. "I know nothing. I'm at your disposal."

"After planning the courses, the three *plats principaux* and side dishes will fall to you, me, and Clothilde. I'm not too skilled when it comes to seafood. And it wasn't until your grandmother went to the hospital that I took on the main courses, but Clothilde has needed my help." She paused to catch her breath. "The granny brigade is in charge of entrées and the *apéro*. Gustave, once he's finished with lunch service at Le Papillon Sauvage, is our king of desserts. His creations are simply to die for."

"Okay, great," I said. I could do this. It was a no-brainer. "Sounds easy enough and organized."

"So, now that you have the four-one-one, do you know where you'd like to start?"

There I was relying on Phillipa and she still needed my guidance. For the first time in ages, I felt useful—not useless. I needed to get my head in the right place. She helped me to whisk away my problems and focus on the task at hand.

"I haven't worked with duck for a while, but I can handle a *bœuf bourguignon*, and fish is my specialty," I said, thinking fish *used* to be my specialty. Doubt still weighed on my mind. But I wanted to do this. I needed to do this. *Get yourself together, Sophie. Make your grandmother proud. Make yourself proud.*

"What will we have in regards to seafood?" I asked, my voice a bit shaky.

"The *poissonnier* is delivering some of his beautiful *daurades* and scallops."

I let out a sigh of relief. "Perfect. If there's anything I can handle, it's sea bream, lovely and light," I said, nodding my head. I needed to do this. "It's winter. Fennel is in season, yes?" I asked, thinking about what would plate well with the duck, and she nodded.

"Pomegranate? And hazelnuts?"

"Of course," said Phillipa, rubbing her hands together. "I can't wait to see what you've got up your sleeve."

That would make two of us. What was I going to do with the daurade? Something simple like daurade with almonds and a romesco sauce? Did the kitchen even have almonds? The more I thought about this recipe, the more boring it sounded. Roasted daurade with lemon and herbs? Again, typical. I had an opportunity to create something special, something out of this world, on my own terms. I wanted to get creative and do something colorful, playing with the colors of winter and whatever was in season. My imagination raced with all of the possibilities—a slideshow in my mind presenting delicious temptations. A crate of oranges caught my eye. I licked my lips—a light sweet potato purée infused with orange. Braised cabbage. Seared daurade filets. Saffron. The colors, ingredients, and plating came together in my mind. "Do we have edible flowers?"

"I take it you haven't ventured into the greenhouse?"

I hadn't.

Phillipa took my arm, helping me off the stool. "Grab a basket on the way out and let's head over there for some divine inspiration." She glanced at my ankle. "Can you walk?"

"You know what? I've got one good leg," I said. *Fight or flight.*

Although winter was upon us, the grounds remained vibrant and green in some parts, golden in others. A large garden with a sea of waxy oranges, greens, and beiges surrounded the greenhouse. I shuddered as I eyed the round potimarrons, wondering if I'd ever be able to put Cendrillon behind me, and when. I blinked, focusing on the other winter squashes, like butternut, acorn, and spaghetti.

"Jane handles most of the gardening," said Phillipa.

"I can't imagine her getting her hands dirty."

"She may be a pain in the butt, but she's got a green thumb. She's even our head beekeeper. Toward the back of the property are the *ruches*," said Phillipa, pointing. "See those wooden boxes? They're a bit quiet now, but in the summer and spring, they buzz with bees, the noise so loud it's deafening."

We opened the door and walked from a chilly December afternoon into the almost tropical humidity of the greenhouse. My eyes widened at this jungle of freshness, the earth on the ground. The back wall, around thirty feet high, burst with terra-cotta pots filled with every herb imaginable—basil, thyme, coriander, parsley, oregano, dill, rosemary, and lavender. There were tomatoes of almost every variety beaming with colors of red, dark purple, yellow, and green. Lemon trees. Avocados. Lettuces, like roquette and *feuille de chêne.* Zucchinis and eggplants. Fennel, celeriac, artichokes, and cucumbers. Leeks, asparagus, cabbages, and shallots, oh my.

I exhaled a happy breath. This explosion of color, this climate-controlled greenhouse, was every chef's idea of heaven. I ran my hands over the leaves of a *cœur de bœuf* tomato plant and brought my fingers to my nose, breathing in the grassy and fragrant aroma, an unmistakable scent no other plant shared. All of the smells from my summers in France surrounded me under one roof. As the recipes Grand-mère taught me when I was a child ran through my head, my heart pumped with happiness, a new vitality. I picked a Black Krim, which was actually colored a dark reddish purple with greenish brown shoulders, and bit into it. Sweet with just a hint of tartness. Exactly how I summed up my feelings.

I darted around the greenhouse, climbing up ladders to clip fresh herbs on the best of culinary missions. After picking some endive and arugula, I turned to Phillipa. "This place is absolutely incredible," I said, and added a handful of edible flowers to my now full basket.

"I know, right?" said Phillipa. "Do you have everything you need?"

I looked to my left, then my right. "I believe I do."

Clothilde was slicing potatoes with a mandoline when we returned to the kitchen. She dabbed the sweat off her brow with a kitchen towel. "Oh, Sophie, you're here! Wonderful! I'm preparing your dinner," she said.

"Don't worry about me," I said. "I can do it."

"*Ma petite puce*, you have enough on your plate," she said with a no-nonsense stance. "How is your grand-mère?"

"She's doing better. We're hoping she'll be home before Christmas," I said.

"That's the best news I've heard all day." Clothilde wandered over to a corner, returning with my grandmother's poppy-print apron. "I think she'd want you to wear this."

As I held the fabric up to my nose, my grand-mère's scent of cinnamon and nutmeg mixed in with aromas of lavender and Chanel No. 5 washed over me. I almost lost it. Every scent of my happy childhood hit me in waves, nearly pulling me under. But this scent—her scent—offered comfort, as if she were right here in the room wrapping me in one of her hugs.

"Have you planned the menu?" asked Clothilde. "After all, it's your kitchen."

"I have a few ideas—there's so much beautiful produce in season." I clenched my teeth. I was being thrown into the fire feetfirst. "But this isn't my kitchen."

Again, my grandmother's words rang in my ears. I shut my eyes, trying to keep panic from taking over.

After I die, the château will be yours.

"Look at the apron you're wearing—it's the one reserved for the head chef."

I glanced at the apron, holding out the edges. This kitchen, although changed from what I'd remembered, felt like home. My heart beat with excitement. People were counting on *me*, and I was going to do everything in my power not to screw anything up. By Clothilde's expectant expression, I knew my grandmother had set up my immersion into the kitchen, and I wasn't going to fail her. Along with fresh produce, a spark of happiness ignited my heart. Wanting to stoke the fire, I couldn't wait to get cooking. This was exactly what I needed.

The first course would be an amuse-bouche, a little taste setting up the flavors to come, a way to whet the palate. The entrée was always the second course. Unlike in the States, where we referred to this dish as the main plate, in France it was more of a small dish, more substantial than an amuse-bouche. I'd heard of many Americans ordering an "entrée" in France, only to be disappointed with the small size of the portion. What they really had intended on ordering was *un plat*, or *un plat principal*—the main course. All of this, *bien sûr*, would be followed by a cheese course or a salad (depending on the menu) and capped off by an exquisite dessert. After much thought and almost wearing out the floor from my frenetic pacing, I came up with a doable menu and stepped up to the board.

MENU

L'AMUSE-BOUCHE
*Pan-Seared Scallops wrapped in Jambon Sec and Prunes with
a Balsamic Glaze*

L'ENTRÉE
*Pan-Seared Foie Gras with a Spiced Citrus Purée, served with
Candied Orange Peel and Fresh Greens*

OU

Velouté of Butternut Squash with Truffle Oil

LE PLAT PRINCIPAL

Bœuf Bourguignon à la Maison served with a Terrine of
Sarladaise Potatoes

OU

Canard à l'Orange served with a Terrine of Sarladaise
Potatoes along with Braised Fennel, garnished with
Pomegrante Seeds and Grilled Nuts

OU

Filet of Daurade (Sea Bream) served over a Sweet Potato
Purée and Braised Cabbage

LA SALADE ET LE FROMAGE

Arugula and Endive Salad served with Rosemary-Encrusted
Goat Cheese Toasts, garnished with Pomegranate and
Clementine, along with a Citrus-Infused Dressing

LE DESSERT

Poached Pears in Spiced Red Wine with Vanilla Ice Cream

When I finished marking up the menu, I wiped the chalk off my hands and looked to Clothilde for her approval. "Do we have everything? Do you foresee any problems?" I asked. "Should I change anything?"

Clothilde stood silent for a moment, her lips pinched together. My nerves were about to go haywire until she smiled. "It's a beautiful menu, one your grandmother would be proud of," she said, scribbling notes. "Time to type them up and print them out on the beautiful linen paper for the guests and Bernard so he can plan the wine pairings."

I blew out a sigh of relief.

Jane swaggered into the kitchen with her perfect French twist and twisted smile. She eyed the board. "Lovely menu," she said. "Clothilde, I'm assuming you planned it."

"No, it's all Sophie's doing," she said.

Jane's eyes met mine. "I see. Well, I hope you can pull it off." She glanced at my sneakers. "We don't need a repeat of the run-away chef."

I bit down on my tongue as she turned on her kitten heel and left. I knew she was trying to throw me off my game; I just didn't know why.

All I needed to do was push back any panic, breathe, and focus. So, it took the death of my career and Grand-mère Odette's stroke to get me here, but there was an unforeseen benefit. As I surveyed the kitchen—this perfect kitchen—with the excitement I felt rushing through my veins, I knew the scars left from Cendrillon would eventually heal. My cooking mojo: it was coming back to life. I could only hope the same for grand-mère.

17

poached pears and a poached chef

ON FRIDAY AFTERNOON, the granny brigade and Gustave arrived early, and after a round of *les bises* and chatting about days gone by from the last time they saw me at the age of thirteen, the kitchen buzzed with activity. I was almost feeling back to my old self. The distraction that came with cooking—really cooking— was exactly what I'd needed to move my mind to a better place.

This was by far the strangest kitchen staff on the planet, or at least in this corner of France. Gustave, an older man in his sixties with a scruffy beard and wild red-tinged eyes, sipped on a bottle of pastis, a potent anise-flavored liquor, as he poached the pears for the dessert. Most people mixed pastis with water in a glass, but, clearly, Gustave cut straight to the punch. The gray-haired granny brigade, comprising *les Dames* Truffaut, Bouchon, Pélissier, and Moreau, were all dressed similarly to Clothilde, although their shoes were not covered with ladybugs, and they chatted away like chickens as they deveined livers for the foie gras and prepared the entrées, occasionally dropping a few. They all sat on stools. Add in the English twin and me, the American, and we were one motley crew.

"Phillipa?" I asked when we finished prepping. "Where do I find the fish?"

"They're in the walk-in on ice." My head darted in every direction. I didn't know this kitchen that well. When my face pinched with confusion, Phillipa broke into a grin and said, "Come on, I'll show you around."

AFTER A QUICK refresher tour, we lugged out the crate filled with the daurade, and hoisted it on the prep table. I pulled one out, surveying it. Known as gilt-head bream in the United States, this fish was found in the Mediterranean Sea and the eastern region of the Atlantic Ocean. Needless to say, I knew this fish well. I'd often prepared the dark, silver beauty at Cendrillon. I let out a loud sigh, trying to suppress the nightmare. I unrolled my knife case, the steel blades glistening in the sunlight. My hands shook as I grabbed one of the custom knives my grand-mère had given me when I'd graduated from the CIA. If anything, I was cooking for grand-mère tonight. I had something to prove, not only to her but also to myself.

Phillipa tapped my shoulder. "You okay?"

I'm fine, just zoning out." I brushed my hands on my apron and snapped to attention. By Phillipa's eager expression, she needed some guidance. "Have you ever filleted a fish?" I asked.

"No," she said. "But I'd love to learn. I'm usually just prepping vegetables and the like. After all, I didn't go to a cookery school. I started out on the waitstaff and I'm ready and willing to learn whatever you're willing to teach me. Your grand-mère doesn't like people looking over her shoulder. She's like a dog guarding a prized bone with her kitchen secrets. Aside from Clothilde, we're lucky if she lets us glance at her kitchen notebooks."

"Filleting a fish isn't exactly a kitchen secret," I said, nodding perfunctorily. I handed Phillipa a knife and a set of kitchen gloves. "First, lay the fish on the table, holding it by the tail. Using your knife, scrape, starting at the tail and moving toward the head. Good. Now we run the slippery sucker under water," I said, and we did. "Okay, it's time to empty out the organs. Make a cut, slicing into the belly of the fish like this. Ready for the fun part?"

"Ready as I'll ever be," she said, grimacing.

PHILLIPA'S FAITH IN me had bolstered my confidence, and we set to work.

When we finished filleting, Clothilde handed me one of my grandmother's kitchen notebooks, the pages with the recipes for the *bœuf bourguignon* and *canard à l'orange* bookmarked with a red ribbon.

"I'm not the young girl I used to be," she said. "I could use a little help gathering the ingredients for the *canard à l'orange*."

While I searched for Clothilde's ingredients, I found a few bottles of juniper eau-de-vie in the dry storage area, nestled among hundreds of glass jam jars filled with Grand-mère Odette's homemade compotes—fig, cherry, apple, strawberry, apricot, raspberry, pear, and peach. When he saw me gripping the eau-de-vie, Gustave's eyes lit up and he raced over, scooping the bottle from my grip. I gave him a look.

"*Pffff. C'était moi qui l'ai fait.*" (It was me who made it.) He unscrewed the cap, chugged a sip, and then knocked his chest with his fist. Gustave held out the bottle. "*Essaye-le.*" (Try it.)

"*Juste un petit goût*" (Just a little taste), I said. The moment I took my little drop of a sip, the alcohol burned my throat. So potent, this was the kind of alcohol that could put hair on your chest. I hacked out a cough and my hands flew to my throat. Fire water.

"*Ah, oui, c'est bon*," he said.

I coughed. "Did my grandmother hide the bottles from you?"

"*Bien sûr*," said Gustave. "But what was lost is now found." He walked away, bottle in hand.

An hour later, Clothilde walked up just as I was finishing the sauce for the fish. I held out a spoon. "Taste this."

"*Impeccable*," she said. "You have your grand-mère's talent. Maybe even better. You've done her proud."

I let out the breath I'd been holding in. "How are the potato terrines and *canard à l'orange* coming along?"

"Absolutely fine! Everything is prepped for the duck and it will *mijoter* for two hours, so I have about an hour before cook time. I just need to sauté the potatoes for the side dish in duck fat and parsley, season them, and place them in their individual baking dishes. Perhaps while I finish up you could check in on the rest of the staff?"

Hesitantly, I walked up to Gustave.

As if reading my mind, he said, "Dessert is almost complete. The pears are chilling in the *frigo* and then I'm going to take a nap," he said. "But before I do, come, I made one for you to taste, like I always do for your grand-mère Odette."

He placed the dish in front of me and I almost fell down from the shock. Gustave had created a work of art and I hadn't even realized he'd worked so quickly; I thought he'd only peeled the pears. He'd plated one of the desserts in a beautiful glass bowl, complete with what he said was the homemade vanilla bean ice cream he'd made the previous night, and garnished the pear with the sauce, a cinnamon stick, sprigs of thyme, vanilla bean pods, and pomegranate seeds.

"The sauce?" I asked, dipping in my spoon.

"Vanilla bean seeds, red wine, sugar, and nutmeg," he said. "If there's anything I know, it's how to make sauces with wine."

I dipped my spoon in and tasted it. Oh my God, heaven on my tongue. I eyed him warily.

"You really do know sauces. It's simply delicious," I said. "But I taste a few more ingredients? Orange? Star anise? A dash or two of pastis, maybe?"

"Your palate is just like your grandmother's. I can never get anything past her either." He laughed and added a whole star anise to the garnish. "Do you like it?"

"What's not to like? It's perfectly delicious and beautifully brilliant."

Gustave let out a hearty laugh and slapped me on the back. "It is, isn't it?"

Who would have thought the town drunk would be a maestro in the kitchen? By the end of the evening, we'd have poached pears and a poached chef.

WHEN I WASN'T dropping utensils or tripping over my two feet, the rest of the evening went by without a hitch. Somehow everything worked. There were no uniforms—no toques, no ugly checkered pants. And, oddly, there was only one man. It was an alternative cooking universe to what I'd grown accustomed to, and I enjoyed every moment, every second.

Sébastien, one of the servers and, apparently, also the caller, alerted us when the guests were seated in the main dining room for dinner service. He yelled out orders, tucking sheets of paper in the rack. My heart nearly stopped when he said, "We have a full house and it seems most of the guests are ordering the daurade tonight—twenty-seven out of forty plates."

"We just need to focus," I said, mostly to myself. "It's go time."

Phillipa and I plated the amuse-bouche and set out the entrées.

An hour later, it was time for *le plat principal*. I wiped the sweat off my brow. "The sweet potato purée is ready. I wanted to show you how to prepare the daurade. First, into two pans, melt a little butter and add a dash of olive oil so the butter doesn't burn. Add some minced garlic into one of them; it's for the cabbage. Sauté for two minutes." I paused. "Am I moving too fast for you?"

"No," she said.

"Rub the fish with lemon and parsley. Season with *herbes de Provence* and a bit of ground pepper." I slid four daurade filets into one pan. "Cooking fish can be tricky. You don't want it to cook for too short a time, or for too long. These filets aren't very thick, so I'm thinking about two to three minutes each side until the fish is opaque and golden." I added butter and a dash of olive oil into another heated pan. Then I flipped the filets. "Onto the braised cabbage. Add the cabbage to the other pan with the garlic. Let it wilt and stir. Add in more. Wilt. Add a dash of balsamic, season with a pinch of *fleur de sel*, three or four twists of pepper, and some grated nutmeg. It's time to plate." Phillipa shot me the thumbs-up. I pulled out a four-inch circle tool and placed it on a plate. "First we add the cabbage, press it down, then a ladleful of the sweet potato purée, also pressed. Finally, we place a filet on it. Set the dish under the heat lamps." I turned to Phillipa. "Your turn. Five minutes. Go."

I showed her how to garnish, placing the edible flowers and herbs with kitchen tweezers. Admittedly, the plate was a piece of art, so beautiful Monet and his water lilies would have been jealous—just as wonderful and colorful as I'd imagined it would be.

"Thank you for having confidence in me, Chef," said Phillipa.

This was the first time anybody had called *me* chef, and it felt great. More than great. But I wasn't about to take all of the credit when this was a team effort.

"You're a chef, too. Now hit the counter and yell, 'Service!'"

"Service!"

The smile spreading across her face, the pride lighting her eyes, told me I'd won over her cooking heart, and I also felt mine sparking back to life. For me, being back in the kitchen and cooking was liking being zapped with a defibrillator, delivering a dose of electricity right into my soul.

After all the main courses had been delivered, Jane sashayed into the kitchen. "The guests would like to meet the chef," she said. I grinned until she continued, "although it's not a good idea and I made an excuse for you."

"Why?" I asked.

Jane's cold blue eyes sparked to life. Her lips twisted into a half smile. "Because half of the guests are from New York, and I overheard one of them talking about you."

"Wha-what did they say?" I stuttered.

"That they heard that the sabotaging chef is the granddaughter of the Grand Chef here," she said, turning on her kitten heel and leaving the kitchen. Over her shoulder, she said, "I'd strongly advise you not to follow me in."

I froze. Phillipa clasped my hands into hers, squeezing them.

"Don't pay mind to one word she uttered," said Phillipa. "Nobody knows the truth."

"That's the problem," I whispered, trying to hold back the tears. "My name is ruined, and if I stay here, I'll only bring the château down with me. I can't do that to you guys. I can't do that to my grand-mère."

Before Cendrillon, I'd never been a crier—not even when I burned my hands or cut my fingers—but all I seemed to be doing lately was drowning in an ocean of salty tears. I didn't shed one tear when my mother died. I didn't cry when I'd found Eric had cheated on me—multiple times. Something in me had changed, and I wasn't sure if I liked it. I used to be strong and fierce. Now I was a pathetic weakling.

"The staff in a kitchen is called a brigade, right?" asked Phillipa, and I let out a grunt. "Okay. After the guests leave, save for Valentine's Day and private events, we have three months until the château opens to the public and the truth will come out," she said. "So if the ship goes down, which it won't, because I'm going to make it my mission to clear your name, we'll all go down with you. We're a family here and, if I know your grand-mère, she wouldn't have it any other way."

"I bet Jane thinks differently."

"Jane isn't the heir to this château. You are," she said. "Fight for it. I saw the way your eyes lit up in the kitchen. I could almost feel the energy, your love for cooking. You taught me how to fillet a fish and I'm sure you can teach me so much more."

Phillipa stared at me, waiting for a response. My mind reeled. "You said you wanted to help me clear my name?" I finally said. "How?"

"I have a few ideas, but I need to sort them out first," she said, wiggling her eyebrows. She tilted her head. "So, what's it going to be?"

I squeezed my eyes shut. "I did have fun tonight."

"That's the spirit," she said.

"Why are you being so nice to me?" I asked.

"Because I know what it's like to be judged—especially when you're constantly being compared to your *perfect* sister," she said. "But there's no such thing as perfect. We all make mistakes. We're human." She rocked back and forth on the heels of her sneakers. "Look, the granny brigade and Gustave are nice and all that, but we don't have much in common. You showed up. And I really need a friend, one I can talk to, and one who speaks English. All the French makes my head swim."

"Me, too," I said.

I wiped my runny nose with the sleeve of my shirt and nodded, putting the toxic emotions invading my system to the side. Phillipa hip-bumped me. "I may have to lean on you, too, one day— especially when it comes to cooking."

"Lean away," I said, thinking I'd been self-dependent for so long that I wasn't wired to depend on anybody, only myself. After my mother snapped when I was thirteen, I kept everybody at arm's length, cutting off any friendships I'd had. Maybe it was time for me to change, to let my guard down, to let people in. Maybe I could shed my self-defense mechanisms and actually trust somebody. I wanted to. And I really wanted to trust my instincts and myself. But, still feeling like a train wreck, I also didn't want to make false promises to Phillipa.

"Phillipa?" I asked.

"Yes?"

"If things don't work out, don't say I didn't warn you."

18

friends and foes

S OMEHOW I SURVIVED the rest of the weekend, namely by avoiding the guests, steering clear of Jane, and skulking down the stairwell into the kitchen like a rat. Alas, I didn't see the bride or the groom, any of the floral arrangements, or the reactions when the guests ate my creations. Although I was incognito, I knew I was making my grand-mère proud. And, just for that, my confidence swelled. It wouldn't be long before the old Sophie was back; I missed her.

A text alert buzzed and I pulled out my phone, looking at the name. Relief flooded my body: Walter.

> Walter: It's almost Christmas! We miss you. When are you coming back?
>
> Me: I'm not sure.
>
> Walter: If the mountain will not come to Muhammad, then Muhammad must go to the mountain.

Me: Huh?

Walter: We're coming to France. First Paris, then on to you
for two days. I hope you have room for visitors.

Me: You'll have your choice of rooms. There are 26 of
them. When r u thinking?

Walter: The 23rd and the 24th, if that's okay.

Me: It's more than okay. I'll have somebody pick you up at
the airport. Send me your flight details. Love you.

Right when I set my phone down, Phillipa knocked on my door
and entered my room, carrying a tray of croissants, a variety of the
château's *confitures*, and, to my delight, coffee. She set the tray down
on the dressing table. "All the guests are making their way down to
Le Papillon Sauvage for breakfast, and I wanted to bring you something before everything's eaten up."

"Thank you," I said, slipping out of bed and throwing on my
bathrobe and slippers.

"I overheard one of the guests talking about the daurade," she
said.

My heart plummeted into my stomach. "Oh no—"

"Stop looking like an abused puppy," she said. "I'm pretty sure
'heaven on a plate' is the highest of compliments."

I couldn't help but smile. "It is."

"To celebrate, I'm thinking that after you eat, we should head
over to the Christmas market in Gaillac. Get into the Christmas
spirit. Ho-ho-ho and all that. Plus, I need to pick up some things for
Clothilde."

"Is Jane coming?"

"No, she'll need to check the guests out." Phillipa raised her nose and spoke with a hoity-toity accent. "And she thinks the market is for simpletons. It's beneath her."

It seemed my fate had been decided. "It's not beneath me. I crave simple. I'd love to go."

"Meet me out front in fifteen minutes," she said. "Is that enough time for you to get ready?"

I bit into a croissant and nodded.

"Great. See you in a few."

"Wait! What if one of the guests recognizes me?" I said, but Phillipa was already out the door. My heartbeat accelerated. I'd already agreed to accompany her to the market, but guests were still lingering around on the property. How would I make an escape without notice? I really needed to get away from the château, though, even if it was just for an hour or two. I couldn't stay holed up in my room. Like Clothilde had said, I needed to join the world again. It was then I decided to wear a disguise—big black sunglasses, a hat, and a scarf wrapped over my head. Once again, I skulked down the servant's stairwell and then I made a dash for it, right out the front door.

Phillipa burst into laughter when I breathlessly approached her car—a rusty burgundy Citroën with precarious-looking wheels. "Here comes secret chef."

"Shhhh," I said. "I'm not here."

"Oh, but you are, and you look ridiculous," she said, opening the door. "Jump in. Your chariot awaits. *On y va.*"

Phillipa was a worse driver than Clothilde. She didn't keep her eyes on the road at all. We almost ran over the rogue sheep. By the time we reached Gaillac, dainty snowflakes floated in the air, swirling around with grace. Phillipa latched her arm onto mine, and we walked to the center of town. We traversed a narrow street, finally arriving at the market, where little log cabins had been set up, selling everything from candles and soaps to spices and sausages. Among the old and the young, we ambled through the market, me enjoying all the sights, smells, and sounds of Christmas.

She giggled. "I feel like we're on a date."

"I wouldn't know," I said. "I've never been on one. Eric and I just jumped right into a relationship."

Her jaw dropped and she nudged me with her hip. "We are not talking about him. He's dead to you. Got it?"

"Got it," I said with a laugh. "What about you, Phillipa?" I asked. "Do you have a love in your life?"

"It's hard meeting people like me in a small French town," she said.

"People like you?"

"People that like girls instead of boys," she said, scrunching her nose. "Don't worry. You're not my type. And I hope you're okay with my confession. Some people aren't when I tell them."

I couldn't help but laugh.

Phillipa's eyes widened with fear. "What's so funny?"

"I was a beard for my best friend, Walter. He was terrified to come out to his family. I pretended to be his fiancée for two years to throw off his mother. I lived with him."

"No," she said. "You?"

"Yep. Me," I said. "Don't look so surprised. He and his partner, Robert, finally came out to his mom. Anyway, a lot of stuff went down in New York. I flew here to—"

"Earn a thousand points of respect from me," said Phillipa.

"Well, you'll meet them. Walter and his partner will be here for Christmas Eve." My grin stretched across my face until I realized I'd told Walter I'd have somebody pick him up. Asking Rémi or Clothilde was out of the question. "I have a favor to ask you."

"Anything."

"I don't know how to drive. Plus, I will probably need to visit with Grand-mère. Would you be willing to get them at the airport?"

"Of course," she said. "I'd be happy to."

I blew out a sigh of relief. "Thank you so much."

"No need to thank me," she said, her grin wide. "Let's celebrate our friendship with a *vin chaud*. My treat. Go peek in on Santa. I'll be right back."

I watched her walk away with a smile stretching across my face, realizing I'd actually made my first real friend in France and maybe my first true female friend ever. She didn't judge me. She bolstered my confidence. She accepted me for who I was. I accepted her. I closed my eyes, listening to the festivities in the market, feeling rather festive myself. My holiday spirits were up. A little girl's excited screech pierced my ears. "*Papa, papa, le Père Noël! Le Père Noël!*"

"*Oui, oui, ma puce!*"

Her father brushed past, bumping into me. "*Désolé,*" he said. I knew that voice. I turned to face him. An older woman with chocolate brown hair peeking out from her winter bonnet scooped a little girl around two or three years old out of his arms. The mother? But no, this woman was far too old to be of childbearing age.

"Rémi?" I questioned.

Rémi's face blanched and he whispered, "What you just saw, you didn't see." A heavy silence filled the air. I blinked the confusion and snowflakes from my eyes. He turned on his heel and walked away, leaving me stunned and hurt by his attitude.

There was more to Rémi's story than I'd imagined. I shivered, thinking about the fun we'd had as kids—picking cherries and swimming in the lake. He was so different now, and I wondered what, besides being a father, had happened to him. The only problem was that he was shutting me out in the cold and not letting me in.

A minute later, Phillipa sauntered up and handed me a paper cup of *vin chaud*, and the scents of orange, nutmeg, and cinnamon permeated my nostrils. "Are you okay? You look like you've seen a ghost."

I wanted to confide in Phillipa, but a nagging feeling in my gut kept me from betraying Rémi. The fact that he had a daughter was his business, not mine. "I'm fine. Just a little cold," I said, shifting uncomfortably. "What did you need to pick up for Clothilde?"

"Clothilde? Oh my God. I almost forgot. I need chocolate and nougat for the thirteen desserts."

"Thirteen desserts?"

"It's a tradition in France representing Jesus Christ and the twelve apostles, always displayed on Christmas Eve and enjoyed until December twenty-seventh, consisting of a combination of dried fruit, fresh fruit, nuts, and sweets. *Voilà*. A total of thirteen desserts. It's for the party."

"Party?"

"Another tradition. The Christmas Eve party for the staff and, pretty much, every villager within a twenty-mile radius of the château," she said. "Clothilde told me you were in charge of planning the menu. She said Grand-mère was counting on you. Didn't they tell you about it?"

"No, they didn't," I said with a sigh.

So much for the simple life.

THE NEXT FEW days were beyond awkward. Every time I ran into Rémi, he always looked as if he wanted to say something, or kill me, but clamped his mouth shut and stormed off before doing so. He'd ignore me and go back to doing whatever he was doing, like decorating the twenty-foot-tall Christmas tree in the entry or installing lights in every front-facing window of the château for the party. It seemed every time I turned a corner he was there.

One afternoon, when I walked into the kitchen to plan the menu, Rémi was unloading crates into the walk-in refrigerator. His eyes locked onto mine. I wrung my hands.

"Thank you for taking care of the delivery," I said, not knowing what else to say during an awkward and tense silence. I wasn't about to bring up his daughter, though it crossed my mind until I thought better of it.

"*Pas de problème*," he said with a shrug. "It's my job."

These were the least loaded sentences we'd exchanged so far. Maybe he'd gotten over whatever it was he needed to get over. Maybe he was going through a shitstorm, too. "So, what have we got?" I asked with a hesitant smile.

"You'll figure it out," he said. "Or, then again, maybe you won't." He clomped out the back door. I flipped him *le doigt d'honneur*—my middle finger—as he left.

Take a deep breath. Get back to cooking. Get back to yourself. You can't let your grandmother down. You can't let yourself down.

After slamming my roll bag of knives on the counter, I headed into the walk-in to plan the menu and opened the crates. The fish vendor had delivered a sea of heavenly delights. *Les gambas*, large shrimp, were the size of my hand. Once cooked, they'd be lovely and pink. The oysters were enormous and beautiful, the briny scent conjuring up the sea. I couldn't remember the last time I'd swum in open water. Six years ago on a Sunday trip to the Hamptons with Eric? Oh God, I didn't want to think about him.

Besides the work of shucking more than three hundred of them, oysters were easy. They'd be served raw with a mignonette sauce and lemons, along with crayfish, crab, and shrimp, accompanied by a saffron-infused aioli dipping sauce.

I lifted the top of another crate, and fifty or so lobsters with spiny backs greeted me—beautiful and big, and the top portion freckled by the sea. I loved working with lobster, the way their color changed from mottled brown and orange to a fiery red when cooked. I'd use the tails for *le plat principal*, flambéed in cognac and simmered in a spicy tomato—my version of my grandmother's recipe for *langouste à l'armoricaine*. The garnish? A sprig of fresh rosemary.

The other crates were filled with lovely mussels, scallops, whelks, and smoked salmon filets, along with another surprise— escargots. Save for the snails, this meal would be a true seafood extravaganza.

The more I thought about the meal, the more inspired I became, and hunger set in. With these incredible ingredients laid before me, it was a dangerous situation, kind of like going to the grocery store when you're famished and buying everything in sight. I couldn't help but open an oyster, digging into its side with an oyster knife and popping the top shell off. I loosened the meat and it slid down my throat, all salty and sweet.

As I licked my lips, inspiration set in. Whatever happed to the château, whatever happened with my grandmother, I was going to tame these ingredients into tasteful submission, giving the guests an unexpected gastronomic experience. Pleased with my plan, I darted to the board, grabbed a piece of chalk, and wrote out the menu.

CHRISTMAS EVE MENU

Foie Gras with Caramelized Apples

Salmon with Lemon, Cucumber, and Dill, served on
Small Rounds of Toasted Bread

Escargots de Bourgogne

Oysters with a Mignonette Sauce

Oysters with Pimento Peppers and Apple Cider Vinegar

Oysters Rockefeller, deglazed with Pernod, served with
Spinach, Pimento Peppers, and Lardons

Sophie's Spiced Langouste (Spiny Lobster) à l'Armoricaine

Crayfish, Crab, and Shrimp with a Saffron-Infused Aioli
Dipping Sauce

Moules à la Plancha with Chorizo

Selection of the Château's Cheeses

Three Varieties of Bûche de Noël

The kitchen staff walked in as I threw the chalk on the counter. Phillipa snuck up behind me. "Oh my God. That menu looks wicked incredible. I'm already drooling."

Clothilde nodded her head with approval. "It's perfect. You've made your grandmother proud."

"How many *bûches* do you think we'll need?" asked Gustave, referring to the celebrated and traditional log cakes served in every French restaurant and household sometime during the holiday season.

"Twenty?" I answered.

"Good thing I started on them a few days ago," he said. "Pineapple and mango, chocolate and praline, and vanilla and chestnut."

"No alcohol?" I asked.

"Maybe just a pinch of Armagnac." He held up his forefinger and thumb. Looked like more than a pinch.

"Desserts are your specialty." I clapped my hands together. "The menu is set."

"You forgot about the *chapons* and the *faisans*," said Gustave.

"Wow, what a feast. Capons *and* pheasants, too?" I asked.

"*Oui*. I'm roasting them tomorrow morning, and *les dames* are making the *farce aux marrons*. Not everybody is a fan of seafood."

The granny brigade whispered in a corner, nodding their heads in unison. By their smiles, everybody seemed happy with the plan. I was proving I could do this—to me and to them.

"Are we all ready to get to work?" I asked.

"*Oui*, Chef," came the shout, the two little words sending tingles and shivers down my spine.

Phillipa tapped me on the shoulder. "I'm taking off to pick up Walter and Robert. You've got things covered here?"

"I do," I said. "And thanks."

"No need to thank me," she said. "I'll be back in a few hours."

WALTER AND ROBERT stood in front of the château, mouths agape. Naturally, they both wore their matching Façonnable shirts, Robert showing his personal sense of style with his ascot. "This is your grandmother's house?" asked Walter with a gasp. "Why were you slumming it with me?"

Robert brought his hands to his chest as if he were having a heart attack. "We are so getting married here." He thrust his hand in my face, showing off a simple black ring. "Walter and I are engaged!"

"Congratulations! This is amazing news. I'm so happy for the two of you, and I wouldn't expect you to get hitched anywhere else," I said, but something caught my attention. My gaze shot to Rémi. My smile turned into the hardest of frowns. Rémi's expression was harder.

"Oh *mon Dieu*, who is that?" asked Robert, fanning his neck dramatically.

"It's not a who," I said, glaring at Rémi. "It's a what."

"Then what is that?" asked Walter.

"A giant asshole," I said.

"Is that your childhood sweetheart? Rémi? What happened to him?" asked Walter, knowing all of my stories.

"He changed," I said. "And not for the better."

"I don't know about that. His ass is Adonis-like," said Robert. He snorted out a laugh at my look. "What? You know Walter and I have a look-don't-touch policy. I'm a one-man guy. Sophie, you should do something about that."

Walter let out a groan. "The last thing Sophie needs right now is that kind of distraction. Look at her, she's finally back. She looks great. She doesn't have that crazed look in her eye. She looks happy."

Admittedly, I watched Rémi's ass as he walked away. No, I didn't need that. For now, having my two closest friends in France was the best distraction in the world. It was nice bantering with them and, minute by minute, I was feeling back to my old self.

"Come on," I said, locking my arms through theirs. "I'll give you a quick tour and then take you to your room."

joyeux noël

T HE SKY DARKENED and thick clouds rolled in, giving the château's grounds an ominous feeling. The leaves on the bushes and the moss on the trunks glowed with a haunting hue. A van rumbled down the gravel driveway, snaking its way among the plane trees. The doors opened. A ramp lowered. There sat Grand-mère Odette in a wheelchair dressed in her Chanel skirt suit with an orange Birkin bag on her lap, surveying all from behind large black Chanel sunglasses. I raced up to her and we swapped *les bises*.

"Clothilde told me she brought you your clothes this morning," I said. "I'm so glad you're home. It finally feels like Christmas."

She lifted her shoulders into a shrug. "The doctor didn't want to release me, so I discharged myself," said Grand-mère. "I couldn't stand another moment in that dreadful room—especially during the holidays." She clasped her hands together and straightened her posture. "Unfortunately, I have to deal with this Agnès creature."

She pronounced Agnès like *ahn-yes*.

"Who?"

Grand-mère tilted her head toward the van and scowled. "My dreaded nurse."

A heavyset woman wearing thick-soled white shoes and pale blue scrubs jumped out of the passenger seat with two male aides beside her. In a flash, she disappeared, rounding the corner of the van to the other side. She had rosy cheeks, and kind but nervous brown eyes. Her brown hair was falling out of its ponytail. She was frazzled, as I could only imagine. When she made her approach, Agnès spoke softly. "We tried our best to keep her in the hospital, but she insisted on coming home. Actually threatened on having the hospital closed down if we didn't comply," she said. "I'm sorry. I'm Agnès, you must be Madame Valroux de la—"

"Please call me Sophie," I said, thrusting out my hand.

Agnès blinked repeatedly as she took it. "The hospital is afraid of lawsuits and I've been given strict instructions to stay with her," she said, the quivering in her voice making it clear she was petrified of losing her job.

"We'll have a room made up for you," I said.

"But I have to be with her 24/7," she said, her voice catching. "Is there a possibility to have a cot? Or is there a couch?"

"She has a full suite. We'll work something out," I said. "Thank you for taking care of her."

Rémi opened the front door to the château and swaggered over to us. After glowering at me, he embraced my grand-mère. "I was finishing up the Christmas lights on the top floor and saw the van pull up. I'm so glad you're doing better and you're home, Grand-mère."

"My darling boy," said Grand-mère with so much sweetness and love, I cringed. "It's wonderful to be home. I'd like to speak with Sophie and then I'd like for you to visit with me, *d'accord*?" She lifted her head toward me. "Oh, *ma chérie*, can you take me up to my room? I've had enough with this Agnès creature. She's very bossy. And she isn't family."

Agnès blinked again and said, "Actually, Sophie, if you could take her up, that would be great. And, Rémi, if somebody could help us with all this equipment, I'd appreciate it." She motioned to the machines and monitors and drips filling the inside cabin of the van.

"Did you bring the entire hospital here?" asked Rémi.

"Just what's needed for her care."

"Sophie," said Grand-mère impatiently. "I'd like to be in the comfort of my room."

"Yes, Grand-mère," I said, gripping the handles of her wheel-chair.

As I wheeled her up the ramp, Grand-mère asked, *"Ma chérie,* what in the world is going on between you and Rémi?"

"Rémi? There's absolutely nothing going on," I said, thinking, aside from the fact that he hated my guts.

"Ah bon, I see," she said, her voice a question. "Sophie, he's a good man, a bit rough around the edges and a bit of a loner, but a good man nonetheless. I think of him like a son."

"But he isn't family," I said. "He just works here."

"Everybody under my roof is family to me—especially Rémi," she said. "His whole world changed when his parents died in that horrible car accident. He had nowhere to go, and I took charge of him."

I froze midstep, almost launching my grandmother out of her chair. "What? When did this happen?"

"The fall after your last trip to Champvert."

No wonder Rémi hated my guts. I'd just left him in Champvert after promising I'd come back. "You never told me this? I mean, I'm thinking it's pretty important."

"I told your mother to tell you. She said the farm boy from next door was of no interest to you. She was livid I'd taken Rémi in and was more concerned with her inheritance. It was on this call when she told me you never wanted to see me again."

"She lied," I said. "I wanted to spend my summers with you more than anything."

"I know, *ma chérie*," she said. "But I don't want to talk about Céleste. The subject upsets me," she said, her voice shaky. "Tell me, what have you planned for the celebration?"

I swallowed back the information I'd just learned and told her about the menu I'd concocted, looking for her approval. "Is that okay?"

"Darling, you're the seafood expert, and when I'm not in the kitchen, it's yours."

We took the lift up to the third floor. "The key to my room is on the ledge," she said. "With all the guests milling about, I don't take any chances. A few years ago, a very drunk and very naked man stumbled into my suite."

I snorted out a laugh as I grabbed the key. "How—how enlightening?"

"It was quite the shock," said Grand-mère. Judging by her tone, the incident wasn't funny to her at all.

I stood in my grandmother's room: similar to mine, but decorated in pale blues instead of greens—and nothing at all like the other rooms in the château. It was a time capsule from the past, photographs covered the walls and her dresser. Some of them were old and faded, yellowing at the edges from time, like the pictures of her and my grandfather on their wedding day. Although she still carried elegance and grace, she was drop-dead gorgeous when she was younger, especially in her lace wedding dress. I picked up the photo.

"Wow, you're so beautiful," I said.

"Not so much anymore," she said. "But I was, as they say, quite the looker back in the day."

"You're still beautiful."

"*Ma chérie*, you're being kind," she said. "As you are not blind, you can see that I'm not the woman I was in that picture."

I ran my fingers across the image. "Grand-père Pierre was really handsome, too. He has broad shoulders, but holds them with grace. Kind eyes." I paused. "How did you meet him?"

"Ah, well, that's quite the story. It won't be as romantic as you might think. My parents came from a powerful shipping family in Bordeaux. We also ran a lovely vineyard. One night, they had a large gala and invited everybody within the region, including Pierre's parents. Pierre came along and, apparently, fell head over heels in love with me. A *coup de foudre*, he called it, a bolt of lightning that shocks the system. Love at first sight. I, however, didn't feel the same way about him. I thought he was pompous. Plus, he was also fifteen years older than me."

I'd always envisioned her and Grand-père having a whirlwind fairy-tale romance, the kind from the movies—filled with parties and champagne and dancing.

"But you married him anyway," I said. "Why?"

"Our marriage was arranged," she continued. "There were few options of proper women for Pierre to choose from in Champvert. It was decided we'd be a good match—a nobleman and the girl from a rich family. Plus, my parents wanted to get me away from one of the vineyard workers I'd fallen for. He was beneath my family's social stature. Well, there was that fact, and also my parents' shipping business wasn't doing well. They needed money. I had to be the good daughter."

"So you didn't love Grand-père?" I asked, shocked.

"In time, I grew to love him as well as my life here," she said. She dabbed her eyes with a handkerchief. "I miss him every day."

I choked back my surprise. "I never knew any of this."

"*Alors*, it's not the kind of conversation one can have with a child. But you are an adult now—a beautiful young lady at that."

"Do you regret not marrying for love?"

"*Non, comme Edith Piaf chantait, non, je ne regrette rien.*"

The lyrics to this song floated in my mind as I took in the life Grand-mère had carved for herself—how there were good things and bad things in the past. And how neither of them could affect you. How you could restart your life from ground zero. I knew the words to the song by heart; my mother used to sing it to me—on her good days, on her bad days, all the time.

"Bernard said he saw a lot of Grand-père in me."

"I'm sure he was talking about your strength, the conviction in your eyes," she said, clasping my hands. "I, however, see more of me in you."

"Me, too," I said, staring at the photo. I'd always wanted to emulate my strong grandmother, not my weak mother. Maybe now that she was home, some of Grand-mère's strength would rub off on me. "I've always felt connected to you. But Grand-mère, I'm not feeling so tough lately."

"Oh, darling, I'm so glad you're back in Champvert, where you belong. You'll find you're very powerful. It's in your blood. You can overcome anything."

Maybe not anything. "I'm not exactly fitting in here."

"But you will," she said. "Take a look at the other photos. I'd like for you to remember the wonderful times you had when you visited with me. I think about them often."

Pictures of me from every summer I visited Champvert were scattered all over her room, decorating her walls and her dressers. I didn't even know she'd taken them. In one photo, I hung upside down from one of the willow trees, seemingly acting like a chimpanzee. In another, I licked a spoon, chocolate dripping down my chin. There was even a framed picture of me and Rémi. We were laughing with a big basket of cherries in front of us. All the pictures held one thing in common: they proved I'd been happy in Champvert. I wondered if I'd ever find that kind of happiness again. A surge of something sparked in my body. I wasn't sure what it was. Maybe it was hope?

As I surveyed the shots somebody had captured of days gone by, I wondered why there weren't any pictures of my mother displayed. The relationship between my grandmother and her only daughter couldn't have been that bad. With her health on the upswing, maybe now she'd talk about it.

Agnès and Rémi walked into the suite, wheeling in equipment. Rémi grunted and pushed by me without an apology, almost crushing my feet with a heavy machine. I jumped out of the way just in time.

"Don't worry, I can take things from here," said Agnès, her eyes sweeping the room. "My goodness, this château is magical. You must love living here, Sophie."

"I'm only a visitor for now," I said.

"Then why have you invited male guests to stay on at the château?" said Rémi with a huff.

"Guests?" questioned Grand-mère.

"My two best friends from New York," I said, turning my back on Rémi and facing Grand-mère. "I should have asked you if it was okay—"

"Oh, don't be a silly girl," said Grand-mère. "It's a lovely surprise, and I can't wait to meet your friends." She straightened her posture. "One day the château will be hers and she'll be staying here for good, Rémi. She can invite whomever she pleases to stay with us," said my grand-mère. "Isn't that right, Sophie?"

I didn't want to upset Grand-mère with my indecisiveness when she was getting her strength back, so I simply agreed. "Yes, yes, of course."

As I left her chambers, I felt like I was being forced into an arranged marriage to the life my grand-mère had created for me—a life I hadn't worked for and didn't deserve. I wandered to the kitchen, wondering if I could learn to love it here like my grand-mère had done with Pierre.

20

let the wild rump roast begin

B Y NINE P.M., the party was in full swing, people sipping on the château's ancestral-method sparkling wine and eating to their hearts' content. There must have been close to two hundred guests. If I'd thought the château was magical before, I hadn't experienced it at Christmas. Lights twinkled, winding down the staircase and flickering everywhere, and the silver decorations on the tree sparkled. I wouldn't have been surprised to see a flute-playing faun jump out to join the festivities. I was thankful Jane had hired an outside staff to serve and man the party; after cooking up a storm, I could relax and enjoy myself. The château, along with all the Christmas lights and the roaring fire, had never looked so beautiful. As did my grand-mère, although she was a bit pale. Much to Agnès's chagrin, she'd insisted on joining the Christmas revelry, and she'd worn an elegant silver gown. With a spark lighting her eyes, she said, "It was the only thing I had in my closet to match this dreadful wheelchair."

"You look beautiful, Grand-mère," I said.

"*Merci*," said Grand-mère as she gave me the once-over. "And you're quite the vision tonight. I'm glad to see your dress doesn't have holes in it. You look lovely."

I didn't think she'd noticed my attire when I first visited her at the hospital. Apparently, nothing slipped by her eagle eyes, which were currently taking in every last detail of the party. I'd gone with a basic black sheath and kitten heels, which obviously Grand-mère approved of. "I threw those jeans away," I said.

"Good," she said. "Remember, you are a lady, not a tramp. You are a Valroux de la Tour de Champvert, and appearances must *always* be kept up."

Walter and Robert sauntered over and hugged me. I introduced them to Grand-mère. Her eyes widened with surprise when Walter and Robert clasped hands, and then she said something that surprised me. "You two are a very handsome couple," she said.

"It's wonderful to finally meet you," said Walter. "Sophie's told me all about you."

"I see," she said, but was cut off.

People buzzed around Grand-mère, kissing her cheeks and then mine, while I stood awkwardly by her side, fidgeting.

"The buffet is incredible. *Merci*, Grand-mère Odette," said somebody.

"The lobster is divine—just the right amount of spice," said another.

The compliments came one after the other.

Grand-mère Odette lifted her chin and nodded to me, pride sparking her eyes. "As you can see, I'm a bit incapacitated. My beautiful *petite-fille* is responsible for everything. It seems her skills have surpassed mine."

"Impossible," I said.

"Not impossible," said Walter. "Just take a look around. Watch everyone's expressions. Your cooking is so magical, I think a few people have been transported to another dimension."

I surveyed the party. A few guests were closing their eyes, heads tilted back as they ate, supreme pleasure on their faces. I wanted to jump into their minds to see what they were thinking. I wondered if, when they ate oysters, they thought of their childhoods by the sea. Or, when they ate the spiced lobster, if it brought memories of pain or love. Were they here right now with us? Running on a beach with reckless abandon? Curled up by a fire in a passionate embrace? At Cendrillon, I was always stuck on the line, and never saw how people reacted to my food. Eric had always taken credit for my creations. I could get used to this. Was this my new wonderland?

Grand-mère smiled. "My Sophie is a force to be reckoned with."

"Now, that's the truth," said Walter, and Robert agreed. "And I want to see what all the fuss is about. We've really missed her cooking."

"That's for sure," said Robert.

"Go, go, enjoy yourselves," I said, happy they didn't bring up the *œufs cocotte* and hash browns I'd managed to ruin. "We'll catch up later."

Walter kissed me on the cheek and excused himself, making his way over to the buffet, Robert in tow.

"Your friends are lovely," said Grand-mère.

I didn't have a chance to respond. Right after Robert and Walter meandered away, Phillipa bounced up to us with an older couple. They all exchanged *les bises* with Grand-mère Odette before turning their attention to me.

"Sophie, these are my parents, Hank and Lizzie," said Phillipa.

"Sophie, it's an honor to meet you," said Hank. He gripped my hand hard, pumping up and down for far too long.

Lizzie embraced me in a tight hug. She smelled strongly of tea rose perfume—so much of it I had to hold my breath until she released me. "Phillipa cannot stop talking about you," she said, air-kissing my cheeks. "It's Sophie this, Sophie that. She's thrilled you're giving her a chance to experiment more in the kitchen. I'm delighted to meet you."

"Yes, it's wonderful to meet the enigmatic Sophie from New York. Now tell us, my dear—" began Hank.

Phillipa interrupted her father, saving me from what looked like was about to become a barrage of questions.

"Mum, Dad, let's join up with Sophie's friends Walter and Robert. I'll show you exactly what we've been up to." She winked and whispered out of her parents' earshot, "Once they get started, they don't stop. You owe me."

"I do," I said. *More than you know,* I thought.

With a smile on my face, I watched them walk away, wondering if Jane was really part of this family. Not only did she not resemble either of her parents, or her twin, she wasn't nice or welcoming. My eyes scanned the crowd for Jane until I found her. I watched her greet guests and straighten her posture. I could almost hear her snooty, affected Queen's English accent—one that had probably taken her years to master. She was from Bibury, after all.

What could Grand-mère possibly see in Jane?

"Jane?" came my grand-mère's raspy voice. *Putain de merde.* I thought the words I'd uttered had been in my head. "She's very efficient. A vision of elegance and grace. Before you came back to Champvert, she was the face of the château, instead of my old one, and I couldn't run things without her. But you're back now. Look, just look how happy the people are."

My stomach catapulted to my throat. I now knew why Jane was gunning for me. She wanted my life. She'd said it herself. She'd said she'd been a better granddaughter to Grand-mère than I was. And she could certainly work a crowd, flitting from one guest to the next. She caught me staring and glared. I gulped, swallowing hard.

"*Ma chérie*, go get something to eat," said Grand-mère. "Enjoy the fruits of your labor."

After all the hard work of preparing for the party, I was starving. "Will you be okay?"

"Isn't that Agnès creature behind me?"

"I am," said Agnès. "And I really wish you'd stop calling me a creature."

Grand-mère turned her head toward Agnès. "I rather like you," she said. "You're growing on me like the mold of well-aged Roquefort cheese, but I like you." Grand-mère smiled at me, her teeth and eyes bright. She winked. "This Agnès creature doesn't put up with my shenanigans or insults."

"I'm just doing my job," said Agnès with a long sigh.

Grand-mère pulled out a string of pearls from the pocket of her wheelchair. She handed them to Agnès. "These are for you, my little creature. For putting up with me. *Joyeux Noël.*"

"I can't accept these," she said, her hands clutching the pearls. She blinked repeatedly. "They'd fire me."

"You can and you will accept my gift," said Grand-mère. "What nobody knows won't hurt them. And saying no to me isn't an option."

"Thank you." Agnès kissed Grand-mère on the cheek. "You can call me creature."

Grand-mère's pale green eyes locked onto mine. "Sophie, your gift is right here, right here in this moment."

"I don't understand, Grand-mère."

Again, she reached into the pocket of her wheelchair, pulling out a set of keys. She placed them in my hands, clasping both her hands around mine tightly. "The château is yours. I'm not fit to run things—not anymore."

I stood stunned, staring into her eyes, my heart racing.

Did I have any control over my life? No, because it was spiraling out of control, I wasn't at the wheel, and the only thing I could think of doing was bracing myself for another crash. "I—I don't know what to say," I stammered, practically choking on my tongue.

"*Merci* would be a start," she said. "Now go get something to eat. You're going to need your strength."

There was no arguing with Grand-mère—not now, not in front of two hundred people. Not with Jane shooting me the stink eye. I had to keep myself calm, cool, and collected, even with my trembling hands and the sweat pooling in the small of my back.

"*Merci*, Grand-mère," I said, gripping the keys with a heavy heart. "I hope I won't let you down."

As I made my way to the buffet, I heard somebody playing the piano quite well. I followed the melody into the salon to find Rémi playing, switching from Christmas music to French classics like "*Je t'aime . . . moi non plus*" by Serge Gainsbourg and Jane Birkin and "*Mourir d'aimer*" by Charles Aznavour. He noticed me holding my *coupe de champagne* with my jaw wide open.

"I told you it's rude to stare," he said.

"You play?"

Rémi shrugged. "When I was a troubled teen, your grand-mère signed me up for lessons."

"You're really good," I said with a pause. "Rémi, I'm sorry, I didn't know about your parents until today."

He slammed the lid of the piano closed. "We need to talk."

Good God. I couldn't take any more. Not now, not when I was finally enjoying myself. Here's your nightmare before Christmas, Sophie. An angry man who hates you. A pompous witch who has made it clear she doesn't want you around. A sick grandmother. The pressure of taking over the château. All wrapped up in a neat bow.

Rémi stood up and latched onto my wrist, my champagne spilling on the floor. He practically dragged me through the kitchen to the servant's stairwell. He crossed his arms over his chest with defiance. Although we didn't have guns, we were in a Mexican standoff of sorts, our eyes shooting daggers. I placed my hands on my hips. "What? You wanted to talk, so talk."

"If you were thinking about telling Grand-mère Odette about Lola—don't bother," he said. I could only assume Lola was the little girl I'd seen him with at the Christmas market. Rémi continued, "Grand-mère, Clothilde, and Bernard know about her, but the others don't—and I'd like to keep it that way."

I was thrown for a loop. "Why?"

"Because I'm a single parent," he said, his breathing labored. "Do I seem like the type of man who welcomes pity? After my parents died, that's all I got, and I'm not going through it again. And I certainly don't need it from you." He paced and clenched his fists. "And how could you not have known about my parents? I must have written you two dozen times and you never wrote me back."

"I never received *one* letter from you. Not a one—" I began, but then it dawned on me. By his attitude, the hurt look on his face, I knew he'd written. "My mother," I said, cringing with her memory. "When she moved us to New York, she wanted to put Champvert in her rearview mirror and never look back. I was eighteen when I found out she threw away Grand-mère Odette's letters. She probably threw away yours, too."

Rémi uncrossed his arms and stopped pacing. He turned to face me, his long eyelashes blinking back his surprise. "You swear?"

"I do," I said.

Rémi went silent for a moment. "*D'accord*. But why didn't you come back to Champvert? Did you hate it here that much?"

"I loved it here, but my mother wasn't right in the head," I said with a gulp. I sank down to sit on the cold concrete steps, trying to keep my feelings at bay. "She was really bad off that last summer I came back from France, and went on a downward spiral from there. She told Grand-mère Odette that I didn't want anything to do with her and vice versa. She was a selfish mess. Her acting career never took off like she'd envisioned, and she lost all direction—hung out with all the wrong people, drank too much, and popped pills like they were candy. There were so many men, I lost track of them all. Me? A child? I had to take care of her—cook, pay the bills, and wipe up her vomit. For the remainder of my teen years, she was in a co-matose state—her eyes glassy and open, there but not present in the way I needed her. At school, I kept to myself, cut the ties to any friendships I had. My mom was an embarrassment, a mess."

A pause hung in the air while Rémi took in all the information I'd spouted out. A surge of emotion shot through me. I took a deep breath and swallowed. I choked back the memory and continued, "She committed suicide when I was eighteen."

He blew out the air between his lips. "*Bon Dieu,*" he said, his tone gentle and peppered with concern. "I knew she died, but I didn't know how. I'm really sorry you had to go through all that. I don't know what to say."

"I don't either," I said. "Believe me."

Rémi gripped my hands. "This may sound silly to you, but when you never came back to Champvert, especially after my parents died, I felt like I was a nothing, a complete zero. I was angry with you. I felt betrayed and, most of all, I was hurt. Look, I'm sorry about your mother," he said, straightening his posture, "but you never came back to Champvert after she died. *Pourquoi?*"

A knot of guilt twisted in my stomach. I felt horrible for eschewing my roots, for not being there for him when he'd needed me. A lone tear made its way down my cheek. Rémi brushed it away with the back of his hand. Our gazes met and he raised an eyebrow in a question.

"Sophie, why didn't you come back? I need to understand your reasons."

"I was accepted into the Culinary Institute of America, one of the best cooking schools in the world. After Grand-mère Odette helped me sell my mother's apartment, I had the money to do so. Cooking was the only thing that made me happy, and the kitchen was the only place where I didn't think about my mother. I became obsessed with my culinary career."

Rémi sat on the stoop. "So neither of us have parents. Anaïs, Lola's mom, died during childbirth, and Lola only has me," he said. "Which makes me wonder. Did you ever find your father?"

My father? I remembered telling Rémi I'd wanted to find him. Apparently, he'd left my mother when he found out she was pregnant with me. But what kind of man just abandons their child? There had to be another reason he wasn't in our lives, something missing from her story. She'd probably driven him away because the only person she truly cared about was herself. Finding him was all I'd talked about when I was younger, a need to complete the family circle, a need to find out where I came from. I'd wanted answers. But all the winding roads I'd traveled down led to dead ends.

I forced a strained laugh. "Kind of hard to figure out who he is when your mother told you Zeus was your dad and that you were hatched from a giant swan egg in Central Park. Either that, or she just referred to him as some worthless Frenchman she wanted to forget. I gave up the search years ago," I said and, feeling uncomfortable, I changed the subject. "Just so you know, I didn't sabotage the restaurant."

"I know," he said. "I overheard you talking to Phillipa."

I let out a breath. "You were spying on me?"

"No, Sophie, I was in dry storage and I didn't want to interrupt your private conversation." Rémi lifted his shoulders. We stood in silence for a moment, me assessing his words, him regarding me with doubt, as if I wasn't being truthful. Finally, he spoke. "The real question is: are you staying on in Champvert?"

"Do I have a choice?" I held out the keys. "Grand-mère handed over the kingdom tonight. It was completely unexpected."

"I guess that makes us business partners," he said, showing me another set of keys, an exact replica of the ones shaking in my hand. "When Grand-mère passes away, you will be receiving eighty-five percent of the estate. I get fifteen," he said.

"I don't know what to do. This has all been thrust on me," I said.

"Lord knows, I don't know what to do either," he said. "But the facts are the facts; she's sick. We've got to prepare ourselves."

"I'm not prepared for any of this."

"You'll figure it out," said Rémi. "But tonight isn't exactly the night to do it with the party going on. We've been gone for a while. We should head back in . . . for Grand-mère."

I shrugged. "So, can we be friends again? I mean, I'd like to be. Friends."

Silence. His eyes met mine, not cold, not judging, but not exactly warm. My stomach pitched.

"*Alors*, we have a new start. I'll come by tomorrow and we can talk some more," he said. "*D'accord*?"

Rémi's arm snaked its way into mine and we rejoined the festivities, me not feeling so festive. Over Rémi's shoulder, Jane caught my eye. In addition to her fitted designer dress, she wore a wicked frown on her face. She made a beeline for us, her mouth twisting into one of her fake smiles. After shooting me a nasty sneer, she turned toward Rémi and pulled him in for *les bises*.

"*Joyeux Noël*, Rémi," she said, placing a possessive hand on his shoulder. "I'm glad I caught you. The guests have been wondering where our delicious piano player had gone. They were so enjoying your talents—the way you tickle the ivory keys. Would you be a dear and play some more? Something lively and fun?"

Rémi's posture straightened and he wore a guilty, lost-puppy look on his face. I couldn't help but wonder if he and Jane had been a thing. I wouldn't have blamed him. Jane was a looker, especially in her tight red Hervé Léger dress, which highlighted her more-than-ample cleavage. An odd feeling washed over me. It wasn't anger, but something else I couldn't pinpoint.

"*Oui, bien sûr*, Jane," he said. "What's a party without music?"

Jane and I watched Rémi walk into the salon, and then her eyes blazed into mine. "One doesn't get their meat where they get their bread." Her voice came out in a low hiss.

"What's that supposed to mean?" I asked.

"Are you not a smart girl?"

I clenched my teeth together. "I get it. You and Rémi were a couple."

"No, I don't mix business with pleasure. And neither should you." Her blue eyes turned colder than ice. "We're running low on oysters. Could you shuck some more?"

I took a step back. "Didn't you hire a staff to take care of every-thing?"

"I hired them to serve, not to prepare. Are you not the chef?" she asked. Jane let out a snort and placed her hands on her hips. "You don't want to disappoint the guests or your grand-mère, now, do you?"

I plastered on a fake smile. "If the guests want more oysters, they will get more oysters," I said, and then spun around on my heel, making my way to the kitchen, my nails digging into my palms. Once my anger settled down, I commandeered a crate of oysters from the walk-in and slammed them on the table.

"How about you go shuck yourself, Jane," I muttered, and grabbed a knife.

"That's a good one," somebody said.

I looked up. Walter and Robert stood in the kitchen. My tears exploded, and through wheezes and stutters, I let loose. I told them about Grand-mère and how I couldn't watch her die and how I couldn't take over the château. "I want to come back to New York," I said, my emotions churning and boiling. "I can't take all of this pressure. I'm going to explode. When does your flight leave? I'm coming with you."

Walter took in a deep breath. "Sophie, as much as Robert and I miss you, and as much as we'd welcome you back, your grand-mère obviously needs you and loves you. I know you. If you ran away, you'd regret it for the rest of your life."

"Honestly, I don't know what to do," I said.

"Be the Sophie I know and love. Stop crying. You're not a crier. I thought we got rid of that Sophie. Be strong for your grand-mère."

I lifted my chin and wiped away my tears with the sleeve of my dress. I stopped pacing and flopped down on a stool, thinking about how I could find this elusive strength that people seemed to think I had. Walter, knowing me, let a long silence pass before he spoke.

"So tell us about life at this wonderful château. It can't be that bad living in a beautiful castle in southwestern France."

"Where do I begin?" I asked.

"With the good things," he said.

My sigh came out in a whoosh. "Can I just tell you everything? Because there's some good . . . and some bad."

"That pinch-nosed Jane?" questioned Robert with a grimace.

I nodded.

"She's extremely jealous of you," said Walter.

"Why should she be? She's pretty, smart, and—"

"Think about it, Sophie. She thinks she runs the place and then you, the only heir, come waltzing through the door after years of being away. She's threatened by you."

"Yeah, that thought crossed my mind. But she shouldn't be threatened. I'm a mess."

"The good thing about messes is that they can be cleaned up."

"I need a whole crew," I said.

"You have us," said Walter, and Robert nodded. "And you also have Phillipa. She worships the ground you walk on, and I really like her. Focus on the good things, like her, and pray your grand-mère gets better."

I placed my hands on the prep table, steadying myself. "Why do you always have to be right?"

"Because I'm on the outside looking in. I have no idea how I'd handle everything you're going through."

"One bite at a time," I said. "Truth be told, shucking oysters will help me to sort out my thoughts."

"We'll help you," said Robert, and Walter grimaced.

"You're wearing Armani," I said. "And I'm pretty sure neither of you knows how to shuck."

"True," said Robert. "But we'll stick by you and we'll watch, chanting, 'Shuck Jane, shuck Jane.'"

I let out a laugh and picked up an oyster, preparing to stab it. "I missed you guys so much."

21

the hidden journal

O N CHRISTMAS MORNING, Walter and Robert returned to New York without me. Although part of me wanted to sneak myself into one of their suitcases, for now I had to stick it out in Champvert for Grand-mère. Save for two members of house-keeping, the rest of the staff had taken off for a break and would return to the château at the beginning of February. I was going to miss Phillipa like crazy, as she and her family were jaunting off to England, but was happy I didn't have to deal with Jane and her nasty attitude.

Rémi came over with Lola on one arm, a baby bag on the other. She was adorable, with chubby sausage legs ensconced in pink tights, and her *châtain* (medium brown with a bit of blond) hair was tied into two little pigtails on the top of her head like the antennae of a fuzzy caterpillar. As Rémi took her sparkly Christmas coat off, I noticed the golden specks in Lola's hazel eyes, the shape of her lips. My gaze blasted from Lola's cherubic face to Rémi's. "Rémi, I thought we were continuing our talk?"

"We can talk in front of her," he said. "She doesn't understand much. And I wanted you to meet her."

"Why?"

"I'm tired of keeping her a secret. It's not fair to her," he said. "I made a mistake. I'm fixing it. After we spoke last night, I did a lot of thinking and I realized keeping secrets does more harm than good."

"What about the others?"

"*Pffff*, who cares? This is France. Unless it's family or close friends, people don't pry into other people's business. Let them talk. They always do—especially *les dames*."

"You're scaring me, Rémi," I said.

"*Pourquoi?*"

"Because you've completely changed overnight," I said. "And you have a wild look in your eyes."

"But this is the old Rémi, the one who used to believe in happiness. He saw a sliver of what things could be like last night," he said, thrusting out his hand. "*Bonjour*, Sophie, it's Rémi, your childhood friend. I missed you."

I squinted at him with confusion.

"That's what I should have said at the airport when I picked you up."

"Oh, I get it, Mr. Hyde, we're backtracking now."

Rémi's face pinched with confusion. "Mr. Hyde?"

"Never mind."

Lola stretched her arms out to me. "*Maman*," she said.

"I'm not your *maman*," I said, and she started to cry and squirm in Rémi's arms, reaching out for me.

"Sophie, *s'il te plaît*," said Rémi. "*Évidemment*, she thinks you're Anaïs."

"Why on earth would she think that?" I asked.

"She's seen pictures," said Rémi. "You both have black hair."

I studied his face anxiously. What was his point? Why did he have to say Anaïs and I had anything in common? It was then I realized I wasn't angry; I was jealous, and that was the feeling I'd had last night with Jane. "*Le Père Noël* clearly has a twisted sense of humor."

Lola wailed and held her arms out to me. I sighed and scooped her up. She nestled into my neck. Her hair smelled like strawberries and sunshine. "I'm your Aunt Sophie," I said, trying to figure out a solution to this conundrum. "*Tatie* Sophie."

"*Tatie?*" she questioned, sucking back her tears. She placed her chubby, sticky hands on my cheeks, her little mouth twisted with confusion. "*Pas Maman?*"

"*Non, pas Maman,*" I said. "*Tatie* Sophie."

Rémi blew out a sigh of relief.

"How would you like your *tatie* Sophie to make you a *chocolat chaud* before you visit with Grand-mère?" I asked, emphasizing "*tatie*" again, and looking to Rémi for his approval. I didn't know what this child was allowed to eat or drink. I didn't know a thing about children.

"*Oui, Tatie* Sophie," she said, bouncing in my arms. "*Oui, oui, oui! Chocolat chaud! Chocolat chaud!*"

Lola bounced in my arms like a jumping bean. I adjusted my arm under her bottom so I wouldn't drop her, and that's when a wetness saturated my arm. I handed Lola back to Rémi. "I think somebody needs their diaper changed," I said.

"We'll meet you in the kitchen, *Tatie,*" he said, lifting up Lola like she was on an airplane ride. "A pretty baby girl needs her diaper changed."

They zoomed into the salon. Thankful for the distraction, I headed into the kitchen, washed my arm with soap, and then rubbed on a gel disinfectant. Then, I pulled out a pot and gathered most of the ingredients—milk, crème fraîche, sugar, vanilla, and cinnamon. I was about to head into dry storage to grab the chocolate when Rémi came in with Lola.

"Can you hold her for a second?" he asked. "I need to grab a high chair."

Lola was squirming in my arms before I could respond and I hoped she wouldn't pee on me again. She grabbed my braid, pulling it. *"Mon chocolat chaud, s'il te plaît, Tatie."*

When I was in New York, I hadn't given motherhood much consideration, thinking I'd be a terrible mom, but with Lola cuddling up to me with her sweet baby breath, the foreign concept crossed my mind for a second. But why was my head even going there? The answer returned with a high chair. I found myself staring at every inch of Rémi's body. The way the dimples formed in his cheeks when he smiled and set Lola in her chair. The way his strong hands buckled her in. The way his broad shoulders shifted when he straightened up to face me. I'd also felt the same way last night when we had our talk. My God. I couldn't be falling for Rémi, the ward of my grand-mère and, although not a blood relative, a member of the family. He had a little girl to take care of; this was too much. An angel without wings, Lola came with extraordinary responsibilities. I shook my head to clear it. I had enough responsibilities now, like making sure my grandmother got better. Auditioning to be a replacement mom wasn't in the cards.

"You're staring at me again, Sophie," said Rémi. "And with a look of disgust. Is it because of what just happened?"

"No, no, no, it's fine," I said. "I just don't know where to find the chocolate for the *chocolat chaud.*"

"Do you always make such funny faces when you're thinking?"

"I guess," I said, heading into dry storage, where I could hide the blush reddening my cheeks. "By the way, what's going on with you and Jane?" I called out. Damn it. I hadn't meant to be so forthright. I'd wanted to work this nagging question naturally into the conversation. My hand swept over a glass jar filled with peppercorns as I grabbed the chocolate bar, and little black balls scattered across the floor. I sank down to my knees and did my best to pick the grains up.

"Jane?" he asked, standing in the doorway. He paused, his lips pinched into a smirk. "What about her? And what are you doing?"

"I spilled some pepper. I'm picking it up," I said. "Speaking of spices, Jane is very pretty."

"She's not my type," said Rémi. "While I may be a man with urges, I'm first a *papa*. The next woman I'm with will be the one— one who accepts me and my daughter."

I straightened up, trying to regain my composure. "Well, I'm sure that woman is out there somewhere."

"I'm sure she is," he said.

The chocolate bar I'd commandeered dropped from my hand to the ground. It was a good half hour before the *chocolats chauds* were made, me fumbling and evading Rémi's eyes. Instead of focusing on his lips and wanting to kiss them, I fussed over Lola. Finally, I asked, "Can we really talk? In front of her?"

"Sophie, she's two and a half. She doesn't understand anything but *chocolat* and toys. We can talk about anything you want. Just don't swear. She's like a parrot and repeats things." He whispered in my ear, his breath all chocolaty and delicious. "Thanks to me, she oftentimes says *merde, merde, merde,* or *putain.*"

I should have laughed, but couldn't. I had too much on my mind—this nagging attraction to Rémi, and my grand-mère's "gift." I was a nervous mess. "Rémi, what am I going to do? I can't take over the château. I just can't do it."

"Then you might be a little bit crazy," he said.

"Please, don't use that word," I said, and his shoulders slumped.

"*Désolé*," he said. "No offense."

"It's fine. But what, worst-case scenario, what do I do?"

"After the *notaire* calls us in, we'll have around four months to make the decision to accept or reject our inheritances." He wiped the chocolate dribbling down Lola's face with a napkin.

"Can I just sign over the château to you?"

"Sophie, as you may have noticed, I'm not exactly a people person," he said. "I like being behind the curtain, not the star. Plus, you are the rightful heir, and Grand-mère wants this for you. It's a family business. And you are her family."

"You're her family, too," I said. "She thinks of you like a son."

"You just can't gift an estate of this size—the taxes would be extraordinary. Also, selling a château of this size would be quite difficult, not to mention you'd be letting down all the people who work here, including me."

"The entire village of Champvert," I said with a sigh. "So you're telling me that I basically have to accept my inheritance or I'll ruin everybody's lives." He shrugged. "What if I accept it and have Jane run things? She could hire a new chef—"

Rémi's jaw dropped. "Jane? Please don't give that woman that kind of power," he said. "She's already a snob. Imagine if she truly ran things around here; it would be hell, and the château would go down in flames." He paused. "Plus, where would you go? Back to New York?"

"It's where I'm from," I said. "It's where my roots are."

"Roots can be replanted. Don't forget you were born in France." Rémi's eyebrows furrowed. "Give this decision great thought, Sophie. It's not only yourself you have to think about. And, although I wasn't exactly kind to you in the beginning, I'm kind of hoping you'll stick around."

"So, we're friends again?"

"For now," he said with a bashful grin. Was he flirting?

EVERY DAY GRAND-MÈRE seemed to be getting her strength back. On New Year's Eve, she was propped up in her bed, Agnès checking her vital signs. Her eyes darted to Agnès's. "Are you finished with poking and prodding me yet, creature?"

"Yes, my queen," said Agnès, shooting me a surreptitious wink.

"Please leave," said Grand-mère.

Agnès gave me a panicked look. "I really should stay."

Grand-mère Odette's voice rang loud and clear. "I would like to have a private conversation with my granddaughter," she said, and Agnès stiffened.

"I'll be right outside the door," said Agnès. "If she needs me—"

"I'll be fine," said Grand-mère. "I'm not dead yet. Sophie, be a dear and get the fire going. I'm quite cold."

Agnès left the room and I stepped over to the fireplace, my hands trembling from nerves as I lit match after match. I could feel her watching me. Finally, the fire sparked and the flames lit up my grand-mère's eyes.

"Sophie, I spoke with Rémi. He told me that you know of Lola, his darling little girl. And what I have to say is this: A child should never have to lose her mother. And a mother should never have to lose her daughter," she said. "I know I haven't wanted to talk about Céleste when you've asked—it hurt me to think about her. But I realize I've been hurting you, too. I've given this great thought, and it's time for you to learn the truth."

I sank down into the window seat. Although I was the one who'd pushed the subject, I felt as if I'd climbed up a jagged, rocky cliff and the only way to get down was to jump into the roiling sea below, not knowing the outcome. I shuddered. I'd wanted to have this conversation for so long, but wasn't sure if I was ready for the answers. But I knew I needed them. I pulled my knees to my chest, preparing to dive in. "We're finally going to talk about her?" I asked.

"Non, *ma chérie*," said Grand-mère. She gripped her rosary beads. "Not exactly."

I snapped to attention, my spine rigid. "I don't understand."

"Under a plank in the closet, hidden in the floor, is my journal," she said, pointing to the door with a shaky hand. "I don't know how to speak of the shameful secrets of my past. The journal will be our starting point. Go get it."

With questions pulling and tugging at my brain, I headed into the closet. My heart raced as I stooped down onto my knees and ran my fingers over the wood, trying to find a knotty board in the floor that would be easy to lift like the one in the kitchen. Bingo. I found it and lifted the board, setting it to the side.

Just like the kitchen notebooks, the cover of the journal was made of rustic leather. Unlike the others, this one was marked *Céleste*. I stroked the cover, rubbing my fingertips over the grain of the leather, wondering what I'd find inside the journal's pages.

"Did you find it, *ma chérie*?" Grand-mère called out.

"Yes, Grand-mère," I said, returning to her side, my hands trembling.

"Sit down next to me. We're going to read it together, but only one or two pages a day. I'm afraid that's all I can handle," she said, pausing. "Sophie, I love you with all of my heart. I may not have made the best decisions in the past, but I did whatever I could to protect our family—some of my actions were unspeakable, but I think, once you have the full story, forgivable."

My palms went damp as I traced the letters of my mother's name with my fingers, and, after a deep inhale and exhale, I opened the book. On the left side of the page there were two grainy black-and-white childhood pictures of my mother mounted into the book with triangular photo edges. She wore white underwear and danced in the garden. On the right-hand pages were journal entries. My voice shook as I read the first one.

18 April, 1980

My sweet Céleste—

Strawberries are in season! It's a warm, beautiful day—around 25 degrees in the sun—and the Gariguettes are ripe and ready for picking, but you've already discovered that, ma puce, *haven't you? Soon the Charlottes, my sweet favorites, will follow. When they are ripe, we'll pick and eat them together. For now, I'm just enjoying watching you from the kitchen window.*

You have just ripped off your flowered sundress, the one with the poppies that matches my apron, and you are running around the garden in your white underwear, the ones with the lace trim on the bottom. Bright red juice drips off your face and chest from the Gariguettes you've been stuffing into your mouth. You are spinning and turning, whirling with your arms outstretched to the sun.

A dragonfly just zipped over your head. He's the size of my hand and, from what I can tell, sapphire blue. His wings sparkle and flutter. You stop twirling and try to catch him. He flies by your astonished face. And, as you laugh, you start dancing again. Call me crazy, but I think the dragonfly is joining in with your whirly-twirly ways.

I want to capture this moment forever. Such freedom is a feeling I've never experienced, the way you're blowing with the wind, your arms swaying in the breeze. Sometimes I feel enchained. But this is the life I chose. Or perhaps this life chose me. Or maybe I wasn't given a choice? But on days like today, just watching you, I realize what a wonderful life I have. And, Céleste, I want you to have choices—the choices I've never had.

Tonight, for your dessert, I'll make a crème brûlée with the Gariguette strawberries from the garden. It's one of your favorites—at least this week.

Many bisous,
Ta mère

A deep sadness crept into my heart as I stared at the photos. There was a time when my mother was truly happy, when her eyes sparkled. There was a time when she giggled and laughed. I never knew that person; I only knew a shell of the person she once was. Although I wanted to read more, I closed the journal as my grandmother instructed. She squeezed my hand.

"She was beautiful, wasn't she?" she said, her eyes filling with tears. "Such a happy and joyful little girl."

Visions of my depressed mother floated in my mind. Cleaning up her vomit. Longing for a hug or a motherly touch. Taking care of her. For most of my life, my escape was the kitchen, trying to do something—anything—to make her smile. When I was fifteen, I turned to making French recipes—all of her favorites, like crêpes, *bœuf bourguignon*, coq au vin, hoping my mother would come back down to earth, that she'd love me; she never did.

"She was never happy," I said, thinking, at least not with me.

"*Non*, perhaps not always, but I so love remembering her when she was like this."

"Those days for me are really hard to come by," I said, squeezing my eyes shut.

"They are hard for me, too. Which is why it's so hard for me to talk about her."

I snapped to attention. Would she talk about herself then? "Grand-mère, you wrote you felt enchained to the château. Was it because of my mother? Grand-père?"

"*Ma chérie*, things were simply different back then. Women were expected to trail after their husbands—bear children and not follow their dreams of having a career. Plus, being married to a noble came with a different set of challenges and rules."

"You didn't follow your dreams?"

Her eyes brightened. "Why, yes. After your grand-père died, I bought the pied-à-terre in Paris and I attended Le Cordon Bleu. Like you, I found my heart in the kitchen. But it's my desire for you to know much more than that."

Of course, I'd found her diploma when I was snooping in her office, but we'd never talked about it. Apparently, we were going to talk about everything now. This was what I'd wanted. Wasn't it?

"You said you did everything at the château for me. Is that true?"

Her gaze flicked to the side. "I'd be lying if I didn't say I did a lot of it for me, too. But you are my granddaughter, and I have a feeling we share more than a few dreams. I just didn't get to follow my heart until much later in life."

"I don't even know what my dreams are anymore," I said. "All I ever wanted to be was a Michelin-starred chef, but that dream was taken from me."

"If you want that dream, you'll have to fight for it. Les Libellules, our flagship resturant, is worthy of stars, and perhaps your stars will come to you," she said. "Tell me, *ma chérie*, are you not happy here?"

"Yes. No. I don't know," I said, thinking all my dreams could fall right into my lap—dreams I hadn't worked for. "It's so easy and simple here but complicated at the same time. What do I know about running a château?"

"You'll learn," she said. "If anybody can do it, it's you. Just get to know it better, at least while you're here." She yawned, her head lolling to the side. "I believe we've covered enough for one day, yes?"

There were so many questions, so many doubts, so much sadness swimming in my mind. The truth of the matter was that if I was truly running the château, it would mean my grand-mère had died. And I didn't want that to happen, especially when I was getting to know her again.

"You've invited Rémi, Lola, Clothilde, Bernard, and Agnès for the New Year's Eve celebration?" she asked, and I nodded. "Although I'm looking forward to the meal you've planned, after reading about it, I'd simply adore a crème brûlée."

"Yes, Grand-mère," I said.

"One day, when I'm feeling better, I'm looking forward to joining you in the kitchen. I'm sure you're a force to be reckoned with."

"I'd love that, Grand-mère." I kissed her on the cheek and made my way downstairs, thinking about my mother, my grandmother, and the château.

I rubbed my eyes with my fingertips. At Cendrillon, I'd been stuck adhering to rules and regulations and rigid recipes, and my creativity got lost in the process. I'd been telling somebody else's story when all I'd ever wanted was to tell my own. But what if I didn't like my story? Would the rest of Grand-mère's diary provide me with the answers I needed to make my decision?

In the journal entry we'd read, the one with the dragonfly, my mother had been happy, and my heart had filled with joy. I wanted—no, needed—to wrap myself in her happiness, if only for a few minutes. I crawled into the corners of my memories, trying to remember something sweet she'd said. The past flooded my core, bringing me back to a day when she'd looked at me and said, "I don't deserve something as wonderful as you."

"You think I'm wonderful?" I'd said with surprise.

"Of course," she'd said. "You are the best thing that's ever happened to me."

Until now, I'd forgotten this conversation. I supposed I'd blocked out any of the good memories, the sweet things my mother had said and done, with bad ones as a self-defense mechanism, trying to protect myself from the pain of when I lost her. But the memories came flooding back. When she wasn't doped up, life with my mother really wasn't all bad. I choked back my tears. It was then I realized I really missed her. I never hated her. I may have loved her too much.

AFTER ALL THE stress and surprises, our New Year's Eve celebration was a nice way to wind down the year—a simple meal among family and friends. Well, a simple meal—the French way, almost an exact repeat of Christmas Eve, but for seven people, and it included the addition of a clementine-infused crème brûlée. After tucking a very tired and stuffed Lola into one of the window seats, we sat by the fire waiting for the clock to strike midnight, chatting and drinking the château's ancestral-method sparkling wine. Grand-mère was getting stronger every minute. She even made it out of her wheelchair, walking slowly toward me, each step purposeful.

"*Ma chérie,*" said my grand-mère. "You are a wonderful chef. When I'm gone, I know the château will be in your capable hands. You've made me happier than I've been in a long while. *Bonne année.*"

"I hope you'll be around for a while," I said as we swapped kisses. "Look how great you're doing. That day isn't coming anytime soon."

"But one day it will come," she said. She clasped my hands in between hers before making her way over to Clothilde. A knot formed in my throat—so tight it was difficult to swallow.

Rémi was the last to exchange *les bises* with me.

"Thank you for being so kind to Lola and for being such a great friend," he said. Rémi poured some sparkling wine into our glasses. "Here's to the New Year. *À ta santé.*"

We toasted, and my heart wobbled a little bit.

22

there's heat in this kitchen

THE NEXT FEW days were spent fulfilling duties at the château, such as polishing silverware, turning over mattresses, and maintaining the grounds, Rémi doing the latter when he wasn't running into town picking up diapers for Lola. The weather was cold and dreary but there was some heat sparking my body, namely my growing feelings for Rémi. I liked how he fawned over Grandmère. I liked his dimpled smile, especially when it was directed at me. I liked how he was a doting father to Lola. What I didn't like was the fact that we'd barely spoken since New Year's Eve. He was friendly enough, yes, but reserved and always rushing off to take care of something.

Then something happened between us. The snow fell hard again, covering the grounds of the château in a sugarcoated wonderland. I was coming back from the greenhouse and Rémi was hauling wood in one of the ATVs. He didn't stop or even wave. So I threw a snowball at him and it landed, smacking him right on the back of his neck. The ATV stopped and Rémi jumped off it, racing toward me, his face twisting in what looked like anger. I turned to run, but slipped in the snow. His laughter boomed. He ran up, stretched out his hand to help me off the ground, and I was almost up when he released his grip.

"What'd you do that for?" I asked.

"You threw a snowball at me," he said.

"Because you've been ignoring me," I said and, not knowing what else to do under his gaze, I started making an angel, my legs and arms swooping in the snow.

"I could never ignore you, Sophie," he said with a grin, and spread out next to me. "You really are an angel." He propped himself up on his elbow and leaned over me. I swear our lips were about to touch. I could feel the heat of his breath. I really wanted him to kiss me, ached for his lips on mine. Instead, he jumped up. "Grand-mère needs her firewood. She's cold."

So was I, especially after the heat sparking my body. He winked. "I'll see you later."

"Later," I said with frustration.

The fantasies infiltrating my brain when I watched him walk away—his broad shoulders, his tight rear—were so wrong, especially at a time I shouldn't be thinking about him. I reminded myself: I was here for my grand-mère—not for me, and not for him. I headed into the kitchen to prepare my grand-mère and Agnès a meal—a simple leek quiche. A few hours later, after ushering Agnès to another room, we read more of Grand-mère's diary and I found myself coming closer to my mother and to my grandmother with each passage I read.

"Ah, yes," said my grand-mère with a laugh, pointing to a photo accompanying an entry. "I remember that day. One day, Céleste brought baby goats into her bedroom and jumped around with them on the bed until I burst into her room and said, '*No goats in the house. And no jumping on the bed.*'"

Her laughter came strong, as did mine.

I traced my mother's image with my finger, wanting to see her in person again, even for a few seconds. She was so beautiful in these photos, so full of life, so full of laughter, which made me realize I never truly knew her when she was alive.

"Could we read one more?" I asked, even though we'd already gone through dozens.

Grand-mère nodded. "Just one more," she said, and I read.

19 December, 1988

My darling Céleste—

You're now thirteen years old and quite the beauty. Your figure is blossoming and it makes me so very uncomfortable to see the way men—older men—look at you. Your father isn't too keen on letting you hang around boys—even ones your age. I don't blame him.

Many bisous,
Ta mère

How many men had fallen in love with my mother? I knew the answer: too many. It was hard to keep track of them all, one swinging through the front door while another one left through the back. When I was sixteen, I just called them all Bob under my breath. How many men had she loved? Zero. She used her lovers like toilet paper on her rise and fall to an unclaimed stardom, and they probably used her, too—sucked the life right out of her.

Although she did land a few bit parts in a few films, always playing roles like the unnamed French maid or waitress, her career never took off, no matter how hard she tried. I could say one thing: she was driven, maybe too driven. Perhaps I was more like her than I realized.

"Grand-mère," I asked. "Did she ever talk to you? Tell you about her first loves? Tell you anything? She was always so distant with me."

"*Non, ma chérie*," she said. "Look at this picture, the one when she was fifteen. Look at her eyes."

My mother was sitting on a swing, head down, her jaw clamped into her famous closed-lip smile. This photo was different than the others. It was as if she was no longer present. This was the mother I remembered.

"What happened to her?"

"We're getting to that part soon," she said, closing the notebook, her eyes glistening with tears. "Please, I'm doing what I can for now."

One of the machines buzzed and beeped, the noise deafening. Agnès rushed into the room. She huddled over my grand-mère and attached a blood pressure monitor to her arm. "Did something cause her stress?"

"Yes, yes, yes, I'm sure of it," I said, bracing my hands on my knees. "We were . . . we were . . . talking about my mother. She— she doesn't like to—"

"I'd avoid the subject," said Agnès, worry creasing her brows. "Her blood pressure is through the roof."

"I will talk to my granddaughter regarding topics I want to discuss," said my grand-mère with a wheeze. "It's my dying wish for her to know the truth. You, Agnès, won't take that away from me."

I latched onto Grand-mère's trembling hand. "Maybe it's too hard on you. I can live with not knowing. Your health is more important to me. You're here. And she's gone."

"*Hors de question*" (Out of the question), said Grand-mère, her voice strong and unwavering. "Our good lord won't let me into his kingdom unless I confess all of my sins. I'm so sorry. I'm so sorry."

Confess? Confess what? I knew my grand-mère was religious, went to church every Sunday, but I didn't think she believed in the wrath of God. What would have rattled my grand-mère so badly that she would say such terrible things? My heart raced so fiercely I thought it would explode from my rib cage.

A loud sound came from another one of the machines. Agnès scrambled over to a tray, returning with a vial. "I'm giving your grand-mère a sedative," she said as she injected a liquid into the IV. "She really needs to stay calm, and I need to make sure her blood pressure stays stable or she could have another aneurysm rupture."

This setback was my fault. I'd instigated a painful conversation when I should have just left it all alone. Could I live without my answers, especially since Grand-mère could die giving them to me?

In seconds, Grand-mère's eyelids quivered to a close and her chest rose and fell softly. I stood panicked, my breathing rapid. "Will she be okay?"

"If I get her stabilized," said Agnès.

My eyes shot to the diary splayed out on my grand-mère's lap. I didn't want to be the cause of her death, but after what she said about confessing, I wanted to know why. What had she done to my mother that was so terrible? Instead of putting Grand-mère through emotional turmoil, I could get my answers on my own. Before I could reach for the journal, Agnès picked it up, closed it, and tucked it on Grand-mère's nightstand, out of my reach.

"Sophie," said Agnès. "We need to keep your grand-mère strong. Can somebody bring us dinner in a few hours? I'd make something myself, but I can't leave her. Not for a second. Something light and healthy, chock-full of nutrients—like a soup?"

"I will," I said, fighting back my tears.

—◦◦❦◦◦—

FOR THE MOST part, the château was quiet and empty. I rarely saw
the housekeepers. If I did, the ladies would say a quick *bonjour* and
scurry off. All I could think about were loneliness and guilt—mine
and hers. I don't know how my grand-mère survived the winter
months without anybody around in the past—including me. Instead
of her diary and the confession it contained, I thought of her kitchen
notebooks. I pulled them out from their hiding place in the floor,
searching for one recipe in particular. If my grand-mère was on the
cusp of death and needed to face her ghosts to move on, I could,
too. We were already talking about my mother, which eased my
pain; I needed, for my sanity, to do something else.

    After finding the recipe, I dashed over to the greenhouse with a
basket, and I eyed my nemesis growing in the garden to its side: the
potimarron. The wind picked up and the orange squashes bobbed
on their leaves, taunting me. Still, I needed to be strong for my
grandmother. She needed to see I could do more than bring up croissants and baguettes. She needed to feel she'd done something important by teaching me what she knew. She needed to know she was
always by my side even when we were oceans apart. She had to let
go of her guilt. I needed to let go of my guilt. I ambled into the field
of winter squashes and picked eight waxed beauties, releasing them
from their leafy green vines, and placed them in my basket. Then I
opened up the door to the greenhouse, feeling alive and inspired. I
grabbed stalks of leeks, carrots, and fresh herbs, including lavender.
Lavender—healing and calming, just what she needed. After picking the purple stems and placing them in my basket, I brought my
fingers to my nose. Healing and calming—just what I needed, too.

    Back in the kitchen, I set to work, laying out the ingredients
before me in a perfect line. I grabbed a cutting board and, not even

thinking, I slammed my knife into one of the potimarrons. And it felt good, like I was taking out my frustrations and hate on Eric, the guilt I felt for leaving Grand-mère. By the time I was finished, the squash was butchered, but still usable.

"Remind me to never get you angry," came a voice, and Rémi sauntered into the kitchen.

Embarrassed, I dropped my knife. It clattered onto the prep table. "How long have you been standing there?"

He held up his hands in mock fear. "Long enough."

I couldn't meet his eyes. "Did you need something?"

"I wanted to know if you were free tomorrow."

"I'm always free. I'm American," I said, instantly regretting my sarcastic response.

"Don't forget you were born French. I thought you might like to get away from the château, see a bit more of the area. Laetitia will be watching Lola," he said. "I kind of need to get away, too. I thought we could catch up."

I had to keep my distance. But I couldn't. Not with Remi's long eyelashes blinking away. "As friends, right?"

"No, as mortal enemies," he said with a smirk. "Is there a problem? You're acting really bizarre, Sophie."

"I'm just worried," I said, trying to hold myself together. "Grand-mère isn't doing well. She had a setback."

"*Merde*," he said, his face paling. He turned abruptly to exit the kitchen. "I need to visit with her."

I grabbed his shoulder. His strong, muscled shoulder—my hand quickly recoiled. "Rémi, I wouldn't. Agnès gave her a sedative. We can't disturb her now."

"But I have to do something," he said.

"You can help me, if you want to." I rocked back and forth on my heels, anxious. "I'm making dinner for her, something healthy to keep Grand-mère strong. It's a healing potimarron velouté. Do you know how to cook?"

His beautiful lips pinched together. "Of course. I was under Grand-mère's tutelage for years. But she never taught me how to murder a squash. What on earth did you learn from her over the summers?"

I had to laugh—at myself, at this situation. I also had to remind myself I couldn't fall for Rémi. Out of the question. But we could be friends. "Grab a cutting board," I said. "And cut the squash. I'd like to serve her and Agnès bowls made from the roasted squash, so after we cut the tops off, they'll have to be carefully de-meated and deseeded."

He pointed to the cutting board, to the seeds splattered everywhere. "What about the victim?"

"Perfectly roast-able, but definitely not a bowl."

"Besides watching you murder squash, I'm looking forward to seeing your other skills." He picked up my knife from the counter and handed it back to me. Our hands brushed, giving me chills. I wondered what skills he had.

I walked to the sink and rinsed the knife off, looking over my shoulder. Rémi smiled and held up the squash. "I'm waiting for more instructions, Chef."

Stop smiling at me like that.

"The leeks, carrots, and onions need to be chopped," I said with too much force.

"What are you going to do?" he asked skeptically.

"I'm heating up the ovens and looking for Parmesan. And I'm making the other soup I'll expect you to taste. You're going to be my guinea pig and tell me which one's better. Okay?"

He eyed the notebook, still open to Grand-mère's recipe. "Parmesan? It isn't listed here."

"What can I say? I need to get creative. For Grand-mère, I'm making Parmesan crisps and I'm making the ginger-infused lobster for the other dish. With homemade stock, of course."

"Why another soup? Isn't one enough?"

"No. Same idea. Different recipes. I want to follow O'Shea's. I need to know which one is better. One soup is for Grand-mère, the other one is for me and my peace of mind."

"I understand. It's bizarre, but I understand," he said, holding back his laughter. "Let's do this."

Over the next hour, Rémi and I worked together, me supremely impressed with his knife skills, him listening to my every instruction and calling me Boss Woman. Sometimes we'd bump into one another, or our hands would touch, and my heart would feel like it was going to leap out of my chest. But no. Rémi and me couldn't happen. I couldn't, wouldn't let it happen. Still, fighting my attraction toward him was going to be so damn hard. Why did he have to be so good-looking and know exactly what to say to make me laugh?

Finally, I pulled out the immersion blender. Two large pots stood in front of me. It was go time. "Okay, Rémi, I'm seasoning one with O'Shea's recipe. And adding in the lobster," I said. I ladled a spoonful into a bowl. "Taste it."

He grabbed a spoon and swallowed back a mouthful. "I like the addition of the lobster, but the velouté has no flavor. I don't like it. He served it like this?"

"He did."

"What got you fired?"

"Adding in more spices to the velouté, upon Eric's instruction."

"Do it," he said, and I did. He tasted the soup again and looked up. "It's even worse. Why do I taste so much cumin? It really overpowers everything. I'm really hoping the other velouté is better," he said. "For Grand-mère's sake."

"I hope so, too," I said, ladling another bowl. I topped it off with the Parmesan crisp. "*Voilà*. Tell me what you think."

Rémi took the bowl and took a bite. His head dropped back and he closed his eyes with pleasure. "It makes me fall in love with the chef who cooked this," he said, and my jaw went slack. "But it's missing something."

"What? What's it missing?" I asked, panicked, hoping I hadn't messed up.

"The lobster. But with more orange sauce and less ginger. And maybe flambé the tails with a bit of Armagnac. She loves lobster prepared like that."

"You don't think that would be too much? It's alcohol."

"*Non*," he said. "Alcohol burns down. Try it."

I lit a match and flambéed the lobster tails, the flames heating my body for a quick second. Or was it Rémi's close proximity?

Rémi dipped the spoon into the pot, and as he fed me a bite, our eyes locked for a moment. I had to close mine. He was right. The soup was beyond delicious. So was he—his long eyelashes, the golden sunbursts speckling his caramel-colored eyes. And, damn, those perfect bow-shaped lips, offset by dimples when he smiled. I couldn't control the blush creeping across my cheeks.

Did I just lick the spoon your beautiful mouth was just on?

My entire body sparked, wondering what it would be like to kiss him. With Eric, his mouth was like a sucking octopus, one with very bad halitosis from smoking too many cigarettes. I'd never been that giddy girl, the kind who fretted and fawned over a man. But, when I looked at Rémi's lips, I was becoming that silly girl. I needed to pull myself together.

"Did we just create a new recipe together?" I asked.

"I believe we did."

Rémi pulled me in for *les bises* and my knees nearly crumbled. "I've got to head home. Can you spare some for me, Lola, and Laetitia?"

Right.

"Sure, there's plenty," I said. After scrambling around for a container, I handed it over.

"*Merci*, Sophie, I'll pick you up tomorrow morning at nine."

Rémi left and I stood there for a moment, pushing back indecent thoughts and shaking my head. After making sure everything was perfect, tasting it again, I ladled the velouté into the roasted potimarron bowls, added the lobster and Parmesan crisps, and set them on a tray.

Please love this, Grand-mère. I need your approval.

Anxious, I knocked on Grand-mère's door and Agnès opened it. She eyed the soup.

"Wow," she said. "I was expecting something wonderful, but not pure magic."

"Do you think this is too much for her?"

"It's perfect. She's stable, but not one mention of whatever you were discussing before, please." Agnès paused. "Do you want to feed her? Or should I?"

"I'll do it," I said.

"I'll have to stay by her side."

"I understand," I said.

Agnès set up the hospital tray, placing it over my grand-mère's lap. After setting Grand-mère's meal on it, Agnès sat on a chair and dug right in. Grand-mère opened her eyes. She looked at me and then at the velouté. "You created this?" she asked. "It's beautiful. I hope it tastes as good as it looks."

"Yes, we made this for you. Rémi helped." I picked up a spoon, holding it out with a napkin placed under it so it wouldn't drip onto her dressing gown.

Her mouth puckered and opened like a baby bird's. Strange, how I was once the child and she used to feed me. This role reversal was bizarre and unnerved me so badly it broke my heart. I reminded myself I needed to be strong for her. I sucked in a breath and, trying to keep my hands from shaking and spilling orange soup on her nightgown, I fed her a spoonful. Grand-mère licked her lips. "Oh, *ma chérie*, this is absolutely wonderful. I taste each and every ingredient. Oh, lavender. Turmeric? The lobster. Wonderful! How on earth did you bring all these flavors together?"

"I learned everything I know from you," I said. "Honestly, cooking school was a cakewalk."

"I could never have created anything like this," she said. "You are far more creative than I am."

"This is a soup," exclaimed Agnès. "A soup? And it's the best meal I've ever had in my entire life."

"I concur with Agnès," said Grand-mère, and a deep pride set in. "Now, tell me. You said Rémi helped you? I take it you've settled your differences?"

"We did," I said. "And we're friends again. He thinks it's a good idea for me to get away from the château," I said. "See life outside the gates. If that's okay with you. Of course, if you need me, I won't go."

"The château isn't a prison," she said. "Don't worry about me. I'm not dying any day soon. Stop digging my grave and get out, have some fun."

This was an order.

"But not too much fun," she said with a soft cackle.

I blushed. "Grand-mère, we're *just* friends. He only wants to show me around."

"I see," she said with a twinkle in her eye. "I'm glad the most important people in my world are *just* friends." She opened up her mouth. "More of this deliciousness, *s'il te plaît*." Spoonful after spoonful, as I fed her, I hoped she couldn't read my mind, because I was thinking about Rémi and how I really didn't want to be "just friends."

23

in and out of the friend zone

AFTER A VERY sleepless night, I woke up at six in the morning. Every fiber of my being was telling me to stay far, far away from Rémi—to keep him at arm's length, to accept his friendship. My dream, the one I was controlling in my head, said otherwise.

"Yes, he has a child," one voice would say. The other voice said, "Sophie, you need to see if something is there—look at his lips, his gorgeous kissable lips." And then the other voice said, "Sophie, your life is still in the crapper. You can't bring them into this." I scrambled out from underneath my covers, feeling like I was on the verge of going schizophrenic.

Nerves set in until I reminded myself this wasn't a date. Rémi wanted to show me life outside the château. That was all.

I dressed, pulling on a green cashmere sweater, jeans without holes in them, and my black woolly boots. Casual. Cool, calm, and collected, my hair blown dry and down. A little mascara. A little blush. I was me. Just me.

Rémi, as promised, waited for me in the foyer at nine a.m. He looked gorgeous, wearing black slacks, a gray sweater, and a fabulous steel-gray cashmere coat—like he'd just stepped off the pages of *GQ* magazine.

This is not a date.

"Wow, you should wear green more. It brings out the color of your beautiful eyes," he said, and I smiled bashfully. "But those boots? Did you steal them off a homeless *gitan*? Or a babushka?"

"What's wrong with my boots?" I asked, a bit insulted.

"Everything."

I looked down at my feet. "Should I change?"

"No, I don't think you should change. I think you're wonderful just the way you are—even in those ugly boots."

He'd just complimented and insulted me at the same time. I liked it. "Do you always say what's on your mind?"

"Not always, but I'm French. You are family. I'm allowed to tease you," he said. "Are you ready to go?"

Family. Right.

"Where are we going?"

"I was thinking of taking you to Cordes-sur-Ciel, voted one of the prettiest villages in France, and afterward taking *la route des bastides*, where medieval villages thrive, to show you a little history, but then I thought you'd like to be in the city."

"Toulouse?" I asked.

"*Oui*, Toulouse," he said. "Have you ever been?"

"Aside from the hospital, no," I said.

"Toulouse it is then," he said. "It's only forty-five minutes away. *On y va?*"

"Yes, let's go."

"Maybe you can find some new boots," he said, opening the door.

As we walked to the truck, I looked down at my boots again. They were ten years old and way out of style—just like the rest of my wardrobe. I needed more than shoes. I needed more than a new wardrobe. I needed to take charge of my life. But one baby step at a time. "How do you feel about shopping, Rémi?"

His laugh came hard. "I'll help you find new shoes. And jeans without holes in them."

"I threw those jeans away," I said, and lightly slugged his arm. "My style isn't that bad."

Rémi held the passenger door open for me. I hopped in and he closed it. I liked this Rémi. I wanted to know more about him. I did share a lot of secrets with him as a child, like me searching for my birth father. I remember lying in the fields with him, hidden among the wildflowers, telling him about my dreams of becoming a chef. Funny, I didn't remember him sharing anything with me; he just listened with his head tilted toward the sky. Maybe he'd talk to me—really talk to me.

"Rémi, can you tell me about Anaïs?"

"What do you want to know about her?" he asked.

"It must have been so hard to lose her," I said, really wanting to know everything.

"*Bien sûr.* It was terrible." He blew out the air between his beautiful lips, *pffff*, and his shoulders slumped. "I'd like to be honest with you."

I nodded for him to carry on.

"When Anaïs fell pregnant, Grand-mère, of course, wasn't happy about it and she told me I needed to take responsibility for my actions. We decided I'd marry Anaïs so the baby could take my name. My plan was to divorce her after Lola was born, to take care of them both financially and to be a part of Lola's life as her father."

This didn't sit well with me. "Didn't you love Anaïs?" I said, thinking she must have loved him. Did he just leave her high and dry?

"No, Sophie, we were together, but we were not in love," he said matter-of-factly. "She only agreed to marry me for the same reasons I just explained." He gripped the steering wheel tightly, his knuckles turning white. "When Lola was born and Anaïs died, my world changed. I changed."

His statements weren't computing. "I don't understand."

"I've only been in love with one woman—my first love, a girl I thought I'd never get over, but eventually did. Or I thought I had." Rémi brushed a strand of loose hair away from his eyes. "Sophie," he said, glancing at me. "It was you, and I'd like to get to know you again."

I didn't know how to respond. Of course, I'd been thinking the same thing, too, but words wouldn't come to me. I narrowed my eyes into a mock glare, my heart racing. "Why would you ever want to put up with the likes of me?"

Rémi laughed. "You don't put up with my crap—you never did. I remember when you dunked me in the lake. All those memories, all the fun we had, rushed back when you lobbed me in the head with that snowball." He swallowed hard, his Adam's apple bobbing. "Taking you to Toulouse was my way of getting you alone," he said sheepishly. "I wanted to know if you think there could be a chance. For us?"

"Oh," I said, and his posture crumbled.

"That's not the answer I'd hoped for." His shoulders, the broad ones I'd been staring at with lust, caved.

"Just give me a minute to gather my thoughts," I said. "What you just said was completely unexpected."

My neck prickled, thinking about what I'd learned in Grandmère's diaries. Until I had all my answers about my mother, I wasn't sure what I was going to do, if I was even staying in Champvert, although I now had another reason to stick around. I was definitely developing feelings for Rémi and he was helping me move on from thoughts of Eric and New York, I wasn't sure if it was just the idea of him, the fantasy I'd created in my head like a perfect recipe. Even though the sparks of the Rémi I'd known when I was a young girl flashed in my memories, in a way it was almost as if my grandmother had been grooming him for me over the years—taking a farm boy and turning him into a prince, an Elijah Doolittle. Part of me wanted him to go back to being Mean Rémi; it was easier then and I wouldn't have to fight my feelings for him.

"Sophie?" said Rémi. "I just poured out my heart and you're just sitting there silently."

I clasped my hands together, head down, voice low. "There's a chance, but I think we should take things slow."

His beautiful bow-shaped lips curved into a sexy smile, flashing white teeth. "Slow? I can do that."

"I mean really, really slow," I said. "We're starting off as friends."

"Just friends?" he questioned, and I nodded. "I guess I can do that, but it will be hard, considering how much I want to kiss you right now."

I focused on his perfect jawline. No kidding.

"So, friend," he said with a grin. "I've told you all about my shameful past. How many boyfriends have you had?"

"One," I said, cringing as I thought of him. "Eric."

"Impossible," he said, sucking in his breath. "You're so beautiful you must have had to fight the boys off with sticks."

"It's completely possible and completely true," I said. Damn it. He'd complimented me again. "What can I say?"

"This Eric? Was he the chef who set you up? And the reason you murdered a potimarron? The velouté thickens—"

"Look, I really don't want to talk about Eric," I said, my shoulders tensing. "But since we're telling stories, I will share one of mine. I had a fake fiancé in New York."

"Fake?" questioned Rémi. "*J'ai mal compris.*" (I don't understand.)

"Walter is my best friend, and he is gay." Rémi's lip curled with confusion and he motioned for me to carry on. "I was only pretending to be his fiancée because he was petrified to come out to his parents. We lived together for two years."

"You didn't have relations with him?"

"Aside from friendship, no. We had separate bedrooms," I said, driving my point in. "You saw him and his partner over Christmas."

He let out a hearty laugh. "And to think I was a bit jealous," he said. "I thought one of those men was your boyfriend."

I let out an awkward donkey-like laugh.

Rémi pulled into a parking lot marked Esquirol, right in Toulouse's *centre-ville*. I sat in the car for a few moments, trying to catch my breath, until he opened the door and helped me jump out of the truck. I took his hand and hopped out, only to misjudge my balance and land straight into his chest. He smelled like the woods, cedar and musk. He raised a flirtatious eyebrow as I pushed myself away, flushing with embarrassment.

We ambled up the steps, making our way to Rue d'Alsace-Lorraine, the main shopping drag. There must have been hundreds of people rushing down the street, all carrying bags filled to the brim, which I found odd. "It's *les soldes*" (the sales), explained Rémi. "The stores hold them twice a year in France—right after Christmas in January and in July." He took my hand, pulling me. "*Regarde*, a shoe store. You'll get a good deal."

As we entered the shop, all eyes turned on us—men, women, and young girls, mouths agape. Probably because Rémi was so damn hot. He pointed to a pair of over-the-knee boots with four-inch heels. "Those are very nice," he said. "I can see you in them."

"Completely inappropriate for life in Champvert," I responded. They were so sexy I could only imagine what he was thinking about because I was doing it, too. I cleared my throat and made a beeline to a pair of more practical boots with a flat heel, black—riding boots. Normally €300, they'd been marked down to €150. A salesgirl came over and I asked for my size. In minutes, they were on my feet. "I'll take them," I said.

Rémi was over at the register paying before I could stop him. I caught up with him.

"You shouldn't have done that," I said, tapping him on the shoulder.

"It's what *friends* do," he said. "Plus, I had them throw your old boots away."

"You hated them that much?"

He nodded his head. "*Elles étaient méga moches.*"

"*Méga moches?*"

"Not just ugly, but super ugly," he said. "I believe I did you a favor."

"*Merci,*" I said with a laugh, wondering if I should air-kiss his cheeks.

"*Ce n'était rien.*" (It was nothing.) "*On y va.* I have much to show you."

We exited the shop into swarms of people and the energy was exactly what I'd needed, although, with the crowds, I felt myself longing for the quiet of Champvert. Still, it was nice to know that if I needed a dose of the city, Toulouse was spitting distance away.

We traversed narrow streets flanked by beautiful buildings with iron balconies and carved wooden doors, finally arriving at our destination—a large square surrounding a bevy of cafés, where the outside terraces heated with lamps were filled with people eating and drinking, facing an enormous brick and limestone neoclassical building adorned with impressive sculptures.

"This is Place du Capitole," said Rémi, pointing. "The big buildings over there house the *hôtel de ville*, the mayor's office, and the opera. Do you know why they call Toulouse '*La Ville Rose*'?" he asked.

"No," I said.

"Because of all the pink brick buildings," he said. "*Tu as faim?*"

I wasn't hungry just yet. "Not really," I said.

"Good, because we are not eating here. I have a special place I want to take you. But first we will visit the Basilica of Saint-Sernin, one of the largest Romanesque structures in the world."

"You make an excellent tour guide," I said.

"What can I say?" he replied. "I'm a very good *friend*."

With that, he turned on his heel and began to walk away. He looked over his shoulder as I stood in the center of the Occitan cross, one of the symbols of the region, not moving. "Are you coming, Sophie?"

OUR MORNING ENDED at Marché Victor Hugo, at one of the restaurants over the market. We sat across from one another in silence, me looking at the menu.

"What do you want?" asked Rémi.

Well, that was a loaded question. I couldn't focus on the menu because I was looking at his beautiful lips and wondering how they'd feel pressed onto mine. I knew what I didn't want. I didn't want to be "just friends" with Rémi, and the lustful feelings I was fighting were confusing me beyond belief.

"Sophie," said Rémi. "I don't know about you, but I'm starving."

After a very awkward lunch with me staring at Rémi and vice versa, we meandered through the market at Victor Hugo, filled with butchers, cheese, fish, and vegetable vendors, along with quite a few bakers. He bought a few things—a roast beef and some vegetables. We stopped in front of a pâtisserie and Rémi pointed to some cakes.

"Have you ever had a *galette des rois?*"

"No," I said. "What is it?"

"It's a tradition in France," he said. "On January sixth, which is today, we celebrate the Epiphany, when the baby Jesus was presented to the Three Wise Men. In the past, the cake was cut into portions, plus one. This extra slice was known as the *part du pauvre*, the slice given to the needy. After that, under the reign of Louis XIV, *une fève*, a small porcelain figurine depicting Mary or another nativity figurine, is hidden inside the cake. Whoever finds the *fève* is crowned queen or king for the day, the paper crown supplied by the local pâtisserie. We have two choices—the brioche flavored with *fleur d'oranger* or stuffed with frangipane. Which one would you like to try?"

"Frangipane," I said, loving this tradition and wondering why my mother had never told me about it.

"But you can't eat it now," he said.

"Why? We didn't have dessert and that looks delicious."

"I was hoping you'd join us for dinner," he said, casting his eyes downward. "Lola keeps talking about her *tatie* Sophie. I'm cooking." He pointed to his shopping bags. "Do you like *rôti de bœuf?*"

"What about Grand-mère?" I asked.

"I've already cleared my plan with her."

Of course he had. I was being set up again. And this was fine by me. I was feeling back to my old self, and I didn't want this day to end.

24

too much, too soon, too fast

RÉMI'S HOUSE WAS quaint and charming, and I remembered visiting it as a kid. An old stone farmhouse with wooden beams, it held none of the glitz or glamour of the château, and I immediately felt at ease. He'd obviously done some renovations since I'd last been here, opening up the downstairs completely—American style. Rustic. Charming. Simple.

We stepped over dolls and toys, and after a quick tour of Rémi's five-bedroom home, he ushered me into the large kitchen, complete with a beautiful red Lacanche stove. The dogs, D'Artagnan and Aramis, slept on the floor in rather luxurious burgundy velvet dog beds with a brocade fleur-de-lis print. The dogs rolled on their backs, tongues lolling, wanting belly scratches. Happily, I obliged.

Rémi lit a fire, put on classical music, and opened a bottle of wine. As he handed me a glass, I realized there was something missing. "Where's Lola?" I asked.

"She's at her music class." He eyed his wrist. "Laetitia will be bringing her home any minute. It's only a bit past five. I hope you don't mind eating so early. We usually eat at six."

"It's fine," I said, taking his arm and eyeing the mark on his watch. He wore a gold Rolex with a black dial.

"Circa 1980s. It was your grandfather's. Grand-mère Odette gave it to me for my twentieth birthday," he said. "Does it bother you that she gave it me?"

"No," I said. He'd been here for Grand-mère. I hadn't. "You deserve it. And more."

"Go, relax. Sit on the couch," he said. "I'm going to get started on dinner."

As I watched Rémi cook, peeling potatoes and chopping, I thought that while I may be flipped-out with the magnitude of the château, I could grow to like it here. I could get used to this. To a life with him. But his situation was far from simple. A smiling photo of a woman on the mantel stared down at me, and I could only assume this was the famous Anaïs. While she wasn't my spitting image, in a way, she did resemble me. She was thin. She had black hair. She had a hard look about her. I tucked my knees into my chest, thinking about how I was in way over my head.

Just then, the door opened. The dogs barked, and when Lola saw me, she squealed with joy. She toddled over to me and jumped into my lap. She latched her arms around my neck, nearly pulling me over. "*Tatie* Sophie!"

"My little Lola," I said, breathing in her strawberry and sunshine scents.

Laetitia followed her in. "She did wonderful today! I think our little girl is a budding violinist."

Her gaze met my curious one. This woman seemed so familiar to me, and I couldn't place her until I recalled seeing her at the Christmas market. I knew she was older, midfifties, by my guess, I just didn't remember her being so pretty—the kind of French-woman carrying a certain *je ne sais quoi*. She took off her coat, hung it on a hook, and fluffed up her chestnut-colored hair. Her warm, chocolate-colored eyes locked onto mine. "Sophie, I assume?"

"*C'est moi*," I said. "Nice to meet you. It's Laetitia, right?"

After swapping the required air-kisses, she grabbed the bottle of wine and sat down next to me, pouring herself a glass. "I've been dying to meet you." She tilted her head toward Rémi. "He always smiles at Lola, but not much else. I'm thrilled he's no longer keeping us a secret. It's not good for a child."

"No," I said. Did she say "us"? "It isn't."

"Of course, we often visit with your grand-mère, or she comes here, but it's been difficult with her health. Is she doing better?"

"She has some good days, some bad," I said. "I'm hoping she pulls through."

"It must have been hard for you, coming back to all this after being gone for so long."

"It's been a challenge," I said. How much did this woman, this stranger, know about my life? It was disconcerting.

"*À table*," exclaimed Rémi.

It was time for dinner.

"Let's eat," said Laetitia. She commandeered Lola from my arms. "This one is a gourmand, and her *papa* cooks wonderful meals, doesn't he?" She tickled Lola's tummy.

"*Oui*," said Lola as she squealed.

"You'll sit there, Sophie," said Laetitia, pointing.

The table, like the house, was rustic—a long slab of mahogany wood. Simple. Charming. I took my seat as Rémi brought the dishes over: potatoes cooked in duck fat, the roast beef, and a salad with pan-seared foie gras. He winked at me as he carved the roast. "We're doing it American style for our American guest. How do you like the temperature of your meat?"

"*Saignant*" (Rare), I said. I liked mine bloody.

"Phew. If you said otherwise, I'd wonder if you were really born French." His dimples puckered his cheeks.

"See?" said Laetitia. "He's smiling. I'm so happy to see him like this."

I wondered why a nanny would care so much for an employer's happiness. I supposed they'd just become close, him being a single father needing somebody to take care of his child. I stared at Laetitia, my mother coming to mind. If she were alive, my mother would have been about the same age, maybe a little younger. Her eyes were a liquid brown, the color like maple syrup, and filled with kindness, not darkness. If my mother hadn't been so sick, would she have been filled with warmth and light like Laetitia?

"I hope you like garlic," said Rémi as he carved the meat. "I stuffed the roast with quite a few cloves."

Over a conversation about what we'd done that day and Lola's music lesson, we finished a delicious dinner, and I was impressed with Rémi's cooking skills. The roast was perfectly cooked. The potatoes were moist, delectable, and savory, and the salad was the perfect accompaniment. I'd forgotten how good pan-seared foie gras was.

Rémi brought out the dessert and Lola clapped her hands. "*Galette des rois! Galette des rois!*"

As Rémi served the galette, Laetitia winked at me. "She really likes her sweets. All she's been talking about is your *chocolat chaud*. She told me '*non*' the other day, 'it's not like *Tatie* Sophie's.'"

Rémi placed a slice of cake in front of me. "We're going to be like savage Americans. It's okay to eat this dessert with your hands."

I took a bite and my eyes went wide as I cringed with pain. "I almost broke a tooth! What in the world is in this dessert?"

"I think Sophie found *la fève*," said Laetitia with a grin.

I spit out a small porcelain hedgehog into my hand. It was blue.

"I thought religious figurines were supposed to be hidden in the cake?"

"Commercialization," said Laetitia. "All sorts of branded characters. Mickey Mouse, Les Lapins Crétins, you name it."

Rémi placed a gold paper crown on my head. "You're the queen," he said. "At least for one day."

"*La reine, Tatie* Sophie," squealed Lola. She clapped her hands with delight. "Can I be a princess?"

"Of course," I said.

"She takes after her mom," said Laetitia, squinting at me. "You really do remind me of her in a way."

I blinked like Agnès—repeatedly. "You knew Anaïs?"

"Why, of course," said Laetitia. "I'm Anaïs's mother. Did Rémi not tell you?"

My eyelashes had a life of their own. I couldn't stop blinking.

"I may have forgotten to mention it," he said, like it was no big deal. "But now she knows."

I jerked my head, the crown falling onto the floor. I didn't know why, but this news came as quite the shock.

"Rémi needed help. I moved in, wanting to be close to my granddaughter," said Laetitia. "And, on that note, it was lovely to meet you, Sophie. I've got to get the little one bathed and into bed," she said. "I'm looking forward to seeing you again."

Laetitia scooped up Lola. "Give your *tatie* Sophie a *bisou*," she said.

Lola leaned over and kissed me on the lips.

"It was so nice to meet you, Laetitia," I said, grabbing my coat. "Rémi, I've got to go check on my grand-mère. Thanks for today. And thanks for dinner," I said. I lifted up a foot. "And thanks for the boots. I'll pay you back."

"Sophie—wait," said Rémi. "I can drive you."

"That's okay. I can walk. It's not far. And you've done enough already. Really, perfect day. Perfect meal."

"But it's dark out. What about the *sangliers*? They forage at night and in the early morning. They can be quite dangerous."

"I'll take my chances," I said. "I have to get back to Grand-mère."

"It's not an option." He grabbed his keys and his coat. "I'm driving you."

I didn't say a word in the truck, just stared straight ahead. Two minutes later, we pulled in front of the château. I shook my head, irritated. "Don't you think it might have been a nice idea if you told me Laetitia was Anaïs's mom before I met her, Rémi?"

"I really don't see what the problem is. She's a very kind woman, and I don't know what I'd do without her. She has every right to be in Lola's life."

"She does. But I don't like surprises, especially important ones," I said, jumping out of the truck and storming up to the château's main entry, standing there for a moment, waiting to hear him drive away. Rémi snuck up behind me. He gripped my arms and whirled me around to face him.

"I'll keep it in mind that you don't like surprises," he said. And then he pulled me toward him and he kissed me. Chills shimmied down my spine. Fireworks exploded in my brain. I could almost hear my heartbeat, throbbing and beating in my ribs. When he pulled away, my body trembled. The kiss was supernatural—like nothing I'd ever experienced, and better than I imagined. Rémi whispered, "I've been wanting to do that for thirteen years."

"What happened to moving slow, Rémi?" I spluttered.

"You said there was a chance for us." He crossed his arms over his chest. "What's really holding you back from taking it?"

I swallowed one gulp at a time. I had the opportunity to tell him the truth. "It's the stars."

"Stars? Look up, Sophie, we have plenty of stars here."

I sat down on the front stoop. "Not those stars. Michelin stars. It's been my lifelong dream to become part of the one percent of women at the the helm of a starred restaurant. I need to clear my name in New York. It was destroyed."

Rémi ran his hands through his hair. "*Bon Dieu*, Sophie. You'd trade in the possibility of falling in love for reigniting a destroyed career?"

This was absolutely insane. He was moving too fast for me— way too fast. I opened the front door to the château. Rémi's hand swept out, closing it. Although I was definitely developing feelings for him, and we had a magnetic physical attraction, my head and my heart, while pounding wildly, weren't quite open to the concept. "Love? We've only just met again."

He crossed his arms over his chest and said, "I said the *possibility* of love. And if you want to reach for the stars, you could do that here."

"I feel like everything is just being handed to me on a silver platter," I said, opting not to add, "including you."

"And that's a bad thing?" he asked, looking at me like I was nuts.

"Yes. No," I said. "I don't know."

"You need to figure out what you want," he said, turning on his heel. He sauntered down the steps and headed back to the truck.

I yelled after him. "Which is exactly what I told you. I need to figure *everything* out. It's why I told you I wanted to move slow."

"So you're just going to ignore your feelings?"

"No, Rémi, I just need time to sort them out."

25

vindication and
perspiration

IN THE MORNING, I wanted to clear my head from a sleepless night spent tossing and turning over Rémi, Grand-mère's health, and the stress of taking over the château. I was about to head out to the greenhouse—that sanctuary of goodness, filled with calming lavender—when my cell phone buzzed. I pulled it out from my pocket, shocked to see Cendrillon on caller ID. Odd. It was one thirty in the morning in New York. My finger shook as I accepted the call.

"Hello," I said, my voice just above a whisper.

"Sophie?"

I'd recognize his gruff voice in my sleep. "Chef," I said, leaning against a stone wall in the gardens to retain my balance, preparing myself for an onslaught of threats. I stayed quiet, listening to the sound of his heavy breath and rubbing the nape of my neck.

"Sophie, are you there? Do we have a bad connection?"

"I'm here," I said.

"And I'm an overreacting hothead," said O'Shea. "I owe you an enormous apology, and not just for calling at such a late hour."

Oh. My. God. Somebody must have fessed up. My hands shook

and my jaw went slack. "I see," I said, tilting my head toward the sky, squeezing my eyes shut.

"I received an anonymous letter about you, Eric, and the star loss," he said. "I wasn't going to read it at first, but Bernadette insisted, practically forced it into my face. I don't think she's Eric's biggest fan."

"No, she isn't," I said, wondering who had come to my defense and what their motives were.

"At first I thought you sent the letter, but not with words like 'dodgy wanker,' 'tosser,' and 'knobhead.'"

I couldn't help but stifle a laugh. When Phillipa told me she'd been adamant about wanting to help me clear my name, I didn't know she'd actually do something about it.

"You know who sent it, don't you?"

"I have a pretty good idea who wrote it," I said, "but, I assure you, I didn't know about it."

"Intrigued, I read the contents of this strange letter, sent from Bibury, England, to the brigade, and most of them laughed it off—except for Miguel. He came into my office, saying he needed to confess or he was going straight to hell. I didn't realize he was so religious."

O'Shea cleared his throat. "He admitted that he'd seen and overheard Eric and Alex conspiring against you, that Eric told you to spice the velouté. He also told me there were rumors circulating around town that Cendrillon may lose a star. Those two douchebags took the opportunity to sabotage you. I couldn't fire Eric, considering he left a few months ago to start a flagship restaurant to call his own."

"Eric wanted me to work for him. I said no, Chef," I said. "I wanted to tell you, but I didn't get a chance to."

"That's my fault," said O'Shea. "Like I said, I'm a hothead." He let out a huff. "I fired that bastard Alex on the spot."

"Good."

"With that said, the chef de cuisine position is yours if you want it. Can you come in today to discuss?"

"I can't." My heartbeat quickened. Wait, he was *actually* offering me the promotion? My dream? "I'm in France."

"France? With your grandmother? When are you coming back?"

The barn swallows—*les hirondelles*—swooped in the sky in a joyous, orchestrated dance. The sun beat down on my head and dizziness set in. There was no way I could leave Champvert now—no matter how much my heart ached to do so. The *chac-chac-chacs* of the magpies reminded me of that.

"About that. I'm not sure. She's taken ill and I'm helping her out here until she gets better."

"Look, I can hold down the kitchen for a while, months even. I'm planning on getting everything back on track. And, if you saw it, don't worry about the article in the *Times*."

"I did. See it," I said, not wanting to think about it.

"I'm sending in my retraction," he said. "I have more clout in the culinary world than Eric does. He's a talentless, disloyal twit, and I'll take care of this. I'm going to clear your name and bring him down." O'Shea laughed a hearty laugh. "Blackbird may have the shortest opening in history. I'm sorry those two boneheads did this to you."

"Me, too, Chef. Me, too." A happy tear slid down my cheek.

"I'm sorry I lost my temper like that, Sophie. I'm ashamed of my behavior. I promise. It won't happen again." His voice sounded pained. I felt terrible. "So, will you think about my offer?"

"I will, but I don't know when I'll be back in New York."

"Take as much time as you need," he said. "I'll be waiting for your response."

"Thank you for calling, Chef," I said and hung up, sinking to my knees.

I surveyed the grounds, now coming back to life. The buds on the magnolia trees were already tinged pink. One day soon, the flowers would bloom, just like I, in a way, was blooming, too. Could I leave all of this behind? Still, if I took him up on his offer, I'd be back to telling O'Shea's culinary story, not mine. I didn't know if I should be celebrating or what. Part of me was happy, and the other part of me felt extraordinarily guilty for even thinking about leaving Champvert.

My grand-mère couldn't die. If she did, she was counting on me to take over the château, and I couldn't do it without her. All of this was just being given to me. I hadn't worked for it. In addition to the reservation system and the two kitchens, there was so much to manage here. The château made and sold the honey and *confitures* to outside vendors. Add in the wine business, and it was far too much for one person to handle without going crazy. At least I knew what waited for me at Cendrillon—the long hours and sexual harassment were a cakewalk compared to the stress that came with the château. I needed to talk with Grand-mère. Now. I needed the answers to the rest of my questions.

I took in a deep breath, knocked, and entered her room. I didn't say a word, just stood there trying to figure out what I was going to say.

"*Ma chérie*," she said, looking up from her magazine, "you look out of sorts. Is something wrong?"

"Yes and no. I've been vindicated. Chef O'Shea just called me. He received a letter that cleared my name," I said, not meeting her eyes.

"I see," she said pointedly. "I'm assuming O'Shea's apology came with a job offer. Are you thinking of moving back to New York?"

I shrugged. "I need time to process everything that's been going on."

"What do you need to process?"

For a moment, I couldn't speak. I just held my breath. But it was now or never. She seemed to be doing well. I wanted answers. I whipped around and met her gaze. "To make my decision, I need to know why Mother left Champvert and never looked back."

The silence that followed my statement was punctuated with heavy breaths—mine.

"I knew this day would come," she said, struggling to pull out her diary from her nightstand. "Sit down next to me," she commanded, and I did. "Forward a few pages. No more. Now read." Her eyes met mine. "Yes, here's where we shall begin." She inhaled deeply. "I've been dreading this day."

My voice shook as I read the words.

21 April, 1993

Céleste—

I've just gotten back from the doctor with you. You are pregnant and I am aghast. On the car ride home, you told me you wanted to have an abortion. That, my darling, will never happen. You're not in the right frame of mind.

Ta mère

"'Right frame of mind,' Grand-mère?" I said, every bone in my body so tense I thought I'd crumble to pieces, to dust.

"At the age of sixteen, Céleste was diagnosed with clinical depression. The doctor prescribed lithium to control these mood swings. When she fell pregnant with you, it got worse. I've always assumed that she stopped taking her medications when she did what she did."

Although my grandmother refrained from using the word "suicide," this explained everything. Almost everything. But if she knew my mother was so sick, why didn't she do anything about it? Why didn't she save me from her and the misery I'd lived with?

"She took me away from Champvert and I didn't have a choice in the matter. I was too young, couldn't even walk or talk. Why didn't you try harder to take me away from her? She was sick."

I'd pointed the finger of blame at her and I couldn't take my words back.

"I tried. The courts ruled in her favor. This put another wedge in our relationship, as you can imagine. There is a file under the plank in my closet. You can read the judge's ruling." Grand-mère's eyes filled with tears. "Taking you away from her would have killed her."

"But she killed *herself*," I said, the memory of her blue and bloated in the tub flashing in my mind.

"*Ma chérie*, she was sick long before you were born. Did you ever notice the glazed look in her eyes when she'd smile, as if she was never really there? The way her moods would switch from abnormal highs to severe lows?"

When my mother was on an upswing, she was the belle of the ball. She'd take me shopping to buy clothes. Sometimes she'd brush my hair, telling me how beautiful I was. One time, she came home with seeds, dirt, and terra-cotta pots, with the thought that I'd like to plant a garden on our small terrace because I liked cooking so much. I did. On these good days, her eyes were clear and she was full of life. But her bad days were terrible. She'd hole up in her room with the curtains drawn, barely moving. Looking back, these days were marked when she lost out on an audition to an actress younger than her.

"Keep reading," said Grand-mère, squeezing her eyes shut. "There's more you need to know."

14 July, 1993

Céleste—

Jean-Marc Bourret came by looking for you. I didn't like the looks of him. He was dirty, unshaven, and not a proper fellow. You were in your room, sleeping. This pregnancy has been tough on you. You are always with morning sickness and on bed rest. Jean-Marc insisted that I wake you from your slumber. He told me that he was the father of your baby, and that he wanted to marry you.

I told him to wait on the front steps. And then I grabbed my checkbook. He didn't want to accept the check at first. He argued and pleaded to see you. And then he looked at the sum. Oh, you should have seen his smile, the glimmer in his eye as he surveyed the château. I told him there would be more coming for every year he stayed away from you. Of course he agreed. I suppose this is my confession. And I don't feel bad about it. I did what was right for you. A marriage to the likes of him would never have worked. Today is Bastille Day. And I've just claimed your independence.

Ta mère

The notebook slipped from my hands. I rubbed my eyes. This couldn't be real. The answer I'd been searching for half of my life just appeared on the page, right under my nose, written in Grand-mère Odette's loopy handwriting. Although I now had some answers, more questions loomed. Rivulets of sweat dripped down my neck. Was this Jean-Marc Bourret really my father? Was he still in the area? If so, could I find him? Did I want to? My tears fell, smattering the notebook with tiny droplets. I'd been looking for truth and I'd found it. But sometimes the truth was hard to swallow, a jagged pill.

"How much did you pay him?" I asked.

"At the time, it held the equivalence to ten thousand euros."

"I can't believe he took the money," I said.

"He did," she said. "But he only cashed the first check."

My throat tightened. All this time, my grandmother had known who my father was and hadn't told me. I took a deep breath, trying to keep my emotions at bay. "You've been keeping his identity a secret from me. Even if he is a money-grubbing jerk, I had a right to know."

"When you were a child, it wasn't up to me to tell you who he was; it was your mother's."

My nails dug into my palms. "But after that? After she died?"

"You never asked me," she said. "And it's not exactly a conversation one has over the phone."

She had a logical answer for everything. If I was being honest with myself, she'd only been trying to protect me from a distance. And perhaps grandmothers did know best.

She raised a frail hand. I took it in mine. "*Ma chérie*, we both know I'm in the process of dying. I may have a few days. I may have a week. Maybe a month. You have your answers. I got my last confession in before I transition over to the other side. Your mother tore my heart apart when she did what she did," she said with a sob. "I'm sorry I wasn't there for you more. I'm sorry I didn't tell you about your father. I'm sorry for so many things. I need to put the past behind me. Isn't that what you want so we can both move on with peace—not resentment or hate—in our hearts?"

"I'd like that," I said, wiping away my tears.

"Me, too, my love, me, too." Her customarily steady voice shook with vulnerability; I knew she was telling the truth.

I spent the next few weeks with Grand-mère, looking through photo albums and talking about days gone by, and preparing her meals. We'd just finished eating our galettes, which were savory versions of crêpes, when she dabbed her napkin to her lips and said, "I have something else to show you. It's the letter your mother wrote to me before she left this earth."

"She wrote you?" I asked, my heart thumping against my ribs. "Where is it?"

"In my nightstand."

I scrambled over to the other side of the bed and opened the drawer, finding the letter immediately. Water droplets had turned the paper thin in some places—tearstains, either my grandmother's or my mother's.

"Please don't read it out loud," said Grand-mère. "I know each and every word by heart."

Dear Mother,

You and Father were right about everything. I want to be clear for Sophie, but it's impossible through all the pain I've brought onto myself and onto her. Perhaps I should have followed your advice and stayed on my medications. But I never listened to you even when you were right. I should never have taken her from Champvert. It was selfish of me. The money I've received means nothing to me. I spend it on frivolous things and I haven't taken care of my daughter. The truth of the matter is that Sophie takes care of me. I'm a failure—as a woman, as a mother, as a daughter. I'm sorry for all the harsh words we've exchanged over the years. I'm sorry for not listening to you. I've never hated you. I've always loved you. I was just too messed up in the head to see it. Something is wrong with me and I can't fix it. So I'm doing something about it. Please take care of Sophie; she deserves better.

> *All my love,*
> *Céleste*

My breathing slowed down. My mother loved me. She'd left a note. Her death hadn't been my fault, like I'd thought all these years. I held up the letter, waving it, tears streaming down my cheeks. "Of all the secrets you've kept from me over the years, why this one? I thought maybe she did what did because of me. Don't you realize I needed this?"

"Because it hurt too much," said Grand-mère. Like me, she was crying, gasping and wheezing. "I lost her. I couldn't do anything to stop her. By the time her letter arrived, it was too late. She was gone. Please don't be angry with me. All I've ever wanted to do was to protect you from the pain I felt."

"I'm not angry, Grand-mère," I said. "I'm hurt and I'm confused and I'm upset."

"*Ma chérie*, I understand. Please, forgive me."

Forgiveness. Perhaps I would have found out all these truths if I'd come back to Champvert sooner. But I hadn't. And I realized my grand-mère shouldn't be the one asking for forgiveness. It was me. I gripped her hand. "Grand-mère, please forgive *me*."

"For what?"

"For not being here for *you* when you needed me."

"You are here now, *ma chérie*," she said.

MIDNIGHT. I SAT in the window seat, looking up toward the stars, wondering if my mother was up there looking down on me, wondering about the stars I'd always craved. My cell phone buzzed. I looked down at the caller ID, expecting it to be Walter, but it was a text from O'Shea.

> Dug in a little bit more with my foodie spies. Found out Trevor Smith is one of Eric's investors. He's going down. Bad news—the Times isn't going to write my retraction. Good news—they want me to write an op-ed. I've written it and it'll run in a few weeks. Bad news—Eric's restaurant opened to glorious reviews. Good news—Trevor Smith wrote the review. Everything is being sorted out. Think about my offer, Sophie.

I was thinking about his offer, and it pulled my head and my heart in different directions. I bolted to Grand-mère's office and pulled up the review of Blackbird in the *Times*. On the home page, there was a picture of Eric, with the headline: MICHELIN WILL SOON BE KNOCKING ON ERIC ROMANO'S DOOR.

"What the hell?" I said, muttering to myself.

My eyes scanned the page, words jumping off the screen like "two-starred master chef," "culinary masterpiece," and "seasonal seductions." But the slap to the face came when I locked onto the photo of the meal they were raving about. It wasn't Eric's recipe; it was mine, the one for the filets of daurade—every layer of every ingredient I'd used all exactly the same, the garnish complete with edible flowers like lavender. I seethed with anger. There was only one person at the château who could have been responsible for such betrayal, and she'd be returning in one week.

26

---

new york state of mind

I T WAS HARD keeping Rémi at a distance, especially when he smiled at me like a puppy dog waiting for a treat, his hazel eyes shining and expectant, like I'd race into his arms and say, "Rémi, I'm ready. I've had enough time to think. Take me into those strong arms of yours and carry me away!" As much as the notion tempted me, I wasn't ready for a relationship. Far from it.

So I definitely wasn't prepared to find Rémi in the kitchen with Lola, both of them covered in flour, a few days after I'd received O'Shea's text. Lola had a bowl in front of her and she was whisking away—flour and milk splattering on her face, her mouth covered in chocolate.

"What in the world are you doing?" I asked.

"Making crêpes," Rémi said, his voice not overly warm, but not exactly distant. "Today is February second. It's *la Chandeleur*."

"Crêpes, crêpes, crêpes," repeated Lola. "*Miam-miam.*"

"It's another French tradition—like the *galette des rois*—but better," said Rémi by means of explanation. "In addition to being a religious celebration for Catholics, when Jesus was presented at the temple in Jerusalem, it's also France's national crêpe day."

"Stop smiling at me like that," I said, my eyes narrowing into a mock glare.

"Stop staring at me and help us make the crêpes. We're making them for Grand-mère," he said, turning his back to me and whisking the batter. "Ever done a pan flip?"

"Of course," I said. "Just not with a crêpe, but I'm a quick learner." I shoved him on the shoulder and gave him the stink eye. "You do realize I'm a seasoned chef?"

Rémi brushed by me and grabbed a pan. He placed it on a burner, turning the heat up to medium-high. I watched him rub the oil onto the pan. He ladled a spoonful of the batter, lifted it up, and swirled it around, coating every inch. He placed the pan back on the burner.

"The trick is to let the edges turn golden," he said. "Then you take a spatula and lift the edges lightly, like this, see? *Voilà!* Then we flip." He jutted out his arm a few times, the crêpe lifting from the pan. And then he flipped it. "Your turn."

"Oh, I can do this. Easy peasy," I said. I rubbed oil on the pan with a paper towel, as he had. I ladled the mixture, swirled it, and placed the pan on the burner. I waited for the edges to brown, and lifted them. I was ready for the pan flip. "One, two, three," I said. "Flip."

My crêpe didn't land in the pan; it landed on the burner, the flames burning it down into a sticky mess. As I put the pan down, I could feel the blush rushing to my cheeks. Rémi came up behind me, wrapping his arms around me, and my body went still. "Slow, Rémi. I'm still figuring things out."

"I'm trying to help you," he said, pulling me in closer and kissing the nape of my neck.

Damn it. I had no willpower. I wanted to feel his lips on mine. Just as I turned to melt into his embrace, a snooty voice rang in my ears, ruining the moment. "It appears I'm interrupting something."

Jane. Every bone in my body went rigid. I jerked away from Rémi and turned to face her. Her eyes locked onto mine with what I could only describe as a death stare. "We're just making crêpes," I said, throwing my hands up in defense. "When did you return?"

"This morning," said Jane, her steadfast gaze accusatory and unflinching.

"And Phillipa?"

"She's helping my parents unpack. She'll pop by in a bit." Jane regarded Lola with disgust. "Why is there a dirty child covered in chocolate in this kitchen?"

Rémi puffed out his chest proudly. "This is Lola, and she's my daughter."

Jane jolted as if she'd been electrocuted. "What?"

"Are you hard of hearing?" he said. "I said this is Lola, and she's my daughter."

"I'm sorry," said Jane. "I don't know what's going on. Have I fallen into some strange alternate universe?"

It was now or never. "No," I said, straightening my posture, "and I need to have a word with you in Grand-mère's office."

"Brilliant." Jane turned on her kitten heel and stormed off. "Because I'd like to have a word with you, too."

JANE PACED IN the office, her heels clicking on the polished floor. She whipped around to face me, her eyes like steel daggers. "Everything always works out for you, Sophie. Doesn't it?"

"Not really, Jane," I said. "And I need to know why you have such a big problem with me. Why are you trying to ensure my failure? Everything you do or say has one ultimate goal: to bring me down."

Her posture stiffened. She raised her chin so high I could see into her flaring nostrils. "I have no idea what you're talking about."

"I think you do. And I know what you did." I clenched my fists into tight balls, an attempt to keep me from slapping her uppity attitude right out of her. I reminded myself that she was in the wrong and I was in the right. "Why did you send Eric my recipe?"

"Eric? Who is Eric?"

"Right," I said with a snarl. I stepped over to the computer, fired it up, and opened a browser, pulling up the article from the *Times*. "Explain this. Explain why the chef who destroyed me is making his mark with the daurade recipe I created." I stepped away and pointed to the photo.

Her eyes scanned the article and she sank into the chair, her head drooping. "I swear to God, I had nothing to do with this. I'd never do that to your grand-mère or the château."

"But you would do it to me," I said. "Let's face it, we both know you don't want me here. You want me to fail. Why?" I asked, already knowing the reason but wanting to hear it from her thin lips.

Her eyes widened with disbelief, as if she thought I was an idiot. "How do you expect me to feel?" she said. "I've been running things around here for five years and then you just show up—out of the blue. I've been building my life here. You don't deserve to take over."

There was a truth to her statement. I had just shown up. I hadn't worked for any of this. But I did have my pride. My body trembled, but I remained strong.

"That isn't your decision to make," I said. "It's my grand-mère's. She handed over the keys to me on Christmas Eve."

Her posture crumpled. "Just be done with it then. Fire me."

"I told you I didn't know how to run things around here," I said. "Firing you isn't up to me while Grand-mère is still alive." I paused, my voice catching. "Are you going to tell me why you sent Eric the recipe so I can make a decision as to whether I tell her about your betrayal or not? Unless you want to tell her yourself."

"I already told you I didn't do it," she said, placing her hands in her hair, her French twist unraveling. "There has to be another explanation."

I didn't have one. "Like what?"

"As I recall, we had a full house the night you made the daurade dish, half of the guests from New York," said Jane. "Maybe we can cross-check the reservations, see if any names pop out to you. If they don't, I'll Google each and every one of them."

"Do it," I said, my hands on my hips.

Jane tapped the keyboard with her perfectly manicured nails. After a few clicks, she pulled up the names of the guests who had stayed at the château that weekend. I scanned the list and exhaled a deep breath.

"You see something?" asked Jane.

"Yep," I said, not believing my eyes.

"Who?"

"Trevor Smith, freelance critic for the *Times*," I said. "His palate knows food, he wrote the article praising Eric's restaurant, and he's also the one who destroyed my reputation by printing a story when he didn't have all the facts."

Jane pulled up a browser and ran a quick search. "I thought food critics were supposed to be anonymous, but here he is, right on Google Images. And you'll never guess who he's with."

I didn't have to guess when I already knew. "Eric."

"I recognize this Trevor," said Jane, pointing at the screen. "He was the guy who was talking about you."

Back then, I didn't make the connection, figuring it was a coincidence, and the news of Cendrillon hadn't yet fizzled down. "Eric must have sent him," I said under my breath. "He needed to poach my recipes because he's the zero with no talent. He doesn't know how to create recipes, he only knows how to follow them," I said. "That's why he wanted me to come work for him."

"Yes, Phillipa told me about that, but why was this Trevor Smith here? It doesn't make sense," said Jane. She clicked though a few more articles. "*Et voilà*. Found it. He was covering the wedding for some social magazine," she said, pointing.

"His article doesn't even mention the food or the château," I said, reading it quickly.

"You have your answer," she said. Jane's eyes met mine. "But I don't have mine. What are you going to do with me?"

I didn't respond at first. My brain was churning like a crazed hamster on a wheel. Although I didn't trust Jane, I did need her until I figured out what I was going to do. She looked at me expectantly, cheeks sucked in, mouth puckered.

"Grand-mère told me you were very efficient. I'm going to respect her wishes."

I could have sworn I heard her mutter, "Respect is earned, not given." Oh, the things I wanted to say to her, but didn't. I clamped my mouth shut.

Phillipa bounded into the room. She gave me an exuberant hug. "Rémi told me the two of you were in here. What's going on? What did I miss, aside from the fact that he has an adorable daughter, Lola? Did you know about her? Where is her mum?"

"I know about her now," I said. "She's a really sweet little girl. And her mother died in childbirth."

"I hope you and Rémi will be happy together," said Jane stiffly, cutting off Phillipa.

"We're not a couple," I said.

"But you will be," she said. "Or did I imagine what I saw in the kitchen?"

Phillipa slugged my arm. "What happened in the kitchen?"

"Nothing," I said.

"Nothing?" said Jane with a snort. She raised a defiant and perfectly manicured eyebrow. Phillipa's eyes went wide with anticipation.

I let out an embarrassed sigh. "Fine, we almost kissed."

The almost kiss I wanted to share with Rémi, but then Jane ruined it with her unexpected interruption.

"Love is in the air!" Phillipa squealed. "I knew something about him had changed. He smiled at me, and he never smiles."

"Whoa, whoa, whoa, we're taking things slow," I said.

"Slow? Good luck with that," she said, raising her hands like claws and squeezing her fingers, making the perky butt motion. "Straight people and their wacky issues. No wonder I'm queer. So, tell me about this almost kiss."

"It was nothing." I cleared my throat, quickly changing the subject under Jane's wicked glare. "Apparently, somebody in this room sent O'Shea an anonymous letter. He dug into it and found out the truth. He wants to destroy Eric," I said with a grin. "Karma *is* a bitch and her name is Phillipa. Thank you."

"Oh my God," she said. "That's incredible! Your name has been cleared!"

"Not yet, but he's working on it, thanks to you."

"Brilliant," said Jane, eyeing me hopefully. "Are you thinking about going back to New York?"

"O'Shea offered me the chef de cuisine position," I said. "Honestly, I don't know what to do."

"Unless you are committed to your life here, you should seriously think about taking him up on his offer," said Jane. Her expression said what her mouth didn't say: I'll push you upstairs, help you pack, and drive you to the airport.

Phillipa stomped her foot with defiance. "What in sod's sake? I only wanted to help you clear your name so you'd stay on at the château, not leave it, Sophie. You can't be thinking about going back to New York. Because you can't," she said, racing out of the room. "I'm not happy for you anymore, I'm bloody livid."

I stood shell-shocked, considering my options. I wanted to run after Phillipa to explain my feelings to her, the confusion swirling in my head, but I was rendered immobile.

"Don't worry," said Jane. "She'll get over it."

"I won't."

I turned around to find Rémi standing in the doorway with Lola in his arms. "What's this about New York?"

27

confidence and creation

WITH THE ADDED STRESS OF Grand-mère's health taking a turn for the worse, the next few weeks were beyond uncomfortable. If, for some reason, Rémi and I found ourselves standing in front of one another, he'd ask with a hopeful look in his eyes, "Have you made a decision?" and I'd shrug.

"Until you know what you want, I'm giving you your space," he'd say and saunter away.

One morning, on my way back from the river, where I often went to think and get away, even with the *pies bavardes* taunting me with their loud *chac-chac-chacs*, I ran into him. I had a question, one that would aid me in the decision-making process. Rémi was about to turn on his heel, but I grabbed his arm. "Do you, by chance, know a Jean-Marc Bourret?" I asked.

His face pinched with confusion. "The mechanic in Sauqueuse? What about him? Of all people, why are you bringing up his name?" Rémi pressed his palms to his forehead. "There's something going on—something you're not telling me. I can tell. You're acting all twitchy."

I couldn't stop the words before they leapt out of my mouth. "I think he may be my father."

Rémi's hazel eyes, the concern darkening them, told me all I needed to know about his feelings for me. "How did you learn of this?"

"Grand-mère and I have been talking about my mother, Rémi. She has a diary. And, until I fully understand what I've learned in it, I need for you to understand that I'm not ready for a relationship— with anyone. I need to figure myself out first."

"Why didn't you tell me this before?" he asked.

"Because it's something I need to come to terms with on my own."

"Sophie, you can't just bottle up your feelings inside. You'll explode," he said. "I know. Because it's what I did."

His concern was enough to crack my wavering control, and I burst into tears. Through gasps and sobs, I told him everything. When I got to the part about Grand-mère paying off Jean-Marc Bourret, his eyes narrowed. "Do you want to meet your father?"

"One day," I said. "But I need to be ready. And I'm just not ready now."

I took Rémi's hands into my own, feeling the warmth. His hands were rough and calloused, and so large they dwarfed mine, but they were gentle and his fingernails were trimmed and manicured. He stroked the knuckle of my index finger with his thumb, easing the tension and anxiety sparking my body.

"I understand, Sophie," he said. "And, regardless of what happens between us, I want you to stay in Champvert, so I hope you find your answers."

A BIT SCATTERED, I was in the process of planning the Valentine's Day menu when Phillipa placed her hand on my shoulder. "You're here in the kitchen. That's a good sign, right?" she asked with hope.

I hung my head. "I guess. And I have a question. If somebody offered you your dream, one you worked so hard for, what would you do?"

"I'd reconsider my dreams, because they can change with the wind," she said. "Look, your life isn't so bad in Champvert, is it?"

"No, aside from Grand-mère's health, it's mostly been great," I said. "But I don't know jack shit about running a château. It's kind of a lot to take on. I'm kind of missing my life in New York."

"I get that, but you have me. I'm here for you. Let's go through the pros and cons. What about friends in New York? Did you have a lot of them?"

God, I was going to sound pathetic. I didn't have one friend in the brigade, never did. Miguel was friendly enough, but he worked under me. At least he had confessed about Eric sabotaging me. Monica dumped me the first chance she got, but she didn't even live in New York. "Two. Just Walter and Robert. Funny, I guess I have more friends here. You, Clothilde, Bernard, Gustave . . . and Rémi when he's speaking to me."

"So, let me get this straight. You were in New York for most of your life, and in four months here, you have more friends, and maybe a more satisfying life?"

"Yes," I said. "Maybe. But every time something good happens, it seems something bad is waiting for me around the corner."

"That's called life," said Phillipa. "And we need you in ours." She blinked. "Tell me what you like about Champvert and the château."

I thought about it.

"I love the greenhouse. I love being able to invent meals and getting my crazy on during the process. I like the idea of running this kitchen but wonder if I can handle it. I love the changes in the seasons and cooking with fresh produce. I love the sounds of the river flowing and the birds singing. I love the team here. I'd like the chance to tell my story—"

"And what do you like about New York?"

"I love Walter and Robert, but I'd have to find a new place to live. I love the buildings and architecture, but I don't like the pollution or the noise, O'Shea's temper, the long hours. The sexual harassment in the kitchen is annoying, but I can deal with it."

"Do you realize everything you've said about New York is kind of negative?"

Phillipa was right. I'd been so wrapped up in my career and all the drama, I'd lost sight of the things truly making me happy.

"Yeah, I guess you're right," I said.

"Then what's stopping you from grabbing on to the reins here?"

"My pride, I guess," I said. "Everything is being given to me. I didn't work for it."

"I suggest you get over your pride and get to work," she said. "Prove to yourself you deserve it, because I think you do. You need to believe in yourself."

If anything, cooking would help me sort out my thoughts, my scrambled emotions. And if there ever was a time for experimentation, to let my cooking flag fly, it was now, and right when I needed it most. "Let's get crazy, wild, and inventive this weekend."

Phillipa raised her hands with joy. "Yes! I believe I've convinced you to stay on in Champvert." She looked at me expectantly, her hands on her skinny hips.

"You were pretty convincing," I said, and she let out a whoop. I bit down on my lip, hating to lie to her. Truth be told, I didn't know what I was going to do. One thing was for sure, I wasn't abandoning the ship just yet. "Let's take it one meal at a time."

She made a goofy face, nose and lips scrunched. "Slow, right. Gotcha. That's gonna work."

"I need all hands on deck in the kitchen tonight to ensure success," I said, brushing her comment off. "Is there anybody we can call in?"

"Sébastien," she said. "And I'm on it." Phillipa raced to the phone.

Jane walked into the kitchen carrying a basket of herbs—mostly mint, fresh and peppery. She set her basket down and placed her hands on her hips. She glanced at the board. "Where's the menu? It's almost two, and I'll need to print them up."

"Tonight's meal wouldn't be complete without chocolate," I said. At the moment, my feelings were hot and cold, sweet, spicy, bitter, and sour. I wanted to balance flavors, taming them into tasteful submission, and give the guests an unexpected gastronomic experience.

Whatever happed at the château, whatever happened with my grandmother, whatever my decision, I was going to tell my story while I had the chance. Pleased with what I'd come up with, I darted to the board, grabbed a piece of chalk, and wrote it down.

MENU

L'AMUSE-BOUCHE
Chocolate Parmesan Tapioca with a Pan-Seared Scallop

L'ENTRÉE
Salad with Chèvre Chaud, Honey, and Mint Dressing

OU

Roasted Butternut Squash and Cacao Soup

OU

Oysters with a Mignonette Sauce

LE PLAT PRINCIPAL

Armagnac-and-Chocolate-Infused Daube de Bœuf à la Gascogne

OU

Sweet Potato Curry with Mussels

OU

Chocolate Pasta with a Gorgonzola Cheese Sauce

LA SALADE ET LE FROMAGE

Moules à la Plancha with Chorizo served over a bed of Arugula

Selection of the Château's Cheeses

LE DESSERT

Mousse au Chocolat spiced with Pimento Chili Peppers and Chocolate Flakes, garnished with Mint

I spun around on one heel, excited to get prepping. Unbeknownst to me, the rest of the kitchen staff had arrived, their jaws agape as they stared at the menu. As usual, Phillipa was the first to speak up. "That menu looks wicked incredible."

"I don't know about adding hot peppers to the *mousse au chocolat*," said Jane, and the granny brigade nodded in agreement.

I was so sick of her know-it-all attitude. I knew a thing or two and I was going to stand by my decision. "The combination has Aztec roots. To honor the fertility goddess they drank *xocolāt*, a chocolate concoction spiced with chili pepper and vanilla. It's delicious and unexpected."

Jane rolled her eyes. "You're the chef."

"I am," I said, wanting to challenge her. "And this is the menu."

"I think the hot peppers sound interesting," said Gustave. "But the recipe is missing something."

"Alcohol?" I asked knowingly, and he nodded. "Add in a bit of cognac."

"Can I do something interesting with the chocolate shards? And what about a little bit of pear?"

"*Bien sûr.* Desserts are your specialty." I chalked his additions onto the board and then wiped my hands on my apron. "The menu is set."

I turned to Sébastien. "I heard you'd like to move from the waitstaff to the kitchen. Is this true?"

"Yes, madame," he said, his eyelashes lowered. "I've been cooking my entire life."

"How old are you?"

"Eighteen."

"The same age I was when I started cooking school," I said. He had a cherubic face, slender hands, and sensitive eyes, and I couldn't help but think how the brigade at Cendrillon would have chewed him up and spit him right out. I'd have to toughen him up. "But schools aren't the real learning arenas, right, Phillipa?"

"Amen!" she said. She put her hands together toward the sky.

Choking back my laughter, I turned to Sébastien. "Have you ever used a plancha?"

"I'm half Spanish. *Mon nom de famille* is Rodriguez," he said with fierce pride. "I can cook using a plancha blindfolded. And please, call me Séb. All my friends do."

I liked his attitude. "Ready to prep, Séb?" I asked.

"Yes, Chef!"

As he darted off to his station, Rémi snuck up from behind me and whispered, "I understand your concept for the meal."

"You do? Am I that transparent?"

"Don't get me wrong, she loves to cook and cooks with love, but Grand-mère doesn't cook with her emotions. The sugar, the chocolate, and the pears. All sweet. Maybe your feelings for me? Or am I being presumptuous?"

"You're not." I turned to face him. "Go on."

"Sour, bitter, and hot. It's the worry you're feeling for Grand-mère."

"And her ingredients?"

"Vinegar, arugula, hot peppers—a few more."

"I guess you have me all figured out," I said.

His hand ran up my back, quickly. "No, not at all. But I want to."

"Rémi, like the recipes I'm making tonight, it's all about creating the perfect balance."

His mouth came close to my ear. "Which is what we're going to have if you stay in Champvert." I froze. "Sophie, you've gone quiet."

"I'm thinking," I said.

As I looked into his eyes, New York, the stars, and making my mark as the comeback chef faded from my desires. I had everything I needed in Champvert, including the possibility of falling in love.

RIGHT BEFORE SERVICE, Jane tapped me on the shoulder. "The guests want to meet the chef."

"Are you sure that's a good idea?"

Jane lifted a well-shaped eyebrow. "It's a tradition at the château, and it's now or never. And that's the truth."

The truth.

The truth was, I loved every moment in this kitchen. And I loved to be able to talk to somebody openly about extremely personal issues and to have them share their problems with me. I loved every second my heart beat. I loved the feeling of falling in love. Because, with my heart closed off to everything but the kitchen, I'd never really felt it before. My confidence was back.

"Let's go," I said.

One careful footstep at a time, I followed Jane to the dining room, which gleamed in silvers and whites. Jane grabbed my hand and we stood in the doorway, me willing my heart to stop racing and surveying the room. Wildflowers and fresh herbs from the château's gardens surrounded the white roses on the tables. Jane had outdone herself, celebrating the changing season.

Perhaps I'd misjudged her as much as she'd misjudged me.

"I'd like to present our wonderful chef at Les Libellules here at Château de Champvert," Jane exclaimed, ushering me in. In that moment, with her words not speckled with sarcasm, I knew I'd gained at least one ounce of Jane's respect, and after seeing what she'd accomplished, she had at least two ounces of mine.

The sound of applause thundered in my ears. I brought my hands to my wildly beating heart, not knowing what to say. I closed my eyes, thinking of my grand-mère. "My grand-mère taught me that meals are supposed to be cooked with love, each ingredient celebrating this exquisite emotion. Tonight, we are celebrating love, are we not? And it's my greatest hope you'll love what we've prepared for you. *Toujours l'amour. Encore l'amour*," I said. "*Merci*."

Forks and spoons clanged on glasses.

THE NEXT FOUR hours were frenetic and fast-paced. Séb, now a chef and our caller, remained calm and cool as he belted out the orders *and* managed his station. The air in the kitchen was so electric, even the granny brigade and Gustave stuck around to see how the service went. During dessert, Jane returned to the kitchen.

"I think it would be a good idea if you came into the dining room again," she said.

My heart raced. "Is there a problem?"

"Quite the opposite," she said.

"Everybody, follow me," I said. "We're a team here."

"Yes, Chef."

Before entering the room, I snuck a quick peek and watched the guests' faces as they cracked the chocolate dragonfly and dipped their spoons in the spiced chocolate mousse with cognac-drunk pears. The sounds of pleasure filled the room. Séb, Phillipa, the granny brigade, Clothilde, and Gustave followed me in and we stood in front of the fireplace. "Ladies and gentlemen," I said. "I'd like to introduce you to all of the people responsible for creating tonight's meal—my family."

If I thought the applause I'd heard earlier was loud, this time the sound reverberated in my chest, so powerful it felt like an earthquake.

"Best meal I've ever had in my life."

"You cook with your heart."

"I feel love in every delicious bite."

"Worthy of not one Michelin star, but three."

I lowered my head and placed my hand on my beating heart, thanking my lucky stars and Grand-mère, whose presence I could feel embracing me. If I took O'Shea up on his offer, my dream of becoming one of the one percent of female chefs running a Michelin-starred restaurant would come to fruition in the blink of an eye, but I'd be back to telling O'Shea's story and following his rules. Grand-mère had said I could reach for the stars here.

Did I dare become a rule breaker?

Yes.

Forget about Eric. Forget about New York and Cendrillon. I felt more alive and at home in Champvert. This girl was finally going to rise from the ashes like a culinary phoenix. For the love of cooking, I had the chance to create and the chance to reclaim a passion I'd lost somewhere along the way. I had a chance to tell *my* story. I was happier in Champvert than I'd been in a long while. Not only did I have a kitchen, I had a chance at love.

It was in that moment I truly understood how far people go to achieve success and just how far they go to protect the ones they love. I forgave my mother, I forgave my grandmother, and, most important, I forgave myself. I had closure. In a way, my grandmother had given me my life back, and I was going to claim it. After the applause died down, I raced to Grand-mère's room and tapped on the door. Agnès opened it.

"Is she awake?" I asked.

"Yes, why? Is something wrong?"

"No, Agnès, everything is all right. More than right." I twirled her around and scurried over to my grand-mère.

"I've made my decision. I'm not going back to New York. I'm staying in Champvert. For good," I said, taking her hands.

Grand-mère tried her best to smile. "Oh, I was so hoping to hear those words. I couldn't imagine what the vultures would do if you sold the estate. They'd probably turn the grounds into one of those horrendous theme parks." Her green eyes went clear as she took my hand. "You've given a dying woman her greatest wish."

"For me to take over the château?"

"Non, *ma chérie*, my only wish was to see my granddaughter take charge of her happiness. It's the only thing I've ever wanted for you."

III

spring

At home I serve the kind of food
I know the story behind.

—MICHAEL POLLAN

28

famous for being infamous

SPRING, THE SEASON of renewal and new beginnings, had sprung in all her glory one month early. Everything was coming back to life and thriving—including me. In the morning, I sprinted over to Rémi's home, eyeing the bushes for *les sangliers*. I couldn't wait to tell him of my decision. Breathless, I knocked on the door, and Laetitia, after a second or two, opened it, smiling a wide, toothy grin. "Sophie, it's wonderful to see you, but are you okay?"

"I'm fine. I just ran over from the château," I said, panting and placing my hands on my knees. "Is Rémi here?"

"Yes," she said. "He's upstairs getting Lola ready for the day. Come in, have a seat on the couch. I was just making coffee. Would you like one?"

I nodded, although with my heart racing like it was, maybe it wasn't a good idea. Laetitia headed over to the Nespresso and plunked a capsule into the machine. In less than sixty seconds, both of us had coffee in hand.

"I'm sorry you didn't know I was Lola's grand-mère," she said. "I'm sure it was quite the shock."

"In a way, it was," I said.

"Don't get me wrong, I miss my daughter every day, but I always knew the truth. She didn't love him. He didn't love her. But they did the right thing by Lola."

I gulped. "What was Anaïs like?"

"Stubborn. Full of life. A bit of a party girl. I could never keep track of her," she said, smiling with remembrance. "She was like me, back in my wild days in the eighties."

"And your husband?"

"Let's just say Anaïs was a lot like me, but her father didn't do the right thing."

"Oh," I said.

"Yes, but I don't hold him any ill will. We were young and foolish and sometimes things just aren't meant to be," she said. "Am I making you uncomfortable?"

"No," I said. "You're refreshing. You're speaking your mind, telling personal things to a stranger."

"But you're not exactly a stranger to me. Rémi has told me much about you."

I couldn't help but think of my own father. "Was Anaïs's father's name Jean-Marc Bourret?"

Laetitia laughed. "No, his name was Armand. Rémi told me you were searching for your father." She paused. "If you do approach him, make sure you're prepared, because he might not want to have a thing to do with you. Sadly, that was what happened when Anaïs confronted hers."

I shuddered. I don't know what bothered me more. Her warning or the fact that Rémi had told her all about me. Then again, I couldn't really blame Rémi. Who else was he going to confide in?

Lola scurried down the stairs on her knees—one at a time. Her eyes lit up when she saw me. "*Tatie* Sophie!" She ran up and flung her strawberry-scented body onto mine like a miniature linebacker, but one wearing a pink tutu and tights. "*Chocolat chaud*?"

Laetitia scooped her up. "No, my darling, not now," she said. "But maybe *Tatie* Sophie will make you one when we return from ballet class." She winked at me. "I'm taking the tiny dancer. You and Rémi will talk. *Voilà*. I'm off."

Before I could blink, Laetitia and Lola left, and Rémi sauntered downstairs, his eyes widening in surprise when he saw me. "What are you doing here?"

"Who, me?" I asked.

"Yes, you," he said, crossing his arms over his chest.

"Well, I-I-I wanted to tell you that I'm sticking around," I said, stuttering. "For g-good."

His eyebrows raised curiously or accusingly. I couldn't tell. "What about your stars?" he asked.

"I'm tired of chasing them. Maybe they'll come to me?" I said. "Plus, like you said, we have plenty of stars here, the sky fuller and clearer than in New York. We'll lie on our backs and look up at them tonight."

My last statement brought a smile to Rémi's formerly stoic expression. He tilted his head to the side. "You're not going back to New York?"

"I'm not."

"Does your decision have anything to do with me?"

"Maybe," I said.

"Maybe?" he asked.

I straightened my posture and took a deep breath. I could open myself up to him instead of pushing him away. I was ready to take the risk, to put everything, put my heart, on the line. My shoulders trembled. "Fine. It has a lot to do with you. I want to give us a chance. I know what I want now. Can you forgive me?"

"For what? Being scared? Being human?" His voice came out so strong I thought he was going to lay into me for being such an indecisive twit when I had everything I wanted right in my grasp.

"Yes," I said, lowering my head. I rocked back and forth on my heels. "So, is there still a chance?"

"For what?" he asked, and my heart catapulted into my stomach.

My gaze leapt to his. "For us?" I said, my voice rising. "Isn't that what you want?"

He went silent for a moment, watching me wring my hands and fidget. He took a step forward. I took a step back. He took another step forward, a wild look in his eyes. I didn't know what was going on, his movements and his expression intense. I took another step back and Remi followed. He took me in his arms and we shared an out-of-this-world kiss, me exploring each ripple of his back, him with his hands in my hair, pulling me closer. When we finally broke apart, we were both panting and wide-eyed. Breathless with lust and the heart palpitations of the beginnings of love, I said, "You didn't answer my question."

"Ah, *mais oui*, Sophie, I believe I did," he said, a seductive grin twisting his lips. "And I'd really like to answer your question again."

My knees went weak and I fell into his embrace, his muscled arms wrapped around me.

PHILLIPA AND JANE waited for me in the salon. Floating on a cloud of happiness, I meandered into the room in a state of complete euphoria. Phillipa pointed to a bouquet of roses, at least two dozen of them. "Somebody sent you these. Maybe lover boy?"

"Rémi and I are still moving slow," I said, and Phillipa rolled her eyes dramatically. Blushing, I snatched the envelope from her hands and ripped it open.

The flowers are from Miguel. I hope you enjoy the gift I've enclosed and that you are still thinking about my offer. O'Shea

"Where is the box the flowers were delivered in?" I asked.

Phillipa pointed to the bar. The card fell to the floor as I raced over and pulled out a copy of the *Times* magazine from the bottom of the box, gasping so hard I started to hiccup. O'Shea was featured on the cover and almost every article in its glossy pages was dedicated to the food world. I flipped to his piece on fearless female chefs, where he not only wrote about what happened at Cendrillon, he destroyed Eric and Trevor Smith in the process.

I thumbed through the pages.

Chefs, most of them female, wrote the other articles with headlines like "Misogyny in the Kitchen," "Michelin Can Take Its Star Back," and "Why There Is a Lack of Female Chefs." It was as if the entire cooking world had leapt to my defense.

"What's going on?" asked Jane.

I waved the magazine triumphantly over my head. In between excited hiccups, I said, "My name has been cleared and then some."

Phillipa picked up the card off the floor and read it, her lips mouthing the words. "Bloody hell! You better not be thinking of going back to New York," she said.

I wrapped my arms around her. "I'm not going. I'm staying here, right here where I belong."

Her head twisted to the side and she shot me a wicked smile. "So, since you're not taking up O'Shea on his offer, don't you think it might be a good idea to tell him?" asked Phillipa. "Like right now?"

"Yes," I said. "It is."

I pulled out my phone. "It's too early to call him. It's two-thirty in the morning in New York."

"Text him," said Jane.

"Yes, we need to see it with our own eyes," said Phillipa. "At least I do."

Chef—Thank you for clearing my name. Thank you so much for everything. While I appreciate your offer, I unfortunately can't accept it. My grand-mère's health is in decline and I'm taking over her kitchen at Château de Champvert. I finally have the chance to tell my story. I hope you understand. The best of wishes, Sophie. P.S. If you ever find yourself in France, please visit Champvert and we'll take care of you!

Within seconds, my phone buzzed with a response from O'Shea.

Sophie, I understand. And I'm very proud of you. You are going to light the cooking world on fire. And I will take you up on your offer . . .

Phillipa sandwiched me in a hug.

"Is it too early to celebrate?" I asked.

"It's never too early for champagne," said Jane. "I'll pop open a bottle."

MY MUSCLES DIDN'T want to listen to my mind. For at least five minutes, maybe more, I stood in front of the carved oak door of my grandmother's quarters tracing the acorns ingrained in the wood. My arm raised, my hand balled up ready to knock. Inside, I could hear her rustling around. Suddenly, the door opened, and I clamped my jaw shut.

Grand-mère Odette's hair was coiffed. She wore a beige Chanel pantsuit with matching ballet flats. Her cheeks were tinged rose. Her wheelchair was pushed to the far side of her room. "Sophie, *ma chérie*, why are you just standing there gawking at me like that?"

"You're up?" I said, stating the obvious.

"Yes, I was feeling better and thought I'd head to the kitchen to see what you were up to."

"She should really stay in bed," said Agnès. "But she won't listen to me."

Grand-mère ignored Agnès and latched her arm onto mine. "Would you please tell that woman that this is my house and I'm not dead yet."

I shot Agnès an apologetic look over my shoulder as we made our way down the hall.

"The château opens in a month and I'd love to hear all about your plans," she said. "Just make sure you share a joyful tale—I think we've had enough pain and sadness around here to last us a lifetime."

"I agree," I said.

Slowly, we walked into the salon to find Clothilde and Phillipa sitting on the settee, and Jane pacing. Jane whipped around. "The reservation system crashed last night," she said with a screech. "O'Shea's article mentioned Grand-mère Odette and the château, along with the name Jean-Jacques Gaston. Who is he?"

"He was O'Shea's mentor," I said.

"He was also a professor of mine at Le Cordon Bleu," said Grand-mère. "And he's a very famous chef now."

I'd only skimmed the article, locking onto the bits about me, Eric, and Trevor, and hadn't read it fully. "Why is this a problem?"

"Jean-Jacques Gaston wrote about how Grand-mère was one of the most talented chefs he'd ever encountered and that, if she'd learned how to cook from her, her granddaughter—that's you, Sophie—would be just as magical, too. He even went as far as to see he recommended you for your *stage* at Cendrillon."

I knew that from the emails I'd found. "Jane, slow down, what's going on?"

"We're booked solid from May first of this year to the end of the season. And because the reservation system is blocked, emails demanding requests have been pouring in." She gave me the once-over. "A member of La Société des Châteaux et Belles Demeures will be visiting with us soon."

"Your comeback is the biggest thing out there. Everybody wants a piece of you," said Phillipa.

Jane cleared her throat. "I'm afraid it's more serious than that," she said. "Since word has gotten out that Sophie is now the chef here and Grand-mère is ill, they want to make sure everything is up to par. It's an audit."

Part of me had to accuse Jane. "Did you have something to do with this?"

"So we're moving backward instead of forward now?" she asked, raising her hands in surrender. "I thought we were in the process of getting over our differences. Believe me, I'm not out to sabotage you, Sophie."

"Do you blame her?" asked Phillipa. "You've been nothing but cruel to her."

Jane twisted her head to the side, nostrils flaring. "How dare you take her side. You're my sister."

"Really?" said Phillipa. "Because you don't act like one. You hoity-toity snob."

"Ladies," yelled Grand-mère. "*Ça suffit!*" (Enough!) "There is no sense in arguing among yourselves when you're going to have to work together." She pointed to the magazine. "I think the audit might have something to do with that."

The room fell silent, all of us shocked with the force of Grand-mère's voice. I slumped onto the settee, feeling the color rushing out of my cheeks. I rubbed my temples in disbelief. "This can't be happening."

"Unforunately, it is," said Jane as she paced, wringing her hands. "What if I fail?"

"Then the château will lose its status . . . and a lot of business," said Jane, her eyes panicked. "Plus, we pay lofty membership fees, which won't be reimbursed."

"Not only will they be looking at you to take over my reign as Grand Chef, you'll also become the *maîtresse de maison*," said Grand-mère. "You'll have to know every nook and cranny of the château, its history, its wine, its tenets and values, and share your knowledge with the guests."

"What do I do?"

"Do what we know you can do. Prepare memorable meals and share your heart. And don't forget everything must be linked to the château, its history, and the terroir," said my grand-mère.

"But you're not feeling well," I said. "Who is going to teach me everything there is to know about the château? I can't do this on my own."

"I'll help you," said Jane.

I recoiled. "You?"

"I know we haven't exactly gotten along," said Jane, "but this château is my life, and I, for one, won't let Grand-mère down. We have to rise to the occasion together."

I bit down on my bottom lip, concerned about the visitor coming from La Société des Châteaux et Belles Demeures. If they didn't like the new management, me, or the new Grand Chef, also me, this entity could destroy the château's reputation. I'd already experienced my name being dragged through the mud; I hoped it wouldn't happen again. My only hope of succeeding hinged on trusting Jane's guidance when I didn't fully trust her.

29

hopping into the flames

SINCE I'D COMMITTED to this new life in Champvert, there was no turning back, no changing my mind, and I had less than two months to learn everything about the château inside and out. I'd ventured out early to enjoy the peace and beauty of the morning. The sun was just rising, and the vineyard sprawled before me, lit with an unearthly light. Bernard ambled up to me. He stood silent, taking in and breathing in the moment with me. The vines sparkled, glistening with buttery yellow drop, the canes coming to life before my eyes.

"We just pruned the vines so their productive life is lengthened. It's vital for the upcoming season," he said. "The magnificent miracle of nature you're looking at right now is called the weeping of the vines, or teardrops, when the vine's sap flows upward from the trunk and drips from the cuts of the fruiting canes. It only lasts for one or two days."

There had been many moments when I'd felt I'd come back to life in Champvert. And many moments when I'd wished I could hibernate forever.

"It's beautiful," I said wistfully.

Jane marched up to us like a drill sergeant. She wore khaki pants and a matching jacket, clipboard in one hand, a wicker basket filled with bottles of wine in the other. "How many bottles does the château produce each year?" she asked.

"I have no clue," I said.

"You need to know. You need to know everything." She handed me a set of printouts from a folder. "Study this. I'll quiz you tomorrow."

One by one, Jane placed seven bottles on an oak barrel. In between the iron rings holding the barrel together, spilled wine stained the oak, the residue coloring the wood an earthy red. The side of the barrel was etched with the château's logo, a dragonfly, and the name, Château de Champvert. Bernard meticulously opened the bottles one at a time.

"We have five different kinds of grape varieties for the whites, the terroir friendly to the Loin de l'Oeil, Muscadelle, Sauvignon Blanc, and Mauzac varieties," said Bernard. "For the reds, the terroir is favorable to Merlot, Cabernet Franc, Cabernet Sauvignon, Braucol, Duras, and Syrah grapes."

I knew enough about wine, having worked in a Michelin restaurant, and I knew how to pair wine with food, but I didn't know about the grapes themselves.

"We cultivate three whites—one semisweet, one dry, and one sweet—three reds, and one sparkling using *la méthode ancestrale*, our version of champagne, but because we're not located in the Champagne region it can't be considered as such. Semantics. Per French laws, our wines are geographically tied into our terroir."

He poured me a glass. "This is the 1984 Gaillac dry white. Hold it up to your nose. What do you smell?"

"A clean and sweet scent?"

He nodded. "Now this wine is comprised of forty percent Mauzac, thirty-five percent Loin de l'Oeil, and twenty-five percent Muscadelle grapes. *Goûte-le maintenant*" (Taste it now), he said. And I did. "*Et alors? Dis-moi.* What flavors tickle your taste buds?"

With my palate and mind somewhat clear, I savored the sip. "Apples. A creamy texture, but a dry finish. Wonderful acidity, not too strong. Fresh and clean. Lovely."

"You'll make a fine vintner one day." Bernard beamed from ear to ear. "This mélange of *cépages* was your grandfather's first in 1973. And over the years, it just got better and better. We have bottles from every year since the winemaking began in *la cave*. Thousands of bottles. Your grandfather was a genius. I learned everything I know about winemaking from him."

After tasting all of the *cépages*, Bernard excused himself, and Jane handed me another set of printouts. "Here are the tasting notes. You did well, but missed a few key elements."

"Let me guess," I said. "I have to study. And you'll be quizzing me tomorrow."

She jutted out a hip. "Sophie, I'll be quizzing you every day. This visit isn't a joke. Grand-mère wasn't kidding that you have to know everything about the château."

My hands flew to my eyes, covering them. "I know. And I'm freaking out."

"You have to remain cool, calm, and collected. Ready for your next lesson?" she asked, and I nodded. "When you meet them, you'll have to address each and every guest," she said. "By name."

"How on earth do you do that?"

"It's a little trick and part of the château experience," she said. "People are always impressed when you address them by name. First, the porter sneaks a peek at their luggage tags. He calls me up with a walkie-talkie before they get to the front door. I open it and say welcome to Château de Champvert, introduce myself, and ask them if they have any special requirements and if they are celebrating any special occasions like an anniversary or birthday. When I check them in, I quickly note everything down in the computer. If we have a birthday or an anniversary, we usually comp a bottle of the ancestral-method sparkling wine and dessert."

"Okay," I said. "But how do you remember them after the first introduction?"

"I focus on unique features," she said, shrugging. "Sometimes I make up strange little expressions. Like Monsieur LeBlanc with the *moustache blanche*. He's the one you'll have to keep your eye out for."

"The auditor?"

"Yes, and don't worry, I'll take special care to point him out to you, as well as all the other VIPs."

My mind boiled with information overload. I had to approach this immersion like one of the lame jokes Walter and Robert had told me when they were trying to cheer me up.

"How do you eat an elephant?" he'd asked, and I'd shrugged. "One bite at a time."

"Jane, just to let you know, I'm really serious about this," I said.

She placed her hands on my shoulders. "I know you are. And I'm going to do everything in my power to help you through this."

"And I'm thankful for your help," I said. "Really, this château wouldn't run without you."

"Or you," she said. I swear a smile crossed her lips before she turned serious again. "On to the next lesson?"

We didn't need words to apologize to one another. Earning respect, as I learned that morning, was a two-way street, and bygones were bygones.

ASIDE FROM STEALING the occasional kiss, I didn't see much of Rémi, save for when we visited Grand-mère together with Lola. I was in total immersion, learning about everything the château offered—from the honey production to the *confitures* right down to the history of the château, which Grand-mère enlightened me on.

"Napoléon Bonaparte himself bestowed your great-great-grand-père with his title in 1813. Back then the titles were used to distinguish the nobility from the middle class, just after the French Revolution. Your great-grand-père was a magistrate—*noblesse de robe*—and originally came from Paris where he served in the *parlement*," she said.

"Was the château affected by the war?" I asked.

"We were all affected by the second world war," said Grand-mère with a pained breath. "I was just a young girl of three when the Germans took over our home in Bordeaux. Before they arrived in 1940, I remember my parents hiding everything of value," she said.

"Under the floorboards," I said.

"*Exactement*," she said. "*Alors*, the Germans had no interest in taking over our home, but they did have interest in our wine. They looted the cellar, taking every last bottle. Times were tough. Food was rationed and it was scarce. I remember my father talking to my mother about moving us to America. As you know, he was in the shipping business. Unfortunately, the Germans had taken over the port and there was no way to escape from their strong grip."

"Wow," I said, clasping her hand.

"It was in 1942 when some of the surrounding areas of Toulouse came under direct German rule. Your grand-père and his parents weren't forced off the property when the Germans took over the château, but were asked not so politely to move into the clock tower," she said. "Pierre was around twenty then. He joined the Resistance— a dangerous thing to do with the Germans a breath away, but he wanted to fight for his home and his country. I don't know the details of what he did, since Pierre didn't like to discuss this troubling time, as many of us don't, but I'll never forget the day when all of France was liberated in 1944. There was a grand celebration at Place du Capitole in Toulouse; I was seven years old. When we married, Pierre told me the Germans left the château in near ruin."

Compared to what my grandparents had gone through, the audit from La Société des Châteaux et Belles Demeures was a walk in the park. The troubles I'd faced in New York were ancient history. I kissed Grand-mère on the cheek. "Thank you for sharing all of this history with me," I said. "I'll fight for the château, for our family's home, for you."

"I have no doubt you will," she said. "You are a Valroux de la Tour de Champvert."

"That I am," I said, lifting my head up high. "And I've never been prouder."

That afternoon, I wandered the grounds, breathing in everything I'd learned about the château. I was fighting for the past. I was fighting for the future, one I desperately wanted to win. As I made my way down to the river, I realized I was walking in my grand-mère's footsteps, and a deeper pride set in.

I WAS IN the process of studying when Phillipa banged on my door and barged into my room. "You have to come with me now," she said. She grabbed my arm, lifting me off the window seat. My papers scattered on the floor. "We need you downstairs."

"Is there a problem?"

"You could say that," she said.

We raced down the stairs and into the salon, where Clothilde, Bernard, Rémi, Lola, Laetitia, Grand-mère, and Agnès waited, all of them facing the doorway and watching my entrance with stoic expressions. I was about to ask what was going on when Jane entered the room carrying a chocolate cake, the glaze shimmering like silk, decorated with candied purple pansies with happy faces and lit with candles.

"*Joyeux anniversaire*," they sang.

I didn't remember the last time anybody, save for Walter and Robert, had wished me a happy birthday, let alone sang. I didn't even remember it was my birthday. Before I lost it, Lola scurried up to me and pulled at my skirt. "*Tatie* Sophie," she said, pointing. "*Gâteau*."

"*Oui*, Lola, *un gâteau au chocolat*," I said, wiping my happy tears away with the sleeve of my dress.

"Blow out the candles and make a wish," said Phillipa.

I closed my eyes and I blew. This time my wish wasn't to become a three-starred chef, nor was it to impress La Société des Châteaux et Belles Demeures when they came for the audit. I wished for more days like today, to share happy times with my friends and my family. I sliced the cake, handing Lola's piece to her first. She plopped down on the floor and dug right in, chocolate covering her face in less than thirty seconds. Phillipa popped open a bottle of the château's sparkling wine and poured glasses for everybody. We sat down on settees or at one of the smaller tables and after a toast, ate the cake.

"Who is responsible for this masterpiece?" I asked. "Clothilde?"

She shook her head no. "I made it," said Phillipa, her mouth full. "It took me three days."

Jane handed me a large white box wrapped with a silver silk bow. "This is from me. I thought it was appropriate, considering." She tilted her head to the side.

I undid the ribbon and lifted the top off the box, throwing it to the floor and pulling out a chef's coat with embroidered poppies surrounding the cuffs. It was a modern version of my grandmother's apron. As I traced the flowers with my finger, I couldn't hold back my ragged breath.

Jane placed a tender hand on my back. "You hate it that much?"

"No, I love it that much," I said, standing up, and we swappd *les bises*. "Thank you."

"Brilliant," she said, tears glistening in her eyes. "I've had similar ones made for Clothilde and Phillipa, too."

Grand-mère nodded, her chin lifting with approval. "The coat is absolutely beautiful, Jane. I'm sure Sophie will wear it with honor."

"I will," I said.

Once we were finished eating, Rémi pulled me to the side. "Do you have a minute? I'd like to speak with you alone," he said, leading me into the entry. He stood quietly, fidgeting.

"Yes?" I asked.

Rémi rubbed the nape of his neck and then pulled out a jewelry box from his inside coat pocket. "*Joyeux anniversaire*, Sophie. Open it."

I lifted the lid of the box and nearly fainted when I saw what was nestled inside—a white-gold chain with three pavé-diamond-encrusted stars dangling off it.

"You now have your three stars. I know it isn't the same, but this is me bringing you closer to them."

A tear crept down my cheek. "Rémi, I don't know what to say. Thank you."

"I'm the one who should be thanking you. Since you've come

back to Champvert, I've had visions of what could be. Happiness. Lift your hair," he said, taking the necklace, and with gentle hands, he clasped it around my neck.

"This is the most thoughtful gift I've ever received. How did you know my birthday was today?"

"I have my informants," he said.

"Grand-mère?" I asked, and he nodded.

I gave him a kiss on the cheek, inhaling his woodsy, masculine scent. "You know what? Maybe I never found my heart in the kitchen. Maybe I found my heart right here in Champvert many years ago," I said.

"Are you quoting a romance novel?"

"No," I said.

"Are you saying you might be falling in love with me, too?"

"I am," I said, looking into his caramel eyes. "We strays need to take care of one another."

"What are we going to do without the drama?" he asked.

"Live our lives—love, laugh, and eat cake," I said.

Rémi pulled me in for a kiss—a spine-tingling, toe-curling kiss. When we returned to the salon, his arm was still wrapped around my shoulders. Laetitia grinned. Clothilde and Bernard exchanged confused glances. Grand-mère raised her eyebrows knowingly.

"I guess our relationship is out in the open," I said.

"As if it was such a big secret?" said Grand-mère with a huff. "I may be old and sick, but I've never been blind."

"What do you mean 'never'?" I asked.

"*Ma chérie*, if you're asking if I saw you and Rémi kiss down by the lake when you were thirteen, then my answer would be yes. I also saw you locking eyes on that snowy day."

Busted.

30

opening day

IN MID-APRIL WHEN the château had its first official event before the season started, the entire world would be waiting to
judge me, this time not as a person at the heart of a scandal, but as
a Grand Chef and the *maîtresse de maison* of this château. Of course,
I'd always wanted people to recognize me as a culinary talent, just
more organically. I felt like a reality star who the press had thrust
into the limelight with no rhyme or reason. The public glommed on
to the morsel that the château was, for the most part, a woman-run
business with a woman-run kitchen. We were getting emails of support every day, which, thankfully, Jane answered. I sat at the edge
of the lake, putting my game plan together. Being in nature, in
quiet without all the constant chatter, put me at ease. As I watched
two male mallard ducks try to chase a female guarding her ten adorable buttery and caramel ducklings, my phone buzzed—a text from
O'Shea.

Blackbird is closing down. Aside from Trevor, Eric's other
investors pulled out. Word on the street is his food was

inedible, all remakes of my recipes, but loaded with too
many spices. He came in begging for his old job. I said no.
Thought you'd like to know.

Part of me felt bad for Eric, but he'd already consumed too much
of my time. It wasn't up to me to figure his life out. After texting
O'Shea a quick thank-you, I skipped over to the greenhouse with a
basket. Phillipa and I had our work cut out for us.

When she saw me smiling like a fool, Phillipa beamed. "You're
in a good mood. How's it going with you and Rémi?" she asked,
bumping her hip into mine.

"A lady doesn't kiss and tell," I said, blushing. Although Rémi
and I had been arranging secret midnight trysts when Lola and
Grand-mère were fast asleep, we wound up falling asleep, too exhausted from preparing for the soft opening. "We're still taking
things slow and getting to know one another."

She snorted and raised her hands in resignation and then shot
me the okay sign. "Right. Slow."

"Slow for him. Fast for me. And, on fast, ready to get planning?"

WE OPENED THE door to the greenhouse to find a plethora of
strawberries—big, bright, speckled beauties, kissed and almost rip-
ened by the climate. It was as though they had burst like fireworks
overnight. "Technically, these shouldn't be in season yet—not for
another month," I said. "Should we use them?"

"Rules are meant to be broken," she said, licking her lips. "How
many varieties do you think there are?"

"At least three. I spy Gariguettes, which have sweet and acidic
tones. Clerys, which are sugary. And Charlottes, which are more
woodsy," I said, handing her one of each.

A few seconds later, we were stuffing one strawberry after the other into our eager months, fighting back groans of complete and utter delight by giggling. As the sweet flavors burst on my tongue, I thought of the photo of my mother dancing in the garden in her underwear. The memories of her now made me happy, not sad. I twirled around, thinking of her and my summers in Champvert. I was free. I opened my eyes to find Phillipa leaping like a strange ballet dancer, kicking up dirt. She fell to the ground, gripping her stomach, laughing and wheezing.

"What in the world are you doing?"

"Whatever you were," she said. "It looked like fun."

"If Jane could see us now," I said, shoving another strawberry into my mouth.

"She might have joined in," said Phillipa.

"No way," I said.

"Since you guys started getting along, she's changed. I think feeling less threatened by you is doing good things for her personality. She's way less uptight. She's even let her hair down. I think her tight French twist was pulling at her brain." Phillipa sat upright. "You're the best thing that's ever happened to this château, you realize that?"

I took her hand, helping her off the ground. "I don't know about that," I said.

"I do. Here's to the future," she said.

When we exited the greenhouse, a kaleidoscope of butterflies floated over our heads, whirling in the sky. They were beautiful, their wings a creamy butter speckled with black. The top portion of the wings had stripes, similar to tiger markings, and the hind portion was marked with inlaid sapphire-blue crescents and one golden orange spot. One landed on my shoulder and fluttered its wings.

"Those are flambé butterflies. It's how your grand-mère came up with the name for the other restaurant," said Phillipa. "I Googled the English name: scarce swallowtails."

"I prefer flambé," I said. One of the butterflies hovered over an ocean of green stalks. I pointed. "What's growing over there?"

"Wild asparagus," said Phillipa, eyes wide. "Are you thinking what I'm thinking?"

"Do you, by chance, have a knife on you?"

"Always," she said, pulling it out from her pocket and flicking the cover open. "A Laguiole switchblade."

"I believe we have our theme for the menu."

After Phillipa harvested some of the *asperge sauvage*, throwing them in her basket, we raced back to the château. "Last one to the kitchen is a rotten egg," I said.

BY THE TIME Phillipa caught up to me, I'd planned the menu in my head. By my expression, she knew it and handed me a piece of chalk.

"French classics. Fusion. The coming of spring!" I exclaimed.

MENU

L'AMUSE-BOUCHE
Strawberry Gazpacho served in Chinese Spoons,
garnished with Deep-Fried Goat Cheese and Basil

L'ENTRÉE
Zucchini Cakes with Lemon Prawns and Braised Wild
Asparagus, garnished with Edible Flowers

OU

Cream of Wild Asparagus Soup

OU

Roasted Cauliflower and Beets with Capers, served over
Spinach in a White Wine Lemon Sauce

LE PLAT PRINCIPAL

Drunk Shrimp, Flambéed in Cognac, served over a Terrine of
Tomatoes, Avocado, Strawberries, and Creamy Lemon Risotto

OU

Confit du Canard, served with Roasted Baby Carrots and
Sweet Sautéed Radishes

OU

Bœuf en Croute with Foie Gras and Mushrooms, served with
Grilled Wild Asparagus and Sweet Sautéed Radishes

LA SALADE ET LE FROMAGE

Strawberries and Wild Asparagus, served over Arugula with
a White Wine Vinaigrette

Selection of the Château's Cheeses

LE DESSERT

Crème Brûlée with a Trio of Strawberries and Cognac

Chalk in hand, I whipped around. "For every meal, we're cooking from the heart. I want to feel love, taste it, and experience it in every dish. Are you with me? Love," I said. "That's our story."

"Yes, Chef," said Phillipa. "On love, I have something for you. It's a belated birthday present. I meant to give it you before. Hold on, I'll be right back."

Phillipa headed into the servant's stairwell and returned a few seconds later, carrying her dirty old backpack. "Sorry, I didn't wrap it."

"You're giving me your backpack?"

"This old thing? Heavens no," she said, grimacing. "I'm giving you what's *inside* it."

Phillipa unzipped the pack and reached in. She held out a leather-bound notebook with a red ribbon, similar to my grandmother's. "I thought you'd like to keep up with tradition."

I just stared at the notebook for a minute, realizing whatever story I told, even if I didn't follow every single one of her recipes, or if I changed them, was also my grandmother's tale. The tears threatened to explode.

"Don't get all weepy and emotional on me," she said. "You know rule number one—"

"Yeah, yeah, no crying in the kitchen," I said. "I've been breaking that rule all the time."

The flambé butterflies floated by the window, reminding me I was in charge of my fate. This time, I wasn't going to go down in flames. Also, sometimes, it really felt good to cry, especially when I'd held all of my emotions deep inside for most of my life.

FINALLY, JUDGMENT WEEKEND arrived. Although I'd prepared myself for the occasion, my nerves were wound so tight it took a good fifteen minutes to pull myself out of bed. It was as if all my muscles had locked up. It was seven thirty a.m. and I hadn't slept much, if at all. Before heading to the kitchen, I scrambled up the stairs to visit Grand-mère. She smiled a feeble smile when I entered her room.

"Grand-mère, are you feeling okay?"

"I'm fine, *ma chérie*, just tired," she said. "Don't worry about me. You've got plenty of work to do." She straightened up a bit. "Before you leave, I wanted to ask you what you will be wearing to the Sunday lunch. All the VIPs will be here, including our special visitor, and you'll be representing the château. Do you have anything appropriate?"

"What would be appropriate?" I asked, wondering why nobody—not even Jane—had mentioned this before.

"This is France. This is a château," she said, making a popping sound with her lips. "Chanel. It never goes out of style."

"Grand-mère, I don't own one stitch of Chanel."

"*Alors*, it's a good thing I do," she said. "Go into my dressing room and choose something. My suits are arranged by size. The ones when I was petite like you are located on the right." She waved me away. "*Vas-y*, take a look."

I entered her large closet, a room in itself, and thumbed through my grandmother's clothes, quickly realizing she must have at least forty Chanel suits and over one hundred pairs of shoes and white blouses. So many couture choices, so little time. I ended up claiming a celery green and ivory tweed skirt suit with ivory grosgrain ribbons and black piping trim, with black buttons. When I carried it out in the light to show my grandmother, the tweed sparkled with a touch of iridescence. "Is this one okay?" I asked. For me, it was magic.

"Ah, *oui, ma chérie*, that was one of my favorites," she said, clapping her hands together with delight. "Pierre bought it for me in Paris because he thought it would bring out the color of my eyes. It did. You'll look lovely in it. A true vision. Your eyes will sparkle, too."

I kissed her on the cheek. "*Merci*, Grand-mère."

I exited her room, holding the fabric to my nose; it smelled of her—a mix of lavender and Chanel No. 5.

WE WERE STARTING preparations early today—not overlooking any exquisite detail. As I headed downstairs, I heard Jane's voice echoing in the servant's stairwell. "The flowers just arrived. Ladies! Now." I passed by Jane and she took me by the arm. "Come," she said. "I'd like your opinion on my arrangements."

Was confident Jane as nervous as I was? Was her bossy demeanor all a front? I really liked this new Jane. Once the veneer was cracked, she was charming, likable. My, how things had changed.

She led me into the salon, where buckets of mostly white flowers bloomed in every corner of the room like fluffy clouds, making it a magical olfactory experience for my nose and my spirit, the sweet aromas potent. There were roses, tulips, and peonies, as well as a few containers bursting with blood-orange flowers with saffron-colored filaments, similar in form to an amaryllis.

"I mostly ordered white flowers," said Jane, pointing to an arrangement. "The clivias offer a dash of color—my concept for the exciting change to come." She smiled. "This is my favorite part of my job. What do you think?"

"I think you've outdone yourself," I said, not realizing Jane was so creative. I should have picked up on that fact when she'd bestowed me with my gorgeous chef's coat.

"The smaller arrangements will be placed in the guests' rooms and on the tables in the dining room. The medium arrangements are placed just about everywhere—in the spa, in here, in the hallways—and the large one is displayed in the foyer on the marble table."

"How are you going to get them all completed before the guests arrive?"

Jane placed her hands on her hips. "All the rooms were prepared yesterday," she said and then bellowed, "Ladies! 'Now' means *maintenant*!"

The housekeeping team scrambled into the salon, said *bonjour*, and set to work, chatting amicably among themselves and copying Jane's prototypes. Jane wiped her hands on her slacks. "Do you need me to quiz you again?"

"No, I've got it."

"Good," she said. "I think it was Ina Garten who said, 'The most important thing for having a party is that the hostess is having fun.' Sophie, you're the hostess. Take a deep breath and have fun. You can do this. I have complete and utter faith in you."

"Thank you," I said. "It means the world to me."

"Don't thank me. I should be thanking *you*."

"And why is that?"

"Family," she said, grinning. "Whether you like it or not, we're going to be like sisters now."

THE NEXT FEW hours prepping were frenetic and fast-paced. Even in the madness, the brigade had found a rhythm working together. It was an odd rhythm, with spills and other minor kitchen catastrophes, but it worked. There were a few moments when nerves started to kick and churn inside me like the immersion blender in my hand, but, breathing deeply, I was able to calm down. I remained focused, as did the rest of my motley brigade. By five p.m., all of the ingredients had been prepped, and I asked the team to prepare eighteen of each of the dishes they were responsible for.

Gustave chortled. "Why?" he asked.

"For the family meal," I said. "We'll all be tasting each and every dish on the menus this weekend. The extra dishes are for Grand-mère and Agnès," I said. "We, as a team, as a brigade, need to be sure everything is perfect. If it isn't, you'll tell me and we'll change it."

"Yes, Chef!"

Finished with their duties for the evening, the granny brigade and Gustave scurried out of the kitchen at six thirty, murmuring how much they enjoyed the best staff meal they'd ever had—the best meal they'd ever had, period. Rémi disappeared to play piano at the wine tasting and *apéro* while Séb, Phillipa, Clothilde, and I were left to make final preparations for the dinner service.

I closed my eyes, preparing myself, giving myself a pep talk in my head. *I can do this.*

Somebody tapped me on the shoulder. Agnès stood to my side, holding a note. "It's from your grand-mère," she said. "I've got to get back to her."

As she left the kitchen, I read the note.

Ma chérie, your skills in the kitchen have far surpassed mine. I felt your heart in every dish. I felt your soul. I'd say good luck for tonight, but you won't need it. All my love, ta grand-mère.

With my confidence blazing, I tucked the note into the pocket of my chef's coat and smiled. "Are we all ready to make this weekend a memorable affair?"

"*Oui*, Chef."

Tingles shimmied down my spine right into my toes. We set to work, chopping and sautéing and slicing and dicing—each of us with our set tasks. I'd never seen the faces of a brigade look so concentrated. At seven thirty on the nose, Jane approached me. "The guests are seated. Are you ready for your big entrance, Sophie?"

I'd never been more ready for anything in my life. I walked into the dining room to a slow movie applause that escalated to a thunderous roar. Once it settled down, I did what I'd planned; I spoke from the heart.

"*Merci beaucoup.* Considering we have an international crowd, like the Changs who have joined us all the way from Hong Kong and the Goldbergs from San Francisco," I said, nodding to their tables, "I'm going to speak in my native tongue, which is English. I'd like to personally welcome you to the château, and its flagship restaurant Les Libellules. As you're probably aware, all of this, everything you see, was my grandmother's vision, and a beautiful one at that. My grand-mère was the reason I decided to become a chef. From the age of seven, I learned everything I know and love about cooking from her. She also taught me about the importance of family and how far we'll go to not only protect it, but also savor it. Here at the château, we are a family," I said, eyeing the man with the white mustache. "We are also deeply rooted to this land, our terroir. All of the wines you have to choose from are the château's, some of the vintages dating back to the 1950s. If you'd like a tour of the vineyard and our winemaking facilities followed by a tasting during your stay, please speak with Jane, the château's brilliant manager."

I took a deep breath.

"We are a garden-to-table outfit, the produce grown right here on the property. All of our meats and fishes are sourced in France. A lovely team of women makes all of our cheeses. We support our neighbors, who are family. And while I've taken creative liberties with tonight's menu, I'm not straying from my grand-mère's teachings. She always told me that recipes were guidelines, not necessarily to be followed word for word or ingredient by ingredient. With that said, I'd like to welcome you, dear guests, to our family, and it's my greatest hope you enjoy the meals we've planned for you and your stay."

A few women dabbed their eyes with napkins. The lone diner

with the white mustache was the first to grab his spoon and clank it on the *coupe de champagne* glass. Every single table joined in.

"*Merci*, but if I'm going to feed you, I'd better mosey on into the kitchen," I said, my statement followed by laughter. "Enjoy your meal. The first round of drinks to accompany the amuse-bouche is our sparkling wine and is compliments of the château."

As the waitstaff popped open the sparkling wine, I floated back into the kitchen to the sound of roaring applause. To my delight, the next night played out the exact same way, and I savored every moment. The only worrisome thing was that the man with the white mustache, Monsieur LeBlanc, never approached me.

"*Ne t'inquiète pas*" (Don't worry), said Grand-mère. "Perhaps he's seen and experienced all that he needs to make his decision."

31

sunday lunch surprises

I SHOULD HAVE been exhausted by the time the Sunday lunch rolled around, but adrenaline and excitement had taken over, jolting me with energy. There were no complaints of any kind, only accolades, as I'd learned when mingling with the guests the previous day. Plus, per tradition, on this day I wasn't allowed to step foot in the kitchen. In addition to the granny brigade, the villagers of Champvert brought in the traditional dishes of southwestern France. Still, I hadn't met the most important person, the man who could bring down the château—and me—with his decision. I tried to relax, but it was beyond difficult.

The courtyard bustled with activity—people laughing and eating. The large stone tables had been covered with beautiful French linens with poppy patterns. A self-serve buffet had been set up with every quiche and *tarte salée* one could imagine, like a beautiful *pissaladière* made with onions, shiny black olives, and slippery anchovies, or the one with tomato, honey, and goat cheese. There were many salads, and foie gras, and roasted chickens. Most of the men played *pétanque* on the court. Phillipa, Jane, Laetitia, and the granny brigade chatted amicably with the other ladies from the village and the guests, drinking tea. Lola played in the garden with the other children, hunting down the chocolates I'd hidden, placing them in cute white wicker baskets—an Easter egg hunt. Toward the back of the terrace, Gustave manned the large spit turning the *méchoui*— a full roasted lamb, his bottle of pastis in hand.

I watched all of this from Grand-mère's suite. People smiled and waved to the window, my grand-mère looking like the Queen of England sitting on her wheelchair throne.

"*Ma chérie*, I'm quite cold. Could you put a fire on? There are logs just over there." She tried to motion with her hand. But couldn't.

As I got the fire going, a sadness tore at my heart, my stomach. So did fear. The truth was, she wasn't getting better. She was getting worse. Agnès had told me she'd pushed herself too far. Right about now, I couldn't have cared less about the audit.

"*Ma chérie*, go join the others," said Grand-mère. "I'll be fine. Agnès is with me. I want you to enjoy yourself after working so hard. You've made this old woman very proud."

"Are you sure? I'd kind of like to sit with you."

"I'll be falling asleep in no time," she said, waving me away. "Off with you."

There was no arguing with Grand-mère. I headed outside to mingle with the guests, catching up with Rémi. When he saw me, he placed his hands over his heart. "*Ouah*, I didn't think it was possible for the most beautiful girl I've ever met to look even more beautiful. Green really is your color," he said, eyeing me up and down, stopping at my legs. "Is that Chanel?"

"It is," I said. "It's Grand-mère's."

"You're a vision of grace and beauty."

"I'm not sure about grace," I said, stumbling. "But I'll take the compliment."

The moment Rémi put his arm around me, the granny brigade pointed at us and whispered. Clothilde's voice rang clear. "Quit your clucking," she said. "Rémi and Sophie are now a couple and that little girl over there is Rémi's daughter."

Each member of the granny brigade's eyes widened and they clucked on and on. All of the guests, around eighty of them, took notice. Normally, I'd have shied away from such attention, but this time I wasn't the center of a scandal and I was proud of myself—and the handsome man standing at my side.

"No more secrets," said Rémi, squirming a little bit. "In a way, it feels good. Awkward, but good."

"It does," I said with a slight smile.

As an outside observer, I thought it seemed that everyone was having a good old time, save for the man standing with a beer in one hand. He might have been good-looking when he'd been younger, but time had not been kind to him, and the effects of the sun had taken its toll on his weathered face.

I nudged Rémi. "Who is that man? The one staring at me? Clothilde and Bernard don't look like they are all too thrilled to see him."

"Oh," he said. "Him? That's Jean-Marc Bourret."

My vision blurred. I couldn't focus. "What?"

"I invited him."

"Wasn't meeting him supposed to be *my* decision?"

"It is yours. You don't have to talk to him if you don't want to, but I wanted to give you the opportunity. You told me you were looking for answers," he said. "I can tell him to leave."

I didn't know if wanted to hug Rémi or kill him. Of all the days he'd invited Jean-Marc, it was when we were under audit by La Société. "We'll talk about this later."

As I approached Jean-Marc, he smiled a feeble smile. I don't know how my feet moved toward him without falling down. I don't know how I found my voice, but it came out strong. "My mother was Céleste Valroux de la Tour de Champvert," I said. "I believe you knew her."

"I did." His eyes flashed with the incredible sadness of deep loss, one that I knew. "I was very hesitant to come here today. Your grand-mère isn't my biggest fan, but Rémi was insistent. There's no easy way to ask you my question." He straightened his posture. "Is it true? Are you my daughter?"

"I am," I said, though wondering a bit as I took in his face. Aside from the shape of his jawline and his hair—now gray, but which had probably been an inky black like mine in the past—we didn't share any similar features. "My name's Sophie."

"Please forgive me. I was young and stupid. Believe me, I'm not a bad man," he said, not meeting my eyes.

It was time to walk my own path, to choose it. My battle scars had healed; his could, too.

"Everybody has a story, and I want to hear yours," I said, thinking of Phillipa's nonjudgmental reaction toward me. It was now my turn to listen to his words, even if I didn't like what he said. I braced myself.

Jean-Marc straightened his posture. "What would you like to know?"

"Did you ever try to find me?" I asked.

His mouth curved into a sad frown and his eyes darkened. "I wanted to. But I was a man of little means. I barely had enough food on my table."

"But wasn't my grand-mère paying you?"

"She was," he said. "But I only cashed the first check."

He was telling the truth. Grand-mère had told me this after one of our reading sessions.

My eyes went wide and I motioned for him to carry on. He swallowed hard. "I worked here at the château as a seasonal picker during the grape harvest to make extra money." His lips curved into a wistful smile. "Sometimes, Céleste would help collect the grapes. I thought she was the most beautiful woman I'd ever seen. It was, as they say, *un coup de foudre.* Love at first sight, and I did everything in my power to get her attention."

"You loved her?"

"With all my heart," he said with a sigh. "But she didn't love me."

"What makes you say that?"

"She told me," he said. "She was eight months pregnant with you when we met by the river. I had to scale the fence on the far side of the property to get there, cutting myself in the process. I told her I wanted to take care of you, to take care of her. I told her I accepted the money from your grand-mère so I could do just that. When I asked her to marry me, she laughed in my face and told me she had other plans." His face crumpled. "Big plans, she'd said. Then she looked me straight in the eyes and told me she wasn't sure who the father was and shouted at me to leave."

He didn't need to mince his words. All of this had come from her mouth; I knew it. I swallowed my guilt back; I'd had big plans, too. But my plans had metamorphosed.

"She was a sick woman," I said, grabbing his hands. I told him about her bipolar disorder, how her actions and moods would flip on a dime. "In the end, she committed suicide."

Jean-Marc let out a breath as if somebody had sucker punched him in the gut. Finally, he spoke. "Before she died, did she tell you that I was your father?"

"No," I said. "Grand-mère Odette did."

"Your grand-mère didn't like me. Why? After all these years?"

"She wanted me to know the truth, even if she herself didn't like it," I said. "It's my choice now. Like I said, I'd like to get to know you." I paused. "Did you ever marry? Have kids?"

"No," he said. "I've been a bit of a loner ever since she left me." He tried to regain his composure.

I wanted to get to know him. I needed to. Aside from Grand-mère, and who knew how much time she had, this man was the only blood relation I had left. And I believed his story. In this moment, I was truly free of the past. I nodded to Rémi, who had been watching the exchange from a distance like a hawk. He sauntered over to the table, exchanged *les bises* with Jean-Marc as men do in France, and sat down. Just then, the man with the white mustache caught my eye and waved me over. I knew the timing of this was all wrong, but I didn't have a choice.

"Excuse me, Jean-Marc, I really do want to get to know you," I said, "but, unfortunately, duty calls."

"I understand," he said. "I'll have Rémi give you my contact information. That's if you wish to see me again."

"Of course I do," I said, giving him a kiss on the cheek.

Slowly, I made my way over to the auditor, smoothing out my skirt and hair on the way. Although I loved the suit I was wearing, I felt like a little kid playing dress up. Would he think so, too? Was he going to take the château's status away? I let out a few deep exhales and picked up my pace. Confident Sophie needed to get back on track.

"Monsieur LeBlanc," I said, thrusting out my hand, which he took with a surprised smile.

"You know my name?"

"It's part of the experience here at the château. As I said in my opening speech, all of our guests are like—"

"Family," he said. "You've certainly made your grand-mère proud. I'm hoping she's feeling better. She's in our thoughts and prayers." He handed me a heavy box. "Open this after I leave. We had a feeling about you, and let's just say, I came prepared. It was lovely meeting you, my dear."

With that, Monsieur LeBlanc walked up the steps and turned the corner. For a moment, I stood stunned, wondering if I'd imagined the whole exchange—surreal as it was—and I hoped his feeling about me had been a positive one. I ripped open the package, finding an elegant embossed card placed on a large wooden plaque.

Félicitations, welcome to La Société des Châteaux et Belles Demeures family. We're looking forward to getting to know the new maîtresse of the château and its Grand Chef.

My sigh of relief whooshed with the lilac-scented spring breeze, warming my soul. I'd done it. I could put all past stress behind me. I'd never been prouder of anything in my life. I was a chef again. I traced the brass fleur-de-lis and the words inscribed, LA SOCIÉTÉ DES CHÂTEAUX ET BELLES DEMEURES, with my fingertips, focusing on my name. Sophie Valroux de la Tour de Champvert, GRAND CHEF.

Soft breaths whispered on my back. Jane and Phillipa peered over my shoulder. I turned, raising the plaque triumphantly. "We did it!"

"No, you did it," said Phillipa.

"We're a team," I said.

"I'll take credit when it's due," said Jane.

"I couldn't have done this without either of you," I said with a laugh, hugging both of them. "I have to go tell Grand-mère. Can you tell Rémi and Jean-Marc I'll be right back?"

"Jean-Marc? The mechanic from Sauqueuse?" asked Phillipa, squinting in their direction. "Why is he here?"

I'd forgotten Phillipa and Jane's parents lived in the next town over. Surely, Phillipa took her beat-up car to his garage.

"Long story," I said. "I'll tell you all about him later."

I raced up to my grand-mère's room, opened the door, and held out the plaque from La Société des Châteaux et Belles Demeures. "I wanted you to see this."

Her eyes glistened with proud tears. "*Ma chérie*, I knew you could do it. You must have Rémi take my plaque down and put yours up at the front gate."

"No, Grand-mère," I said.

"It's your château now, and it's your kitchen. You are the Grand Chef now and the master of this home," she said. "If you want to keep my plaque in memory of me, hang it in your office."

"You mean your office," I said.

"Not anymore."

"Grand-mère—"

"Darling, be like the woman O'Shea called you in his article. Be fearless."

"But I'm scared, Grand-mère," I said, slumping. "I don't want to lose you. Not now—not when I'm getting to really know you."

"I know. But I'll always be here for you, even when I'm gone. We have to face what's coming with strength." She closed her eyes and squeezed my hand, her head lolling slightly to the side. "The ring you wear around your neck?"

I sucked back my sobs, wanting to be strong for her. What was supposed to be a celebratory day had taken a turn. "It was yours, wasn't it? My mother stole it?"

"It was mine," she said. "And she did. I'd like to hold it one last time. It's quite beautiful."

I undid the clasp of my necklace, slipped off the ring, and tucked it into her hand. She looked longingly out the window. "I did grow to love your grandfather and my life here," she said wistfully.

"Grand-mère, there's something I need to tell you," I said.

"*Oui, ma chérie.*"

"I met Jean-Marc Bourret, my father," I said. "He's downstairs now with Rémi in the gardens."

"If you're wondering if I told Rémi it was a good idea to invite him here, I said it was," she said. "And what do you think of this man?"

"He has kind eyes. He's had a tough life, it seems," I said, thinking that of course my grand-mère had been in on the plan. Nothing escaped her. "I'd like to get to know him. He's, um, he's my family."

"As you should," she said, her eyes locking onto mine. "It was important for me to make amends with everything I'd done in the past before I move on to the other side. Please offer Monsieur Bourret my sincerest apologies." She gripped my hand. "*Je t'aime, ma chérie.*"

"*Je sais, Grand-mère*" (I know, Grand-mère), I said. "*Je t'aime aussi.*"

One of the machines buzzed, jolting my heart along with it. Agnès scurried over, pushing by me, her smile feeble. "Sophie, I've got to get her stabilized. There's nothing more you can do here. Please, go join the party."

I agreed, but it didn't feel like a celebration anymore. My grandmother's words felt like a final *adieu*. With the plaque in hand, I headed to my room. Instead of joining the others, there was something important I needed to do. I rolled out my mother's suitcase, unzipped it, and unpacked her things, hanging her dresses in my closet and placing her jewelry box on my dresser.

I was going to kiss any remnants of past pain goodbye before I had to deal with any more of it.

32

---

sad goodbyes and happy beginnings

GRAND-MÈRE ODETTE'S FUNERAL would take place three days later, right at the château. In between sniffs, sobs, and sudden breakdowns, Rémi, Clothilde, *les dames*, Gustave, Séb, Phillipa, Jane, and I were going to cook up a celebratory feast—exactly how Grand-mère would have wanted it. I didn't wear her poppy-print apron, but tucked it away in the closet, wanting to guard her vanilla, cinnamon, and nutmeg scent, which was already fading. We stood in the kitchen.

"We are cooking everything in her notebooks," I'd said, and then quickly corrected myself. "Everything we have ingredients for. She'd kill us if we cooked out of season."

"How in the world are we going to prepare all of her recipes?" Clothilde asked.

"I've called in reinforcements," I said, nodding at Laetitia and Lola. I picked Lola up and placed her on a stool. "This was my favorite place in the kitchen when I was a young girl just like you," I said. "I'd watch my grand-mère cook and sometimes she'd let me help. *Tu peux m'aider*, Lola?"

"Oui, Tatie."

Grief came in waves, but I was in charge of my emotions now, aside from the occasional breakdown when I'd pick up something that reminded me of her, like an old wooden spoon with burn marks on the handle, or her favorite copper pot.

People from all over France were due to arrive for the ceremony—from Gaillac to Toulouse, Paris to Bordeaux, and even New York. I ran down the front steps when Walter and Robert's taxi arrived, tripping over my feet. Rémi shot out his hand, lifting me off the ground.

"I think I need to buy you a helmet," he said.

"Very funny," I said. I left Rémi in my dust as I ran up to hug my best friend. Walter spun me around, lifting me off my feet.

Rémi joined us.

"Which one of you was my girlfriend's fake gay fiancé?" said Rémi, pretending to be serious or mad, which worked for about five seconds. Robert pointed at Walter. Rémi crossed his arms and his chest started heaving up and down with laughter. "It was the most bizarre thing I've heard come out of Sophie's mouth."

"He had me going there for a minute," said Robert, fanning his face dramatically. "He's drop-dead gorgeous and has a sense of humor. Wait, I thought this was the—"

I cut Robert off before he could continue. Rémi didn't need to know I'd called him a what, not a who, or worse, an asshole. With a wild laugh that I couldn't believe came from me, I made the introductions. Once they finished slapping one another on the backs like frat boys or long-lost friends, Walter pouted and said, "We're never getting her back to New York."

"Not a chance," agreed Robert.

This was true. New York was a distant memory and the farthest thing from my mind.

"Life in France has apparently done wonders for you," said Walter. "I know we aren't here under the best of circumstances, but all things considered, I'm thinking our Sophie is back and she's stronger than ever."

"You know what?" I said. "I am. On that, sorry to skip out on you, but I've got to get changed before everybody arrives and check in on the kitchen," I said. "Rémi will show you to your room, okay? We're giving you the best one in the house. And remember, we are celebrating my grand-mère's life—no black."

CAR AFTER CAR rumbled down the driveway, filling all the parking spots and lining the long driveway. For mid-April, the weather was more than agreeable, not too hot or too cold. I wore a navy-blue silk sheath and one of my grandmother's scarves, cream with her signature poppy pattern, around my shoulders. Rémi stood beside me and we greeted the guests. Murmurs of condolences accompanied gracious words about my grand-mère.

"She helped us through a tough time in our lives."

"She was such an inspiration."

"An incredible woman, so full of life."

Even Jean-Marc Bourret showed up to pay his respects, looking rather respectable himself—all clean-shaven and wearing a suit. "Did you mean it when you said you'd like to get to know me?" he asked.

"I did."

"*Merci*, Sophie." His eyes glistened. "I know right now isn't the right time, but I'm looking forward to that day."

"Me, too," I said, gripping his hand.

There were many times I choked back my tears, but I held myself together, hiding the ones that slipped out behind Grand-mère's black Chanel sunglasses. Soon, it was time for the procession to the small chapel. Rémi, Lola, and I led, followed by Clothilde, Bernard, and Laetitia, the rest of Grand-mère's closest "family" behind them. Once gathered in front of the doors, Father Toussaint, a kind man with graying hair and unruly eyebrows, began the service. As he spoke, I surveyed the guests. Some dabbed their eyes with handkerchiefs, wiping away their tears. Some cried, like Clothilde and Jane, gulping back ragged sobs. I loved my grandmother and it was nice to see how much others loved her, too.

Behind the chapel, there was a field ablaze with *coquelicots* (wild poppies), the flowers blowing in the breeze, butterflies soaring over a sea of red. I could feel Grand-mère with me, telling me not to be sad, but to focus on the beauty.

When Father Toussaint finished delivering his sermon, Rémi and I walked up to Grand-mère's gilded casket, polished wood with carvings of flowers, to say our final goodbyes. Her face was still and peaceful, beautiful even though ravaged by the effects of time.

"I'm going to miss you fiercely," I said, stroking her hand. "I wish we'd spent more time together, but I'm thankful for the time we had."

Rémi put his arm around me. "Don't worry, Grand-mère Odette, I'll look after Sophie and take care of her for the rest of my life."

I nudged him softly and whispered, "Who says I need to be taken care of?"

"You are definitely your grand-mère's *petite-fille*," he said. "And she made me promise her that."

We each grabbed a single red rose from a basket and tossed it into her casket, me thinking about the lessons Grand-mère taught and would keep teaching me. When I opened my eyes, a flash of blue caught my attention: a dragonfly the size of my palm, flittering his wings just over her casket. He landed on my arm, but flew away so quickly, I'd thought I'd imagined it. Rémi latched his arm onto mine and we walked across the grounds to the château.

"Did you see that?" I asked Rémi. "The dragonfly?"

"I did," he said. "I read somewhere once that if a dragonfly lands on you, a good change is coming."

"I'd like to believe that," I said.

He blew out the air between his lips and winked. "Then believe it."

IN FRANCE—AND it didn't matter if there were ten guests or two hundred—as a matter of *la politesse*, people milled about waiting for all the guests to arrive, eyeing drinks and food ravenously. I nodded to the servers carrying trays of *coupe de champagne* glasses filled with the château's sparkling wine—*la méthode ancestrale*—and they distributed them. I tapped my glass with a spoon.

Once I had everybody's attention, I spoke. "Thank you all so much for joining us on what is supposed to be a sad day. But if any of you knew Grand-mère Odette, I'm sure you'd agree she'd be extremely angry if we moped about and cried. My grand-mère, my fierce and strong grandmother, would want us to celebrate her life."

"Hear, hear!"

"Grand-mère loved to entertain, and it was through food that she expressed her love. From the time I was very young, she instilled this love of cooking into me. And I'm eternally grateful for her lessons. She was a Grand Chef, the grande dame of this château, and an even better grandmother. She didn't let titles or money affect her friendships. She opened the doors of this château to everyone. So in honor of my grandmother, I'd like to carry on that tradition. We've re-created many of the recipes she's served us throughout the years. The buffet is open. Please join me in celebrating my grandmother's life." I raised my glass. "To Grand-mère Odette, may she soar among the wild butterflies and dragonflies."

A few guests burst into tears; I stood strong, feeling my grand-mère's strength fill me. I met the eyes of my family, my gaze shooting from Clothilde and Bernard, to Gustave and the granny brigade, to Laetitia and Lola, finally settling on Jane and then Phillipa. Love vibrated from every corner of the room, pulsing in waves. I fingered the necklace Rémi had given me for my birthday, thanking each and every one of my lucky stars.

Once the applause died down, I took in a deep breath. Rémi pulled me to the side, away from the others. "I thought we'd end today with something special. Can you come with me?"

I nodded, wondering what he was up to. He led me out the front door and stood quietly for a moment, head down. From his pocket, he pulled out my grandmother's engagement ring; it sparkled in the sunlight like a beacon. "You had the ring? I've been looking everywhere for it."

"Grand-mère Odette wanted me to give you this," he said. "Under one condition, though."

"Condition?"

He dropped to one knee and smiled his fantastic, dimpled smile that made my knees turn to butter. "I know we've been moving at the speed of light, and you wanted to take things slow, but when you know you're in love, you know. I've loved you from the first moment I laid eyes on you when I was only nine years old. And I never stopped loving you. Sophie Valroux de la Tour de Champvert, will you marry me?"

Grand-mère Odette had calculated and manipulated and connived, right up to her last breath. She'd never wanted to hold the ring again. She'd wanted to give it to Rémi so he could give it to me. And if that didn't prove her love for me, I don't know what did. I was ready for change, to ride on the wings of dragonflies and butterflies. I was ready to start my new life. No looking back, only forward, but just a little slower—one breath at a time, and I couldn't find mine, so I didn't say a word and stared at my feet.

Rémi lifted up my chin. "What? Too fast?"

I met his eyes and said, "Can we just be engaged to be engaged?"

"*J'ai mal compris*" (I don't understand), he said.

"Yes, I want to be your fiancée, Rémi," I said, hunching my shoulders. "But we really need to get to know one another better. Marriage is a huge, forever commitment. I want to be with you and want that for our future eventually, but can we take our time? Maybe we could take a vacation together first? I read somewhere that that's the best way to get know somebody. You know, stuck in a room."

"We'll leave tomorrow," he said.

"I can't. The château is booked solid and there won't be any breaks until after Christmas," I said.

"You're talking about schedules now? *Bon Dieu*, you really are Grand-mère's *petite-fille*."

My posture straightened proudly. "I am."

After holding up his hands in surrender, Rémi pulled me in for a passionate kiss. "By the way, your grandmother also wanted me to tell you that rings are supposed to be worn on fingers, so when you're ready, let me know, because it's going on your left hand. Until then, wear it on your weird necklace, so I know I'm still in the running," he whispered as he pulled away.

"*Merci*, Rémi," I said, tears of happiness glistening in my eyes. "Thank you for understanding."

"What's to understand? Some people need more time than others. I get that about you, Sophie, but you'll come around. Love always wins in the end," he said. He wrapped one arm around me and pointed to the orchard with the other one, to flowering trees exploding with white blossoms dancing in the wind. "Cherries will be in season soon. Do you know what that means?"

"I do," I said. "We can make Grand-mère's clafoutis."

It was then I realized that Grand-mère would live on through me, through her recipes, through everything she created at the château. She would always be here with me; she wasn't *really* gone. She would always live on in my heart—the one I discovered outside of the kitchen, thanks to her. But Grand-mère had passed her dreams on to me. And I wasn't quite sure how I felt about that, because I used to have dreams of my own.

Rémi clasped his hand around mine. "Ready?"

"For what?" I asked.

"To go back in," he said.

Rémi kissed me, pulling me in close, his breath a whisper on my neck, before he opened the door. My thoughts melted like butter on a hot skillet. Aside from Grand-mère, didn't I have everything? I was a woman. I was a chef. And I could have both love *and* success on my own terms.

"I'm as ready as I'll ever be," I said.

Le Dessert

⚜

This is my invariable advice to people: Learn how to cook—try new recipes, learn from your mistakes, be fearless, and above all, have fun.

—Julia Child

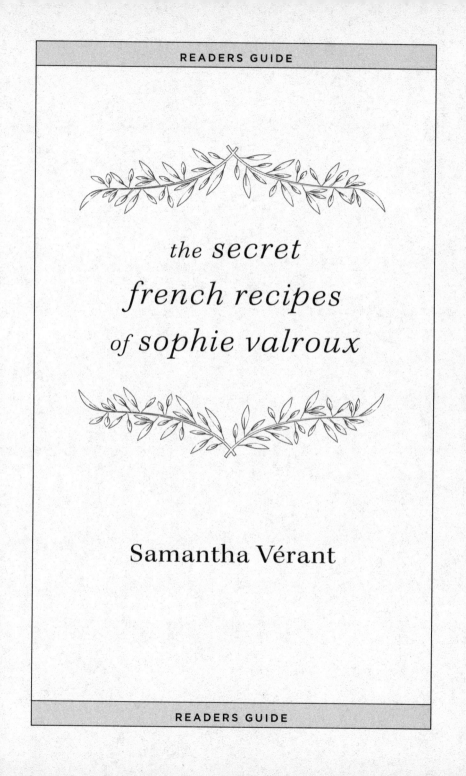

the *secret*

french recipes

of sophie valroux

Samantha Vérant

discussion questions

—◦◦◦—

1. In the beginning of the novel, Sophie is chasing her one
    and only dream, but it's snatched from her grasp. Have
    you ever chased a dream that didn't come to fruition?
    What did you do to make amends with yourself? How did
    Sophie pick herself up from the beginning of the story
    until the end? How did she change? How did you change?

2. Sometimes people come off as strong even when they feel
    quite the opposite. They put up a front. Sophie knows
    this about herself but then encounters her tipping point
    and finds herself facing a storm, not just with her conflict-
    ing emotions, but also with her past. Has this ever hap-
    pened to you?

3. Sophie's one true love is cooking, and she cooks with her
    emotions. As she spirals into depression, she ends up
    blaming herself and locks away most of her feelings, end-
    ing up with self-pity and wavering grief. How would you

have reacted to the sabotage she faced? Do you empathize with her?

4. Do you think there is misogyny in most professional kitchens? Do female chefs have to work harder than their male counterparts? Discuss current events and books, news, or articles you may have read about this.

5. The theme of food and recipes passed down from relatives is threaded throughout the story. Do you have culinary traditions in your family? Did you inherit recipes from a family member? Discuss how food can tie you to the past and the nostalgia it invokes.

6. Phillipa accepts Sophie from the get-go because, as we learn, she knows what it's like to be judged. Jane doesn't trust Sophie and thinks she'll be the ruin of the château. How do both of these friendships evolve? Have you ever judged somebody in the beginning only to find that you misjudged a person's intentions?

7. Recipes from Sophie are included in the book. Do you feel that added to the narrative? Once she gets her cooking mojo back, did you feel her passion for it? Which recipe would you want to make for your family or friends?

8. Family—three generations of women—are presented in this book. Sophie, as a young girl, had to take care of her mother, Céleste, who was estranged from her own mother, Grand-mère Odette. Did Sophie's backstory make you sympathize with her or did you find her selfish for chasing her dream?

9. After Sophie finds out she's to inherit a twenty-eight-room château in southwestern France with two working restaurants, she's not too keen on the idea because she feels unworthy. She thinks Grand-mère has handed over to her a world Sophie has never really been a part of. Would you feel daunted or up to the challenge of the opportunity?

10. Rémi is none too thrilled that Sophie is back in Champvert, because she (unknowingly) hurt him in the past. Both of their stories are similar, and they do eventually find a connection. Did Rémi's actions make you feel sympathy for him? Did you relate to him?

11. After meeting her father, Sophie realizes that she needs to open her heart up to him, and to everybody in her world, something she feels conflicted about. What traits does Sophie share with her father? What attributes or

flaws do you share with your parents, and how does that make you feel about yourself and about them?

12. Grand-mère Odette kept secrets from Sophie with the notion that she was protecting her from a painful past. Discuss this. Was Grand-mère right?

sophie's recipes

Dear Reader,

Grand-mère Odette taught me that recipes are only guidelines. Throughout the years, I've learned to season to taste (and to taste while cooking, never overseasoning), to add or omit ingredients depending on my likes, and to get creative in the kitchen. Please remember that every kitchen is different. One oven may run hotter or cooler than another. Pots and pans may cook differently at the same heat. As Jacques Pépin has said: "Cooking is about the art of adjustment."

When entertaining, the French do follow certain rules for a formal sit-down dinner. Instead of an amuse-bouche, most French serve an apéro, or apéritif—cocktails or champagne along with small appetizers such as canapés, olives, cherry tomatoes, or potato chips, and one or two standout dishes. After the apéro, the host calls the guests to the table. The dinner starts with the entrée (the first small plate), followed by le plat principal (main course), then the cheese and/or salad course, and, finally, dessert.

With that said, I hope you enjoy the recipes I've chosen to share with you. If you'd like to offer your dinner guests a cheese course, I'd suggest Roquefort, a Cantal, goat cheese, Brie, or a Tomme. Throughout the meal, the wine you serve is up to you. Bon appétit!

Many bisous,
Chef Sophie

L'Amuse-Bouche (*Apéro*)

Pan-Seared Scallops wrapped in Jambon Sec and Prunes with a Balsamic Glaze

SERVES 8

PREP TIME: 20 MINUTES

COOK TIME: 10 MINUTES

INGREDIENTS

16 nice-sized sea scallops, around an inch in circumference,
with or without the coral

Juice of 1 lemon

Fresh ground pepper

4 to 6 slices *jambon sec* or other dry-cured ham like prosciutto

8 sprigs fresh rosemary

8 dried prunes*

2 cup balsamic vinegar

Extra-virgin olive oil

1 tablespoon butter

16 leaves fresh sage

TECHNIQUE

If using scallops with the coral, peel off the coral and set aside. Drizzle the lemon juice on the scallops. Season with fresh ground pepper to taste. Lightly toss and set aside.

Slice the dry-cured ham in half lengthwise.

Take a rosemary sprig and spear one scallop, followed by one prune, and then another scallop.

Wrap each scallop with half a slice of dry-cured ham.

Pour the vinegar into a small pot and cook over high heat until it reduces to a syrup-like consistency, approximately 5 to 7 minutes. Lower heat to keep warm.

Combine a dash of olive oil, the butter, and the sage in a large frying pan over medium-high heat. Once the pan is hot, add the scallop spears, along with the coral, if using, and cook about 2 to 3 minutes per side, until the scallops are cooked through and firm to the touch and the dry-cured ham is browned.

Place the browned sage on a small dish, topped with the speared scallops and prunes. Drizzle with the balsamic glaze, and garnish with the coral, if using, and fresh ground pepper to taste. Serve immediately, one sprig per plate.

*Chef's Note: *In the summer, fresh figs can be substituted for the dried prunes.*

L'Entrée

Velouté de Potimarron with Flambéed Lobster Tails and a Parmesan Crisp

SERVES 8 TO 10 FOR AN ENTRÉE OR 4 TO 6 FOR A MAIN
COURSE

PREP TIME: 30 TO 45 MINUTES

COOK TIME: 1.5 HOURS

EQUIPMENT: PARCHMENT PAPER, BAKING SHEET, LARGE POT,
CHEESE GRATER, KITCHEN SCISSORS, FOOD PROCESSOR OR
IMMERSION BLENDER, LARGE FRYING PAN, LONG KITCHEN
MATCHES, SPATULA

INGREDIENTS FOR THE VELOUTÉ

2 medium-sized potimarron (Hokkaido squash) *or* butternut
squash

Extra-virgin olive oil

Salt (*fleur de sel*, sea, or kosher)

Fresh ground pepper

4 teaspoons cinnamon

1 medium leek, sliced into thin rounds*

1 onion, peeled and diced

2 celery stalks, diced

2 carrots, peeled and diced

2 garlic cloves, peeled, degermed, and finely minced

6 to 7 cups homemade chicken broth *or* canned chicken *or*
vegetable stock

1 to 2 teaspoons ground cumin

1 tablespoon paprika

1 tablespoon ground turmeric

3 healthy pinches *herbes de Provence*

Juice of 1 lemon

Sprigs of lavender or rosemary for garnish

Crème fraîche or sour cream (optional**)

Chopped chives (optional**)

INGREDIENTS FOR THE PARMESAN CRISP

7 ounces Parmesan cheese, a nice chunk

INGREDIENTS FOR THE LOBSTER TAILS

4 langoustes (spiny/Caribbean lobsters) thawed—
approximately 4 oz. each

Freshly squeezed juice of 1 to 2 oranges

2 to 3 tablespoons finely minced ginger

Extra-virgin olive oil

1 to 2 knobs of butter (about 1 to 2 tablespoons each)

¼ cup Armagnac or cognac

TECHNIQUE

Preheat oven to 400°F.

Using a sharp knife, cut the squash in half. Deseed, then cut the squash into large chunks. Place on a parchment-lined baking sheet, skin side down. Drizzle with olive oil. Lightly salt and pepper. Sprinkle with cinnamon. Bake for 25 minutes.

While the squash is cooking, heat 2 tablespoons of olive oil in a large pot over medium-high heat. Add the leeks, onion, celery, carrots, and garlic, cooking until the vegetables are soft, about ten minutes. Add the broth, cumin, paprika, turmeric, and *herbes de Provence*. Bring to a boil, cover, and reduce the heat to a simmer.

When the squash is ready, set aside and let cool.

It's time to make the Parmesan crisps while the oven is hot. Hand-grate the Parmesan using a grater. Each crisp requires 1½ to 2 tablespoons of cheese, totaling 8 to 10 rounds. Bake on a parchment-lined baking sheet for around 7 minutes, until golden. Remove from the oven and set aside.

Using kitchen scissors, cut off the lobster shells. Gingerly remove the meat of the lobster from the shell, aiming to remove it in one piece. Place the tails in a bowl and add the orange juice and the ginger. Mix well, cover in plastic wrap, and set the bowl in the refrigerator until ready to cook.

When the squash is cool enough to handle, peel off the skin and chop the squash into 1-inch to 2-inch cubes. (You should have about 5 to 6 cups.) Add the squash to the pot of vegetables and broth. Simmer for another 15 to 20 minutes. Purée in batches with a food processor *or* all at once with an immersion blender until creamy. Season with the juice of the lemon and salt and pepper to taste. Keep warm.

Add a dash of olive oil to a large pan along with a knob or two of butter. Set the heat to medium high. Place the lobster tails in the pan and fry until the meat is white, flipping to cook both sides. After the tails are cooked to perfection, turn off the heat on the stove and—very important—the evacuation system, if using. It's time to flambée. Pour the Armagnac (or cognac) over the tails and quickly light a long kitchen match, dipping it into the alcohol. If the flames rise too high, grab a pot cover and snuff the flame out. Please note: flambée at your own risk. If you have long hair, tie it back out of the way.

Cut the lobster tails into bite-sized pieces. Pour the soup into bowls. Add a few morsels of lobster, about four to six pieces a person. Using a spatula, lift up the Parmesan crisps. Garnish the soup with one Parmesan crisp and fresh herbs, like lavender or rosemary. Serve immediately.

Chef's Notes: *To clean the leeks, slice off the dark green end, trimming to the part where the color is pale green or white. Cut off the roots. Slice the stalk lengthwise, not cutting through it. Run the leeks under cold water. Set aside until ready to chop and use.

**This soup can be served on its own, garnished with a dollop of crème fraîche, chopped chives, and fresh ground pepper.

Filet of Daurade (Sea Bream) served over a Sweet Potato Purée and Braised Cabbage

SERVES 8

PREP TIME: 25 MINUTES

COOK TIME: 30 TO 40 MINUTES

INGREDIENTS

    6 to 8 medium-sized sweet potatoes, peeled and cut into
        rough chunks

    ½ to 1 cup crème fraîche or sour cream

    Freshly squeezed juice of 1 to 2 oranges

    Ground nutmeg

    3 to 4 tablespoons butter

    Extra-virgin olive oil

    3 to 4 tablespoons finely minced garlic

    1 head red cabbage, sliced into ¼-inch strips

    Freshly squeezed juice of 3 to 4 lemons, plus more if needed

    Balsamic vinegar

    8 filets of daurade (sea bream)

    ½ to 1 cup finely minced flat parsley

    2 to 3 pinches saffron

    Fresh ground pepper

    Salt

    Fresh herbs, like lavender and rosemary, and edible flowers
        for garnish

TECHNIQUE

Bring a large pot of salted water to a boil. Place the sweet potatoes in the pot, boiling for about 18 to 20 minutes, until tender. Drain and place back into the pot. Add ½ cup crème fraîche or sour cream, the juice of 1 orange, and a pinch or two of nutmeg. Using an immersion blender or handheld mixer, purée. The sweet potatoes should have a mashed consistency. If the mixture is too dry or has too many chunks, add a little more orange juice or crème fraîche and mash again. Taste, then season to taste with salt, pepper, butter, and a dash (or two) of nutmeg. Place on a burner and set to low to keep warm.

In a large frying pan, combine a dash or two of olive oil, a pat of butter, and the minced garlic over medium-high heat. Once the garlic has softened, add the sliced cabbage, stirring until it wilts. Add two tablespoons of lemon juice and a dash (or three) of balsamic vinegar, and sprinkle with ground nutmeg to taste. Turn the heat to low to keep warm.

In another large frying pan, heat a dash or two of olive oil and a knob of butter over medium-high heat. Season each side of the daurade filets with one tablespoon of lemon juice, minced parsley to lightly cover, and fresh ground pepper to taste. Sprinkle with saffron. Once the pan is hot, place the daurades in the pan and fry, about 2 to 3 minutes per side, adding a bit more lemon juice if desired, cooking until the fish is no longer translucent. (If you have to sear the fish in batches, keep them warm in an oven on low heat.)

It's time to serve. If you want to get fancy, use a 4-inch circle tool to plate. First, place the cabbage, and press down. This is followed by the sweet potato purée. Again, press down. Place the daurades on top of the sweet potato and garnish with fresh herbs and edible flowers. If you're not feeling fancy, plate it in the above order. Serve immediately and enjoy!

Arugula and Endive with Rosemary-Encrusted Goat Cheese Toasts, garnished with Pomegranate Grains and Clementine Slices, served with a Citrus-Infused Dressing

SERVES 8

PREP TIME: 15 TO 20 MINUTES

COOK TIME: 15 MINUTES

EQUIPMENT: LARGE FRYING PAN

INGREDIENTS

2 tablespoons Dijon mustard

Freshly squeezed juice of 1 orange

2 tablespoons balsamic vinegar

Extra-virgin olive oil

Salt

Fresh ground pepper

1 or 2 French baguettes, sliced in ¾-inch-thick rounds

Butter

Fresh rosemary or *herbes de Provence*

1½ cups lardons (small pieces of salted ham) or chopped
    pancetta

1½ cups leeks, chopped in rounds

2 logs goat cheese (200 grams or 7 ounces), sliced into
    ½-inch-think rounds (two per person)

1-½ cups panko or bread crumbs, plus more if needed

8 cups arugula, around 1 cup per person

4 cups endive, roughly chopped, around ½ cup per person

1 deseeded pomegranate, separated

4 clementine or mandarin oranges, peeled, separated into
    slices, and deseeded

Fresh tarragon, roughly chopped

TECHNIQUE

Prepare the dressing. In a small bowl, combine the Dijon mustard, the orange juice, and the balsamic vinegar. Add in the olive oil to taste and whisk until it's a creamy (but not too thick) consistency. Add salt and pepper to taste. Put the dressing in the refrigerator until ready to use.

Slice the baguette(s) into rounds about ½ inch thick, counting out two per person. Heat a frying pan with 2 to 3 tablespoons of olive oil and a nice knob of butter over medium-high heat. Add the needles from fresh rosemary or a tablespoon or two of *herbes de Provence* to the pan. Place the slices of bread in the pan, grilling both sides until golden. Set aside and repeat, if necessary.

When all the baguette rounds are toasted, in the same pan, add a dash of oil, the lardons, and the leeks. Cook until tender and slightly carmelized. Set aside and keep warm.

Gently encrust the goat cheese slices with the panko or bread crumbs, coating both sides. Fry them in the already greased pan, adding a dash or two of olive oil, if needed, for approximately 2 minutes per side. Place the goat cheese on the baguette toasts and get ready to plate.

Combine one cup arugula and ½ cup endive on each plate. Add the lardons and leeks, splitting the ingredients among each dish. Place two baguette toasts topped with panko-encrusted goat cheese on each plate. Scatter the pomegranate seeds and the slices of clementine or mandarin orange. Drizzle the dressing, garnish with fresh tarragon, and serve.

Le Dessert

Crème Brûlée with Two Seasonal Topping Options

SERVES 8

PREP TIME: 20 MINUTES

COOK TIME: 45 TO 55 MINUTES, DEPENDING ON YOUR OVEN

REST TIME: 4 HOURS

EQUIPMENT: SAUCEPAN, MIXING BOWL, ELECTRIC WHISK OR
BEATER, 8 RAMEKINS, DEEP-SIDED BAKING OR ROASTING
PAN, LADLE, KITCHEN TORCH

INGREDIENTS

2 cups milk

3 cups heavy cream or *crème fraîche liquide*

8 egg yolks

½ cup granulated sugar

1 teaspoon vanilla extract or the seeds from a vanilla
bean pod

½ to 1 cup brown sugar

Seasonal fruit and herbs

TECHNIQUE

Preheat the oven to 215°F.

In a saucepan, combine the milk with the cream and bring to a
boil. Lower the heat to keep it warm.

Combine the egg yolks, sugar, and vanilla in a mixing bowl. Using a whisk or beater, blend until smooth. Temper the egg batter,

mixing in the warm milk and cream mixture one tablespoon at a time. This ensures your egg mixture won't cook. Then slowly add the mixture to the rest of the milk and cream; mix well.

Set the ramekins in a baking pan. Add just enough water so the ramekins are almost halfway submerged—a bain-marie. Using a ladle, fill the ramekins with the mixture. Gently place the baking pan in the oven, careful not to slosh water into the ramekins. Bake for 55 minutes. Take the pan out of the oven, again being careful not to get water in the ramekins. Let the ramekins cool, then refrigerate for a minimum of four hours.

Before serving, sprinkle each ramekin with brown sugar, covering the mixture (around ½ tablespoon). Caramelize the sugar topping using a kitchen torch.

TOPPINGS

In the spring or summer, top your crème brûlée with fresh sliced strawberries marinated in cognac. Garnish with a sprig of fresh rosemary or basil.

In the fall or winter, top your crème brûlée with spicy red wine–poached pear slices and garnish with a star anise.

acknowledgments

Sometimes it takes a "brigade" to write a book. I'm so very thankful for all of the people who believed in Sophie's story and saw it come to fruition. Let's get started, shall we?

Merci to the fabulous Eloisa James. Thank you for your friendship and for connecting me with my dream agents. I am eternally grateful for your kind referral.

Thank you to my dream agents (yep, I got two agents for the price of one!), Kimberly Witherspoon and Jessica Mileo at InkWell Management. Without your guidance and support, this book wouldn't have hit the shelves. We really dug into this story, making it submission-ready. Thank you for believing in me and in Sophie.

Thank you to my dream editor, Cindy Hwang. Truth: when my agents put this book on submission, I Googled all of the requesting editors and found a video featuring Cindy. I fell in love with her. Along with a drawing of a penguin, I immediately wrote the following words down on my kitchen chalkboard: "Berkley. Penguin. Remain positive." As I write this, my chalkboard still displays that drawing and the words in all their glory.

Thank you to the entire team at Berkley, especially Cindy's incredible assistant, Angela Kim, copy editor extraordinaire Christine Masters, and the publicity and marketing teams. I am thrilled you welcomed me into the Berkley family with open arms.

Speaking of family, my mother taught me to write down my dreams and that if you work hard enough for them, perhaps they will come to fruition. Thanks, Mom, they did! Thank you to my father, Tony, who has given me much-needed writerly advice. Thank you to my sister, Jessica, who is my biggest book cheerleader. And thank you to my grandmother, who I've dedicated this book to. I miss her fiercely, but she still lives on in my heart and in the recipes she taught me.

A huge *merci* goes out to my army of sous chefs—my beta readers, especially Karen Burns, who read the book not once, but twice, and to Lizzie Harwood, Leslie Ficcaglia, Jo Maeder, Diane Stevenson, and Cassandra Firemark. Thank you to my chef friends: Mary O'Leary, Mardi Michels, Randall Price, and Didier Quémener, who guided me in the cooking world. Thank you to my Paris Author's Group (PAG), especially Lisa Anselmo, for answering all of my questions. And thank you to my friends: Oksana Richie, Alicia Mattes Rourke, and Kate Elizabeth Redfern. *Merci mille fois!*

Thank you to all the chefs who have shared their stories, either on the page or on the docuseries *Chef's Table*. You all inspired this story, especially Anthony Bourdain, Éric Ripert, Gabrielle Hamilton, Dominique Crenn, and Barbara Lynch. Thank you. By the way, a huge *félicitations* goes out to Chef Crenn, the first woman in the US to receive three Michelin stars. I applaud you. A standing ovation.

I'd be remiss if I didn't thank my biggest inspiration, my French husband, Jean-Luc, and my stepkids, Max and Elvire. Thank you for correcting my French. Thank you for giving me a new lease on life. Thank you for dealing with all my crazy shenanigans. Thank you for being supportive, and thank you for teaching me how to cook French. *Je vous aime. Beaucoup! Beaucoup! Beaucoup!*

Finally, I'd like to thank you, dear reader, for choosing to read this book. *Merci! Merci beaucoup! Merci mille fois!*

Author photo by Susy Barrat

Samantha (Sam) Vérant is a travel addict, a self-professed oeno-phile, and a determined, if unconventional, at-home French chef. Over the years, she's visited many different countries, lived in many places, and worked many jobs—always on the lookout for the one thing that truly excited her. Then one day, she found everything she'd been looking for: a passion for the written word and true love. Writing not only enabled her to open her heart, it led her to southwestern France, where she's now married to a sexy French rocket scientist she met in Paris when she was nineteen (but ignored for twenty years); a stepmom to two incredible kids, Max and Elvire; and the adoptive mother to one ridiculously fat French cat, a Chartreux named Juju. When she's not trekking from Provence to the Pyrénées, tasting wine in American-sized glasses, or embracing her inner Julia Child while deliberating what constitutes the perfect *bœuf bourguignon*, Sam is making her best effort to relearn those dreaded conjugations.

Connect Online

www.SamanthaVerant.com

AuthorSamanthaVerant

Samantha_Verant

Samantha_Verant

Ready to find
your next great read?

Let us help.

Visit prh.com/nextread

the *secret*
french recipes
of *sophie valroux*